REAL TIGERS

MICK HERRON

ISIS
LARGE
PRINT

First published in Great Britain 2016
by
John Murray (Publishers)
an Hachette UK Company

First Isis Edition
published 2018
by arrangement with
Hachette UK

A catalogue record for this book is available
from the British Library.

ISBN 978–1–78541–635–4 (hb)
ISBN 978–1–78541–641–5 (pb)

Published by
F. A. Thorpe (Publishing)
Anstey, Leicestershire

Set by Words & Graphics Ltd.
Anstey, Leicestershire
Printed and bound in Great Britain by
T. J. International Ltd., Padstow, Cornwall

This book is printed on acid-free paper

REAL TIGERS

London's Slough House is where disgraced MI5 operatives are reassigned to spend the rest of their careers pushing paper. But when one of these fallen spies is kidnapped by a former soldier bent on revenge, the agents must breach HQ's defences to steal valuable intel in exchange for their comrade's safety. The kidnapping is only the tip of the iceberg, however, as the agents uncover a larger web of intrigue that involves not only a group of private mercenaries, but also the highest authorities in the Security Service. After years spent as the lowest on the totem pole, the spies suddenly find themselves caught in the midst of a conspiracy that threatens not only the future of Slough House, but that of MI5 itself . . .

SPECIAL MESSAGE TO READERS

To Eleanor

CHAPTER
ONE

Like most forms of corruption, it began with men in suits.

A weekday morning on the edge of the City; damp, dark, foggy, not yet five. In the nearby towers, some of which reached upwards of twenty storeys, random windows were lit, making haphazard patterns in the glass-and-steel grids, and some of those lights meant early-bird bankers were at their desks, getting a jump on the markets, but most were a sign that the other City workers were on the job, the ones who wore overalls and whose pre-dawn tasks involved vacuuming, polishing, emptying bins. Paul Lowell's sympathies were with the latter. You either cleaned up other people's messes or you didn't — and that was the class system for you, right there.

He glanced at the road below. Eighteen metres was a fair distance, viewed vertically. Dropping to his haunches he felt the relevant muscles crunch and cheap fabric strain unpleasantly across his thighs. His suit was too small. Lowell had figured it was stretchy enough that this wouldn't matter, but in the event he felt constricted by it, and graced with none of the power he might have imagined it bestowing.

Or maybe he was just getting fat.

Lowell was on a platform, which probably wasn't the correct architectural term for it, above an arch through which ran London Wall, the dual-lane thoroughfare reaching from St Martin's Le Grand to Moorgate. Above him was another tower block, part of a pair set at an angle to each other, and housing one of the world's leading investment banks as well as one of its most famous pizza chains. A hundred yards away, on a grassy knoll by the side of the road to which it had lent its name, ran a chunk of the Roman wall which had once encircled the City, still standing centuries after its builders had given up their ghosts. A symbol, it occurred to Lowell now. Some things endured, survived changing attitudes, and it was worth fighting to preserve what remained of them. Why he was here, in a nutshell.

Shrugging his rucksack free he placed it between his knees, drew a zip and unpacked its contents. In an hour or so traffic would build, heading into the City or points east, a quantity of it passing through the arch on which he perched, and all those cars, taxis, buses and bikes would have no choice but to bear witness. And in their wake would come the inevitable: the news crews, the cameras, carrying his message to the nation.

All he wanted was his voice to be heard. After years of being denied his rights he was ready to fight, and like others before him, had chosen a particular mode in which to do so. This was how traditions were born. He didn't for a moment think anything he achieved today would make a major difference, but others in his

2

position would see, and learn, and maybe act. Someday, that difference would be made.

There was movement, and he turned to see a figure hoisting itself onto the far end of the platform, having scaled the building from the street below as Lowell had done ten minutes earlier. It took a second for recognition to sink in, but as soon as it did he felt a thump of excitement, as if he were twelve again. Because this was what every twelve-year-old wanted to see, he thought, as he watched the newcomer approach. This was the stuff young boys' dreams were made of.

Tall, broad and purposeful, Batman strode towards him through damp ribbons of fog.

"Hey," Lowell called. "Nice one."

He looked down at his own costume. Spider-Man was hardly age-appropriate, but it wasn't like anyone would be offering style points: making the evening news was the aim, and superhero suits ticked the right media boxes. It had worked before and would work again. So he was the Amazing Spider-Man, and the comrade he was meeting for the first time now, with whom all arrangements had been made anonymously through a message board, was Batman, and the pair would be a dynamic duo for one morning only, and blaze through newscasts for the rest of the week. One hand on the roll of canvas he'd unpacked, Lowell levered himself to his feet and extended the other, because this too was part of an ancient narrative: men meeting and greeting, and bonding in a common cause.

Ignoring Spider-Man's outstretched hand, Batman punched him in the face.

3

Lowell fell backwards as the world span out of control: lit-up office windows spiralled like stars, and all the air left his body as it hit damp brickwork. But already his mind had slipped into work-gear, and he rolled sideways, away from the edge, as Batman's foot stamped down hard, just missing his elbow. He needed to be upright, because nobody ever won a fight from a prone position, and he concentrated on this for the next two seconds instead of wondering why Batman was kicking the shit out of him, and his focus almost paid off because he'd made it to his knees before he was punched in the head again. Blood soaked through Lowell's Spider-Man mask. He tried to speak. A formless gurgle was all he could manage.

And then he was being dragged towards the edge of the platform.

He shrieked, because it was clear what would happen next. Batman was hauling him by the shoulders, and he couldn't break free — the man's hands felt moulded from steel. He kicked out and hit the canvas lump, which rolled towards the edge, unravelling as it went. He swung an arm for Batman's crotch, but hit muscle-hard thigh instead. And then he was hanging in space, the only thing keeping him aloft the caped crusader's grip.

For a moment they were locked in near-embrace, Batman rigidly upright, Spider-Man dangling, as if posing for a cover illustration.

"For pity's sake," Spider-Man whispered.

Batman dropped him.

4

The canvas roll hit the road before Paul Lowell did but wasn't a roll by then, having unwound itself along the tarmac to become a strip of carpet instead of the banner he'd intended it to be. In foot-high letters, its hand-painted battle cry, A FAIR DEAL FOR FATHERS, blurred as the wet ground soaked into the fabric, along with a certain quantity of Lowell's blood, but remained a gratifyingly newsworthy image, and would feature in many a broadcast before the day was out.

Paul Lowell didn't see any of them, though.

As for Batman, he was long gone.

Part One

False Friends

CHAPTER
TWO

On a night hot as hell in the borough of Finsbury a door opens and a woman steps into a yard. Not the front street — this is Slough House, and the front door of Slough House famously never opens, never closes — but a yard that sees little natural light, and whose walls are consequently fuzzy with mildew. The odour is of neglect, whose constituent humours, with a little effort, can be made out to be food and fats from the takeaway, and stale cigarettes, and long-dried puddles, and something rising from the drain that gurgles in a corner and is best not investigated closely. It is not yet dark — it's the violet hour — but already the yard is shadowy with night. The woman doesn't pause there. There's nothing to see.

But supposing she were herself observed — supposing the slight draught that brushes past as she closes the door were not a longed-for breeze of the type that August seems to have abjured, but a wandering spirit in search of a resting place — then the moment before the door is firmly closed might be one in which an opportunity is briefly open. Quick as a sunbeam in it slips, and because spirits, especially wandering spirits, are no slouches, what follows would happen in the time it takes a bat to blink; a lightning survey of this half-forgotten and wholly ignored annexe; this "administrative oubliette", as it was once dubbed, of the intelligence service.

Our spirit flies up the stairs, no other option presenting itself, and as it ascends notes the contours marked on the staircase walls; a ragged brown scurf-mark, like the outline of an unfinished continent, indicating the height to which damp has risen; a wavy scribble that might almost be taken, in the gloom, for the licking of flames. A fanciful notion, but one reinforced by the heat and the general air of oppression that smothers the house, as if someone — something — were exerting a malign influence over those in his, its, thrall.

On the first landing, two office doors. Choosing at random, our spirit finds itself in an untidy, shabby office; one with a pair of desks on which sit a pair of computers, their monitors' stand-by lights quietly blinking in the dark. Spillages here have gone so long unmopped they've evolved into stains, and stains so long ignored they've been absorbed into the colour scheme. Everything is yellow or grey, and either broken or mended. A printer, jammed into a space not quite large enough, boasts a jagged crack across its lid, and the paper lantern masking one of the overhead bulbs — the other has no shade — is torn, and hangs at an angle. The dirty mug on one desk is missing its handle. The dirty glass on the other is chipped. The lip-ring on its rim is a Goth's kiss; a sneer in grease.

No place then, this, for a wandering spirit: ours sniffs, but not audibly, before disappearing then reappearing in this floor's companion office, and then in the pair on the next floor up, and then on the landing of the floor above that, the better to contrive a view of the building as a whole . . . Which is not, it turns out, a favourable one. These rooms which seem empty are in fact teeming; they froth with frustration, and not a little bile; they roil with the agony of enforced inertia. Only one among them — the one with the classiest computer kit — seems relatively unscathed by the torment of eternal boredom; and only one other — the smaller of the pair on this top landing — shows any sign of efficient industry. The rest hum with the repetitive churning of meaningless tasks; of work that's been found for idle hands, and seemingly consists of the processing of reams of information, raw data barely distinguishable from a mess of scattered alphabets, seasoned with random numbers. As if the admin tasks of some recording demon had been upsourced and visited upon the occupants here; converted into mundane chores they are expected, endlessly, cease-lessly, to perform, failing which they will be cast into even remoter darknesses — damned if they do and damned if they don't. The only reason for the absence of a sign requiring entrants to abandon all hope is that, as every office worker knows, it's not the hope that kills you.

It's knowing it's the hope that kills you that kills you.

These rooms, our wandering spirit has said, but there remains one still unvisited — the larger of the pair

11

on this top floor, which, while shrouded in darkness, is not in fact empty. If our spirit had ears, it would hardly need press one to the door to ascertain this, for the noise emanating from within isn't shy: it is loud and rumbly and might plausibly come from a barnyard animal. And our spirit trembles slightly, in an almost-perfect imitation of a human experiencing distress, and before that noise, part snore part belch part growl, quite fades away, has descended through Slough House again; past the abysmal offices on the second and first floors; down the final stretch of stairs which is all the property boasts of ground level, wedged as it is between Chinese restaurant and jack-of-all-trades newsagent's; and out into the mildewed airless yard just as time reasserts itself, erasing our wandering spirit like a windscreen wiper sweeps away an insect, and so suddenly that it leaves a little *pop* behind it, but of such a small, polite nature that the woman doesn't notice. Instead, she tugs on the door — making sure it's closed, though she's half-convinced she's performed this action already — and then, with that same efficient industry she lends to her top-floor office, makes her way from the yard into the lane and round onto Aldersgate Street, where she turns left, and has barely walked five yards before a sound startles her: not a *pop*, not a bang, nor even an explosive belch of the sort Jackson Lamb specialises in, but her very own name, wrapped in a voice from another lifetime, *Cath* —

"— erine?"

Who goes there? she thought. Friend or foe?

As if such distinctions mattered.

"Catherine Standish?"

And this time came the tremor of recognition, and for a moment she was mentally squinting, though her face remained unlined. She was trying to locate a memory that shimmered behind frosted glass. And then it cleared, and the glass she was looking through was the bottom of a tumbler, empty now, but filmy with residue.

"Sean Donovan," she said.

"You remember."

"Yes. Of course I do."

Because he was not a forgettable man, being tall and broad shouldered, with a nose that had been broken a time or two — an even number, he'd once joked, else it would look even more crooked — and if his hair, streaked with iron now, was longer than she recalled, it was still barely more than a bullet-cut. As for his eyes, they remained blue, because how could they not, but even in this fading evening she could see that tonight they were the stormy blue of his darker moments, and not the shade of a September sky. And tall and broad, which she'd already marked off, twice her size easily, and they must look a pair standing here in the violet hour; him with warrior written all over him, and her in a dress buttoned to the neck, with lace at the sleeves, and buckles on her shoes.

Since it had to be addressed, she said, "I hadn't realised you were . . ."

"Out?"

She nodded.

"A year ago. Thirteen months." The voice, too, was not one to be forgotten: its touch of the Irish. She had never been to Ireland, but sometimes, listening to him, her head would fill with soft green images.

Being a drunk had helped, of course.

"I could give you the figure in days," he added.

"It must have been hard."

"Oh, you have no idea," he said. "You literally have no idea."

For that, she had no reply.

They were standing still, and this was not good tradecraft. Even Catherine Standish, never a joe, knew that much.

He read this in her posture. "You were heading that direction?" Pointing towards the Old Street junction.

"Yes."

"I'll walk with you if I may."

Which is what he did, exactly as if this were what it appeared to be; a chance encounter on a summer's evening, as light began to fade at the edges; one old friend (if that was what they had been) stumbling upon another, and wanting to prolong the moment. In another age, thought Catherine, and perhaps even in some corners of this one, he would have taken her arm as they walked, which would have been sweet, and a little corny, but mostly would have been a lie. Because Catherine Standish — never a joe — knew this much too: that chance encounters might happen in some places, to some people, but they never happened here, to spooks.

14

★ ★ ★

In a bar near Slough House, Roderick Ho was contemplating romance.

He'd been doing this a lot lately, with good reason. The simple truth was, everyone thought Roddy and Louisa Guy should have coupled off by now. Her thing with Min Harper was history, and if the internet had taught Ho anything, it was that women had needs. It had also revealed that there was no scam so risibly transparent that someone wouldn't fall for it, and that if you wanted to cause a shitstorm on a message board, you simply had to post something mildly controversial about 9/11, Michael Jackson or cats — yep: one way or the other, the internet had made Ho the man he was. Roddy was a self-taught citizen of twenty-first-century GB, and all clued up on how to conduct himself therein.

Bitch was ripe was how he read it.

Bitch was *ready*.

All he had to do was reach out and pluck it.

But while theory was nine-tenths of the game, he was having trouble with the remaining fraction. He saw Louisa most days, and had taken to appearing in the kitchen whenever she was making coffee, but she kept misreading his signals. He'd actually commented, and this was over a week ago, that since they were driven by the same caffeine needs it made excellent sense for her to make enough for two, but this had gone whistling over her head and she was still carrying the pot back to her office. You had to laugh at her feeble grasp of mating rituals, but in the meantime he was stumped for ways to get down to her level.

Ho didn't even like coffee. These were the lengths he was prepared to go.

There were strategies he'd come across, heard about: be kind, be attentive, listen. Jesus — did these people still live in wooden houses? That crap took ages, and it wasn't like Louisa was getting any younger. As for Ho himself, frankly, he had his own needs, and while the internet catered for most of them, he was starting to feel a little tense. Louisa Guy was a vulnerable woman. There were men might seek to take advantage. He wouldn't put it past River Cartwright, for a start, to try it on. And while Cartwright was an idiot, there was no second-guessing what a vulnerable woman might do, especially one misreading the signals.

So Ho figured he needed a little practical assistance. Which was why he was in this bar with Marcus Longridge and Shirley Dander, who shared the office next door.

"Spoken to Louisa lately?" he asked.

Marcus Longridge grunted.

They were the newest of the slow horses, this pair, which accounted for their not saying much. Slough House had no rigid hierarchical structure, but it was pretty clear that once you'd ticked off Lamb at the top, you were looking at Roddy Ho — the place ran on brains, not muscle. So these two must regard him as their natural superior, hence their being overawed. Ho'd have felt the same in their shoes. He took a sip of his alcohol-free lager and tried again.

"At all? In the kitchen or anywhere?"

Again, Marcus grunted.

Marcus was into his forties, Ho knew, but that didn't mean you could rule him out entirely. He was tall, black, married, and had definitely killed at least one person, but none of that stopped Ho figuring Marcus probably looked on him, Ho, as a younger version of himself. There must be practical stuff he'd be happy to pass on, which was the reason he'd elected Marcus to join him for a guys' night out. A few jars, a few laughs, and then some opening up. But reaching that stage was an uphill struggle with Shirley Dander sitting the other side of him, like a malevolent fire hydrant. He had no clue why she'd tagged along, but she was cramping both their styles.

She had a packet of crisps in front of her, opened up like a picnic blanket, except when he'd reached to take one she'd slapped his hand. "Get your own." She was levering about fifteen per cent of the total quantity into her mouth now, and once she'd done that she chewed briefly and said, "What about?"

Ho gave her a look that meant *men talking*.

"What's the matter?" she asked. "Lemonade go down the wrong way?"

"It's not lemonade."

"Yeah, right." She used some of her own, definitely non-alcohol-free lager to sluice the crisps down her throat, then returned to topic. "Talk to Louisa about what?"

"Just, you know. Anything."

Shirley said, "You're kidding."

Marcus stared into his pint. He was drinking Guinness, and Ho had spent a few minutes working up

17

something to say about this, about Marcus and his drink being the same colour — observational comedy — but had shelved it until the moment was right. Which might be soon if Shirley shut up.

She didn't.

"You have got to be kidding."

"I don't know what you mean," he said.

"Louisa. You think you've got a chance with *Louisa*?"

"Who said anything about —"

"Ha! That is fantastic. You seriously think you've got a chance with Louisa?"

Marcus said, "Oh God. Shoot me now," but didn't seem to be addressing either of his companions.

Not for the first time, Roderick Ho wondered if he'd made a tactical error in his social life.

Sean Donovan said, "You're not at the Park any more."

As this wasn't a question Catherine didn't answer it, instead saying, "I'm glad you're out, Sean. I hope life's treating you better."

"Water under the bridge."

But he said this with the air of one who spent a lot of time on bridges, waiting for the bodies of his enemies to float past.

They were approaching the junction, where small queues of cars, mostly taxis, waited. Through the windows of the pub opposite she could see heads bobbing in conversation and laughter. It wasn't a pub for serious drinkers; it was strictly for casuals. She was very conscious of Sean Donovan at her side; of his thick soldier's body. Still a physical presence, well into his fifties. Behind bars, he'd have haunted the gym. In his cell he'd have done push-ups, sit-ups, all those crunching exercises which kept the muscles strong.

A row of buses trundled past. She waited until their noise abated before saying, "I have to be going, Sean."

"I can't tempt you to a drink?"

"I don't do that any more."

He gave a low whistle. "Now we're really talking hard time . . ."

"I get by."

But she did and she didn't. Most days she did. But there were difficult passages, in the early summer evenings — or the late winter nights — when she felt drunk already, as if she'd slipped without noticing and woken enmeshed in her old ways, doing *that* some more. Drinking. Which would start an unravelling that might never end.

Taking another drink was not about lapsing. It was about becoming someone she planned never to be again.

"A cup of coffee then."

"I can't."

"Jesus, Catherine. It's been how long? And we were . . . close."

She didn't want to think about that.

"Sean, I'm still with the Service. I can't be seen with you. I can't take that risk."

She regretted the phrase as soon as it escaped her.

"Risk, is it? Touching pitch and all?"

"I didn't mean that the way it sounded. But the truth is, I just can't be with you. Spend time with you. Not because of . . . your troubles. Because of who I am. What I am."

" 'Your troubles.' " He laughed and shook his head. "You sound like my mother, rest her soul. 'Your troubles.' A phrase she'd trot out to a grieving widow or a fussing child. She was never one for making fine distinctions."

That phrase again. Making distinctions.

"I'm glad to see you're well, Sean."

"You're looking grand yourself, Catherine."

It was perhaps indicative of their respective conditions that each left it to the other to affirm their essential road-worthiness.

"Goodbye, then."

The lights were in her favour, so she was able to cross immediately. On the other side she didn't look back, but knew that if she did she'd see him watching her, the colour of his eyes unknowable at this distance, but still that shade of stormy blue they became in his darker moments.

"You look like you could use company."

Louisa didn't reply.

Undeterred, the man slid onto the stool next to her. A glance in the mirror told her he was passable — maybe mid-thirties and wearing it well; wearing, too, a made-to-measure charcoal suit, with an intricately patterned tie, blues and golds, loosened enough to indicate the free spirit blooming within. His spectacles had a thin black frame, and Louisa would have bet her next vodka and lime their lenses would be plain glass.

Nerd-chic. But she didn't bother turning to check this out.

"Only you've been here thirty-seven minutes now, and you haven't once checked the door."

He paused, the better for her to appreciate the cuteness of that specific amount of time, the sharpness of his observation. Sitting here thirty-seven minutes, and not expecting anyone. He'd doubtless counted her drinks, and knew she was on her third.

And now a chuckle.

"So you're the quiet type. Don't get many of them round here."

Round here being south of the river, though not far enough south to be free of made-to-measure suits and classy ties. It was a bus ride from her studio flat, which, since the weather had turned and the streets become heavy with smells of tar and fried dust, felt smaller than ever, as if shrinking in the heat. Everything in it seemed to pulse. Arriving there was a constant reminder she'd rather be anywhere else.

"But you know what? Beautiful woman, all mysterious and quiet, that's an invitation to a guy like me. Gives me a chance to shine. So tell you what, any time you want to chip in, feel free. Or smile and nod, whatever. I'm happy just admiring the view."

So she'd showered and changed, and now wore a denim shirt with the sleeves rolled up, and skinny black jeans over gold sandals. The blonde streaks in her hair were recent, as was the blood-red toenail polish. He wasn't entirely wrong. She was sure she wasn't a beautiful woman. But she was certain she looked like one.

Besides, a hot August evening, and chilled drinks on the bar. Anyone could look beautiful when the context allowed.

She raised her glass and its ice whispered musical promises.

"So I work in solutions. Clients mostly import-export, and a real bastard landed on my desk this morning, two-and-a-half mill of high-spec tablets chugging out of Manila and the paperwork's only been bollocksed . . ."

He chuntered on. He hadn't offered her a drink — he'd time it so he'd finish his own a beat ahead of her then raise a finger for the girl behind the bar, *vodka lime, plenty of ice*, then carry on with his story so as not to draw attention to the minor miracle he'd performed.

This, or something like it, was how it always went.

Louisa placed a finger on the rim of her glass and traced round it before tucking a lock of hair behind her ear. The man was still talking, and she knew, without looking round, that his companions were at a table by the door, alert for signs of success or failure, and prepared to have a laugh either way. Probably they worked in "solutions" too. It seemed a job title that could stretch pretty far in any direction, provided you weren't fussy about the range of problems it encompassed.

Her own problems — the day she'd had, like every other working day of the past two months — involved comparing two sets of census figures, 2001 and 2011. Her target city was Leeds, her age group 18–24, and what she was looking for were people who had dropped out of sight or appeared from nowhere.

"Any particular language group?" she remembered asking.

"Ethnic profiling is morally obscene," Lamb had admonished.

"I thought everyone knew that. But yeah, it's the sand-jockeys you want to focus on."

People who'd vanished and others who'd materialised. There were hundreds of them, of course, and rock-solid reasons for most, and potentially rock-solid reasons for most of the rest, though tracking those reasons down was a pain in the neck. She couldn't approach the targets themselves, so had to come in at a tangent: social security, vehicle licensing, utilities, NHS records, internet use: anything that left a paper trail, or indicated a footprint. And blah blah blah — it wasn't so much looking for a needle in a haystack as rearranging the haystack, stalk by stalk; grading each by length and width, and making them point the same way . . . She wished she worked in solutions. The current project seemed mostly a matter of contriving unnecessary problems.

Which was the point. Nobody left Slough House at the end of a working day feeling like they'd contributed to the security of the nation. They left it feeling like their brains had been fed through a juicer. Louisa had dreams of being trapped in a telephone directory. The fuck-up that had put her with the slow horses had been bad — a messed-up surveillance job resulting in a large quantity of guns being dumped on the street — but she'd surely been punished enough. Except the point was, no amount of punishment was enough. She could set her own terms, serve her own sentence, and walk away whenever she felt like it. That was what she was supposed to do: give it up and walk away. So, like all the rest of them, it was the last thing she'd ever do. Something Min had said — no, don't think about Min. Anyway, without discussing it, she knew they all felt the same way. Except for Roderick Ho, who was too much of an arsehole to realise he was being punished, which, given he was being punished for being an arsehole, seemed apt.

And meanwhile, her brain felt like it had been fed through a juicer.

The man was still talking, might even be reaching the climax of his anecdote, and Louisa was more certain than she was of anything else that whatever this turned out to be, she didn't want to hear it. Without turning to face him, she placed a hand on his wrist. It was like using a remote: his story ended, mid-air.

"I'm going to have two more of these," she said. "If you're still here when I'm done, I'll go home with you. But in the meantime, shut the fuck up, okay? Not a word. That's a deal-breaker."

He was smarter than he'd so far suggested. Without a sound, he waved for the bartender, pointed at Louisa's glass, and raised two fingers.

Louisa faded him out, and got to work on her drink.

24

★　★　★

Shoot me now, thought Marcus again, this time not out loud.

Shirley was having fun with the idea Ho fancied his chances with Louisa. "That is brilliant. Have we got a noticeboard? We are so going to need one." She made a crosshatch sign with her fingers. "Hashtag deludedmale."

The bar was the far side of the Barbican Centre, and Ho thought he'd suggested it because it was a favourite dive of his, somewhere he hung with his friends, but the truth was Marcus had never set foot in it before, and had picked it for precisely that reason. It was exactly the kind of place he'd wager money no actual friend of his would ever set foot, so the chances of running into any of them while in company with Roderick Ho were minimal.

On the other hand, wagering money was what had got him here in the first place, so placing further bets wasn't his wisest course.

A giant TV screen fixed to a wall was tuned to rolling news. The breaking-headline ribbon was unspooling too quickly to follow, but the picture would have been difficult not to identify: blue suit, yellow tie, artfully tousled haystack of hair and a plummy grin you'd have to be a moron or a voter not to notice concealed a degree of self-interest that would alienate a shark. The brand-new Home Secretary, meaning Marcus's new boss, and Shirley's, and Ho's, not that the relationship would bother Peter Judd — to attract his attention, you had to have royal connections, a TV show or enhanced breasts ("allegedly"). Straddling the gap between media-whore and political beast, he'd long since made

25

the leap from star-fucker to star-fucked, stealing the public affection with shows of buffoonery, and gaining political ascendancy by way of the Hollywood-sanctioned dictum that you keep your enemies close. It was one way of dealing with him, but old Westminster hands agreed that he couldn't have been more of a threat to the PM if he'd been on the Opposition benches. Which, if the Opposition had looked likely to win an election soon, he doubtless would have been.

To borrow an assessment, *Dreadful piece of work.*

To coin another, "Honky twerp," muttered Marcus.

"Hate speech," warned Shirley.

"Of course it's hate speech. I fucking hate him."

Shirley glanced at the TV, shrugged, and said, "Thought you were one of the party faithful."

"I am. He's not."

Ho was looking from one to the other, as if he'd entirely lost his place.

Shirley returned her attention to him. "So when did it start, this insane notion you might be in with a chance with Louisa?"

Ho said, "I can read the signs."

"You couldn't read welcome on a doormat. You seriously think you can read a woman?"

Ho shrugged. "Bitch is ripe," he said. "Bitch is *ready*."

Shirley backhanded him. His spectacles went flying.

Marcus said, "That'll be my round, then."

Friend or foe?

There was no getting round it, anyone from that time of her life was a foe.

26

Catherine lived in St John's Wood, but had no intention of heading there yet. Laying a false trail came naturally — alcoholics learn to dissemble. So she walked north, heading vaguely for the Angel; a woman with a destination, but no great urgency about it. Everyone she passed was thirty years younger, and wearing about as much clothing as covered her own arms. Some shot her glances full of wonderment at one or other of these facts, but this didn't concern her. Friend or foe didn't cover all contingencies. These strangers were neither, and she had other things on her mind.

Sean Donovan was a foe, because anyone from that time of her life was a foe, but he was a decent man, or so Catherine's memory suggested. He was a soldier, and while this was in some ways an error of tense — Sean Donovan *had been* a soldier; Sean Donovan was demonstrably, dishonourably, no longer such — it remained the most accurate description Catherine could summon: you only had to look at him. Mid-fifties now, by rights he should be taking salutes on parade grounds, and having his opinion sought by Whitehall mandarins. Not difficult to picture him before cameras justifying the latest military action. But the last time he'd been before the cameras had been as he was led from a military tribunal in cuffs: found guilty of causing death by dangerous driving, and sentenced to five years.

For Catherine, this had been a newspaper item rather than a personal shock. She was sober by then, and part of the process of becoming so had been avoiding the company she'd kept when she'd been otherwise. This meant men, of whom Sean Donovan had been one; not a particularly important one, or no more important than any other man from that period, but then again, that was a long list.

She crossed a road. This made her a little dizzy; not the action in itself, but emerging from her memory to concentrate on doing so. It took effort, peering back into her past. It wasn't pleasant. For some reason an image of Jackson Lamb swam to mind, cloistered in his gloomy office, but it swam away again. Safely over the road, she risked a look back. Sean Donovan was not following. She hadn't really expected him to be. At the very least, she had not expected to be able to spot him doing so.

He was part of her past, but other than knowing that much, she had little to go on. Of their actual lovemaking, if it could be so described, she had no memory. In those days, two drinks in, her immediate future became a blank slate, with everything scrawled thereon erased within moments of its appearance. He could have written her sonnets, or transcribed arias, and it would all be the same to her. But she knew that was never the case; that it had been fuck-buddy sex like always, because in those days anyone would have done, just so long as she had someone to cling to as she slid into the dark. Poems and operas were not required. A bottle would do the trick.

But while it was true that there were many she'd forgotten, of whom she'd barely been aware even while they were inside her, Sean Donovan had at least been there in the morning once or twice. Fond of the drink himself, he'd done her the false kindness of pretending they were as bad as each other. *Man, my head this morning. We pushed the boat out all right*. But what for her had been blackout territory, for him had been a night on the tiles. She'd been a willing enough partner in this, because she was always willing back then. And if she'd been otherwise, Catherine wondered now, if she'd been sober, would they have stood a chance together? But there was no answering that.

She wasn't far from a Tube station. From there she would make her way home, but first she took out her mobile and made a call. At the other end a phone went straight to voicemail. She didn't leave a message.

Phone back in her bag, she continued up the road.

A hundred yards behind her, a black van idled.

Shirley watched Roderick Ho scrambling for his glasses, and wondered whether she should have slapped him like that. A backhander gave you the drop, sure, generally surprising the backhanded, but if she'd made an effort and formed a fist she could have broken the little bastard's nose. After informing him of her intention in writing, if she'd felt like it. Forewarned wouldn't have meant forearmed in Ho's case. Forewarned would have meant being punched in the nose anyway, after worrying about it first.

What was mildly disquieting about the incident, though, was that it didn't seem to have calmed her down.

In the general order of things, getting physical was releasing a valve, releasing endorphins, so afterwards you felt that sweet high, halfway between an ache and a caress — by rights, she should be watching Ho's cack-handed fumbling with a great big grin on her face, at peace enough to lend him a hand even, though the ungrateful little sod wouldn't thank her. Instead, she still felt wound to full pitch, enough to want to give him another slap. Which wasn't out of the question, obviously, but might put a strain on the remainder of the evening.

Marcus wasn't at the bar; he must have gone to the gents, unless he'd snuck off through the side door. Which must have been a temptation for him, but the way things stood, he wouldn't dare.

That morning, he'd said to her, "You know what that little shit's doing?"

There were any number of little shits this might have been, but top of the list was always going to be Roderick Ho.

"Cyberstalking you?"

"Well, duh. Apart from that."

"He's dobbed you in?"

"Not yet. But he says he will."

"Bastard."

"You've not heard the half of it. Guess what his price for keeping shtum is."

Shirley reflected now that it might have been a better idea not to laugh when he told her.

"A night in the pub? That's it?"

"I'd sooner give him cash."

30

"Oh, that is fabulous. Take notes. I'm gunna want to hear all about this."

"That's not a problem. You're coming too."

"Dream on."

"'Cause if it's just me and Ho, who knows where the conversation might lead? Once we've run through sport and politics, we might end up discussing our colleagues. Like, you know, who sneaks off early when they think no one's looking, and who leaves their dirty mugs in the sink."

"Enthralling."

"And who snorts coke."

Shirley dropped her pen. "You wouldn't."

"Won't get the opportunity. Not if you're there too."

"That's blackmail."

"What can I say? Learned from a master."

So here she was, here they both were, suffering the company of Roderick Webhead Ho. No wonder she was feeling . . .

But she didn't want to use "uptight".

Shirley had been at the dentist's the previous week, and flipping through a lifestyle magazine in the waiting room had encountered one of those diagnostic quizzes, *How uptight are you?*, and had started mentally checking off answers. *Do you get annoyed at queue-jumpers, even when you're not in a hurry?* Well, obviously, because it's a matter of principle, isn't it? But other questions seemed designed to rile her. *You discover your partner met his/her ex for a drink, "for old times' sake".* She didn't need to read the rest. This was supposed to show how "uptight" you were? As far as Shirley was concerned it was grading you on common sense . . . She'd hurled the magazine at the door, giving the dental nurse, who was just popping her head round, something of a fright. She got her own back five minutes later, being overzealous with the waterpick.

And yeah, besides that, so she liked the odd toot, but who didn't? Tell her Marcus never snorted a line of the old marching powder — Marcus had been Tactical, the squad that kicked down doors, and once you'd tasted that adrenalin high, you'd want another boost, right? He said he never, but he would say that. Besides, it wasn't like Shirley was an habitual user. It was a weekend thing with her, strictly Thursday to Tuesday.

There was a thump as Roderick Ho sat down. His right cheek was flaming red, and his glasses hung lopsided.

"What you do that for?"

She sighed heavily.

"It needed doing," she said, half to herself, and wished she were anywhere else.

Though maybe, all things considered, not where River Cartwright was.

River was in a hospital room, standing by a window there was no point attempting to open. It had been painted shut years ago, back when the NHS still ran to the occasional lick of paint, and even if it had opened, the air that would have crawled in would have been thick as soup, with a saltiness that caught the back of the throat and left you gasping for a glass of water. He tapped the pane, looking down on a covered walkway. The noise was in brief counterpoint to the blipping of one or other of the machines ranged by the bed, on which a gradually diminishing figure lay, making no greater impact on its surroundings than it had done for the past however many months it was.

"You're probably wondering what I've been up to," said River. "You know, while you've been taking it easy."

There was a fan on the bedside shelf, but the barely wavering slip of ribbon tied to its frame revealed how feeble it was. Several times River had attempted to fix it, this taking the form of flicking its switch on and off. DIY skills exhausted, he settled for nudging the visitor's chair nearer the draught-zone, and slumping onto it.

"Well, it's fascinating stuff."

The shape on the bed didn't answer, but that was no surprise. On three previous occasions River had sat here, sometimes silent, sometimes making one-sided conversation, and there was no indication that the bed's occupant was aware of his presence. Indeed, the patient's own presence was an open question: River wondered, while the body was lying there, where the mind was; whether it was wandering the corridors of its interrupted life, or cast into some nightmare of its own devising; a Dali-world of two-faced jackals and multi-headed snakes.

"It's before your time, and mine too, but there was a Civil Service strike in '81. Went on months. Can you imagine the paperwork that piled up? Everything needing doing in triplicate, and none of it happening for twenty-odd weeks . . . When the firefighters go on strike, they bring in the army. Who do you get to come in when the pen-pushers down tools?"

River was a pen-pusher too. Who would do his job if he wasn't there to do it? He had a sudden, unwanted vision of his own ghost floating round Slough House, sifting through unachieved tasks.

"Anyway. See where this is going? You'll get there, given a minute, and a nodding acquaintance with how Jackson Lamb's mind works. Because what he likes to do is dream up tasks that aren't only boring, and aren't only pointless, and don't only involve months of crawling over lists of names and dates, looking for anomalies that you can't know are there, because you don't know what they consist of . . . Not only all of that, designed not just to bore you rigid but to kill your soul one screaming pixel at a time . . . But you know the worst thing about it? The really worst?"

He wasn't expecting an answer. Didn't get one.

"The really worst thing is the infinitesimally small, but nevertheless conceivably possible chance that he might just have something. That if you do it right, and turn over all the rocks, you might just find something that didn't want to be found. Which is exactly what we're supposed to be looking for, right? Us in the . . . intelligence services."

The intelligence services, which River had joined at a young age, following in his grandfather's footsteps. David Cartwright had been a Service legend. River was a Service joke, having crashed King's Cross at rush

34

hour during a training exercise, and been exiled to Slough House in consequence. The fact that he'd been set up was the joke's real punchline, but not one many people had heard, and not one River laughed at.

"It's the passport office," he said at last. "All that huge backlog of passport applications, hundreds of them ushered through on the nod once the suits went back to work. So maybe someone out there saw that coming, right? Maybe it was a fire sale on the old false identity front. And what better false identity than a genuine British passport? Renewed so many times since, it's beyond reproach."

The machines chittered and whirred, blinked and bleeped, but the shape on the bed didn't move, and said nothing.

"Sometimes I think I'd sooner be where you are," River said.

But he almost certainly didn't mean it.

Catherine didn't see the van. What she saw was the soldier near the entrance to the Tube.

He wasn't uniformed, or she wouldn't have spared him a second glance — there were always squaddies in London. But he had the watchfulness that goes with having occupied hostile territory, a wary stillness, and that made two she'd seen tonight, and any lingering doubt about chance encounters evaporated. He held a rolled-up newspaper to keep his hands busy, and wasn't so much standing vigil as soaking everything in; cataloguing movement, alert for anomaly. Or not anomaly, she corrected. He was alert for her.

In which case he had already seen her; and if he hadn't yet he had now, because she made an abrupt 180-degree turn. Bad tradecraft, but she wasn't a street agent — never a joe — the nearest she'd come to an op was having her tonsils out, and was this paranoia? When the bad old days revisited, when she felt she'd slipped into a dry drunk, anything could happen . . .

She didn't look back; focused instead on the pavement in front of her. A black van rolled past, and she had to step aside for a group of teenagers, but she kept moving. There was a bus stop not far ahead, and if she was lucky her arrival there would coincide with a bus. On the bus, if one came, she'd call Lamb again. If one came.

The streets were far from deserted. People in office clothes, others in T-shirts and shorts; shops were still open, though banks and bookies and so on had darkened their doors. Pubs and bars had theirs propped open, letting heat escape on a tangle of music and voices. The canal wasn't far, and it was the kind of summer's evening when young people drifted that way, and shared picnics and wine on the benches, or unfolded blankets on grassy patches, where they could lie and text each other in drowsy comfort. And all Catherine had to do was raise her voice, shout for help . . .

And what would that get her? An exclusion zone. A woman having a meltdown in a heatwave: someone to avoid.

She risked a look behind. No bus. And nobody following. The soldier, if he'd been one, wasn't in sight, and Sean Donovan was nowhere.

At the bus stop she paused. The next bus would take her back the way she'd come; it would drop her opposite Slough House, rewinding the evening to when she'd emerged from the back lane. None of this would have happened, and in the morning she'd look back on it as a minor blip; the kind of bump in the road recovering drunks learn to negotiate. Up at the junction the lights changed, and fresh traffic began flowing her way; she was hoping for a bus, but the largest vehicle among them was a black van, the same one that had just gone past in the opposite direction. Catherine left the bus stop, her heart beating faster. One soldier, two soldiers; a recurring black van. Some things were echoes from a drunken past. Others weren't.

Why on earth would anyone be targeting her?

A question for another time. For the moment, she had to go to ground.

Before the approaching traffic reached her, she darted across the road.

On his way to the bar Marcus had called into the gents, for the relief of a few solo minutes, and finding the cubicle free had occupied it to contemplate what had happened to his life. This past while — since his exile to Slough House, certainly, but more specifically the past two months — it had been heading down the toilet. No wonder he felt calmer in here than out there.

Back when everything was as it should have been, one of Marcus's combat instructors had laid down a law: control is key. Control the environment, control your opponent. Most of all, control yourself. Marcus got that, or thought he got it, first time of hearing, but had soon discovered it was the large-print version: control didn't just mean keeping a lid on, it meant nailing that lid down tight. Meant making yourself into one of those soldier's tools, the kind that fold away until they're all handle, no blade, and only snap open when needed.

But the thing about training — and Marcus wasn't the first to notice this — was it filled you with skills that remained unflexed. Lots of stuff he'd had crammed into him, like how to bury himself in woodland for forty-eight hours straight, hadn't been called on since. He'd kicked some doors down, and not so long ago had placed a nicely tight circle of bullets inside a human being, but by and large his career hadn't made demands. And now Slough House, the slow annihilation of every ambition he'd ever had . . . The control factor was the only thing keeping him sane. Every day he nailed himself down, did what he was told, as if this might prove worthy of reward in the long run. And this despite what he'd been told by Catherine Standish, right at the start; that every slow horse knows there's no going back, apart from that small part of every slow horse that thinks: *except, maybe, for me . . .*

And control, of course, was where the gambling came in — ceding control was what gave him the kick. No matter how much he kidded himself it was a balancing act, that he only surrendered the environment but at all times maintained control of himself — set boundaries, established limits — the truth was, he was stepping into the unknown every time he entered a casino. Which hadn't mattered until lately, because until lately, he'd not been in the habit of losing.

It was the machines that had got him, those damn roulette machines, that had appeared in bookies it seemed like overnight. One-armed bandits, he'd never had trouble with: the clue was in the name. Those things were always going to rob you blind. But for some unaccountable reason the roulette machine was more alluring, more seductive . . . You started with a few coins, and it was astonishing how close you came to winning without actually winning, so you put a few more in, and then you won. Winning cleared the decks. Once you'd won you were back where you started, though with slightly less money . . . He'd played poker with Vegas pros and left the table walking; had scooped outsider bets on horses that were walking dog food, and here he was, taken to the cleaners by a fucking machine, feeding it twenties like it was his firstborn. He'd once boasted he was the house's worst nightmare: a gambler who played by the clock. As in, *I'm leaving here at ten, ahead or behind*. These days every time he looked at his watch it had skipped ahead thirty minutes, and every time it did, his next payday got further away.

He'd been digging into savings. Had found himself studying the loan ads on the Tube, the ones with rates that annualised at four thousand per cent plus. Cassie was going to kill him, if he didn't shoot himself first.

Worst of all, playing catch-up in office hours — logging onto casino sites in a bid to recoup lunchtime losses — he'd been snared by Roderick bloody Ho,

Slough House's answer to the tachograph. Which was why, tonight, he was Ho's drinking buddy, with only cokehead Shirley Dander as backup. Yep, the toilet was the right place for him, but he couldn't stay here forever. Heaving himself upright, he headed back to the bar.

When he rejoined his colleagues Shirley was asking Ho if his mouth was connected to his brain. "'Bitch'? You're lucky I just slapped you."

Ho turned to Marcus with relief. "You believe that, dog?"

"Did you just call me 'dog'?"

Shirley raised a hand, for the pleasure of seeing Ho flinch. "Mind your fucking language," she warned.

"Did he just call me 'dog'?"

"I think he did."

Marcus plucked Ho's glasses from his nose and tossed them onto the floor. "I'm a dog? You're a dog. Fetch."

While Ho went scrabbling again, Marcus said to Shirley, "I didn't know you and Louisa were tight."

"We're not. But I wouldn't fix Ho up with a nanny goat."

"Sisterhood is powerful."

"Got that right."

They chinked glasses.

When Ho sat back down, he was holding his spectacles in place with two fingers. "What you do *that* for?"

Marcus shook his head. "I can't believe you called me 'dog'."

40

Ho shot Shirley a glance before saying, "Did you forget the terms of our, uh, arrangement?"

Marcus breathed out through his nose. Almost a snort. "Okay," he said. "This is what's what. We're renegotiating terms, right? Here's the deal. You breathe one word about those casino sites, to anyone, and I'll break every bone in your chickenshit body."

"I'm not chickenshit."

"Focus on the broken bones. Are we clear?"

"I'm not chickenshit."

"But you will have broken bones."

"I will have broken bones. But I'm not chickenshit."

"You pick weird places to set your boundaries. And you know what your problem is?" Marcus was warming up now, developing his theme. "You never do anything. You just sit in your office and surf your machines like, like, like a fucking elf. Day in, day out, churning through reams of pointless information, just to keep Jackson bloody Lamb happy."

"So do you."

"Yeah, but I hate it."

"But you still do it."

Shirley shook her head.

Marcus explained, "You're a dweeb, Ho. All you are, all you'll ever be. A woman like Louisa's never gunna give you a second glance, and nor is any other woman without seeing your credit card up front. Me, I don't have that problem. You know why? Because before I was stuck doing this shit, I was doing other shit. Proper shit. You, all you've ever done is this shit, and this is the shit you like doing."

Ho said, "So what are you saying?"

"Give me strength . . . *Do* something, that's what I'm saying. You want to make a mark, you want to impress people, do something. Doesn't matter what, just so long as it's not sitting at a screen crunching . . . *data*."

If that last noun had involved bodily fluids rather than information, Marcus couldn't have put a more disgusted spin on it.

Now he stood. "I'm going. Broken bones, remember? If you take nothing else away, take that. Broken bones."

"Aren't we having another round?"

Shirley did the thing with her fingers again. "Hashtag missingthepoint."

"Stop doing that," Marcus said. He looked down at his unfinished beer, shrugged, and headed for the door.

Shirley reached across, carefully removed Ho's specs, folded them, and dropped them into Marcus's Guinness. "There," she said.

Ho opened his mouth to say something, but wisely changed his mind.

There was construction work on the other side of the road, as there seemed to be everywhere else: an office block had been taken down, a new one would one day go up, and meanwhile the empty space had been boarded off in case anyone noticed that not everywhere had to have a building on it. Catherine hurried past, buckled shoes tip-tapping on the pavement. An approaching man shot her a troubled look, but whether at her speed or her choice of clothing couldn't be determined.

This area was only vaguely on her map, but she knew if she swung right she'd soon join the main road leading to King's Cross; the other way, and she'd be into one of those enclaves London specialised in, whose small pockets of history had been left largely unmolested. This one was Georgian squares, many of them intact; one or two with a side removed due to war or development damage. Parked cars lined the kerbs. It struck her, and felt like an observation somebody else was making, how tranquil London could look, from the right angle, in the right light.

Out on the main thoroughfare loud cries would create confusion, and confusion was the enemy's friend. Here, away from the rapid pulse of traffic, she could knock on a stranger's door and plead sanctuary . . . She risked a look behind. There was no sign of the black van, which would have to travel some way down the road before effecting a turn, because of the median strip. But there was someone, a hundred yards back, or had been — in the moment of her turning he melted in the evening's heat; was an imp of her unconscious, playing with her mind.

Or he was a man, and had dropped behind a parked car.

It might all be a heat dream. Paranoia, the sober drunk's companion, blooming in the swelter of the evening. But it felt real. First Sean, then the other soldier; the van that had looped round, as if coming to collect her. Panic was welling inside Catherine, though it would have taken a pro to notice. She looked distracted, nothing more. At Slough House, this might have been cause to pull up the barricades; here on the streets, it didn't register.

She believed she was being followed, and that he had dropped behind a car.

And she believed that any moment the black van would reappear, and that for some unknown reason it was coming for her — that Sean Donovan had tagged her for a cohort of watchers, who were gathering, and would soon pounce.

On the move, walking faster, she found her phone, re-called Lamb, and went straight to voicemail again. Disconnecting, she once more considered knocking on a stranger's door: but then what? She was not unaware that Shirley Dander referred to her as the Mad Governess. Dangerous territory, snarking on others' appearance when you were five-two high and favoured a buzz cut, but there it was — the mode of dress in which Catherine felt comfortable labelled her eccentric. Would you let this woman into your home? Besides, knocking on a door would mean coming to a halt, and movement felt safest. Lamb, she thought, would keep moving. Not the Lamb he was today, but the Lamb he'd been back whenever, living the life that had turned him into the Lamb he was today.

She hurried through the square and into a connecting terrace. Streetlights were coming on and the quality of the heat was changing, radiating up from the pavements instead of pulsing down from the sky. Night would bring no relief. Still, when it fell she hoped to be home, behind a locked door, wondering what momentary madness she'd fallen prey to, out on the sun-struck streets.

This terrace was thirty houses long, and ended in another square. At the next junction, she'd head back to the main road: hop on a bus, rejoin the transport network that held London together, when it wasn't holding it up. Another look behind. Nobody. The shape that had dropped behind a car had been a falling shadow, nothing more. Two black vans was well within an ordinary margin. A car rolled by, looking for a parking space, and rounded the corner ahead. As it passed from sight the black van turned into the road. Catherine swung on her heels, and Sean Donovan scooped her into his arms like a fairy-tale hero; cradling her and stopping her mouth in a single embrace. The black van slowed, its back doors opened, and Donovan stepped inside carrying Catherine. The doors closed, and the van swept off.

Seven seconds, if that.

The streets quietly smouldered, as the violet hour grew purple.

It was still hot as hell when Jackson Lamb emerged from Slough House into the backyard and, fiddling in his pocket for his lighter, found his mobile phone instead, and noticed he had two missed calls — Standish. Missed calls. A stationery delivery gone astray, or a complaint about a printer not working. Standish persisted in laying such issues at his door, no matter how many times he outlined department policy, which was that he didn't give a toss. Cigarette smouldering in hand he shambled into the lane, a coronet of smoke lingering in the air behind him, like an image of a wandering spirit . . .

Which lasted but briefly, though in the moments before its passing swelled outward, as though pregnant with impressions of the building's inhabitants, weighed down as they were with grief and gambling debts, with drug habits and self-involvement; unburdening themselves to the comatose, squabbling in pubs, hunting oblivion in strangers' beds, or else grown lazy, fat and complacent — sifting through all these as if somewhere among them lay the answer to a question posed recently, quite some distance away: *Which of your colleagues would you trust with your life?*

And then the air shifted, and the smoke was gone.

CHAPTER
THREE

It must have been a nursery at one time, nestling quietly under the eaves, because beneath the plain white of the ceiling Catherine could make out faint shapes from a previous scheme, stars and crescent moons, decorations to enchant the tenant of a crib. But that was in the distant past, judging by the plaster dust lying in icing-sugar drifts by the skirting board. The floor, too, was bare — no protection for infant feet — though a thin rug had been laid next to the single bed, and the padlock on the outside of the door was heavy-duty, beyond what even the most mischief-prone child warranted. A nursery no more. Though not the securest of prisons.

They'd travelled for an hour at least; slowly at first, through the never-empty streets of London, then faster once free of the capital. Just over an hour, she thought, but her watch had been taken from her, and she had lacked the presence of mind to perform a slow count . . . Besides, she'd blacked out on being dumped in the van. Partly the grip Sean Donovan had exerted, a clasping of — was it her carotid? — plus the shock and the heat and, crazily enough, a momentary relaxation at knowing the worst had happened, and she need no longer dread its approach. She had grown dizzy, and life had grown dark. So there'd been no running tally of corners taken; no memorising of audible landmarks. If church bells had rung, they had rung unheard. If the van had passed a waterfall, she'd failed to notice.

There'd been two others. One driving, obviously. Sean himself, who had lifted her from the street like a sack left for recycling; and a third, the soldier she'd seen loitering by the Tube. Being spotted, it occurred to her, had not been his error: she'd been meant to notice him, and turn away. What use would their van have been on the underground?

Here and now, like any prisoner, she checked the window first. Set in an alcove formed by the slant of the roof and mullioned into a diamond pattern, it was closed by a simple latch, and easily large enough to fit through, but there were iron bars set into the external sill which a brief tug told her weren't going anywhere. Not that she was built for scrambling down the side of a house. It wasn't the securest of prisons, but didn't have to be — she was a middle-aged woman who'd never been a joe; a recovering drunk who was PA to a drunk still working on it. Why did they want her in the first place? And who, Sean Donovan included, were they?

Unsuited for squeezing through them, Catherine settled for leaving the windows open instead, causing a slight adjustment in the air. Nothing you could call a breeze. There was a hum of distant traffic, but she couldn't see the road from here. It had felt like a motorway, though that didn't narrow things down

48

much. An hour or so from central London, somewhere off a motorway . . . A house set on its own in what must be countryside, because it was too dark to be anything else.

In the van, she'd been blindfolded and gagged, her hands bound, but none of it roughly — it might have been a sex game, a party promise. And that had been it for the rest of the journey. She'd contemplated thrashing about, but to what end? Best to preserve her strength for whatever came next.

When they'd left the motorway, the terrain had swiftly deteriorated: slip road, B-road — she'd heard bushes swishing the van's panels. Then the crunching of gravel, and the sudden dips and bounces of rough ground. The van had lurched to a stop; no negotiating its way into a space. They'd untied her but left the blindfold on as they helped her out, one strong arm — not Donovan's — at her waist until she'd found her feet. Then out of the country air, which was softer, greener, richer than the city's, and into a house whose floors were wooden, on which her buckled feet sang and produced a faint echo.

"There's stairs."

Again, not Donovan.

There were stairs, yes, and then more stairs; three floors' worth. And then she was in here, this one-time nursery, and the blindfold was removed.

"Your quarters."

It was the second soldier, the one from the Tube: chipped from the same block as Donovan. Before she had time for a more detailed analysis, he was gone. She heard him fitting the padlock in place, then heading downstairs.

Here she was, then. They'd taken her bag: her money, tissues, lipstick, Kindle, travel pass, other stuff; her phone too, of course. Her watch. They hadn't searched her, though, which could easily have proved their undoing, if she'd been in the habit of carrying a concealed weapon or the means of improvising one. And still she had no clue what they wanted . . . The slightest of draughts now, through the opened window. There were hills in the distance, a starless expanse blocking the heavens. A few faraway lights, which must be other dwellings; a more focused blaze of electricity which was probably a garage, servicing the nearby motorway. All plainly visible. Almost an amateur operation, except for Sean Donovan's involvement. No one would call him amateur.

Looking down on the immediate surroundings, she could make out other structures, half-revealed by the pools of light splashing through downstairs windows. They looked like outhouses — barns? — further suggesting that this was a farmhouse. Something else, too, in the darkness; a vehicle the size and shape of a London bus; one of the old Routemasters that were either out of service or about to be reintroduced, depending what the transport policy was on any given morning. Just another touch of the bizarre to throw into the mix. What was going on?

She doubted it was personal. Donovan would hardly put a crew together to kidnap a former girlfriend. Or not even girlfriend; one of his former lays. Some other reason, then . . . He knew she was no longer at the Park, because he'd said as much, on Aldersgate Street. What did he know about Slough House? Did he think it was important? He had a serious disappointment coming if so.

There was a second door on the far side of the room and Catherine tried it now, expecting to find it locked, but it opened without complaint. An en-suite bathroom: loo, sink, bath. There was no cabinet on the wall, though screw marks, and a less-discoloured rectangle of magnolia paint, indicated that there had been once: yes, well, she thought. Give a girl a mirror, she can make herself a knife. Presumably similar thoughts about the weaponising potential of shampoo, tubes of toothpaste, cans of hairspray, etc. had also occurred to her captors, because the only toiletry, a single loo roll aside, was a complimentary-sized bar of soap, still in its wrapper. Stick a hairpin in it, you've got a one-use-only shiv, she thought, but she didn't have a hairpin, and didn't imagine it would take anyone bigger than a Boy Scout to take it away from her if she did.

There was another window in here, a skylight, but it too was barred over, and anyway out of reach.

She returned to the bedroom. It occurred to her that maybe she should try to get some sleep, there being few other activities available which didn't involve pacing and growing scared, but she decided against it. To sleep was to become vulnerable. For the time being, she was in charge of herself, if nothing else. She'd sit and wait. Sooner or later, information would start to flow. Meanwhile, she'd carry on being herself: not drunk, unbowed, and as organised as the situation allowed her to be.

It was perhaps half an hour before anyone came. Catherine had turned the light off, the better to familiarise herself with the view through the window, but no great insights arrived in the dark. Sean Donovan, she remembered, had been in a liaison role when she first met him; had attended a meeting with Charles Partner, her former boss and then head of the Security Service, and various other bigwigs, some from Down the Corridor, as Westminster was locally known; others from Over the River, where Intelligence was supposedly housed. Alone of those gathered, he had looked her in the eye as she handed out the morning's dossiers. One thing had led to another. In those days, it usually did.

And now, hearing someone rattling the padlock, she assumed it would be him, but the man who entered was a stranger; neither Donovan, nor the other soldier, but a third man: younger, stocky. He wore a once white short-sleeved shirt, and up his arms crawled inky designs, which also peeped out from the collar and crept onto the back of his hairless head. He held something in his hand: two somethings. One was the pair of handcuffs she'd been made to wear in the van. The other was a mobile — it looked like Catherine's own.

"Put these on." He dangled the cuffs.

"Why am I here?"

"Lady, just put the cuffs on. And this."

52

He produced the gag from his back pocket.

"Is that my phone?"

"Yes."

His vowels were flat, she noted: northern. She was no expert on regional accents, but thought north-west rather than east. She noted, too, that her own pronunciation had sharpened in response, becoming more BBC. Maybe Lamb was rubbing off on her. That was the kind of trick he'd play.

"What's your name?" she asked.

"Seriously?"

"It was worth a try."

He said, "Let's just get the cuffs on, okay?"

Catherine said, "Well, since it's traditional."

She offered her wrists, then he leaned across her to tie the gag round her mouth. She could smell him when he did this — sweat, inadequately masked by his deodorant, which was marginally less pleasant. When he'd finished, he stepped back and aimed her iPhone at her. She remained still while he took her picture, and stayed that way while he examined the result, nodding to himself. Good lord, who did he think he was?

Perhaps he caught something of this in the blank gaze she levelled at him, because while he ungagged her, he said, "Just checking."

"Thank you, David Bailey."

"Who?"

"Doesn't matter." But he was Bailey now, which pleased her. Information, even the kind you make up yourself, gives you a handle on what's going on.

He uncuffed her and left, padlocking the door behind him. She wondered what time it was, decided after midnight, and wondered if they planned on feeding her. She wasn't hungry, but to feed her someone would have to come back and maybe talk some more . . . Thinking about not being hungry made her thirsty instead, so she returned to the bathroom, where she cupped her hands and drank from the tap. Where would she normally be now? At home; most likely asleep. She didn't always sleep well. Some nights she played music quite late, but softly. Alcohol used to blur the edges of even the roughest days. Now she had to rely on other comforts, and the days never quite became smooth.

She must have dozed, or hovered on the border, because the noise of the door opening startled her; brought her back with a wildly beating heart. She sat up so quickly her head buzzed.

This time, it was Donovan.

He didn't speak at first but surveyed the room, as if she'd paid a security deposit, and he was looking for reasons not to return it. While he did that, she studied him for signs of guilt. It was there, she thought. Whatever was going on, he felt bad about this part, at least.

When he at last looked at her, his eyes were still the bad-times stormy blue.

She said, "Bailey didn't give much away."

"Bailey?"

"Private joke."

"Glad to see you're making friends. I thought you'd given that up."

"Is that what this is about? Have you been nursing a passion for me all these years, Sean?"

"Is that what you think?"

"I don't know what to think yet. What happened to you?"

He laughed, or nearly did. It was a noise, anyway, and had an edge of amusement to it. "We've both come down in the world, haven't we?"

"Oh, I get by. You, though. You look pretty rough."

He glanced down at himself.

"Not your clothes. It's you, Sean. You're not the man I knew. It's like you've taken a slow-acting poison."

"A slow-acting poison."

She gave her signature shrug, which is to say she held her palms upright, to show she had nothing to hide.

"Quite the lady, aren't you? Now you've given up the booze."

There was a looser aspect to his movements than earlier, as if his joints had been oiled. This would have been enough to tell her he'd taken drink, even if she hadn't been able to smell it on him. She pictured him downstairs, the downstairs she hadn't seen. A comfortably shabby room, looking out on that courtyard with its outhouses and its double-decker bus, if that's what it was. There'd be a sideboard, a drinks cabinet: straight out of fifties' rep. He'd have poured from a cut-glass decanter, downed it in one, then poured another for a more contemplative sip-and-savour. Nothing to dull his edge, he'd have thought, because everyone thought that. Like smokers unable to smell their habit on their clothes, drinkers always thought themselves unaffected.

Her hands had curled into fists. Thinking drinker's thoughts could do that.

Uncurling them, she brushed at her skirt, as if it harboured crumbs. There was something very precise about her movements, and this seemed to annoy him.

"All buttoned-up. Who'd think to look at you the times we once had?"

"I'm an alcoholic, Sean," she said calmly. "I had lots of times, did lots of things. I wouldn't do them now."

"Too good now."

"It's not about goodness."

"You were, though. On your back or on your knees, you were always good."

He waited for her to respond, but she said nothing. Just regarded him unflinching, simply being who she was now instead of who she'd been then, and letting him know she felt no shame or self-disgust. Simply the determination never to be that person again.

Only when he looked away did she speak.

"What do you want, Sean? If you're expecting a ransom, you're going to be seriously disappointed, but either way, what brings you upstairs? A chat about the weather?"

That seemed to amuse him, for some reason. But the answer he gave was, "To find out who you trust."

"I'm not in the mood for that conversation."

56

"It's not a conversation. Just a question. Which of your colleagues would you trust with your life?"

"With my life," she said flatly.

He didn't answer.

She said, "I used to trust you. Does that count?"

"Someone from Slough House," he said. "I need a name. Longridge? Cartwright? Guy?"

So this wasn't about her. It was about Slough House.

Probably, when you got down to it, it was about Jackson Lamb.

"Catherine?"

She gave him a name.

He left, locking the door behind him. For a long while afterwards she sat in the same position: upright, with her hands clasped on her knees. A Mad Governess again, and not just mad, but locked in an attic. That would give Shirley Dander a laugh, supposing she caught the reference.

After a while Catherine lay on the bed instead, and after a further while, slept.

However many miles away, in whichever direction it was, Slough House boiled in the morning's heat. Everyone was there by nine save Catherine and Lamb, and the former's unfamiliar absence struck a jarring note. It did with River, anyway, and as he stood by the kettle, pouring a cup of instant coffee, he asked Louisa, who was brewing a pot of the real stuff, if she knew where the other woman was.

She didn't reply.

"Louisa?"

"What?"

"Seen Catherine?"

She shook her head.

Why bother? Since Min's death she was a walking time bomb: not much given to conversation, but if you listened carefully, you could hear her tick.

River took his cup to his office, and contemplated another day of studying ancient passport applications, scanned and pasted into a database so creaky, if it was a boat you'd be watching rats abandon it. Picking up a biro, he tapped it against his front teeth. Eight and a half hours of this, minus whatever he could get away with for lunch. Five times that to make up the week, and forty-eight weeks in the working year . . . He might see this task off before his fortieth, if he really hammered it. Yeah: get a wiggle on, and he could celebrate putting this to bed alongside the big four-o.

Or he could just beat himself to death with a hole punch.

Gathering one up, pumping it like a stress reliever, he crossed to the window whose gold-tooled lettering spelled W. W. HENDERSON, SOLICITOR AND COMMIS-SIONER FOR OATHS for the benefit of those on the street who wondered what poor fools toiled away in here. An oath or two had been uttered in these parts, that was true. The hole punch clacked in his hand. He heard the downstairs door open then close, and thought, *Catherine*, then: no. She comes up the stairs like a ghost. Lamb could too when he felt like it, but this morning he was his usual bothersome presence:

navigating the staircase with the grace of a hip-popotamus steering a wheelbarrow. He thumped past River's office, then into his own room overhead; the precursor, usually, to a one-man-band performance: the farting, cursing, furniture-rattling overture to the day. River returned to his desk, where his pile of passport applications had grown while his back was turned. It wasn't going anywhere, and until it did, neither was he. But he hadn't done more than pluck the topmost sheet off the pile before it occurred to him that the expected overhead symphony hadn't occurred; that what he was listening to now was that kind of silence that descends before a tree comes crashing down . . . He stood. When the thumping started, he was already halfway out of the door.

Lamb eyed his crew — some say "team"; he preferred "minions" — with a malevolent eye, the other being scrunched shut against the smoke from his cigarette. The blinds were drawn as usual, but sunlight had found a little leverage, and was currently painting stripes on the wall, and across the heads and shoulders of said minions, who were bunched like suspects in an old-fashioned film.

In the same hand that held his cigarette Lamb was wielding a Danish pastry, and he waved it now in their general direction. "You know, seeing you all together, it reminds me why I come into work every morning."

Golden crumbs and blue-grey smoke flew in opposite directions.

"It's 'cause I've a cockroach infestation at home."

"Can't think why," murmured River.

"It's rude to mutter. If there's one thing I can't abide, it's bad manners." Lamb bit off some pastry and continued, mouth full, "Christ, it's like being in a zombie movie. You lot need to perk yourselves up. Where's Standish?"

"Haven't seen her," Ho offered.

"I didn't ask if you'd seen her. I asked where she is. She's usually here before me."

"But not always."

"Thanks. Next time I forget what 'usually' means, I'll know who to ask."

"Bathroom?" Shirley suggested.

"Must be the world's longest dump she's taking," Lamb grumbled. "And I speak as an expert."

"None of us doubt that."

"Maybe she has a domestic emergency," Marcus said.

"Like what? Her bookshelves got out of alphabetical order?"

River said, "It's always possible she has a life you don't know about."

"Like you, you mean? How *is* your old pal Spider?"

Meaning Spider Webb, *injured in the course of duty* according to the official report — "injured in the course of being a dick-head, more like" (Lamb) — and still on life support; unlikely ever to make a full recovery, or even regain consciousness. River had visited him a number of times, though how Jackson Lamb knew that was one of those things that made Lamb Lamb: you

60

didn't know how he managed it, but you wished he wouldn't.

Knowing an answer was expected, River said: "He's hooked up to about seven different machines. Nobody's expecting him to wake up anytime soon."

"Have they tried switching him off then switching him on again?"

"I'll ask."

Lamb displayed yellowing teeth and said, "Has anyone actually checked the bog?"

"She's not in there."

Louisa said, "She's probably got a doctor's appointment. Or something."

"She seemed all right yesterday."

"Sometimes people need to see doctors. They don't actually have to be visibly injured."

"This is the Secret Service," said Lamb. "Not frigging *Woman's Hour*. And besides, she should have called in."

"It might be on the chart," Ho suggested.

"There's a chart?"

"On her wall."

Lamb stared at him.

"It says when people are absent —"

"Yeah, I'd worked that out, mastermind. I'm wondering why you're still here. Go and check it."

Ho left.

"Why the big concern?" River said. "Maybe her train's buggered. Happens all the time."

"Yeah, because she was last late when, exactly?"

But Lamb wasn't looking at them when he said this. He'd glanced instead at his mobile, which was on the desk in front of him.

She tried to get in touch, River thought. And Lamb ignored her call.

My God. Is he feeling *guilt*?

Lamb killed his cigarette end in yesterday's half-full teacup.

"Besides," he said. "It's not like her to disappear."

" 'Disappear' is a bit strong," said Shirley.

"Really? What would you call it?"

". . . Not being here?"

"And what would happen if we all did that? What would it be like if I was just *not here* all of a sudden?"

Shirley seemed about to speak, but changed her mind.

"It would be like *Hamlet* without the Prince," River suggested.

"Precisely," Lamb said. "Or *Waiting for Godot* without Godot."

Nobody touched that one.

Ho returned.

"Well?" said Lamb.

"It's not on the chart."

"And that took you five minutes? An idiot would have been back in half the time."

"Yeah, that's because —"

Everyone waited.

Ho slumped.

"Pop it on a postcard," Lamb said. "No hurry."

He glared round the room.

"Any more bright ideas?"

The phone in River's pocket vibrated, and he sent up a prayer of thanks it was on silent.

"Maybe she left a note on somebody's desk," he said.

"When?"

"She might have got here first and had to leave in a rush. I'll go check."

He slipped out of the room.

"Anyone notice a note on their desk?" Lamb asked the rest of them.

"We might have mentioned it," Marcus said.

Lamb's lip curled. "Well, thank you, Action Man. Good to know you've not lost your edge."

Louisa said, "Can we go get on with our jobs now?"

"You're very eager. Discovered a taste for paper-shuffling, have we?"

"Well, it's pointless and boring. But at least we can do it in silence."

"My my. I'm starting to think we should go on one of those team-bonding courses. Though maybe we should wait till your mother hen's back in the coop. What was that?"

None of them had heard anything.

"That was the back door. *Standish!*"

He bellowed this loudly enough, and unexpectedly enough, that Shirley actually felt her bladder release, just a tiny bit. But there was no reply from downstairs, and no Catherine Standish appeared.

"Where's Cartwright gone?" Lamb said suspiciously.

"Bathroom?" said Shirley.

"That's your answer for everything this morning. Something you want to share with us?"

"I'll go look."

"Stay bloody there! Another member of staff goes missing, I'll lose my deposit." He bellowed again, this time for River, but River didn't appear either.

In the quiet that followed, Louisa thought she could hear the windowpanes ringing.

"Jesus wept," said Lamb at last. "It's not like I'm not glad to see the back of you, but we're supposed to be a functioning department."

Marcus snorted, but it might have been hay fever.

"Right," said Lamb. "Enough of this. You" — he indicated Louisa — "go find Standish. And if she's face down in a pool of sick, I want photos. And you two" — this was Marcus and Shirley — "find out where Cartwright's got to and bring him back."

"By force?"

"Shoot him if you have to. I'll sign off on it."

Leaving Roderick Ho.

"I'll go with Louisa," he said.

"No you won't. She can screw up on her own. With you to help, it'll just take longer."

The others were already heading downstairs, but Ho lingered at the door and looked back.

"What?"

Ho said, "That's because an idiot wouldn't have checked as carefully as I did."

"Well, you've saved yourself a stamp. Feeling better?"

Ho nodded.

"Good," said Lamb. "Now fuck off."

64

The incoming message had been from Catherine's phone, and River had opened it heading down the stairs, still congratulating himself on a neat escape. He was expecting a brief explanation for absence: late-running Tube, sudden illness, alien invasion. What he read instead was an even briefer summons:

Pedestrian bridge. Now.

Which didn't sound like the Catherine Standish he knew.

An attachment came with it and he paused on the landing while it effortfully opened — it took half a second to work out what he was looking at: a woman, handcuffed, gagged, like a come-on for an amateur porn site except she was fully clothed and, Jesus, it was Catherine . . .

Why the hell would anyone take Catherine?

Pedestrian bridge.

Now.

There was only one pedestrian bridge it could be; not a dozen yards away, spanning the road between the Tube station and the Barbican. And before checking it out there were alarm bells to ring: slow horse or not, Catherine was an agent of the security services, and Regent's Park ran a full-court press when one of their own came under threat . . . As for Lamb, he'd hang River out to dry if he took another step without putting him in the picture. That was something to think about, so River thought about it as he stuffed the phone away, and took the rest of the stairs three at a time.

It was already stifling outside, the heat much worse in the mouldy backyard. Round the alley and out on the street, and there was a man on the bridge, looking down on the traffic like all this activity amused him . . . Too far away to make out his face, but that was the impression River gained, as he ran up the road, through the station entrance, up the stairs and onto the bridge.

One hand on its railing, the man was waiting for him, and River had been right: he did look kind of amused. He was fiftyish, lean, in a suit the colour of early-morning mist; his dark hair tinged with silver. His yellow tie might have come from a club; his superior smirk, he'd have had drummed into him about halfway through Eton or wherever. And he wore rings on both little fingers, confirming one of River's deepest prejudices.

At River's approach, he removed his hand from the railing. Extended it, as if expecting a handshake.

Instead, River took him by the lapels. "Where's Catherine?"

"She's perfectly safe."

"Not what I asked you." River drew him closer. "Answer carefully. Speak slowly."

"She's. Perfectly. Safe."

Making a joke of it; in vowels, if not cut glass, at least precision-tooled.

River shook him like a stick. "The photo showed her handcuffed. With a rag in her mouth."

"To get your attention. You're here, aren't you?"

"On a bridge above a busy road, yes. You want to go over that railing?"

66

That earned a broader smirk. "You're not going to tell me you don't know how this works, are you? Ms Standish is safe and will continue to be so provided I make a phone call within the next thirty seconds. So I rather think you'd better stand back, don't you?"

Over grey suit's shoulder, River saw a couple on the street below pause, and one of them point their way.

He loosened his grip.

"That's better. Much more civilised."

"Don't push it."

The man produced a phone and exchanged a few brief words with someone. That done, he put the phone away and said, "So you're River Cartwright. Unusual name."

"It means someone who makes carts."

"Ms Standish said she trusted you. With her *life*, as it happens."

"Where is she?"

A mock-sad shake of the head. "Let's move on to how you get her back, shall we?"

He was enjoying this too much, River thought. As if whatever it was he wanted was secondary to the method of acquiring it.

"What are you after?"

"Information."

"About what?"

"You don't need to know about what. You simply have to steal it."

"Or?"

"Do you really want me to go into details? Very well . . ."

He paused and River knew, without turning, that someone was behind him. It turned out to be the couple who'd pointed up at them a minute ago. They walked past, trying not to appear curious; maybe civic-minded types who wanted to be sure a violent assault wasn't under way; maybe locals who were hoping one was. When they reached the Barbican side they looked back, but only once, and then were gone.

"The men holding her have . . . poor impulse control."

"Impulse control," River repeated.

"Poor impulse control, yes. I'd say about eighty minutes short of going critical, in fact. If you wanted to put a figure on it."

River reached out and smoothed down the man's lapels where his two-fisted grip had crumpled them. "You might want to remember this later," he said. "That you once found all this funny."

"Can't wait. Meanwhile, you have an errand to run. And" — he looked at his watch — "seventy-nine minutes before those men I mentioned start loosening their belts. Do you want to waste any more of them threatening me?"

"What do you want?" River said.

The man told him.

Two minutes after River left the bridge at a run, Marcus Longridge and Shirley Dander emerged from the alley onto Aldersgate Street. Marcus looked one way and Shirley the other. Pedestrians, freshly released from the underground, were trooping across the road at the lights, and more were clustered round the entrance to the gym on the corner. There were buses heading in both directions, and a cyclist who, judging by his disregard for other vehicles, had an organ donor card and was in a hurry to use it; there was a woman in council livery pushing a dustcart their way, and a man in a grey suit observing all this from the pedestrian bridge into the Barbican. But there was no sign of River Cartwright.

"See him?" Marcus asked.

"Nope," said Shirley. "You?"

"Nope." He paused, allowing River one last opportunity to reveal himself, then said, "Fancy an ice cream?"

"Yeah, all right," Shirley said.

They headed off towards Smithfield, where they were less likely to be spotted

The man on the bridge had disappeared from sight.

CHAPTER
FOUR

Catherine kept a spare set of door keys in a matchbox taped to the underside of her desk, where Louisa had stumbled upon them quite early in her Slough House career. She collected them now, and headed off to St John's Wood by cab. It was into the twenties already, bright sunlight blindly bouncing off glass and metal surfaces: enough to make you want to sit in a dark room, even if you didn't want to do that anyway. She'd never been to Catherine's flat before. For a while she wondered what that said about her, about the whole of the Slough House crew, and the paper-thin friendships their daily lives were scribbled on, but mostly she concentrated on not thinking; on simply moving in a bubble through London; not being at her desk, not filling the space left by Min.

The flat was in an art deco block, shielded at the front by a well-maintained hedge. Louisa paid the taxi and pocketed the receipt. The block's rounded edges and metal-framed windows lent it a science-fiction air: this had once been how the future would look. Its tiled and shiny lobby made her sandals clack, but that was the only obvious noise. The whole block seemed unnaturally quiet, as if Catherine weren't the only occupant to have gone missing. It was a fate Louisa would cheerfully have wished on her own neighbours. Unnatural quiet wasn't so much of a thing around her way.

Catherine lived on the topmost floor. Louisa rang the bell and waited a full minute before letting herself in, calling Catherine's name as she did so. No reply. She did a quick scoot through, making sure the place was empty. The bed was made, but that was no surprise — Catherine made a place look neater just by being in it. She was never likely to leave havoc in her wake. There was a landline in the sitting room, but no pad for taking messages; a calendar on the kitchen wall, but nothing marked for the month save a hairdresser's appointment two weeks hence. A shopping list on the fridge door gave nothing away, and while a pile of books four deep on the bedside table suggested Catherine was a restless reader, none of the scraps used as bookmarks taught Louisa anything. It wasn't a sterile environment — was a lived-in space — but it held no clues as to where its occupant might have gone. The wardrobe was full, resembling a dresser's rack from a Merchant-Ivory production, and there was an empty suitcase in the hall closet. Nor was there any sign of those things Catherine might be expected to carry round with her: purse, phone, sunglasses, travel pass. At first glance, it looked like Catherine had had an ordinary morning: had got up and left for work as usual, and whatever had kept her from arriving there had happened en route. But when Louisa checked the dishwasher, she found it full of clean dry crockery long since cooled to normal, and there were no breakfast dishes stacked and ready for the next loading. A palm on the kettle came away stone cold. Either Catherine had left without breakfast, or she hadn't been here last night.

"Dirty stop-out," Louisa muttered, but without conviction.

She'd stopped out herself last night, of course. Had got home at seven, time enough to shower and change for work. More than once last year she and Min had spent an evening in a bar, passing comment on the hook-ups happening around them, encounters that increased in desperation the later they occurred, and had congratulated each other on being out of that game. Louisa had been careful never to add "for good" because fate was the kind of attack dog you didn't want to taunt. But tempting fate or not, "for good" didn't happen. "For bad" looked like it had come to stay instead.

Enough of that. She checked the bathroom. The air was dry, and there were no damp towels. Catherine hadn't been here for a day or more.

Louisa returned to the sitting room, trying not to compare and contrast with her own studio flat, which was tiny and crooked and needed serious attention, like maybe arson. Everything here was, if not arranged in straight lines, at least in its proper place, and care had been taken in deciding what that place was. So far, so Catherine. None of this would surprise any of the slow horses, except probably Ho, to whom it wouldn't have occurred to form an opinion. But it didn't tell the whole story. This was where the surface Catherine lived, that was all. Which was why there was no wine cache in a cupboard; no spirits in the fridge, or emergency sherry on a dresser. Or even any glasses, or not proper ones. Louisa frequently ran out of glasses, but that was because glass broke easily, not because she was avoiding the issue. Here, it was deliberate, as if the occasional use of a suggestive receptacle, even for a virgin fruit juice, might nudge a scale that would tip the drinker into a puddle outside the nearest bar.

So now came the obvious thought, that Catherine had fallen off the wagon. She knew Catherine was an alcoholic, not because the two women had ever discussed it but because Lamb made reference to it often enough. And one thing everyone knew about alcoholism was, it wasn't like the flu. You didn't shake it off and carry on; you tamped it down and hoped it wouldn't reignite. Which meant anything could have happened; Catherine could have been on her way home and some tiny incident, invisible to everyone else, could have thrown a switch inside her, redirecting her to oblivion. Louisa wouldn't put it past Lamb, even — who always kept booze in the office — to have tempted her with a taste. Leaving Catherine with an unkillable thirst, and the whole of London mapped with watering holes.

But the image wouldn't stick. Catherine drunk; Catherine passed out under a hedge, or under a stranger — it was like a punchline to an unsuccessful joke. Because all of Catherine's ramrod rectitude — the right-angled efficiency of her office; the primness of her dress; the fact that she so rarely swore — these things didn't make it funny that she'd once been an habitual drinker; they were her defences against ever again becoming one. The same way her flat was, with its places for everything, and all of them filled. Even the private parts of her public life were a form of cover, because they were all joes in the end, all spooks were joes, even those who never set foot outside their secret offices; from the anoracked stoats monitoring phone calls in GCHQ to the intelligence weasels over the river; from the blue-eyed boys and girls on Regent's Park's hub to the slow horses themselves, gradually disappearing under reams of yellowing paper — they were all joes, every last spook of them, because they all knew what it was like to live nine-tenths of their lives undercover. It was why they'd joined the Service in the first place: this sneaking suspicion that the whole damn world was hostile. The only ones you could trust were those you worked alongside, and you couldn't trust them either, because there was no friend falser than another spook. Always, they'd stab you in the back, cut you off at the knees, or just plain die.

Louisa didn't yet know which of those Catherine had done, but she was certain she hadn't gone off on a bender. She guessed Lamb thought that too, but she opened her phone to let him know anyway. There was no such thing as too much information.

Seventy-nine minutes . . .

It had not taken the man long to explain what he wanted. He gave the impression of being used to imparting instructions: a class thing, River thought —

74

the country still riddled with this, and especially London: walking talking suits, inflated by their own self-importance, each and every one of them asking for a good hard kick in the slats —

This the beat in the background as he ran.

Bond would have leaped from the bridge onto a passing bus, or drop-kicked a motorcyclist and hijacked his wheels. Bourne would have surfed the streets on car roofs, or slipped into parkour mode, bouncing off walls and wheelie bins, always knowing which alley to cut through . . .

River threw a quick glance at the nearby row of Boris bikes, shook his head, and ran down into the Tube station.

Not far from Regent's Park, below a recently renovated local authority swimming baths, lurk several subterranean levels unknown to the public. Here, Service members — joes and handlers alike; desk staff too, when their annual appraisals demand — undergo various forms of hand-to-hand combat training, partly to improve their chances of surviving assault by an armed opponent, should such circumstances arise, but largely to ensure they can maim an unsuspecting victim should the opportunity present itself. Pens, coffee cups, spectacles, pocket change: all and any can be used to inflict permanent damage on a potential enemy.

How to do the same to a subordinate is a skill you pick up on the job.

There were six of them at the meeting in the Park, five Second Desks and Dame Ingrid Tearney, but to all intents and purposes four of them might have been the articles of furniture their informal designation suggested. Because, like most other meetings with this cast list, this was all about Tearney and Taverner: Dame Ingrid, who'd helmed the Service for the best part of a decade, and intended to carry on doing so until they gave her a state funeral or made her queen, and Diana Taverner — "Lady Di" — who was Second Desk (Ops), and ruled the hub at Regent's Park, which gave her life-and-death control over joes in the field, but meant she had to hold doors open for the Dame.

It was no secret that she coveted the top job. But, twelve years younger than Tearney, her window of opportunity was closing with every passing day.

The meeting was about resources. Every meeting was about resources these days, whatever their agenda — the bumpy road of austerity having rattled the Service's axles as much as anyone else's — but this one was literally about resources, and how there were going to be fewer of them for the foreseeable future, even though there had already been fewer of them for the recent past. Cuts were in the interests of efficiency, according to a Treasury Department nobody was ever going to mistake for an embodiment of that virtue, and cuts were, more to the point, going to happen, so the Service might as well learn to live with them. Especially since, with the recent reshuffle, the Service had no defender Down the Corridor.

Because their new boss — the new Home Secretary — was Regent's Park's loudest critic. The fact that, decades previously, Peter Judd's application to join the

Service had been given the thumbs down was widely held to have played no small part in fostering this antipathy, but his psychological assessment had been so damning — had basically been written in block capitals, using red ink — that even now, old hands agreed, it cut both ways. On the downside, they were paying the price for having pissed off a narcissistic sociopath with family money, a power complex and a talent for bearing a grudge; but on the up, had Judd actually been allowed into the Service, he'd almost certainly have escalated the Cold War into a hot one, if his intervening years in diplomatic roles were anything to go by. But failures in diplomacy often score highly with the public, and Judd's star remained obstinately in the ascendant. For the moment, at least, the Service would have to live with him.

Besides, while it cut both ways, every two-edged sword has a handle. Which was what Tearney was grasping now, preparing to wield the blade where it would do her most good.

"I know this isn't what any of you want to hear," she said. "But the figures are in on projected spending levels for the next two quarters. There's good news and there's bad news. The good news is that the bad news isn't as bad as it might be." She paused, allowing a rueful grin to sweep round the table like a Mexican wave, breaking only on the stony reef of Diana Taverner. That was fine. Dame Ingrid knew how to play a room, and isolating the troublemaker was always a good move.

She removed her glasses, which were looped round her neck by a chain, and allowed them to drop onto her bosom. Her wig, today, was the blonde halo — a sure indication, for Dame Ingrid-watchers, of serious intent; its downy appearance meant to soften the blows that were coming.

"There'll be no recruitment at Desk-support level for the remainder of the financial year. In fact, come the Autumn Statement, we might well find ourselves having to shed those appointed within the last two years — I know, I know, and I'm sorry." She looked it, too. But this was one of Ingrid Tearney's natural strengths; what she lacked in comeliness, she made up for in apparent empathy. "But these are the realities we're dealing with, and it will do none of us any good to kick against them."

Taverner, of course, was first to ignore that.

"I need admin support."

"But you're doing so well without it, Diana."

"Ingrid, I'm spending half my time chasing up office supplies."

"I'm sure that's an exaggeration."

She was sure it wasn't. Taverner's junior had transferred across the river a while back, and for ten months she'd been holding down two roles: acting as her own assistant, as she'd put it in a memo. Given the tendency of Taverner's assistants to burn out within eighteen months tops, there were those who were anticipating a schizophrenic meltdown soon, but Dame Ingrid wasn't holding her breath. If Diana Taverner

78

ever self-destructed, she'd find a way of doing so to her own advantage.

She said, "Diana. We all know you've been hamstrung by the lack of assistance this past year, but Finance feels it's better to make sacrifices at office level than to risk having to make them on the streets. I'm sure you understand that."

Because not to do so would have been tantamount to declaring she'd sooner put the public in danger than make her own coffee.

"And besides, and this is something I was going to bring up anyway, it's not gone unnoticed what a splendid job you've been doing flying solo. Finance was most complimentary about your solution to the, ah, logistical difficulties we've been facing with Confidential Storage. Most impressive."

Dame Ingrid's use of capitals was a trait all were familiar with. It meant footnotes were following.

She said, "For those of you who don't know, Diana's solution to our Information Overload was actioned as of the end of Q1, and I believe I'm right in saying that your own sector's process has now been completed — Diana?"

Taverner gave the slightest of nods; acknowledging not so much the implied praise as Dame Ingrid's skill in placing it so neatly. *Well played*. She could already sense the killer thrust which was surely on its way.

But which was temporarily diverted by one of her fellow D2s.

"This would be the rehousing of operational records?"

"That's right, George," Ingrid Tearney said sweetly. "So good of you to pay attention. And as we all know, where Ops goes, the rest of us follow, like children trotting after the Pied Piper. There'll be a memo circulated, but, in brief, we can expect our on-site paperwork mountains to become, well, molehills in the near future. If it works for Ops, it'll work for everyone. Operations was always going to be the biggest problem. When Ops goes wrong it creates *so* much paperwork."

"But not as much as our successes do," Taverner said through not-quite-gritted teeth.

"Of course, my dear. I didn't mean to imply otherwise."

"Of course not."

Confidential Storage, to use Dame Ingrid's capitals, had long been an issue. Confidentiality was key, obviously, but the rather more prosaic problem of where to keep everything had grown exponentially. Digitalisation was no cure-all: encryption was one thing, and Ingrid Tearney had enormous faith in Regent's Park's ability to render all and any information in its possession incomprehensible — it was, after all, a branch of the Civil Service. But fear of records being, to employ the modish word, *disambiguated* was a lesser concern: a more alarming threat was the cyber equivalent of a dirty bomb, a virtual attack that would render departmental records so much spam.

The fact was, this wouldn't necessarily be a bad thing. There were documented activities from her years at the helm Tearney would happily see reduced to a pixelated mash, but the Limitations Committee, with a ministerial hand on its rudder, insisted all such were preserved under Freedom of Information legislation. So, since a nasty cyber-scare two years previously, sensitive records were kept off-grid, either on air-gapped systems or in transcript form, hence the storage difficulties. Anything deemed unsuitable for database entry was either in Molly Doran's archive, largely dedicated to personal dossiers, or was the individual department's problem. For Ops, this one had growed like Topsy. Dame Ingrid's sly jab notwithstanding, operations always produced paperwork: the more secret something needed to be, the more arse-covering was necessary for when it leaked. And nothing covered departmental arse like reams and reams of paper.

For once, it seemed, Ingrid Tearney and Diana Taverner had been of one mind. A Confidential Storage facility was required, separate from Regent's Park, and ticking three main boxes: acreage, security, and a potential for plausible damage. In other words, somewhere files could safely be said to have been lost to fire and flood, or eaten by rats, or consumed by mould.

And credit where credit was due, thought Tearney — a firm believer in this principle when it suited her — Diana had come up trumps. Which explained the smile Tearney bestowed upon her now, the smile on the face of the owl before it rips the mouse to shreds.

"One might almost say you're your own worst enemy," she said. "You've been performing these tasks so efficiently, it might almost seem foolish to assign a deputy you can foist them off onto."

Diana Taverner nodded, upgrading her *Well played* to *Fine shot.* Paper-shuffling and throat-clearing from the others, who recognised a shafting when they saw one. Diana Taverner's chances of getting an admin assistant were being buried in real time, with Ingrid Tearney stamping down the dirt.

At length, Taverner said, "It's always nice to have one's efforts appreciated."

"You're an ornament to the hub, Diana. I honestly think the Service would grind to a halt without your input. If it weren't so early, I'd suggest we raise a glass to you. As it is, we really have to press on now and deal with the rest of these matters."

Diana said, "So there's no chance of relief, then?"

Dame Ingrid was one hundred per cent concern. "Relief? My dear, you're not feeling *stressed*, are you? If you're feeling *stressed*, then obviously we'll have to do something about it."

"I'm not feeling stressed, Ingrid."

"You're sure? There's a very good medical package available, you know, Diana. Absolutely no stigma attached. Just say the word. We'll ship someone in to man the hub and damn the budget! All that matters is that you're fighting fit and in full control of all your very commendable abilities."

A silence fell.

She was not one to fly the white flag, Diana Taverner, but she knew when to make a tactical retreat.

"I'm fine," she said. "Really."

"Then let's continue, shall we?" Dame Ingrid said, and the meeting progressed.

River had read stats on how much of the average Londoner's life was spent waiting for, travelling on or stuck in public transport: he had a pointlessly good memory for figures, but he'd deliberately suppressed it. Some days you could feel yourself growing older, going nowhere . . . Two minutes on the platform before a train had arrived, six minutes inside it since, leaving what, seventy minutes until deadline? The picture of Catherine seared into his eyeballs: sitting cuffed on a bed, a gag in her mouth. Seventy minutes before her captors *loosened their belts* . . . His fists were clamped between his knees. He wanted to hit something, ideally the bastard on the bridge. But that would have to wait. The train lurched and hauled itself forward a few yards, then stopped again. He swore to himself, or nearly to himself. It didn't seem to help.

"This should test your ingenuity," the man had said.

His tone had that same punchable quality you heard when government ministers dripping with inherited wealth lectured the nation on the culture of entitlement.

Another lurch, and this time the train began to move.

Reaching his destination was one thing; how to go about fulfilling his task once he got there was another. This was one place where his Service ID would be less than no help: he'd stand a better chance if he pulled a gun . . . It was a measure of his state of mind that he gave this more than a moment's thought. But the nearest gun he knew of was in his grandfather's safe, miles away.

He unbunched his fists, and stretched his fingers as far as they'd go. Words he'd spoken last night swam into mind, the description of his job he'd favoured James Webb with; that it was designed not just to bore him out of his mind, but to kill his soul one screaming pixel at a time.

Yeah, well, today was turning out a bit different.

And he couldn't quite quell the little starburst of pleasure this thought gave him, even though that image of Catherine hadn't left him yet, and even though he hadn't a hope in hell of fulfilling the task he'd been assigned.

Which of your colleagues would you trust with your life?

None of them would have been the short answer, but Catherine didn't think that would have sufficed.

But then, parental bonds aside, how many people could answer that without doubt in their hearts? Perhaps there were marriages that strong, though she suspected there weren't many, and fewer than many married couples thought. Friendships, perhaps. But colleagues . . . ?

Early in her career, she'd had Charles Partner as her boss. Partner had been a rock of a kind; not the sort you'd want to dash yourself against, but one it was good to know would always be there. Except, of course, he wasn't, because she'd arrived at his flat one day to find his corpse in the bathtub. This had been after her drying out. Where almost anyone else would have shunned her on her return to Regent's Park — how could First Desk have a recovering alcoholic as a PA? — he'd simply allowed her to slip back into place, and had never spoken of it again. Catherine supposed that that was the greatest act of trust she'd ever had bestowed upon her. Either that, or the way he'd arranged it so she'd be the one to discover his body. It was a difficult call.

And now, instead of Partner, she had Jackson Lamb. Lamb had been Partner's joe once upon a time, and as fairy tales went, that must have been grim indeed. Where Partner had been bank manager straight — the old kind of bank manager, from the days when they'd been trusted — Lamb was as tightly wrapped as a fart in a colander. This, anyway, was the Lamb who'd come back from his wars, all those years he'd spent hopping this side and that of the Wall. *He's one of a kind*, Partner had told her. And so he was, to everyone's relief. But maybe the Lamb Charles Partner had known had been a different man, one who hadn't buried himself inside a self-made monster.

In his way, she thought, Lamb had protected her the same way Partner had. When Charles died her career should have died too, but when Jackson Lamb was sent into exile in the reshuffle that followed, he'd taken her with him. And it was true, she knew, that Lamb would never leave a joe in the lurch — having been one himself; having been left there himself, more than likely. So maybe she should have nominated Lamb as the colleague she'd trust with her life, except that there wasn't much else she'd trust him with. The collateral damage didn't bear thinking about.

River, though. He'd keep it together. Whatever they asked of him, he'd do his best.

This might turn out to have to be quite good.

Off the train, River took the stairs three at a time, ignoring the "Watch it, mate!" thrown at his back. The sudden brightness of the street pulled him up short: loud traffic, a quantity of pedestrians, the glare and dazzle of a summer's morning. The heat as thick out here as in the underground, and accompanied with smells of tar and rubber. A clock thumping in his head, reading forty-eight minutes . . .

He crossed the road against the lights, and was nearly clipped by a cyclist — and that too, like the stalling Tube train, and the trembling in his knees, seemed familiar, as if racing the clock was an everyday experience, or an everynight one — yes, he thought, running now, leaving the main drag, heading for the leafier areas: that was it. This was the stuff of his dreams. Everyone knew what it felt like, struggling to reach somewhere that receded with every effort made, so your heart felt ready to burst from sheer frustration, though for River it was more of a memory than a suppressed fear; it was what he'd been through, years before, when King's Cross crashed, and it was all his fault. A training exercise that went wrong, a misidentified "terrorist"; twenty minutes of slapstick in the morning rush-hour . . .

That was how you got to be a slow horse.

Mind you, he'd had help.

Thank you, Spider Webb.

The pavement widened. There was parkland to his left, behind iron railings, and branches overhead mottling everything with patchy shadow. A couple sat in a parked car, having what looked like a row. River's lungs were punishing him. Forty-four minutes. He stopped to calm his breathing: no point arriving like a damp rag. He had to look like he belonged, which was exactly what he might have done if not for King's Cross and Spider bloody Webb . . .

Sometimes, a career went off like a volcano. Somewhere under the ashes of his own hid the glowing coals of what might have been, but only River himself, and possibly his grandfather, still believed they might yet spark back to life. And River only believed that sometimes, and not today.

Today was where he was, though. He ran a hand through his dirty-blond hair, and approached the front door of Regent's Park.

The meeting had drawn to a close and the Second Desks dispersed, all but Diana Taverner, whom Dame Ingrid addressed on her way out of the door.

"Diana? Could you spare a moment?"

Leaving Diana hovering while Tearney fussed: looking for her glasses, which remained on the chain round her neck; collecting her papers; pausing interminably for no obvious reason, as if struck by an idea whose genius demanded immediate inspection, in absolute stillness. All of it, Diana had no doubt, for the pleasure of making Diana hover.

It was grim. From almost any angle, she knew she held the advantage. Looks: no competition. Height: ditto. Ingrid Tearney was a hobbit of a woman, one Y-chromosome short of being a trainspotter. She did her best — she could afford to — but all the designer labels in the world couldn't disguise a coypu on a catwalk. Squat body, short legs; and the trio of wigs she regularly rotated, grey, blonde and black, to cover the hair loss she'd suffered in her teens, though moulded by experts to look soft and buttery, still resembled something you might ask to borrow if you needed a bike helmet. Wealth, okay, Tearney had the edge there, but her education was so-so (LSE, as against Diana's Caius, plus a year at Yale), and her upbringing was Staffordshire or somewhere, one of those counties that only existed because otherwise there'd be gaps on the map. In all those areas Diana Taverner had Tearney beat cold, and if there were any way of making a fair fight out of it, which Diana had been known to resort to when desperate, the result would hardly be in doubt.

But Tearney had other strengths. She was smart — desk smart — *committee* smart — and what she lacked in sex appeal, she made up for in a nanny-knows-best briskness which cowed the public schoolboy still cloistered inside those other Second Desks, not to mention the weak-kneed politicos of all stripes Down the Corridor. And she had, too, a bred-in-the-bone instinct for knowing how to needle, humiliate and frustrate her underlings. Like now: Diana hovering in the doorway, waiting for her Dameship to finish gathering herself together, which she'd only do once satisfied that Diana was starting to twitch.

Dame Ingrid said, "There. Sorry about that. Walk with me?"

They headed off down the corridor.

"Terribly dull these meetings can be," Tearney said. "I do appreciate your taking the time to attend."

Attendance was compulsory. The Service was a corporation like any other.

"I should be on the hub," Diana said. "Will this take long?"

"I just wanted your confirmation that the records transfer has been completed satisfactorily."

"As of last month, yes."

"And we're talking about records up to Virgil level, yes?"

"As per the brief."

The grading system changed on a biannual basis, but Virgil was currently the second-highest classification. The Service being what it was, this meant that a lot of sensitive data was logged Virgil, on the grounds that those most likely to wangle access to intelligence — oversight committees, Cabinet ministers, TV producers — tended to focus their attentions on the highest grade, Scott level, on the assumption that this was where the hardcore secrets were. Virgil level, being more accessible, was generally overlooked. Which didn't mean Ingrid Tearney wanted those records stored off-site.

"Ingrid, I thought you already knew all this."

"Merely dotting i's, my dear. You'll be warmly acknowledged in HR's weekly catch-up this morning, I can assure you."

"I'm so grateful. Was that all?"

"You know, one of the burdens of leadership," Tearney continued, as if Diana hadn't spoken, "is not being privy to the gossip below stairs. It can be difficult to take the temperature, if you know what I mean."

Assuming she was not genuinely being asked if she understood a common idiom, Diana said nothing.

"And it would be good to know precisely how things stand."

"Well, we're over-worked, under-resourced and under-appreciated. The general mood more or less reflects this."

Dame Ingrid laughed, a rather more tinkling sound than you'd expect the warthog to make, Diana thought grudgingly. She said, "I can always rely on you to deliver uncomfortable truths, Diana. That's one of the reasons you're such a valuable Second Desk."

"Is there a problem, Ingrid?"

"Our new overlord is rattling his sabres. He's spoken of the need for fresh starts, for — I think he said a *reboot*. Always keen to appear savvy."

"All new ministers say that."

"This one means it. Too many skeletons falling out of closets, apparently. As if it were possible to maintain an effective security service without an occasional blurring of the boundaries."

Which was a polite way of describing, among other faux pas, the wholesale illegal surveillance of the nation's online footfall, not to mention the toothless surrender of same to a foreign power.

Diana made a non-committal noise.

"We're not natural allies, are we? You and I."

"I'm fully committed to the Service," Diana said. "Always have been. You know that."

"And you're currently wondering how best to make that commitment known in the event that Peter Judd succeeds in removing me as head."

Issuing a denial would have been tantamount to confession. Instead, Diana said, "What makes you think he wants to do that?"

"Because it's the most obvious way of flexing his muscle, which he's going to want to practise doing before taking on the PM. Or did you think Home Secretary was the pinnacle of his ambition?"

Nobody over the age of three thought Home Secretary the pinnacle of Peter Judd's ambition.

"So I thought it best to advise you that any assault PJ makes on the Service won't stop with lopping off the head. I have it on good authority he's not keen on the Second Desk role. That he wants an intermediate level built into the command structure, to allow for greater political oversight. This would be by ministerial appointment, you understand. And almost certainly filled from outwith the Service." She glanced sideways. "As I said, we're hardly natural allies. But there's an adage that fits."

My enemy's enemy is my friend, Diana supplied mentally. She said, "And I remain fully committed to the Service. As I said. We've weathered ministerial interference in the past, Ingrid. Judd might be one of the big beasts when he's on home ground, but he's going to have his work cut out for him if he's taking on Regent's Park."

At that moment, her pager buzzed.

Dame Ingrid said, "Thank you, Diana. I'm glad we had this little chat."

She thinks we've made an alliance, Diana thought, as the Service chief nodded in farewell, and moved on down the corridor.

Then she reached for her pager, recognised Security's number, and called the front desk on her mobile.

"Ma'am? We have a walk-in, an off-site agent. He says you're expecting him. But there's nothing on the time sheet."

"I'm not expecting anyone. Who is it?"

"One River Cartwright." Security reeled off Cartwright's Service number.

"Sign him in," Diana said. "I'll be on the stairs."

CHAPTER
FIVE

Thirty-nine minutes . . .

Being in Regent's Park always gave River a hollow feeling; the same you might get on stepping inside the marital home once the divorce had come through. Well, he said "always". There'd been a time when that might have been the right word, early in his career, when it was still a "career"; before he'd become *persona non grata*, which was Latin for slow horse. Since then, he'd been inside its precincts, what, twice? On one of those occasions, summoned by Spider Webb. That had been Spider rubbing it in; letting River know he might as well be in Siberia. Well, Siberia might as well be where Spider was now: all those endless white spaces, bare of life. Was that what being in a coma was like? River hoped never to find out.

At the desk he showed his Service card, and said he was there to see Diana Taverner. An all-or-nothing play; one she'd go for, he hoped, if only to find out what he thought he was doing, turning up at head office — she might let him in just to have him beaten up.

While the security woman paged Taverner, he looked around.

Thirty-eight minutes.

What struck River, as ever, was the dual nature of the building; the Oxbridge kerb-flash a nod to the best traditions of the Service — its history of civilised thuggery — while the modern aspects were sunk below pavement level, safe from dirty bomb and prying eyes alike. On one of its upper corridors hung a portrait of his grandfather. He'd never been that high. You had to be some sort of mandarin.

His attention was being sought.

". . . Yes?"

"Ms Taverner will meet you on the staircase."

This being handy in case she wanted him thrown down it, he surmised.

The woman handed him a laminate on a lanyard, VISITOR, and pointed him in the right direction.

They'd settled on an Italian place near Smithfield, and were upstairs eating ice cream out of tin bowls: Marcus strawberry and pistachio, Shirley peach and stracciatella. Cutlery scraping against tin was as much conversation as they made until both were about finished, then Shirley nodded towards Marcus's bowl and plucked her spoon from her mouth with an audible pop.

"That's a stupid combination. Strawberry and pistachio don't go."

"Go well enough for me."

"Then your taste buds are wrong. Strawberry needs chocolate or else vanilla. Pistachio's not even a real flavour. They only invented it in like 1997."

"You've been dumped, haven't you?"

"What do you mean, dumped? What kind of question's that? We're talking about ice cream."

"Right."

"And no, I haven't."

"Right."

"And even if I had been, it wouldn't be any of your business."

"Right."

"And anyway, how can you tell?"

"Christ, I don't know," Marcus said. "Maybe it's the way you're such a bundle of fun."

"Piss off."

"What happened, she meet someone else?"

"Piss off. Why do you assume I'm gay?"

"You're saying you're not?"

"I'm saying how would you know? Do I bring my private life into work?"

"Shirley, sharing an office with you lately's like having my own personal thundercloud, so yes, on balance, you bring your private life into work. Which gives me the right to hear the dirt. Did she meet someone else?"

"And again with the 'she' . . ."

Marcus laid his spoon on a napkin and licked away the hint of a strawberry moustache. "It's like in books," he said. "Thrillers, whodunnits, you know? You read much?"

"You got a point to make?"

"In thrillers, when the writer says the killer this, the killer that, and never says if it's a he or a she, it's always because it's a she. And you're like that with your girlfriend. You never say if it's a he or a she. Which means it's a she."

Shirley sneered. "Maybe I'm just messing with your head."

"You might be, except you're not. So what happened? She meet someone else?"

"I don't want to talk about it."

"Fair enough. But that means you have to drop the angry victim act. Deal?"

"You really are a hardarse, you know that?"

"Yeah, that used to be my job description."

"Well not any more it's not," Shirley said. "Now you're a desk jockey, like the rest of us. Get used to it."

"That's what I was told months back," Marcus said, picking up his spoon again. "Still got to shoot someone, didn't I?"

"I doubt you'll get that lucky twice."

"Well just in case I do," Marcus said, "you know what I don't need? I don't need a partner pissing and moaning behind me. That shit throws your aim off."

Shirley picked up her spoon too, but her bowl was empty. Watching her tap the one against the other, causing a high-pitched note to ring around the room, Marcus was struck, not for the first time, by how intense her concentration could be. With her near-buzz cut and her broad shoulders, an idiot might think her mannish, but there was nothing remotely masculine about her skin tone or her deep brown eyes. Still. Crouched over the ruins of her ice cream, she might almost disappear into androgyny. Either way, she had a right hook that could knock you off your feet.

She looked up at him. "Is that what we are? Partners?"

"In the absence of a better offer," he said.

"In that case, I'll have another one of these, *partner*. Butterscotch and mint."

"Seriously?"

She stared at him, unblinking.

Marcus went to fetch more ice cream.

"Cartwright."

Taverner, as promised, was on the staircase, a feature which fell on the kerb-flash side of the line, being wide enough to dance down, and boasting, on this particular landing, a narrow window which must have been eight foot tall. Dusty sunlight slanted through it, catching Lady Diana's hair and roasting a chestnut tinge onto its curls, momentarily distracting River. His mind had blanked. What was he supposed to call her? "Ma'am," his mouth supplied. A glimpse of her wristwatch, as she glanced at it, reminded him: thirty-six minutes.

She said, "You're not supposed to be here, you do remember that?"

"Yes, but —"

"And you look a mess."

"It's hot out," he said. "Ma'am."

It was cooler in here, though; air-con and marbled floors.

". . . Well?"

They had history, River and Diana Taverner. Not the kind of history people usually meant when they said history, but not far off: treachery, double-dealing and stabbing in the back — more like a marriage than a love affair. And most of it at a remove, so their actual face-to-face encounters hadn't been frequent. Here and now, on this landing, his shirt clinging to his back, River was remembering how distracting her presence could be. It wasn't just her physical attractions; it was the way she visibly weighed up every situation she was in, calibrating the moment to maximise her own advantage.

He said, "It's about James. James Webb."

"Ah."

"I've been . . . visiting him."

Spider had been Taverner's protégé once, though he'd split what he'd have no doubt called his loyalties fairly evenly between her and Dame Ingrid. At the precise moment he'd been shot by a Russian hood it was hard to tell whose side he was on, though as he'd been mostly on his own back ever since, it probably didn't matter in the long run.

She said, "You were still friendly? I didn't realise."

"We trained together."

"Not what I asked."

River said, "We weren't that friendly in the end, no, but we were close at one time. And he's got nobody else. No family, I mean."

He had no idea whether Spider had family or not, but he was busking here. And banking on Taverner not knowing Spider's family situation either.

"I didn't realise," she said. "So . . . what's his current condition? Any change?"

"Not really."

Just for an instant, he saw something in her eyes that might have been unfeigned concern. And then he mentally kicked himself — why wouldn't there have been? She'd worked with him. And here was River, using his former friend's condition to bluff his way back into the very place Spider had had him exiled from . . . It occurred to him that Spider might have seen the funny side of this. That this small act of treachery was more tribute than revenge.

Thoughts for later.

Thirty-five minutes.

He said, "None at all, in fact. And no real chance of any occurring."

Taverner glanced away. "I've been keeping an eye on the reports," she said vaguely.

"Then you'll know. It's a vegetative state, his brain activity's almost entirely dormant. A flicker here and there, but . . . And his organs, they're not functioning on their own. Take him off the machines, and he'll die in the time it takes a heart to stop beating."

"You obviously have a point to make."

"We talked about it once, the two of us. On one of those endurance courses, up on the Black Mountains?"

She gave a brief nod.

"Long story short —" River said.

"Good idea."

"— if he ever wound up plugged into a wall-socket, if that was all that was keeping him alive, he'd want to be switched off. That's what he told me."

"Then that information will be on his personal file."

"I doubt he ever got round to making an official declaration. He was, what, twenty-four at the time? It wasn't something he was planning for. But it was something he'd given thought to."

"If he'd given it a little more thought, he might have noticed planning doesn't come into it." Thirty-four minutes. "What exactly are you asking me to do?"

"I just wanted to speak to someone about it. How long is he going to be lying there before a decision is made?"

She said, "You're talking about letting him die."

"I'm not sure what the alternative is."

But a Lamb-like crack came to mind: *They could re-skill him. Use him as a speed bump.*

She said, "Look, I don't have time for this right now. Are you sure there's no family? Weren't there cousins?"

"Don't think so."

"But anyway — it's hardly a decision we can make standing on a bloody staircase." She fixed him with a glare, but let it soften. "But I'll look into it. You're right. If there's nobody else to take decisions, the Park will have to do it. Though I'd have thought the medical staff . . ."

"They're probably terrified of liability."

"God. They're not the only ones." She looked at her watch again. "Is that it?"

". . . Yes."

"You're not going to explain why you should be back on the hub? Why Slough House is a waste of your talents?"

"Not right now."

100

"Good." She paused. "You'll be informed. About Webb, I mean. James. Whatever's decided."

"Thank you."

"But don't do this again. Turn up unannounced. Or you'll end up downstairs."

This time there was no softening in her expression.

Thirty-two minutes.

"Off you toddle."

"Thank you."

River walked back down the stairs, sure she was watching him every step of the way. But when he reached the bottom and looked back up, she'd gone.

Thirty-one minutes.

Now came the tricky bit.

The man from the bridge was elsewhere now; in Postman's Park, whose neat little garden was a popular lunch spot for local workers, mostly because of its shelter, the Memorial to Heroic Self-Sacrifice. The tiles on its walls were dedicated to those who'd given their lives in the attempt, sometimes futile, to rescue others, and recalled Leigh Pitt, who "saved a drowning boy from the canal . . . but sadly was unable to save himself", and Mary Rogers, who "self-sacrificed by giving up her lifebelt and voluntarily going down in the sinking ship". Thomas Griffin was fatally scalded in a boiler explosion at a Battersea sugar refinery, returning to search for his mate, while George Elliott and Robert Underhill "successively went down a well to rescue comrades and were poisoned by gas" . . . Sylvester Monteith — "Sly" to those who knew him, or simply suspected his true nature — was drinking iced tea from a polystyrene cup, and wondering why self-sacrifice was deemed so honourable. Every age calls forth its heroes, he supposed. For his own part, he'd come to manhood in the eighties, and his response to any of these emergencies would have been one of pragmatic withdrawal. Later, he would have been among the first to deplore the inadequacy of the equipment at fault, and to enquire about the possibility of furnishing much-improved replacements, at a price that could only be deemed reasonable from the point of view of all future miners, sugar-refinery workers, ship-goers, and foolhardy passers-by. All would be safer, some would get richer, and the world would turn. So it goes.

Meanwhile, to ensure that the world was in fact still turning, Monteith checked his watch. It was some twenty minutes since he'd dispatched River Cartwright on a mission which was as much an act of self-sacrifice as any of those memorialised on the walls of Postman's Park. That was one of the things they didn't tell you when you signed up for duty, Monteith thought. That there was a huge divide between those who lit the cannon, and those who flung themselves in front of it. Lighting the cannon was the path to a long, happy life. The one he'd lit for Cartwright was unlikely to prove fatal, but it would make exile at Slough House seem like an extended vacation.

Even fast horses finish at the knacker's yard. That slow horses get there first was one of life's little ironies.

He finished his tea and reached for his phone.

Sean Donovan answered on the first ring. It sounded like he was driving.

"You're on your way?"

"Yes," said Donovan.

Monteith paused to admire a passing jogger: her hair damp, her T-shirt tight, her head bobbing in rhythm to whatever was pulsing through her earphones.

"How's our guest?"

"How do you think? She's unharmed, a little nervous and very pissed off."

"Well, she won't have to endure it much longer," Monteith said. "Not that there's any harm in giving her a little scare in the meantime."

Donovan was silent for a moment, then said, "That's what you want?"

"It is." The jogger had gone, but the feeling she'd provoked still lingered: a wish to hear a woman squeal. The fact that Monteith wouldn't hear it mattered less than that he'd have caused it.

He said, "What's your ETA?"

"Thirty."

"Don't be late," Monteith said, and ended the call.

Collecting his empty cup, he dropped it into a bin, and paused to look once more at the tiles affixed to the shelter's walls; their fragments of story, each highlighting an ending, because there was nothing to the beginnings and middles that anyone would want to hear about. He shook his head. Then he left the little park and hailed a taxi.

River walked back up the stairs. Behind him, the woman at the security desk called out.

He turned. "I forgot, I need Ms Taverner's signature." He mimed a scribble in the air. "I'll be one minute."

"Come back down. I'll page her again."

"She's just there." He pointed towards the next landing, then waggled his laminated VISITOR badge. "One minute." He reached the landing, and was out of sight of the desk.

Thirty minutes.

Maybe a little more, maybe a little less.

Truth to tell, Catherine Standish was no longer at the front of his mind. The op was the op. This was enemy territory, and the fact that it was also headquarters simply gave it an extra edge.

He pushed through a pair of swing doors. River was coasting on memory, an imperfect blueprint in his head, but there ought to be lifts here. Unclipping the laminate from his shirt, he stuffed it into a pocket, and yes, here they were, in a thankfully unpeopled lobby. What he'd have done had Lady Di been waiting was a question for another life.

Pressing the button, he fished his mobile out. Regent's Park's front desk was still in his contact list: unused for years, but still stored because . . .

Because you always hung on to the numbers, in case your old life was given back.

It was answered on the second ring.

"Security."

"Possible threat," he said, pitching his voice low.

"Who is this?"

"There's a couple in a car out front, twenty yards down the road. Making like a lovers' quarrel, but the male is armed. I repeat, the male is armed. Suggest immediate response."

"Could I have your —"

"Immediate response," River repeated, and ended the call.

That might keep everyone occupied for a little while.

The lift arrived and he stepped into it.

Sean Donovan was entering London from the west. The van's air-con was unreliable, so until Monteith's call he'd been driving with the windows open, the twin blasts nearly cooling the interior. But now he closed them to ring Traynor, who answered in his usual way:

"Here."

He didn't ask Traynor if everything was okay. Benjamin Traynor had served with him in hot places; crouched with him behind walls being pounded to dust above their heads. If Traynor couldn't handle one middle-aged woman in an attic, they should both reconsider their futures. Especially the next twenty-four hours.

He said, "I'm in the city. Everything's on schedule."

"I'll pull out soon. Spoken to the . . . boss?"

Donovan said, "He'd like you to put a scare into the lady."

"Put a scare into her."

"His exact words. 'No harm in giving her a little scare.'"

Traynor said, "Well, he's in charge."

"Where's the kid?"

The kid, whom Catherine had dubbed "Bailey" for some reason.

"Out front. Just in case."

"He's a tryer, isn't he?"

"Doesn't hurt to stay alert," Traynor recited. All those hot places, all those pulverised walls, and he still kept an eye out for the newbies. Of course, he hadn't spent five years counting the bricks in a series of small rooms. "He's a good kid."

"Like his sister," Donovan said.

"Yeah. Like his sister."

He ended the call and wound the windows down again. What came blasting into the cab was all petrol and scorched rubber, but anything that didn't taste of prison smelt like freedom. He glanced at his watch. Twenty minutes before meeting Monteith: a car park off the Euston Road. He'd make it with time to spare.

A lot could go wrong, but it wouldn't be this bit.

Some lifts descended further than River wanted to go. This one didn't — it was standard, staff-for-the-use-of — but there were others which required top clearance and disappeared deep into London's bowels, offering access to secure crisis management facilities, and even a rumoured top-secret underground transport system; a rumour River had regarded with scepticism until he'd learned that it had been officially denied. That there were other areas where deniable interrogations took place, he'd taken as read. Such were the foundations on which security is built.

But he was heading towards the level where the records rooms were.

He'd rarely had occasion to visit these in his time at Regent's Park, but knew from conversations with his grandfather, the O.B., that they'd long been in danger of reaching capacity, containing as they did hundreds of yards, miles even, of hardcopy information: reports and records, personnel files, transcripts and minutes of varying levels of sensitivity. River had affected surprise that physical documents remained the mainstay of the Park's archives, but only to give the O.B. the opportunity of riding one of his favourite hobby horses.

"Oh," the Old Bastard, a purely affectionate monicker, said, "they had to rethink a lot of those early storage protocols, once they realised computers were like bank vaults. Nice and secure, safe as houses, right up to the moment someone blows the doors off and walks away with the loot."

On the most recent occasion on which they'd had this conversation, it had been late evening: rain pattering on the windows, brandy splashing with almost as much regularity into their glasses.

"Because computers *talk* to each other, River — that's what they're for. Your generation can't boil an egg without going online, you rely on them for everything, but you tend to overlook their major function. Which is that they store information, but only in order to divulge it."

Which River had known, of course. Knew that was why the Queens of the Database worked on air-gapped systems, their USB ports gummed up to prevent flash drives being inserted. The Queens had to skip from one row of computers to another to go online — internet and internot being the waggish coinage. Electronic poaching had replaced the nuclear threat as the Big Fear. The Service liked to steal, but it hated getting robbed.

Give a born thief like Roderick Ho five minutes with an internet connection, River thought, and he'd bring back the PM's vetting history, if it was out there to be snaffled.

Which was why the PM's vetting history wasn't held online, but stored in the Park's personnel archive, on the level River was heading to now.

It was definitely a double-decker bus. One of the old-fashioned type, with a deck you could jump onto as it pulled away, if you didn't mind being shouted at by the conductor. It was open-topped, its upper deck shrouded in canvas, and was parked head-on to the house, so Catherine could see its destination window, which read HOP ABOARD! There were no other vehicles in sight. She'd been right about the outhouses, though; three smaller, bluntly functional buildings, flat-sided, windowless, with sloping roofs. Garages or storage units. Nothing looked currently in use. It was as if her captors had stumbled on this place as a vacant possession, and taken advantage. Except that stumbling on things didn't fit into Sean Donovan's worldview.

Any mission he was on would be double-plotted; every detail stress-tested for the unexpected, the potential loose screw.

A sudden bitter thought flared. *A loose screw —* that's all I was to him then.

So what am I now?

She had been awake for hours; had barely slept. Too much confusion flying around her mind, and this question the biggest of them all: *What am I now?* A figure out of Donovan's past, snatched into his present — why? She couldn't pretend it was because of anything she meant to him; it had to be because of what she did. And what she did was nothing much; was only tangentially Secret Service. What she did was Jackson Lamb's paper-shuffling; organising the slow horses' ditchwater-dull number-crunching into what resembled reports, which she then parcelled off to Regent's Park so they could be officially ignored. If anything they'd done at Slough House lately warranted this kind of excitement, it had passed her by . . . Hours ago, lying on the narrow bed thinking all this, she'd heard the front door closing, and had reached the window in time to see Donovan climbing into the van they'd fetched her here in. He'd driven down the track, turned into the lane, and vanished from sight.

Whatever was happening, there was no stopping it now.

The light on this corridor, three levels below where he'd been talking to Diana Taverner, was blue-tinted, as if replicating the effect of dusk in the outside world. It was mildly disorienting, stepping out of the lift: not only the light, but the blank white walls and tiled white floor. Below the surface, everything changed. Wood panelling and marbled surfaces were nowhere to be seen.

Behind him the lift door closed, and machinery murmured.

Twenty-eight minutes.

So far, no alarms. River had left his pass in the lift, in case it was chipped so Security could track him. He hoped they'd been distracted by the pair of armed terrorists down the road, but it wouldn't take long to shoot them and get back to work. And he had twenty-eight minutes, or twenty-seven, to retrieve the file the man in the suit wanted, so his thugs wouldn't vent their poor impulse control on Catherine.

". . . Break into the Park? Seriously?"

"Do I look like I'm joking?"

The thing was, he almost had. It was that supercilious smirk he'd worn, the upper-class sneer.

"I'll keep it simple. You don't even have to steal it. Pictures will do fine."

"They don't let you just walk in," River had said, stupidly.

"We'd hardly have needed to take your colleague if they did."

Through an open door down the corridor, a figure appeared.

She was quite round, with a messy cap of hair, and her face was a thick white mask of powder; a childish attempt to make up as a clown, was River's first

110

thought. But there was nothing childish about her eyes, which were steely-grey as her hair; and nothing of the toy about her wheelchair, which was cherry-coloured, with thick wheels, and looked capable of powering itself over or through any manner of obstacle: a closed door, an enemy trench, River Cartwright.

And this was Molly Doran, of whom he'd heard much, some of it good.

She rolled towards him, head to one side. A faint ping from the closed shaft behind him was the lift stopping on another floor, but could as easily have been this woman beginning to speak: he'd not have been surprised if she vented in a series of pips and squeaks — nothing to do with the wheelchair (he told himself); everything to do with that doll-like face, its porcelain veneer.

But her voice, when she spoke, was standard-issue, no-nonsense, mid-morning BBC.

"One of Jackson's cubs, aren't you?"

"I . . . Yes. That's right."

"What's he after this time?"

Without waiting for a response she reversed through the doorway she'd appeared from. River followed her, into a long room not unlike a library stack, or what he imagined a library stack looked like: row upon row of upright cabinets set on tracks which would allow for their being accordioned together when not in use, and each stuffed with cardboard files and folders. Somewhere along this lot was the file he'd been told to steal. No, keep it simple. He only had to photograph its contents.

Molly Doran slotted neatly into a cubbyhole designed to accommodate her wheelchair. Her legs were missing below the knee. For all the tales River had heard about her, not one had ever laid down the indisputable truth as to how she'd lost them. The only thing all accounts agreed on was that it was a loss — that she'd once had legs.

She said, "Maybe you didn't hear me. What's he after this time?"

"A file," River said.

"A file. So you'll have the requisition form then."

"Well. You know Jackson."

"I certainly did."

She was a bird of a woman, though not the usual bird people meant when they used that phrase. A penguin, perhaps; a short fat bird in squatting mode, head tipped to one side; her nose becoming beakish as her head jutted upward. "What did you say your name was?"

"Cartwright."

"I thought so . . . You've the look of him. Your grandfather."

He could feel himself becoming heavier, as if the time ticking past was accruing weight, loading him down with the consequences of its passing.

"It's around the eyes. The shape of them, mostly. How is he?"

"He's sprightly."

"Sprightly. There's an old person's word if ever there was. Women are feisty and old people sprightly. Except

112

when they're not, of course. What's this file Jackson's after?"

River began to recite the number the man on the bridge had given him, but she cut him off.

"I meant what's it about, dear? What interest does our Mr Lamb have in it?"

"I don't know."

"Keeps you in the dark, does he?"

"You know Jackson," he said again.

"Better than you, I expect." She appraised him. "How did you get in?"

"Get in?"

"Upstairs. Or have they adopted an open-door policy since this morning?"

"I made an appointment."

"Not with me you didn't. Where's your laminate?"

"I had a meeting with Lady Di."

"My, aren't we grand. I didn't know she lowered herself to parleying with exiles. Or does your grandfather's name open doors?"

"I've never relied on it," River said.

"Of course not. Or you wouldn't be a slow horse."

River didn't care to follow this thread. And the seconds were ticking away. It occurred to him to take out his phone and show this woman the image of Catherine. All he'd have to do was ask her help.

And Security would be kicking down the doors a moment later.

She said suddenly, "How is he?"

Without needing to ask, he knew she'd changed the subject.

"Lamb? Same as ever," he said.

She laughed. It wasn't an especially happy sound. "I doubt that," she said.

"Believe me," River said. "There's been no improvement."

Twenty minutes now, if that. And he didn't just have to trace the file and photograph its contents, he had to get somewhere he could transmit them, which meant leaving the Park. Anywhere inside these walls, trying to send an attachment out would be sounding a fire alarm.

The couple in the car would have been checked out by now. His own failure to reappear would have been noted. He doubted they'd put the building into lockdown — he was only a slow horse; could easily have got lost — but they'd send people looking, and soon. He had to make a move. But Molly Doran was talking.

"Jackson Lamb's lived so long under the bridge he's half-troll himself now. But you should have met him a lifetime ago."

"Yeah," said River. "I bet he was a heartbreaker."

She laughed. "He was never an oil painting, don't worry about that. But he had something. You're too young and pretty to understand. But a girl could lose her heart to him. Or other parts of her body."

"About this file."

"For which you don't have a chitty."

"Even when he was young, and girls were losing their hearts to him," River said, "did you ever know him to fill out a form?"

114

"That's smooth. I like that." Without warning, Molly rolled forwards, so her chair was back in the aisle. "You get that from your grandfather, I expect."

"The thing is," River said. He leaned forward, bending so his mouth was near her ear. "I'm not entirely supposed to be here."

"You amaze me."

"But since I had an appointment with Lady Di anyway, and knowing Jackson needed to see this file . . ."

"You thought you'd kill two birds with one stone."

"Precisely."

"Maybe you've picked up a bit of him to go with your grandpa," Molly said. "Jackson was never one for going round the houses. Not when he could drive a battering ram through them."

"I told you he was the same as ever."

"What was the file you wanted?"

He repeated the number. He'd always had a good memory for numbers; he had, too, a good memory for the man on the bridge. He hoped they'd meet again.

"That's curious," Molly Doran said.

"How so?"

"Slough House is all closed cases and blind alleys, isn't it? Nothing live, nothing contagious. That's what I've always heard."

"We crunch numbers," River admitted. "And chase tails. If anything interesting popped up, we'd probably hand it over to the Park."

"Probably?"

"It hasn't happened yet."

Fifteen minutes. Or fourteen. Or twelve. He'd studied Molly Doran's face as he gave her the number, but not by the slightest eye movement had she indicated in which direction the file might be found. And without some kind of clue, he could wander round here for hours without coming close. The last kind of system a Molly Doran would have would be one where the numbers explained where they were.

"Then what's happening now?" she asked. "Because this file's most definitely live. What with its subject being the Prime Minister and all."

Her tone hadn't changed.

Someone walked down the corridor, their heels loud as boots on cobbles. When they paused, River felt his heart do the same. Something hummed and something murmured, and that was the lift door opening. The boots found their way inside, and the hum and murmur repeated themselves in reverse.

All this while, her eyes were breaking him down like Lego.

"Can I tell you the truth?" he said.

"I really don't know," Molly said. "But it might be interesting finding out."

"Jackson's in one of his . . . playful moods."

"He has those," she agreed.

"Right."

"About as often as I go jogging."

"There's a bet involved."

"That sounds more plausible."

"He bet me I couldn't find out the PM's schoolboy nickname."

"And Wikipedia isn't helping?"

"You'd think, wouldn't you? I expect he's got someone wiping it."

"So a quick glance would be all you need."

"That's right."

"And maybe I should turn round while you're doing that. A quick three-pointer."

". . . If you like."

"Well, if I wasn't watching, I wouldn't be involved, would I? So that would save me being your accomplice while you break the Official Secrets Act. And I really can't be doing with a five-year stretch in Holloway. Prison food plays havoc with the digestion, so I've read."

River didn't have to turn to know they had company. As he felt his arms gripped from behind, and the plastic restraints clip into place, he was conscious mostly of Molly Doran's gaze, which was partly pitying, partly curious, as if his behaviour was beyond anything she could readily understand. And this from a woman familiar with Jackson Lamb, he thought. I must really be in trouble.

She didn't speak again as he was taken, moderately politely, from the room.

When Catherine heard the padlock being shifted, she sat up on the bed, feet on the floor. Wasn't this how prisoners responded to a rattle on their chain?

She'd thought it would be Bailey again — the young man who'd taken her photo — but it was the second soldier; the one whose presence at the Angel had driven

117

her back onto the streets. Like Sean Donovan, he had the lifetime soldier's way of entering a room: taking it all in in one sweeping glance. Nothing could have changed since the last time he'd been in here, but that was no reason for taking chances. This done, his gaze rested on Catherine.

She waited.

"Sorry about this," he began.

But he didn't look sorry.

CHAPTER
SIX

Time was, walking up Slough House's stairs made every day midwinter for Louisa. Now, she carried her own weather with her. Stepping through the yard, pushing open the door that always stuck, didn't affect her. It was a mood she was already part of, wherever she happened to be.

On the first landing she stopped at Ho's office. Ho was at his desk, four flat screens angled in front of him as if he were catching a tan. He was nodding in time to something, which the well-padded earphones dwarfing his head suggested might be music, but could as easily be the binary rhythms of whatever code was conjuring the images swarming on his screens. More than once she'd come into this room and he hadn't even noticed, though he'd configured his workstation for a view of the door: when he was in the zone, if the webheads still said that, it was like he'd relocated to the moon. Because while Roderick Ho was a dick, that was only the most obvious thing about him, not the most important. Most important was, he knew his way round the cybersphere. This was arguably the only thing keeping him alive. If he weren't occasionally useful,

Marcus or Shirley would have battered him into a porridge by now.

But today he wasn't on the moon because he was watching her as she stepped into his office. He even pulled his earphones off. That put him in Jane Austen territory, etiquette-wise: Louisa had known him to hold a palm up, as if warding off traffic, if he suspected somebody was about to speak when he was doing something more interesting, like popping a cola can, or preparing to exhale.

He said, "Hello."

. . . That was weird.

"You feeling all right?"

"Sure," he said. "Why?"

"No reason. Can you trace Catherine's phone?"

"No."

"I thought you could do that. GPS. Whatever."

"Not when its battery's removed. Which it is."

"You already tried? Was that your idea?"

He shrugged.

Marcus was standing behind her now; Shirley too. Marcus said, "You didn't find her, then."

Shirley said, "We didn't find Cartwright either."

"I can tell," Louisa said. "Here, you missed a bit."

She touched her upper lip, and Shirley rubbed her own, obliterating a smudge of ice cream. She scowled at Marcus. "You could have said."

"Where's the fun in that?"

Ho was watching all this as if it were taking place behind bars. Louisa said to him, "How about River's phone?"

120

He shrugged again, sulkily this time. "I'd need his number."

Louisa read it out to him off her own.

Ho said, "Have you got everyone's number in there?"

"No."

Shirley nudged Marcus.

Ho's fingers started salsa-ing across his keyboard.

Louisa walked to the window. Same view as from hers, but lower down. She thought: when I joined the Service, this was not what I was expecting. The same view every day, with minor variations.

For a while last year that had seemed less important, but like everything else, this had turned out a false reprieve. Life's cruellest trick was letting the light in, just enough so you knew where everything was, then shutting it off without warning. She'd been bumping into the furniture ever since.

Back in her flat, replastered into a section of wall behind her fridge, was a fingernail-sized uncut diamond, booty from a heist she'd helped derail. She had no idea how much it was worth, but couldn't see that it mattered much.

Min, you stupid bastard, why did you have to die?

And then she shut that thought off because there was nowhere it could lead her that would do anyone any good.

Ho finished tapping. "Cartwright's blocked," he said.

"What do you mean, blocked?"

"His phone's on, but he's somewhere that's scrambling the signal."

"Like somewhere with thick walls?"

Marcus said, "No, like somewhere with the ability to fuck with GPS."

"Golly," said Shirley, who'd been Comms in her pre-Slough House life. "Wonder where that might be?"

The room he'd been locked in was underground; its only window one-way, and that from the other side. From where River stood it was a mirror. About a metre square, it threw back at him the room's blankness and his own oddly calm exterior. Inside his chest his heart thumped like a little drummer boy: all beat and no tune.

The minutes he'd been counting down were long gone, and their deadline history. *These men have poor impulse control ... Soon they'll be loosening their belts.* He watched his reflected hands curl into fists. He'd made more than one poor choice this morning. Principally, he should have stayed on the bridge and dropped the man off it. Whatever happened to Catherine would have happened anyway, but at least he'd have wiped the smirk off that chancer's face.

And why didn't I do that? he asked himself.

He'd have sat, but there was nowhere to sit. The room was bare; a cube, near enough. There was no handle on the door. There was no visible light fitting either, though the ceiling emitted a steady bluish glow, which lent his reflection an alien cast. Alien, except he belonged here. It was where he'd willed himself, as much as if he'd offered his wrists to Lady Di half an hour ago. *Lock me up,* he should have said. *I'm here to steal, and I don't have a prayer.*

There were protocols, and even a slow horse knew them. Slow horses, after all, underwent the same training as any other kind. Threats to fellow officers, actual physical danger, required immediate, official response: the line of command in River's case ran upstairs through Slough House and on to the desk of Jackson Lamb. Who, for all his faults — and that wasn't a short list — would walk through fire for a joe in peril; or make someone walk through fire. By ignoring that, River had stepped across the chalk line, and by bluffing his way into the Park, he'd made things worse twice over.

So they took you in, they trained you up, they prepared you for a life you'd be expected to risk when the occasion demanded, and then they locked you in an office with a view of a bus stop, and made you pour your energy, your commitment, your desire to serve into a sinkhole of never-ending drudgery. Of course he'd gone off reservation. He'd been ripe for it, and whoever had fingered him for this morning's fun and games had known it from the beginning.

Had they also known he'd screw up?

River leaned against a wall, hands on his head, fingers laced, and wondered what his grandfather was going to say. The Old Bastard had steered the Service through the Cold War without ever actually taking the helm — the real power, he'd told River more than once, lay in having one hand on the elbow of whoever was in charge. If not for the O.B., he'd have been out on the pavement after the King's Cross fiasco. But not even his grandfather could protect him this time.

The door opened without warning, and Nick Duffy came in carrying a plastic bucket seat.

Duffy was in charge of the Service's internal police; the Dogs, as they were called. The position was more akin to enforcer than executive, and the Dogs were kept on a pretty long leash, so Duffy's role basically meant he could bite whoever he liked, and not expect more than a tap on the nose. The way he slammed the chair down, and the angry squeak its legs made scraping along the floor, suggested he was in a biting mood. The grim smile he summoned for River confirmed it. Other than the chair he'd brought nothing into the room with him, but when he straddled it backwards, the hands he gripped it with were calloused at the knuckles.

But it was the fact that he was wearing a tracksuit that gave River most cause for concern.

Tracksuits were what you wore when things might get messy.

As mornings go, Dame Ingrid's hadn't been a bad one. Pulling Diana Taverner's tail was always a useful exercise, and sounding her out afterwards had nicely muddied the waters. It was always a good idea to make a predator think you're more vulnerable than you are. When Peter Judd made his inevitable move to stamp his newfound authority onto the Service, Dame Ingrid would at least know where on the battlefield Taverner would be. She'd be right behind Ingrid, looking for her weak spot.

It used to be simpler. There was the Service, and there were the nation's enemies. These changed identity every so often, depending on who'd been elected, deposed or assassinated, but by and large the boundaries were clear: you spied on your foes, kept tabs on the neutrals, and every so often got a chance to fuck up your friends in a plausibly deniable way. A bit like school, but with fewer rules. Nowadays, though, in between monitoring the nation's phone calls and scanning the latest whistle blower's Twitter feed, geopolitics barely got a look-in. If asked to list the greatest threats to the nation's security, Ingrid Tearney would start with ministers and colleagues. Working out precisely where Ansar al-Islam came seemed little more than academic.

But you worked with what you had. Dame Ingrid was a great believer in occupying the here and now: if the Great Game had deteriorated to the status of the Latest App, so be it. So long as there was a podium for the winner, she knew where she wanted to end up.

On her desk was the usual collection of documents for signing: the minutes of the morning's meeting; various reports from various departments. A memo on top, suggesting she ring Security, had appeared while she'd been out of the room. Security meant internal, so whatever had just happened, it probably wasn't a threat to the nation. She rang downstairs anyway; was put through to the Kennel — the inevitable in-house name for the Dogs' office — and given a twenty-second summary of an off-site agent's incursion into the Park.

"And where is he now?"

"Downstairs. Mr Duffy's talking to him."

It was a frequently regretted state of affairs, being talked to by Mr Duffy.

She said, "Is there any obvious reason for — what was his name?"

"Cartwright. River Cartwright."

"Any obvious reason for Cartwright's presence?"

"He's Slough House, ma'am."

"That's context, certainly. I'm not sure it's a reason. Okay, let's let Mr Duffy deal with it. Have him call me when he's done."

Cartwright, she thought. Grandson of, if she wasn't mistaken.

She shook her head. Probably nothing.

She'd barely picked her pen up before the phone rang again.

Nick Duffy said, "Every morning I wake up and think, who's going to mess with my karma today? Because there's always someone. Job like mine, you rarely get the chance to sit back, read the papers and watch the clock till opening time."

For a moment River had thought Duffy was going to mime the sitting-back part of that, but the older man knew what he was doing. He tilted the chair slightly was all, then let its legs slam back down. River didn't blink. This was pantomime. So far, Duffy hadn't said anything he'd not have said a hundred times before.

"No, because there's always someone got his tit in a wringer, and it's Muggins here has to pry it free. Left your Service card in the pub? Let's have Nick sort it out. Unwise conversation with an over-friendly reptile?

126

Let's see if Nick can't smooth over the traces. Shagged the wrong bit of spare at the embassy disco? Don't worry, Nick'll throw a fright into her minder. You know the type of thing. We have a code for it in the Dogs. We call it the Really Dumb Shit."

Hoping to short circuit this, River said, "Am I under arrest?"

"So usually, see, I'm just a glorified au pair, making sure everything's tidied away nicely, no lasting ramifications, no nasty surprises in the tabloids. But what do we have today? Something special. Somebody's ambled into the Park on my watch, and thinks they can take the Really Dumb Shit on to a whole new level."

"Because if I am, I get a phone call, right?"

"And this is a serving agent, I'll grant you, but one with less security clearance than we give the janitors round here. Because the janitors get up close and personal with some nasty crap." He shifted position suddenly, and River knew he was changing gear. "Whereas you, Mr Cartwright, of Slough House, Barbican way, the most classified information you're privy to is whether the 56 bus is on time or not. And you're only allowed to share that if you get written permission from a superior. Which would be just about anybody, yes? Correct me if I'm wrong."

River said, "So I don't get a phone call."

"Of course you don't get a fucking phone call. You'll be lucky to get a blindfold."

"Because it would be handy to have my phone back. There's something on it you need to see."

"What I need and what you think I need are likely to be very different things, Cartwright. Let's see if I've got the order of events straight. You waltz into the Park without authorisation. You drag Ms Taverner out of a meeting, spout crap about Mr Webb, a colleague who might be incapacitated but, unlike you, remains an officer of good standing —"

"He wasn't standing last time I saw him."

Duffy paused. "You've been buddying up to Jackson Lamb for too long. That wasn't funny and doesn't help."

River said, "I came here for a reason."

"I'm sure you did. But I don't fucking care. You were found in a restricted access area, and according to Molly Doran you were planning on putting your hands on a classified file. A *very* classified file. You know the penalty for breaches of the Official Secrets Act?"

"I didn't breach the Act."

"Attempted breach. You know the penalty? They're not going to have you picking up litter, Cartwright. This isn't some ASBO offence. You're a member of the Service, a fuck-up member right enough but you carry a card and you're on the books. Which makes what you did not some petty offence; it puts it into the realm of treason. What were you planning on doing with the file? *That's* what I need to know. Who were you planning on selling it to?"

Lamb had taken his shoes off and his office smelled of socks, which was the fourth worst thing Louisa remembered it smelling of. She took a breath, stepped across the threshold and told him what Ho had just told her.

"He's back at the Park?" Lamb considered this for a moment. "That'd make his grandad proud, if he was still alive."

"He is still alive, isn't he?"

"Yeah, but finding out Junior's been arrested'll probably kill him," Lamb said reasonably.

"What makes you think he's been arrested?"

"If his phone's blocked, it means he's downstairs. And if he's downstairs, it's not because they've opened the dungeons to the public."

Louisa, remembering tales she'd heard of below-stairs interrogations at the Park, wondered what the hell River had done to wind up there. And how he had managed it so quickly. It was only a couple of hours since they'd both been in the kitchen, making coffee. He'd asked her where Catherine was. And Catherine was still nowhere.

She said, "It's not a coincidence."

"What, him and Standish both going AWOL? I doubt it."

"So what do we do?"

"I do what I always do. And you do whatever you were doing yesterday." With dexterity surprising in one so large, Lamb raised his right foot and rested it on his left knee. He began massaging it roughly. "Census project, right?"

"So we all just carry on as normal."

"As if you were normal, yes. Nothing like ambition." He grabbed a pencil from his desk, and began using it as a scratcher, working it between his toes. "Are you still here?"

"What'll happen to River?"

"When they've finished stripping the flesh from his bones, I expect they'll send him back. He'll only make the place untidy otherwise."

"Seriously."

"That wasn't serious? Which part of it did you find funny?"

"You've got two joes missing, and you're just going to sit there making holes in your socks?"

"None of you are joes, Guy. You're just a bunch of fuck-ups who got lucky."

"This is lucky?"

Lamb's lip curled. "I didn't say what kind of luck."

He tossed the pencil back onto the desk, where it kept on rolling until it dropped off the other side.

Louisa said, "We're not joes, no. But we're your joes. You know that."

"Don't get carried away. This is Slough House. It isn't *Spooks*."

"You're telling me. It's barely *Jackanory*." She took a step into the room. "But you think something's happened to Catherine, or you wouldn't have sent me round to her flat. And whatever River was up to has to have something to do with that. So no, I'm not going back to the census project. Not until you tell me what you're going to do about it."

It was dark in Lamb's room, as usual; he'd closed the blinds and turned his low-wattage desk lamp on. This sat on a pile of telephone directories, long since

130

rendered obsolete, and the shadows it cast mostly confined themselves to floor level, where they crawled about like spiders. The ceiling sloped and the floorboards creaked, and such things as he'd hung on the walls — a cork noticeboard on which clipped coupons faded to brittle yellow dustiness, like the corpses of pinned moths, and a smeary-glassed print of a bridge over a foreign-looking river, which had almost certainly come from a charity shop — served to underline the general creepiness. It wasn't a cosy atmosphere he aimed for, and the look he directed at Louisa now underlined that fact.

"I think you're forgetting who's top banana round here."

"No. I'm just reminding you that you are."

She was expecting one of his leers, or perhaps a raspberry, or even a fart — there'd been indications in the past that he could deliver these at will, unless he was just unusually lucky with his timing. But instead Lamb put his foot heavily on the floor, and leaned back in his chair so far it audibly strained. In place of his usual repertoire of grimaces, his face seemed blank, lineless almost; a passive mask behind which she could sense his thoughts rolling around themselves.

At last he said, "I'll make a call," with all the enthusiasm of one preparing to tote a barge, or lift a bale.

Louisa nodded, remaining where she was.

"It's a phone call, not a shag. I don't need someone watching to make sure I'm doing it right."

That wasn't an image Louisa wanted in her head. She left him to it, but didn't close the door on her way out.

"What were you planning on doing with the file?" Duffy said. "And who were you planning on selling it to?"

"I wasn't going to sell it."

"Course not. Going to keep it for a little bedtime reading, right?" Duffy stood and pushed the chair, which fell flat on the floor. "Rub one out while rummaging through the PM's little secrets."

"Does he really have secrets worth rubbing one out to?"

Duffy paused in front of the mirror, pretending it was a mirror. He ran a hand through his cropped hair, maybe checking for bald patches. Or perhaps making secret hand signals to whoever was on the other side.

He said, "What's really funny is you finding this funny."

"I'm not."

"Because this one joke's going to have to last you an awful long time. Couple of years down the road, you might have trouble squeezing any more chuckles from it." He took a step towards River, who was leaning against the wall, and stood directly in front of him. River could smell the fabric conditioner he'd used on his tracksuit. Duffy had put it on fresh from the wash.

He said, "They have Catherine Standish."

"Standish."

"There was a photograph. Came to my phone from hers. It was taken this morning, last night. They wanted the file."

"Standish," Duffy said again. "She's another of your special needs crew, right?"

"Can I be there when you say that to Lamb?"

"You don't get to be anywhere without somebody's say-so, Cartwright. Your whole future's one long yes-sir, no-sir."

That sounded horribly plausible. And River was scared, because Duffy was good at this, but he was scareder, somehow, of letting it show.

Not letting it show was all he had left right now.

"They've got Catherine Standish, and somebody needs to go find her. The picture's on my phone. Whoever's behind that mirror needs to take a look at it *now*."

"This isn't about your amateur porn collection, Cartwright. It's about your attempt to steal the PM's vetting file. Did you really think you'd get away with that?"

"The guy I spoke to was early fifties, five nine. Grey suit, yellow tie, black shoes. Dark hair going silver at the temples. English, white, upper-class accent —"

Duffy slammed his left hand against the wall, an inch from River's ear. "And he's your buyer, right? He's the man instructed you to break into the Park."

"I didn't break in."

"Well you weren't fucking invited. Where'd this happen?"

"Over by Barbican."

"And this toff what, dropped in on Slough House?"

"I told you, he sent —"

Duffy slammed his other hand against the wall, and leaned forward so his forehead was almost touching River's. "You want to know why I'm having trouble believing this fairy story, Cartwright?"

"Look at my phone."

"It's because if any of it even remotely happened, you know where you'd be now? Back at your desk, doing your job. Having reported all these . . . *unusual* events to your boss, who'd have passed them up the line exactly the way it says in the protocols. Because if you'd done anything different, Cartwright, you'd have knowingly endangered the life of your fellow . . . What is it they call you over there?"

River could smell Duffy's breath. Could feel the heat of the sweat forming on his brow.

"Can't hear you."

"You know what they call us."

And then he was doubling over in pain, that familiar terrible pain men learn early and never forget. In a minute or two, it would get worse. But for the moment the impact of Duffy's knee into his testicles wiped out all thought of his future.

Duffy stepped away, and River fell to the floor.

Diana Taverner answered on the third ring and said, "What do you want?"

"No, really," said Lamb. "The pleasure's all mine."

He'd called her mobile, though he knew she'd be at her desk — she had that level of devotion to duty at

134

least partly fired by fear that someone would move into her office if she left it for long.

"Been meaning to call you, actually," she said. "Finance are querying your latest expenses sheet. How come you clock up so much in travel costs when you barely leave your room?"

"How come Finance are passing their queries on to you?"

"Because her high-and-mighty Dameness has decreed that all and any manner of crap be redirected my way." A pause followed, just long enough for her to be lighting a cigarette if that weren't a shootable offence at the Park. "She wants to underline how indispensable I am, which means she thinks she's found a way of dispensing with me."

Because he wasn't at the Park, and because nobody got shot at Slough House without his permission, Lamb lit a cigarette. "You sound quite relaxed about it."

"She'll have to get up earlier than she thinks she has," Taverner said, which would have sounded cryptic from anyone else, but was reasonably lucid for her. "So. These expenses sheets."

"Don't push me, Diana. I have hostages, remember?"

"They're not your hostages, Jackson. They're your staff."

"You say potato," said Lamb. "Anyway, I don't have as many as I used to. A birdy tells me you've got one of mine in your lock-up."

"That would be River Cartwright."

"Yes, but don't blame me. I think his mother was a hippy."

"Smoke a lot of dope while he was in the womb, did she? That might explain today's dipshit behaviour. And I thought he was one of your cleverer boys."

"Mind like a razor," Lamb agreed. "Disposable. Anyway, when you've finished ticking him off, pack him back this way, would you? I've thought of three different ways of making his life hell, and I'm itching to put them into practice."

That he was itching was beyond doubt. His pencil being out of reach he'd grabbed a plastic ruler, and was sawing away at the gaps between the toes on his right foot, a task made easier now the fabric of his sock had given way.

"Yeah, right." Taverner gave her throaty chuckle, famous for making the old boys on the Oversight Committee stand to attention. "You might need to practise your latest . . . *wheezes* on someone else."

" 'Wheezes'?"

"This isn't one of your daily misdemeanours, Lamb. Cartwright attempted to steal, or photograph, a Scott-level document, leaking which would have caused serious embarrassment to both the Service and the government. We're not going to send him back to you with a slapped wrist. Anyway, it's out of my hands. He's with the Dogs. And when they're finished with him, they'll hand him over to the Met."

Lamb took a long drag on his cigarette, noisily enough that Taverner knew what he was doing. He said,

"Scott level? You're still playing Thunderbirds over there?"

"Yes, but don't blame me. Unquote. Tearney thinks they're astronauts." Her chuckle floated into Lamb's room once more, mixing with the cloud he'd just breathed out. "And if you think I don't know when you're processing, you're sadly wrong. You've no idea what your boy was up to, have you?"

"Well, I've got a birthday this year. Perhaps he was looking for that special gift."

"I'll get those expenses details emailed over. You might want to give them some more thought."

"Diana?"

This time, it was more than a chuckle. This time it was an outright laugh. "Oh dear. Sounds like you're about to make a plea."

Lamb said, "Cartwright's not my only joe gone walkabout. If there's anything happening I need to know about, you'd best email those details too. Save me having to come over there and ask you myself."

He hung up, and gave his foot one last vicious tweak with the ruler, which split in half with a noise like a gunshot.

This being Slough House, and Lamb being Lamb, nobody came to find out if that's what it had been.

When he could see again, all he could see was the floor. He spat, and then he could see the floor and some spit, and then his vision went wavy again, and then it came back.

So now you know, a small voice in the back of his head told him, what it's like to be kneed in the balls by an expert.

It's surprising how even the most basic of skills can become, in the hands of an artist, a minor masterpiece.

"I'm waiting," another voice said. This one wasn't in his head; it existed in the rest of the world too.

River hauled himself into a squatting position where the pain didn't exactly subside, but allowed him to think that it might one day do so, and took a deep breath, half scared that doing so would rupture something important. He looked for his voice, and found it a little farther away than usual. "Slow. Horses. They call us. The slow Horses." Even to himself, he sounded like a nonagenarian refugee. "And you know. What they call. You?"

"Everyone knows what they call us," Duffy said. "They call us the Dogs."

"No. They call the Dogs. The Dogs. They call you. A useless prick."

"And yet you're the one lying on the floor."

"You ever. Try that. Outside your own backyard," River said. "We'll see who ends up. On the floor."

It was getting easier again, this old talent of his: making words come out of his mouth. He looked up, and found Duffy looking straight back down at him.

"Maybe we can check that out," he said. "But not anytime soon. You're going to be busy for a while yet."

"Standish," said River. "They have Catherine Standish."

138

"Yeah, well. It's not like we were doing anything with her. And you're going to have one hell of a job persuading anyone she's worth the PM's vetting file." Duffy ran his left index finger over the knuckles of his right hand. "Now get to your feet, and let's try again."

Queasily, River managed to stand.

Duffy said, "Who were you planning on selling it to?"

River said, "They have Catherine Standish. Check my phone, you moron."

This time, Duffy hit him in the stomach.

"Sorry about this," the soldier began.

He didn't look sorry.

"But we're out of milk."

He put the mug of tea he was carrying on the bedside table.

"Room service?" Catherine said.

"Well, we can hardly let you wander down to the kitchen at will. Security issues."

"This is the weirdest kidnapping I've ever heard of," she told him. "Not that I'm an expert. But seriously? Is this your first time?"

The soldier pursed a lip, as if giving it thought. "We've taken prisoners before. But the circumstances were different."

"You're not going to kill me, then."

"We're not animals."

"Can I have that in writing?" She'd hoped for a chuckle, and when she didn't get one asked, "Where's Donovan?"

"Downstairs."

No he wasn't. He'd left earlier, in the van. But it didn't hurt to pretend to believe him.

She said, "I could do with a change of clothing."

"I said we weren't animals. I didn't say we were Marks and Spencer's."

He turned to leave, and Catherine reached for a hook to hold him. She found it just as he was closing the door.

"Does he talk about her much?"

". . . About who?"

"The girl who died."

He paused. Then said, "She wasn't a *girl*. She was a captain in the armed forces."

"My apologies. But she's still dead, right? Does he talk about her at all? I'm sure I would."

Catherine could hear her own voice rising as she spoke — she rarely lost control of her tone, but she was desperate for him to stay, say more, cast light on why she was here, and what was happening elsewhere.

"If I'd been drink-driving the car that killed her, I mean," she finished.

He shook his head, sadly it seemed to her, and left the room, padlocking the door behind him.

After a while, Catherine reached for the tea.

Nick Duffy splashed water onto his face, then gazed hard into the bathroom mirror, finding nothing out of the ordinary there. A morning's work. They weren't all like this — well, they couldn't be. It wasn't a police state.

After he'd dried himself on a paper towel, he checked on Cartwright through the two-way. He'd have expected the kid — not entirely a kid, but Duffy felt entitled — to have parked himself on the chair, which Duffy had left for that specific purpose, to make taking it away from him the next gambit. Cartwright, though, had remained upright. He was leaning against the wall, and if he didn't look happy — looked pale as a fish with stomach pains — he hadn't, Duffy noted, positioned himself out of view of the mirror. In fact, he raised a middle finger towards it at that moment, as if he knew Duffy was watching.

Could have been a lucky guess.

He moved away and released the phone from its hook on the wall. A three-digit extension got him Diana Taverner.

"He's not changing his story."

"Remind me what his story was."

Duffy ran through it: the photograph of Standish, the brief instruction. The man on the bridge who'd worn a suit and had a toff's accent.

"Sounded like he got up Cartwright's nose."

"You believe him then?" Taverner asked.

Duffy looked at his free hand. Nothing about it suggested he'd done anything rougher that morning than carrying a hot coffee.

"I think he'd have changed his story if it wasn't true," he said.

He was used to Lady Di's silences, which generally meant she was assimilating information, dividing it into pros and cons. This one, though, felt different, as if she already had a handle on what was going on.

In the room next door, Cartwright made the middle-finger gesture again. He was on a loop, Duffy decided. A cycle of defiance, because despite all that had happened to him in the past twenty minutes, he hadn't yet grasped the nature or the depth of the shit into which he'd stepped.

Taverner said, "Have you sent anyone looking for this man? The one on the bridge?"

"There was a man, in London, on a bridge, two hours ago," Duffy said. "We could cordon the city off, I suppose."

"Talk to me like that again," Taverner said, without altering her tone, "and you'd happily swap places with Cartwright. What about the woman — Standish?"

"The photo's on his phone. Like he said."

"And it came from where?"

"Her phone."

"Of course it did . . . Any trace?"

"Not that I've heard."

"How badly have you hurt him?"

"Hardly at all."

"By your standards, or anyone's?"

"He might be a slow horse, but he's not a civilian. He'll live."

"Just as well. Lamb can get . . . tetchy when his crew get damaged."

"I thought he despised his crew."

"That doesn't mean he likes other people messing with them. Okay, let Cartwright sweat for the moment. We'll get word from on high sooner or later."

142

"On high?"

"Oh yes. Dame Ingrid's been summoned to the Home Office. And you know how jolly that makes her."

Cartwright was doing the thing with the finger again. He couldn't know Duffy was there, obviously, but it was still starting to get on his wick.

He said, "Look. That crack about cordoning off the city. I —"

"You'd just finished putting the leather to someone. It made you feel cocky. Made you feel invulnerable."

"I guess . . ."

"Trust me. You're not."

Taverner hung up.

Duffy replaced the receiver and stood by the two-way a while longer. Every so often, River Cartwright repeated the finger gesture, but to Duffy's eye, it looked a little less convincing each time. What was it they used knackered horses for again? — oh yeah: dog food and glue. Give it a while, he'd pop next door and remind Cartwright of that. Meanwhile, he deserved a cup of coffee.

He left the room quietly so the kid wouldn't hear. The thought of him standing there, repeatedly offering the finger to an empty room, wasn't quite enough to wipe away the memory of Lady Di's parting shot, but it didn't hurt.

CHAPTER
SEVEN

There were many thorns in Ingrid Tearney's garden — the constant need for vigilance; the ever-present threat of terrorism; Diana Taverner — and here was another: a summons from the Home Secretary. Until recently, such phone calls had been a minor nuisance, requiring her to attend the minister's office and deliver platitudes while maintaining eye contact, as if soothing a worried puppy. But Peter Judd didn't look to her for reassurance, he sized her up for weaknesses. In company he claimed they got on like a house on fire, but it was clear which of them provided the petrol.

It was Dame Ingrid's habit to catch the Tube into work, but she used her official ride for everything else. It took her now through streets that were wilting in the heat. When the freak weather had started it had splashed the capital in colour, but as hot days turned into baking weeks, brightness had faded like old paint. Greenery died, turning parks brown and lifeless. People scurried now from shadow to shadow, wearing the caved-in expressions of trauma survivors, and greeted rumours of rain like news of a lottery win. That the weather was *not normal* was a staple of internet traffic. The streets, meanwhile, were cruel

144

reflections of an unforgiving sky, where everything dazzled and everything hurt.

But inside the car frosted air circulated, and to all outward appearance Ingrid Tearney was unruffled by heatwave or grim thoughts. Her summer outfit was new, the fruit of a recent upturn in her finances, and her mannish features were relaxed into a benevolent-seeming mask. She looked like the friendly grandmother, the one who offers oranges, but behind that mask steam valves hissed. Judd's telephone summons had come from the man himself instead of the usual lackey, but he'd given no clue as to what it was about. His tone, though, had reeked of triumph. Whatever game he was about to play, he'd been dealt a useful hand.

Still, let the chips fall. Dame Ingrid didn't negotiate with politicians.

Unless they had her by the throat.

At the minister's residence, the front door was opened by a pretty young man with the faintest hint of a lisp. Nobody doubted Judd's heterosexuality, which was as enthusiastic as it was indiscriminate, but his entourage tended towards the fey — Judd hadn't dubbed them his camp followers for nothing. It was always possible the quip had occurred to him first, and he'd chosen his retinue accordingly.

"Dame Ingrid," he said now, as she entered his office.

"Home Secretary."

"I've taken the liberty."

Which sounded like a bullet-point summary of his Home Office tenure to date, but was in fact a reference to the tea tray on a nearby table.

Following his guide, she sat in an armchair. The room, she noted, remained much as it had done during his predecessor's ministry, which is to say that not only was it still walnut-panelled, book-lined and Turkish-rugged, but that Judd hadn't even bothered to have the art changed: some drab *nature morts*, a few sea battles, and a large and politically obsolete globe. Given Judd's tendency to leave his stamp on things, Tearney took this as a clue that he didn't expect to remain here long. Which had been true of his predecessor too, but for a diametrically opposite reason.

"Milk? Sugar?"

She shook her head.

Peter Judd poured, placed cup and saucer on a table by her elbow, and lowered himself into the chair opposite.

He was a bulky man, not fat, but large, and though he had turned fifty the previous year, retained the schoolboy looks and fluffy-haired manner that had endeared him to the British public and made him a staple on the less-challenging end of the TV spectrum: interviews conducted on sofas, by scripted comedians. Through persistence, connections and family wealth, he'd established a brand — "a loose cannon with a floppy fringe and a bicycle" — that set him head and shoulders above the rest of his party, and if the occasional colleague had attempted to lop that head off those shoulders in the interests of political unity, they'd yet to find the axe to do the job. Tearney's own file on him was long on speculation, short on facts. So clean of cobwebs, in fact, that she was sure he'd airbrushed his past of serious sins as carefully as he arranged his haystack of hair.

He was eyeing her now in a manner that suggested he was about to enjoy what followed.

"So, Minister," she said, never keen on being made to sign her own punishment slips. "What seems to be your problem today?"

"Oh, I have no problems. Only a bagful of solutions awaiting opportunities."

She pretended not to sigh, or at least, pretended she didn't want him to notice her trying not to. "So this is social? It's always a pleasure, Minister, but I am somewhat busy."

"So I gather. Bit of a rumpus over your way this morning, what?"

"Rumpus" was a favourite PJ-word; one he'd employed to describe a recent tabloid splash about his friendship with a lap dancer. It was also a term he'd used in reference to both 9/11 and the global recession.

"What sort of, ah, rumpus would this be?"

"An incursion."

He meant the Cartwright business, she realised. Which was unimportant and without consequence, which meant there was something to it she wasn't yet aware of.

"I'd hardly call it an incursion," she said. "An off-site agent lost his bearings. The Park can be disorientating."

"So I recall."

"Besides, the incident was done and dusted inside twenty minutes. When I left, the young man was being, ah, chided by our head of security." She sipped again at her tea. "Are you sure such matters are worth your attention? I'd have thought there were weightier issues on your desk."

Though the question of how he'd become aware of Cartwright's frolic almost before she had was a matter Dame Ingrid definitely didn't consider minor.

"I deem few things beneath my attention," he said, adopting the plummier tones ex-public schoolboys use when bringing words like "deem" into play. "And certainly not those issues which call into question the integrity of our national Security Service."

"'Integrity'," she said. "Really?"

He leaned back in his chair. "More tea?"

"I'm fine."

"Sure? You don't mind if . . .?"

She shook her head.

He refreshed his cup, and stirred the contents slowly, not taking his eyes off her.

"Minister, precisely what is this about?"

"Well, it's quite simple, Dame Ingrid. Tell me, are you familiar with the term 'tiger team'?"

Dame Ingrid lowered her teacup.

"Oh dear," she said.

The taxi left Monteith outside the multi-storey car park. It was a drab, soulless building, precisely because of its function: if an architect ever designed a car park the sight of which lifted the heart, civilisation's job

148

would be done. Monteith made a mental note to drop this *aperçu* into conversation next time he was with Peter Judd, and walked down the slope into the structure. Even with heat rising from the pavement, the lower storey carried a grave scent of damp earth and mildew. He stepped around an oil patch on the scabbed concrete, and pulled open the heavy door into the stairwell.

A different splash of odours, urine among them. Civilisation's job was one long uphill battle round here.

He took the stairs two at a time. Into his fifties, he remained proud of his physical condition: barely smoked, and then only good Cuban; never drank port or liqueurs; red wine just three evenings a week (white the rest). If this didn't precisely add up to a fitness regime, it gave him a head start. Besides, he was a leader, not a foot soldier. When River Cartwright had taken him by the lapels earlier, he'd felt no physical fear precisely because of that difference between them. Cartwright was a pawn, and didn't know it. Monteith's place was among the kings, and today's work would serve to consolidate that.

Pawns don't take kings. Basic rule of nature.

Donovan was waiting on the top storey, by the van. Another case in point, Monteith thought. Sean Donovan could have been wearing Monteith's shoes now, near as damn it, if he'd understood the game. But that was the problem with coming up through the ranks — there was a reason the phrase was officer *class*. It came with breeding, wasn't something they could drill into you.

None of that showed in his voice when he called out, "Donovan!"

Donovan didn't respond.

Another oil patch to skip around. The light was better up here; the sides open to the city, technically allowing for airflow. But the midday heat shunted around as if in blocks. Every time you encountered it, it was like walking into a wall.

He resisted the temptation to run a finger around his collar. Appearances: you kept tight hold of them.

"Donovan," he said again when he was no more than a yard away. "Everything in order?"

"So far."

When he'd pictured this moment, Sly Monteith realised, he'd imagined it as one of high-fiving celebration — a plan brought to fruition; the pair of them delighted with each other and themselves. But Sean Donovan seemed, if anything, even less inclined than usual to unbend.

It didn't matter. Monteith didn't need Donovan's approbation. The real celebrations would come later.

Because say what you like about Peter Judd, he knew how to mark a job well done.

"A tiger team," Ingrid Tearney said.

"A tiger team."

"I know perfectly well what a tiger team is," she told him.

That feeling she was getting now was of Judd's fingers round her throat.

Tiger teams were hired guns, essentially. Hired not to wipe out your enemies but to test the strength of your own defences. You set a tiger team to launch a simulated attack: recruited hackers to stress-test security systems, assigned a wet-squad to put a bodyguard team through its paces, and so on. Earlier that year, she had herself overseen a Service-propelled assault on one of the city's major utility providers, to verify concerns that the capital's infrastructure was dangerously vulnerable to attack. The results were mixed. It was, it turned out, surprisingly easy to cripple a large energy provider, but in the wake of recent price hikes, people seemed mostly in favour of doing so. Besides, the populace at large evidently regarded a global wine shortage as a more serious threat to its well-being than terrorism. In rather the same way, Dame Ingrid was now realising, that the greatest threat to the Service — and her own role within it — seemed to be emanating from the Home Secretary rather than its more traditional enemies: terrorists, rival security agencies, the *Guardian*.

"And this was your doing," she said.

He nodded, pleased with himself. This was not in itself an unusual sight — being pleased with himself was Peter Judd's factory setting — but at this close distance, it made Tearney want to throw the teapot at him.

"Can I ask why?"

"Why are these things ever done? I wanted to reassure myself that the Service's protocols are in

151

tip-top order. Not much point in relying on a security provider which can't secure itself, is there?"

"Then you'll have been relieved at the result," she said. "No harm done."

He wagged a finger at her. With most people this would have been a metaphor, but the Home Secretary's tendency towards pantomime ensured that an actual finger was involved. "One of your agents was taken off the street. Another was induced to attempt a data theft from your very own precincts."

"And failed."

"But shouldn't have got even that far. There are procedures, Dame Ingrid. The moment he was approached, your boy should have escalated the matter upwards. He didn't. That's a severe lapse by anyone's standards. And by the standards I expect to attain while I am minister in charge, it's a shortcoming that requires action."

After several years of dealing with a minister who could be reduced to jelly by the very thought of taking action, it was salutary to be reminded that not all politicians covered arse first and made decisions afterwards. It was galling that it had to happen on her watch, though.

"This . . . tiger team," she said. "Who, precisely, are we talking about?"

"Chap called Sylvester Monteith." Judd had the air of one explaining that he'd had a little man from the village round to prune his hedge. "He runs an outfit called Black Arrow. Ridiculous, really. Still, goes with the territory, I suppose."

"Black Arrow."

"No reason it should have crossed your radar. Mostly corporate security, to date. You know the kind of thing, give the company firewalls a rattle, see what's loose. All on home turf, mind. No foreign adventures." Judd placed his cup and saucer on his left knee, which he'd crossed over his right. "Gave the Afghan shenanigans a wide berth, sensibly, if you want my opinion. Plenty of money in that line, of course, but the premiums are crippling."

"How very distressing for all involved," Tearney said. "And you're telling me you hired this man?"

"Damn reasonable rate, too. Are you sure I can't tempt you to more tea?"

"Yes. And I suppose this Sylvester Monteith is an old crony of yours."

"He prefers Sly."

"Which answers my question."

"We both know how Westminster works, Ingrid. It's not called a village for nothing. Obviously we've crossed paths in the past."

"Like I said. A crony."

"That's not a useful term in my book. No successful business, no thriving corporation, can afford to ignore networking. It's how things get done."

"Eton?"

"I'm not going to play this game."

"Twenty seconds after leaving this office, I'll know his inside leg measurement."

"Well then. Yes. As it happens."

"Oxford?"

"No, actually." He picked up his cup once more. "Well, yes, but St Anne's for Christ's sake."

"In the eyes of most people, that would still count."

"That's why we don't let 'most people' take the important decisions."

"An interesting slant on the democratic process."

"Don't pretend to be naive. It doesn't suit you."

"Let's stay on topic then, shall we? You decided, without consultation, to hire an old school chum to set an, ah, *tiger team* onto the Service you have ministerial responsibility for. You don't see any conflict of interest?"

"None at all. Consultation would have undermined the whole purpose. When was the last time you didn't have the minutes of a closed-door meeting in your hands before the principals were out of the gates? The slightest sniff of this and you'd have gone to a war footing."

She couldn't fault his logic.

"Besides," he said. "As you say, I have ministerial responsibility. Confirming the Service's fitness for purpose is well within my remit. An obligation, even."

"One minor lapse in protocol is hardly —"

"One minor lapse is more than enough, even if I agreed it was minor. But you had an unauthorised entry into Regent's Park, which in anyone's eyes is a serious breach of security."

"By a member of the Service. Not by one of your mercenaries."

"It remains an unauthorised entry. And the young man in question is hardly an agent in good standing, is

154

he? From what I hear, he has his grandfather to thank for the fact that he wasn't drummed out before he'd finished his training. He crashed King's Cross, I gather. In rush hour. At the very least, that's a demarcation issue. Buggering up the transport infrastructure is the mayor's job."

A line Dame Ingrid suspected he'd used before, or would again, with a bigger audience.

She said, "I'd take issue with his entry being unauthorised. It was approved by one of our Second Desks. Diana Taverner, I believe."

"And having gained entry, he went walkabout. Let's not split hairs, Ingrid. He was found attempting to access classified information. He should be in a cell. I think we could guarantee him ten years minimum."

"And what about your merry band of friends? They 'took' an agent? Kidnapping carries a tariff too."

He waved a hand as if shooing a wasp. "There'll be a waiver. And it will be signed."

"You're very sure of that."

He graced her with a bland smile.

A loose cannon with a floppy fringe . . . But an important thing about Peter Judd, she reminded herself, was that his affability was polymer-deep. In front of the cameras, in front of an audience, in any kind of best-behaviour scenario, he played the hail-and-well-met card like a pro, as comfortable among punters in an East End corner shop as he was in front of twelve pieces of cutlery at a black tie event. But a very short way below the surface lay a temper that could scorch chrome. It was one of the reasons she

155

knew he'd taken an airbrush to his past. Nobody with his psychological make-up had led a damage-free life.

But right here, right now, he had the upper hand and they both knew it.

She said, "Very well. Wormwood Scrubs for young Cartwright, treble G&Ts all round for the private sector. I assume we can expect to hear that Sly Monteith's about to land some lucrative contract or other? Perhaps he could replace those clowns who did their best to scupper the Olympics."

"Bitterness is so unbecoming."

"Are you expecting my resignation?"

He bared a palm, as if to demonstrate no evil intent. Only one palm, she noted. "Heaven forbid."

"Then what is it you want?"

Unlike many another politico, he didn't waste time pretending he didn't know what she meant. "An, ah, what shall we call it? An understanding. No. An alliance."

"You're my minister. I answer to you on a daily basis. I'm sure we already understand each other, and as for alliances, there should be little doubt that we're on the same side."

"Oh, we're all on the same side. But that doesn't mean we don't pick teams. You're a civil servant. I'm a politician. With a fair wind, you might expect to be head of your Service until retirement. But one way or the other, I don't expect to be in this office for more than another year. If I leave it on my terms, it will be because I'm moving into Number Ten. Otherwise . . . Well, political careers have been known to founder."

"And you're worried yours might."

"Once the PM decides he's in a strong enough position, yes. He brought me inside the fold to forestall a challenge from the back benches. Any such challenge now would seem . . ."

"Treacherous."

"Impolite."

"And thus unlikely to garner support within the party."

Judd blinked in silent agreement.

"Unless his circumstances changed."

Judd blinked again.

It was cool in the office. A fake breeze hummed somewhere, as if it were blowing in off a carpet of ice cubes. But as an undercurrent to that, Ingrid Tearney felt a sudden access of warmth; that of acquired knowledge. Judd wanted to render the Service a sharp kick in the teeth, that had always been clear; a way of both asserting his own current mastery, and revenging himself for a rejection three decades ago. But in addition to that, he wanted — needed — her cooperation. Tearney recognised this ability to layer scheme upon scheme, to allow for maximum benefit. It wasn't so much playing both ends against the middle as securing the middle and flaying anyone within reach with the ends.

She said, "I see."

"I rather thought you might."

"So the file Cartwright was sent to steal — that wasn't a random choice."

157

"For the purposes of the exercise, one file was as good as any other," he said smoothly.

"Of course. I'm just getting an inkling of the use you might have put it to if he'd succeeded."

"Well," he said. "That was never likely to happen, was it? Not unless security at the Park turned out to be in even more parlous a state than was the case." He rose suddenly, and carried his empty cup and saucer to the tea tray. With his back to her, he went on, "Besides, there's no need for me to go to such lengths to examine the contents of an old file housed in a department over which I have ministerial control."

"Subject to the usual limitations," Dame Ingrid said.

He returned to where she sat, and held a hand out. She gave him her crockery.

He said, "Of course. I'm simply seeking an assurance that all and any information relevant to the security of the nation is brought to my attention. That would inevitably include information relating to the reliability or otherwise of those entrusted with the great offices of state."

"Which might then be used to ease those same unreliables out of those offices."

"Well now. Once we've established the unfitness of an office holder, it would be a dereliction of duty not to do something about it."

He carried her crockery to the table and carefully arranged the empty cups and used saucers in as efficient a tableau as possible. Then he returned to his chair and sat once more, smiling pleasantly.

She said, "Have you any idea how many times over the past half-century the Service has been asked to consider doing what you're suggesting?"

He pretended to give it some thought. "I would guess at least once during each administration. But let's not get ahead of ourselves. The important thing is that we both know whose team we're on."

"I see."

An important thing perhaps, but promises of future cooperation were easily given. If the worst that happened here and now was that she be allowed back to the Park to lick her wounds, Ingrid Tearney would count the day a victory. But she knew as well as she knew her own mind that, having manoeuvred her into a corner where she could hardly fail but to indicate surrender, Judd would take it one step further and demonstrate his power. Victory, she had once heard someone say, was about ensuring your opponent never again put head to pillow without thinking with hatred on your face. Tearney, who had never married, had thought this over the top, but had little difficulty accepting it as one of Judd's credos.

It was of small consolation, in such circumstances, to be proved right almost immediately.

Peter Judd picked up a small metal implement from the table by his chair — a cigar-cutter, or some equally ridiculous tool — and examined it with an air of absent-mindedness. For such a dedicated politician, it really was a beginner's tell.

He said, "This Slough House place. Amusing name. I gather it's a decrepit set of offices near the Barbican."

She nodded.

"Somewhere you can send the rejects."

"It's not always politic to fire people."

"Isn't it? Can't say I've ever found that a problem."

It was true that he'd never seemed to worry about lawsuits, whether relating to employment or paternity issues.

"And that's where this Cartwright chap was assigned."

She saw little point in replying when it was clear he knew the answer.

Judd sighed to himself as if enjoying a private little moment of pleasure, and replaced the metal tool on the table where it belonged.

"Well, it's obviously unfit for purpose if its aim was to retrain the morons," he said. "So let's close it down."

"Slough House?"

"Yes," he said. "Close it down. Today."

Jackson Lamb didn't believe in omens. When he got a feeling in his gut, it was generally because of some mistreatment he'd subjected said gut to, though frankly the thing was so inured to his lifestyle, he'd probably have to pour weed-poison into it to provoke a serious reaction. Nevertheless, he didn't like the way the day was shaping up. Cartwright getting arrested at the Park was a serious fuck-up, even for the boy wonder; Lamb didn't doubt Lady Di had meant every word when she'd said they could kiss him goodbye. And while he could contemplate a future without River Cartwright in it with a degree of equanimity, Catherine Standish

160

would have plenty to say on the subject if she ever turned up. And Lamb had learned long ago not to piss off whoever made your morning tea.

If she turned up . . . His gut aside, facts were starting to accumulate. The odds on Cartwright doing something monumentally stupid on any given morning were evens; the chances of Catherine Standish going AWOL were lower. That the two things had happened at the same time meant there was a connection, and if Lamb had to place a bet, he'd put it on cause and effect. Cartwright had learned something about Standish's disappearance that had set him haring off to the Park where he'd hit a brick wall, full tilt.

Time for an older, wiser mind to take charge.

He farted, and settled into Catherine's chair.

Lamb didn't often come into this office. The rest of Slough House he prowled at will, poking into nooks and late-night corners, but Standish's office he left alone. If it contained anything she genuinely didn't want him to find, he probably wouldn't find it without causing structural damage. And by the time he was drunk enough to find this prospect appealing, he was usually beyond putting a plan into action.

The desk was neatly organised, which was no surprise. Front and centre was a pile of reports that should, by rights, have been on Lamb's own desk when he'd arrived this morning; by now, he'd have pawed them out of their pristine state, and spilled enough of one beverage or another onto them, in lieu of actually reading the damn things, to warrant their being reprinted before they were shuffled into secure folders

161

and shipped off to the Park. The knowledge that they'd receive equally scant attention there had never prevented Standish from rendering them as professional-looking as possible. It was one of the ways Lamb could tell she didn't have sex any more.

He picked up the reports, weighed them reflectively as if gauging the intelligence they contained, then dropped them into the wastebasket. "Prioritise," he murmured to himself. Then he stood and moved around the small office.

A faint smell of blossom lingered in the air, or had done until quite recently. The culprit wasn't hard to find: a small muslin bag hanging from the window frame. Lamb tugged at it gently between thumb and forefinger, but not gently enough not to snap the thread it hung from. Letting it fall, he continued his circuit. Two sets of filing cabinets. A coat stand from which a linen tote bag dangled, alongside an umbrella. All of it like a Disneyfied version of his own office: smaller translating into cosier; neater into cleaner. Well, cleaner into cleaner too, to be honest. She'd been here as recently as last night, but already the room was subsiding into a museum piece. He had the strange sensation that, given another twenty-four hours, everything would be laced with cobweb.

Get a grip . . .

There was no point turning the office over, because he already knew there were no clues here. Standish had called him twice after leaving last night, indicating that whatever had happened happened after she left Slough House . . . Still, he went through her desk anyway, on principle. The spare keys to her flat were missing, which gave him a moment's pause before he remembered Louisa Guy had checked her place out. There was nothing else of interest except, in the bottom drawer, a bottle-shaped object wrapped in tissue paper so old it crinkled to his touch. He pulled it free. The Macallan. Seal unbroken. After studying it a moment he rebundled it, and stuffed it back in the drawer.

He looked up to find Louisa leaning on the door frame.

"What?"

"Looking for something?"

"If I was, I'd have found it by now."

He fell back into Standish's chair, which registered its discomfort with a sharp *twang*.

Louisa said, "You don't think she's drunk somewhere."

"No."

"You're sure."

Instead of replying, Lamb fumbled in his jacket pocket and produced a cigarette. He lit it eyes closed, and wheezily inhaled.

"What did they say at the Park? About River?"

"He's under arrest. Something about an attempt to steal a file. You can go clean his desk out if you want."

"Didn't take long, did it?" Louisa said. "Catherine goes off reservation, and we're one down not twenty-four hours later. I'd give us till the end of the week."

" 'Us'?"

"Slough House."

Lamb chuckled.

"You don't think we're a team?"

"I think you're collateral damage," said Lamb.

"And yet here you are, looking for clues. What was the file River was trying to steal?"

"Wrong question. You should be asking, what the hell was Cartwright doing, trying to steal a file?"

"Well, I assume it was a ransom demand," Louisa said. "Whoever took Catherine got in touch with him."

"Has Ho traced her phone?"

"She's taken the battery out. Or someone has."

Lamb grunted.

"So what now?"

"Well it's long past lunchtime," he said. "And no bugger's fetched me a carry-out yet."

"So that's the bigger picture sorted. But what about these other issues? You know, the danger your team's in. That sort of thing."

"Cartwright's not in danger. They might work him over a bit, but they'll give him to the plod soon enough. He'll be perfectly safe."

"But in prison."

"Yeah, well. Silly sod should have thought of that before having his awfully big adventure. He's in MI5, not the Famous Five." Lamb flicked ash onto Catherine's desk. "You'd think he'd have worked that out by now."

"And what about Catherine?"

"Remember what I just said about collateral damage?"

"So whoever's fucking about with Slough House, you're just going to let it happen."

164

The chair creaked dangerously as Lamb leaned back, dangling his arms over the sides. "What do you expect me to do?" he said. "It's not as if we know who's doing the fucking about."

"And when we find out?" Louisa asked.

"Ah," said Lamb. "That'll be a different story."

"Slough House," Judd said. "Close it down. Today."

"Just like that?"

"Just like that. Do we own the building?"

"Yes."

"Better still. We can flog it off now the market's recovered. That'll pay for the odd decoder ring, what?"

"And the agents?"

"Have them put down."

". . . Seriously?"

"No. But it's interesting you felt the need to ask. No, just sack them. They're all retards or they wouldn't be there anyway. Hand them their cards, tell them goodbye."

"Jackson Lamb —"

"I know all about Jackson Lamb. He's supposed to know where some bodies are buried, yes? Well, newsflash, nobody spends a lifetime in this business without stumbling across the occasional corpse. And if he feels like kicking up a fuss, he'll find out what the Official Secrets Act's for. Wormwood Scrubs is more than big enough to hold him as well as Cartwright. Speaking of whom, yes, hand him over to the woolly suits. Don't see why having a grandfather in the business should buy him any favours."

Thus spoke a man whose own grandfather had paid his school fees.

Tearney knew what this was, of course. Slough House meant nothing to Judd; he cared less about it than she did, and she didn't care at all. Were it not that it acted as a thorn in Diana Taverner's side, she'd have erased it without a moment's thought. Lamb was a Service legend, but there were museums full of one-time legends: label them, hang them on a hook, and they pretty soon lost their juju. The slow horses could be history by teatime, and would have passed from her thoughts before supper. But to wipe Slough House out of existence on Peter Judd's word was a different matter entirely. And if she let him get away with it, she'd wind up in his pocket.

Of course, a pocket was a good place to be if you were probing the wearer for soft tissue.

She said, "Consider it done."

Donovan turned away and opened the van, producing something from its depths which for one heart-quelling moment Monteith thought was a pistol with an elongated barrel. A silencer? But when Donovan unscrewed the cap and took a pull from it, Monteith saw it was a bottle of water.

He shook his head. Too much heat, too much excitement. From the bright sun outside to the petrol-fumed air of the car park had been like stepping from one form of battery to another: having been slapped silly by sunshine, he was now being rabbit-punched by pollution. It occurred to him, not

166

for the first time, that London was more than one city. There was the one he was taxied comfortably about in, whose views were spacious and spoke in agreeable accents of wealth and plenty, while the other was cramped, soiled and barbarous, peopled by a feral race who'd strip you bare and chew the bones. The divide itself didn't worry him — it was why the security business paid dividends — but he didn't like being caught on the wrong side.

He remembered a late instruction he'd given, and something tightened behind his waistband. "The woman. Did you, ah . . ."

"Shake her up a bit?" said Donovan, screwing the cap back on the bottle. His voice was flat, but Monteith heard judgement in it.

He bridled. Rank be damned: money went one way, respect the other. That was business.

"Just a joke, man. Is she still at the house?"

"Yes."

"Good. I want to speak to Judd in person before we all stand down." He paused to look around before continuing. "No point changing shirts before the final whistle."

There was nobody in sight, and the only vehicle in earshot was on the level below, and getting lower. Out on the street, traffic noise didn't count; it was simply the natural state of being, like the buzzing round a hive.

Donovan said, "You don't trust him, you mean."

"Why wouldn't I trust him?"

The van's back doors were still open. The soldier put a foot on its floor and began retying a bootlace. "Because he's a sneaky piece of shit."

"I beg your pardon?"

"Your pal. Peter Judd. He's a sneaky piece of shit."

"He's also a senior officer in Her Majesty's Government. So I'd thank you to keep a civil —"

"Where are you meeting him?"

"Did you just interrupt me?"

Donovan put his boot back on the ground, and Monteith was forcibly reminded that the older man was bigger, fitter; altogether more . . . substantial.

He took a step back. "Let's not forget who pays your salary, Donovan."

"Yes, let's not do that."

"You're lucky to have a job at all, with your record."

"Don't kid yourself. My record's the reason you hired me. Puts hair on your balls, doesn't it, Sly? Having the real thing about the place, instead of plastic heroes."

"What did you just call me?"

"Oh, I thought you enjoyed it. Makes you think people like you, doesn't it, when they call you Sly?" Donovan leaned closer, to bestow the following confidence. "I have to tell you, though. That's not the reason they do it."

"Ring Traynor. Now. Tell him to release the woman, and get back to the office. And you can consider that your final act in my employment. You're sacked."

Even Monteith could hear the quiver in his voice, the barely repressed anger. Let Donovan give him one more excuse . . .

168

Donovan laughed. "Sacked? You don't want to try for, what, 'cashiered'? Tinpot little general like you, I'd have thought 'cashiered' more up your street."

"If it wasn't for me, you'd still be queuing up for your Jobseeker's Allowance. Bit of a change from the parade ground, that, was it? Lining up with all the ex-squaddies for your charity handout?"

Donovan shook his head, facing the floor, but when he looked up, Monteith saw he was laughing. For a moment he thought the last few minutes had just been erased, that Donovan had been having a soldier's joke, but that bubble burst in short order. Donovan wasn't laughing with him, but at what he'd just said.

" 'Charity handout'? I swear to God, I've fought wars against people I had more respect for."

Monteith said, "I've had enough of this. Ring Traynor. And give me the keys to the goddamn van."

"Where are you meeting Judd?"

"This conversation is over."

"Not yet it isn't."

Forgetting the keys, Sly Monteith turned to leave, and the next moment the world whipped past him like it was a yo-yo: he was heading for the doorway and its urine-perfumed stairwell, and then he wasn't. Instead, he was slammed back against the van's panels, breathless, his ankles dangling in space. Donovan's fists were scrunching his lapels, and Donovan's voice was drilling into his ear.

"Once more," Donovan suggested. "Where are you meeting him?"

There was a sudden sense of release, several sudden senses of release, and Monteith's feet were back on the ground, and the contents of Monteith's bladder were heading the same way. Donovan's face twisted in contempt, and as much to prevent him expressing it as anything else, Monteith found the words tumbling out.

"Anna Livia Plurabelle's."

"Where?"

"Park Lane. Really quite decent, they do a good . . ." Monteith's memory, or imagination, tailed away. What did they do that was good? A sudden taste of spring lamb in a blackcurrant jus filled his mouth, almost real enough to wash away the smell of his own piss.

Standing in a car park, slumped against a van. Discovering that the scheme he'd been orchestrating had been someone else's all along . . . *Every age calls forth its heroes*: he'd thought that just this morning. Back when he'd been one of the heroes he was talking about, surrounded by memorials to idiots who'd thrown everything away.

At least that had been their choice.

"What time?"

Monteith said, "Half an hour?"

His trousers were clammy, and for a disconnected second he pictured himself turning up at Anna Livia's — *no* one used the "Plurabelle" — steaming in the sunshine. What the hell was PJ going to say? Except PJ wasn't going to say anything, or not to him, because no way was Donovan going to let him walk out of this car park.

He felt the soldier's hand on his neck.

170

"This is what you're going to do," Donovan said. "You're going to lie quietly in the back of the van. Nothing to worry about."

"I don't want to get in the van."

His voice sounded as if it were coming from some distance away. From down the hall, the far side of the kitchen . . . From the pantry where he used to hide when he was small, and things weren't going right.

"Doesn't matter what you want. I'm going to tie you up, but I'm not going to hurt you. No worse than what we did to the woman."

Monteith wasn't thinking about the woman. He was thinking about being left in the dark of the van; tied up and gagged . . .

"What's all this about?"

"Not your concern."

Donovan pulled him round to the back of the van, one of whose doors hung open. The smell was the usual aroma of men and petrol and motorway miles and motorway food. The thought of being locked inside it filled Monteith with horror.

"I'm going to throw up," he said.

He retched, bending double. Donovan swore under his breath, but relaxed his grip a fraction, and Monteith wriggled out of his jacket.

"Oh for God's sake," muttered Donovan, and took off after the runaway.

You didn't have to go back far to recall a culture that said: Yes, we like a drink at lunchtime. The political culture, he meant — Peter Judd was well aware that the culture in general was chucking booze down its neck like a mental hobo. But the political culture, meaning Westminster, had cleaned up its act since the millennium, a shift in which Judd himself had played no small part. A public disavowal of some of the more famous extravagances of his youth had, near as damn it, established a party line, or at least had drawn a line across which his party didn't dare tread. Backbenchers were like those dipping desk-toy ducks — start one off, and it would continue until forcibly stopped. Or in this instance, stop until forcibly started. Once the House's reputation for being more or less sober during daylight hours had been salvaged, and his own status as architect of the "New Responsibility" (copyright, some broadsheet reptile) safely established, Judd was happy to revert to drinking at lunchtime when he felt like it. One of the advantages of being a Big Beast in a Parliament noted for its stunted brethren.

Pygmies, he thought, swirling the quarter inch of Chablis, breathing in the perfume, then nodding at the girl to fill the glass. Anna Livia's chose its staff carefully. This one was a redhead, her hair tamed with a black bow matching the shoelace tie that dangled onto the table as she poured. Flesh-toned bra, so as not to show beneath her blouse. Such observations came naturally to Judd, who could no more look at a woman without assessing her bedability than he could see a microphone without minting a soundbite. She smiled — she had recognised him, of course — then replaced the bottle in its bucket and moved away. He'd leave a decent tip, and get her number. He was supposed to be behaving himself, for reasons of marital harmony, but a waitress hardly counted, for God's sake. He glanced at his watch. Sly was late.

Sly was another pygmy, of course.

"You'll catch yourself using that term in public," his agent had admonished. "Then there'll be trouble."

Judd shrugged such wisdom off. There was always trouble, and he always rose from the resulting miasma looking a lovable scamp: lovable, anyway, to that gratifyingly large sector of the populace to whom he'd always be a figure of fun: breathing a bit of the old jolly into politics, and where's the harm in that, eh? As for those who hated him, they were never going to change their minds, and since he was in a better position to fuck them up than they were him, they didn't give him sleepless nights. The public, on the other hand . . . The public was like one of those huge Pacific jellyfish; one enormous, pulsating mass of indifference, drifting wherever the current carried it; an organism without a motive, ambition or original sin to call its own, but which somehow believed, in whatever passed for its brain, that it chose its own leaders and had a say in its own destiny.

And catch yourself saying any of *that* out loud, he thought as he lifted his glass, and you can kiss the lovable-scamp image goodnight.

But none of this was making Sly Monteith appear, damn the man. He was milking the moment, obviously; the only time in his life he'd have the Home Secretary on hold. If he had any political sense he'd bank the credit, but Monteith had always been a second-rater, with the second-rater's habit of dropping rehearsed reflections into conversation. Ingrid Tearney had suggested he was a crony, which was a joke — Monteith would give his left bollock to be a crony — but he had at least proved useful today, his tiger team giving Judd the weapon he needed to de-fang Dame Ingrid. Cronydom, though; friendship; that was dangerous territory. How could you know someone would never turn out a liability? His glass needed refilling, and the cute waitress was nowhere in sight. Suppressing a sigh, he did the job himself.

Some kind of commotion was in progress on the street, vehicular squealing, and people hurrying past. You didn't expect that round here. Judd sipped wine, and found pleasure in the thought that he'd bent Ingrid Tearney to his will not an hour ago. That ridiculous Slough House: in itself, an unimportant anomaly, but any victory mattered. Tearney's reign as head of the Service would come to an abrupt end if he chose to make a stink about this morning's incursion into the Park, and forcing a policy decision on her served to underline her necessary deference. Besides, if his party stood for anything, it was for defending the right of the strong to flourish, which meant preventing the weak from taking up unnecessary space. Slough House was an excellent example of precisely that. But what was going on outside, and where had the staff vanished to?

Diners nearer the windows were craning forward to see what was happening. Without a clear view from his booth, Judd stood abruptly and dropped his napkin. Sirens were sounding, their distant, interlooping wails a disorganised commentary on city busyness. The irritation Judd had been feeling slipped into something less comfortable. He made for the door, aware that he was drawing glances: might be something, might be nothing, but there was never any harm in showing himself prepared for an emergency. The redheaded waitress was by the door, peering outside, all pretence at professionalism history. A few yards down the road lay a lump, obscured by people crouching round it.

"What's going on?"

"There's been an accident."

"What kind of accident?"

The girl didn't know.

The sirens grew closer.

The lump was wearing a grey suit.

Someone was speaking into a mobile phone: "No, I swear, he was dumped here by a van. Guy got out, opened the back door, and unloaded him like he was a sack of rubbish . . ."

Judd looked both ways, but saw no van.

"Took off like a bat out of hell . . ."

The first police car arrived, and its occupants jumped out and approached the body at a run.

"Okay, okay, let's have some room here. Let's have some room."

"Could everyone please back off, please."

The first officer dropped to one knee by the body and began speaking urgently into his radio.

Judd's first thought was that this was Tearney's work; an emphatic declaration that she wasn't his lapdog. But that didn't survive long. If the Service she headed was this efficient, Monteith's tiger team would have been wrapped in chains and dumped in the Thames by coffee time.

"Did anybody see what happened? Could those of you who saw what happened give your names to my colleague here, and we'll be taking statements just as soon as —"

Judd shook his head, and stepped back into Anna Livia's.

"I'm ready to order," he told the waitress.

"And your guest?"

"Won't be joining me after all."

It meant he had the bottle to himself, of course. But gave him plenty to think about while he waited for his lunch.

Part Two

True Enemies

CHAPTER
EIGHT

You could feasibly throw a tennis ball and cover the distance between Slough House and St Giles Cripplegate, but if you wanted your ball back, it might take a while. For there was no straight route through the Barbican, which resembled an Escher drawing assembled in brick by a spook architect, its primary purpose being not so much to keep you from getting where you were going, but to leave you unsure about where you'd been. Every path led to a junction resembling the one you'd just left, offering routes to nowhere you wanted to go. And set down in the middle of all this, like a paddle steamer in an airport, was the fourteenth-century church of St Giles, within whose walls John Milton prayed and Shakespeare daydreamed; which had survived fire, war and restoration, and which now reposed serenely on a brick-tiled square, offering quiet for those needing respite from the city's buzz and a resting place for poor sods who'd got lost and given up hope of rescue. Today there was a book sale under way, with pallets of paperbacks laid on trestle tables along the north aisle, and an honesty box on a chair awaiting donations. A few moody browsers were picking over the goods. Apparently ignoring them,

Jackson Lamb clumped past and sat on a bench in the nave, near the back. Three rows ahead, an old dear was picking her way through a private litany of petition and remorse. The way her shoulders trembled, Lamb could tell her lips were moving as she prayed.

Separating herself from the book-fanciers, Ingrid Tearney joined him.

He said, "Cripplegate. You think they had their own private entrance?"

"I expect they were beggars."

"You're probably right. Probably both kinds. Lucky and poor."

"I've heard a lot of things about you, Mr Lamb. But never that you were one for whimsy."

"I don't spend much time in churches. It's maybe rubbing off." He raised one buttock off the bench, like a man preparing to fart, but reconsidered, and settled back onto an even keel. "I'm having a busy day. Half my team's gone AWOL, and now I'm missing lunch. What's important enough to let my takeaway get cold?"

"An hour ago, I agreed to close down Slough House."

"Uh-huh."

"You don't seem bothered."

"If it was going to happen, we'd not be sitting here. I'd be in my office, listening to Diana Taverner crowing down the phone."

"Maybe I wanted to tell you in person. A perk of the job. It's not like your department's a jewel in the Service's crown, after all. It's more like a slug in its

180

lettuce patch. There'll be few tears shed in the Park when the memo goes round."

Lamb said, "I don't suppose you can smoke in here."

The old woman glanced back at them, religious irritation on her face.

"It would be the work of a moment to put you all on the street. It's not just that what your team does is barely worth doing. It's that when they start doing things they're not supposed to be doing, the mess they make requires serious attention."

Lamb nodded proudly.

"One of your operatives shot and killed a Russian citizen not long ago."

"I remember," said Lamb. "He's still upset he didn't get a bonus."

"Slough House is supposed to be a punishment posting. Your . . . slow horses?"

"They get called that."

"They're supposed to throw the towel in. Pursue opportunities more in keeping with their talents. Like local government, or petty crime."

"'Petty' is uncalled for," Lamb objected. "They have weapons training."

"I hope you're not making life easy for them."

Lamb paused, and seemed to be contemplating the surroundings: old stone, quiet air, wooden benches. Hymnals were slotted into ledges in front of them, and motes of dust, some of which might have been breathed in and sneezed out by Shakespeare, danced in coloured shafts of light that beamed through the windows. It was almost cool, compared to the bakery outdoors. Compared to Slough House, it was a slice of Paradise.

"I think I can safely say I'm not doing that," he said at last.

"Or too hard."

He looked at her.

"Because overdoing the punishment, letting them know you relish putting the boot in . . . Well. That can be counterproductive, don't you find? The sort of thing that makes some people dig their heels in harder. Alpha types, I mean."

"You've not met Roddy Ho, have you?"

"You keep deflecting."

"And you keep going round the houses. Any chance of getting to the point? I have underlings to bully."

"Peter Judd."

"Our new boss, God help us all. What about him?"

"He's the one wants Slough House shut down."

Lamb shook his head. "I doubt that."

"Trust me. He just got through explaining it."

"Trust you? There's a topic for another day. No, what Peter Judd wants is to wave his dick about. Metaphorically, for a change. And you're the one he's waving it at. Slough House just happens to be in the way. You're not seriously telling me you haven't worked that out for yourself?"

Again, the old woman looked back and glared. Lamb waggled his fingers in return.

Ingrid Tearney looked across at the book-browsers. They'd been joined by an elderly gentleman who'd taken a seat next to the honesty box. Whether this showed lack of trust remained open to question. He might have been planning a heist. She'd lowered her voice when she next spoke:

"I got that far, yes, thank you. It seems Mr Judd has his eyes on a higher prize, and requires my cooperation. This little purge he's suggested is his way of showing me where the power resides."

Lamb said, "Higher prize."

He'd taken a cigarette from his pocket; one of his regular tricks. Few people ever saw him with a packet in his hands. He made no move to light it; instead rolling it between finger and thumb, as if telling a rosary of his own invention.

He said, "If he wants to bring down his own government he'd be better off concentrating on the Chancellor. Coke and hookers were a quiet night in for that lad, back in the nineties. One good splash in the tabloids and he's history. The PM wouldn't last long after that. They've always been a buy-one-get-one-free package."

"The trouble with leaks is, they're generally traced to their source. And if Judd wants the party grassroots on his side, he's got to be seen to be squeaky-loyal. No, he doesn't want to stage a coup, he wants to be acclaimed a saviour. While the leadership falls apart, he'll be glad-handing local worthies and organising charity balls. Not a hint of treachery in sight."

"Charity ball," wondered Lamb. "Is that like a pity fu —"

"We're in a church."

"Fair dos." He studied his virgin cigarette in puzzlement, then tucked it behind an ear. "Well, you didn't bring me here to play Chinese whispers. You've already let his tyres down, haven't you?"

"He punctured himself."

"Tell me."

Leaning closer, Dame Ingrid told him about the tiger team run by Judd's old school chum, Sly Monteith, and about how Lamb's department had been used as a wedge to prise open Regent's Park.

"So they took Standish," Lamb said, his tone neutral.

"That's right. And sent a picture of her, bound and gagged, to your Mr Cartwright as an incentive."

"Unnecessary effort," Lamb said. "Offering him a biscuit would have done the trick. So that was Judd's plan. How many ways did it go wrong?"

"Mr Monteith's body was dumped on a pavement in SW1 about an hour ago."

"And this came as a surprise?"

"The Service doesn't solve its problems with brute force, Mr Lamb."

"Maybe not in SW1," Lamb agreed. "So who left him in the gutter? Let me guess. His own boys?"

"So it would seem," Tearney said. "I had a rather unusual telephone conversation a short while ago with a gentleman who tells me he's, ah, now in charge of Mr Monteith's enterprise. And that the goalposts have shifted."

"The tigers weren't as tame as they pretended, then," said Lamb. "What is it he wants?"

Dame Ingrid told him.

184

All our problems would melt away if we could sit peacefully in a room. Catherine had heard that somewhere, probably at an AA meeting. Fractured pieces of wisdom, cobbled together from half-remembered axioms: put them together, and you had what passed for a philosophy, in the twilight world of the drunkard. And sober drunks could be just as dull as the real kind. Something else she'd learned at meetings.

Sitting peacefully in a room was what she was doing now, but it didn't feel like her problems were melting away.

It must be past lunchtime, she thought. The sun was high, and the heat stifling. The air she'd coaxed through the window tasted more summery than London air, with a sweeter tang, but she was enough the city girl to find it overpowering, and would almost have preferred it if that bus in the yard revved its engines, blasting noisome fumes into the atmosphere. Apart from anything else, country air reminded her of the voices.

The voices had come to her during her "retreat", which had been spent in a perfectly comfortable, perfectly respectable sanatorium in the Dorset countryside; a hideaway for Service casualties. Among all those walking disasters — joes who'd done too much, seen too much, had too much done to them — she'd been far from the only drying-out drunk: it was a jagged brotherhood she'd joined, a shattered sisterhood. Everyone was a walking collection of angles, though the facility itself seemed to have had most of its edges

185

smoothed away. Sudden noises were discouraged, but happened regardless. A tray would drop on a tiled, percussive floor, and the whole community would ring for minutes. When it struck her to wonder what havoc a fire drill would cause, she'd had to bite her tongue to keep from hysterics.

Her room had been about the size of the one she was in now. Through its window was a view of a smooth, very English lawn bordered by ash trees. Occasional twinned piercings in the turf indicated where croquet hoops had been fixed, but this game, being outwardly genteel but actually vicious, had been found too reminiscent of Service life to be a soothing pastime, and the hoops and mallets were disposed of. Those perfectly circular wounds in the lawn remained, a grassy stigmata just barely visible, and maybe they'd heal themselves, and maybe they wouldn't . . . There was no end to the spirals of thought that could catch you; carry you away like Dorothy in her tornado, and drop you into a brighter land where logic eased its grip. The sober world, on the other hand, remained bleached of colour. Even the lawn, even those ash trees, were grim and grey and lifeless. Well, of course the ash trees. Why else were they called that?

But in the absence of colour, new sounds arrived. The voices turned up that first week. It was as if a small crowd of people, forever out of sight, had an awful secret to impart to Catherine all at once, so what reached her was an unbroken mutter of syllables, never approaching clarity. They were her secret sharers, and from the start she had known they existed only in her own delirium, and that the secret they were desperate to share was that she would fall and break at the next opportunity. There was no sadness or triumph in this. It was simply what was bound to happen: ultimately she'd be waved away from this hospital-like seclusion and rejoin the world of noise and lights and sharp edges, where the first thing she'd do would be to open a bottle and jump in.

She'd clung on to this as the first real hope, during those early days. She could stand all of it — the cure, the recovery; the effort demanded of her to regain her pride and her knowledge of who she could be — provided oblivion remained a constant possibility. Even now, most mornings, that thought woke with her. The voices had disappeared in time, and the effort to become herself once again had succeeded in the sense that it remained her daily struggle, but she'd never entirely forgotten them; rather, she'd bundled them in rags and stowed them in the lumber room of her mind. This was not an accepted recovery tactic, but it had worked for her, so far.

And so lost was she in this memory that she gave a small cry when the door rattled, as if her long-ago voices had assumed corporeal form, and were arriving now to take her away.

"You all right?"

This voice was Bailey's.

Catherine composed herself, and stood. "I'm fine."

He undid the padlock and let himself in, a manoeuvre complicated by the tray he was carrying. On it were a cardboard-packed sandwich, an apple, what looked like a flapjack tightly wrapped in Cellophane, its price-sticker visible, a small bottle of water, a 25-millilitre bottle of Pinot Grigio, and a plastic beaker.

"Thought you'd be hungry," he said.

He laid the tray on the bed.

Unable to take her eyes from it, Catherine gestured numbly towards the window. "There's a bus out there."

"I know."

"Why is there a bus out there?"

Even to her own ears, she sounded like she was reciting phrases from a teach-yourself-English book.

"The people who own this place, that was their tour bus, I think."

"They have a band?" Images of an ancient movie swam briefly into focus. Pinot wasn't her favourite wine, but its sudden appearance had displaced previous pleasures. *Summer Holiday.* That was the film.

Bailey laughed. "They ran a tour company. Ferrying folk round local sights?"

"I don't even know where we are."

"No, well. Everywhere's historical, isn't it?"

Catherine said something else. She wasn't sure what.

Bailey said, "Went bust, I suppose. This place used to be a farm. Now it's a holiday let. Next stop, it'll probably be a youth hostel."

"How long are you going to keep me here?"

"Not long."

"This isn't going to end well," she said. "You're messing with serious people."

"Ben and the colonel, they're serious too." He nodded at the tray before turning to go. "I brought you some wine. Little treat."

"I noticed."

"Better drink it before it gets warm."

He opened the door, making the padlock key do a little dance between the index and second fingers of his left hand as he did so.

"Bailey?"

"What did you call me?"

"The others are soldiers, but you're not. Are you?"

He didn't answer.

Seconds later she'd have heard the *clunk-click* of the padlock being fastened if she'd been listening, but she wasn't. All her attention was on the tray he'd placed on the bed, and the toy-sized bottle of wine it held.

The long-ago voices remained silent.

"You're kidding," Lamb said.

Nothing about Tearney's demeanour suggested she was kidding. "It seems that Mr Monteith's scheme was hijacked by someone in pursuit of, ah, a particular worldview."

"He's batshit crazy, you mean."

"That would appear to be the case."

The woman three rows ahead had apparently lost herself in prayer. Or perhaps she had simply given up hope of silencing the background murmur.

"The Grey Books," mused Lamb. "That's the creepy shit, right?"

"We're an intelligence service, Mr Lamb. We keep records on everything. Even, as you call it, the creepy shit."

"And now this tiger, whoever he is, wants a peek." Lamb fished the cigarette from behind his ear, glared at it, and put it back. "And all he has in his corner is Standish. Does he seriously think he can use her as a lever?"

Tearney said, "We value our operatives. It's a moral imperative that we safeguard them from harm."

"Yeah. Besides, if you give him what he wants, you're putting Peter Judd's balls in a vice."

"You have a gift for the pithy phrase."

"So I've been told."

Tearney's own gift was for serenity, it seemed. Talking low, indecipherable to anyone more than a whisper away, her expression had barely changed throughout their discussion. A witchy figure, it was often said, but that wasn't a view Lamb subscribed to. Witches got under your skin. Dame Ingrid was more witches' ground staff: she'd keep the broomsticks in order, though you couldn't trust her not to sabotage them if she felt it was in her interests.

Now she said, "It's not my policy to bow to hostile demands, but it seems the simplest course in the circumstances. The material this man's after is worthless. Once he has his hands on it, and your agent has been released unharmed, he'll be taken care of."

But Lamb was following his own thread, and wasn't about to let it get tangled with hers. "Of course," he said, "it'll have to be under the bridge, won't it? Here's Judd, sanctioning an attack on his own Service that ends with his old mucker dead and a tiger team off the leash. Assist in a cover-up, and you're a co-conspirator. But let the tigers get away with it, that puts Judd deeper in the shit."

"You have an agile mind, Mr Lamb. I don't think anyone ever denied that."

"And it'll be that special bespoke shit. The kind only you know where the shovel is." He leaned heavily back against the bench. "Long story short," he said, "that's why I'm missing my takeaway. You want my crew to deliver the goods to this guy. Off the books. To make sure you've got the Home Secretary where you want him."

"Well, it is one of your own you'll be rescuing. Besides," Tearney said, "there's something appropriate about your, eh, *remedial* group assisting in a frankly demented exercise. What's the phrase I'm looking for? Oh yes: horses for courses."

"Yeah, I know they do," said Lamb. He scratched his thinning hair, then examined his fingernails suspiciously. When he'd finished, he said, "Judd's man wasn't the only one using Slough House as a drain rod."

"Given the nature of the operation, I can hardly order you to undertake it."

"Uh-huh."

"Though if you decide you'd rather not play ball, your department will be history by this time tomorrow."

"Please. Don't tempt me."

He leaned forward, ran a finger round his neck, peered at it, and wiped it on his trousers. Then he looked at Dame Ingrid.

"I assume we'll be collecting the material without the cooperation of those currently holding it?"

She nodded.

"Still. In the current climate, that'll probably be workfare teenagers or rent-a-cop has-beens."

"Either way, it's a live operation and you play by the rules. Your first priority is ensuring that this man acquires what he wants without drawing undue attention."

"Just so we're clear on this," Lamb said. "My first priority is bringing my joe home."

He held her stare until she looked down and fiddled with the clasp on her bag, prior to departure.

"And put Cartwright in a taxi," Lamb added.

"He can catch a bus," were her final words.

He didn't watch as she left St Giles but remained facing the altar. The cigarette had reappeared in his hand, remarkably unbent given its travels, and he rolled it between his fingers as he sat. It was true what he'd told Tearney, he didn't spend much time in churches, but he'd set fire to one once, way back when, behind the Curtain — he recalled the acrid taste of woodsmoke on his tongue, the way it had roiled upwards into the Soviet dark, melting the falling snow. How long do memories last? This one had been with him half his life, and carried on for what seemed like minutes. That noise, that bang, was the first of the rifle shots, as the soldiers realised what he'd done. And then it was merely a book slapping the floor, dropped by one of the elderly readers browsing the paperbacks.

His mobile rang, and the old woman looked round in fury.

"Sorry," he mouthed. "Booty call."

He slipped the cigarette between his lips as he left the church, phone trembling in his hand.

Back at Slough House, the natives were restless.

Standard CD-ROMs are 1.2 millimetres thick, 120 millimetres in diameter, made of polycarbonate plastic, and in digital-data-storage mode contain 2,352 bytes of user data per sector, divided into ninety-eight 24-byte frames. And when laid on the edge of a desk and struck suddenly with a downward motion, they can be made to flip gracefully into the air and drop into a wastepaper bin two yards distant.

"Three nil," said Marcus.

"Cheater."

"Yeah, right. Or just better than you."

Shirley Dander lined her next CD up and chopped at it brutally — recent experience had taught her that time spent calibrating the trajectory required for it to drop into the bin rather than thud uselessly onto the carpet was time she was never going to get back.

It flipped into the air, turned over twice, and fell back onto the desk.

"Crap!"

"What you doing?"

They looked to the doorway, where Roderick Ho was standing, a folded-over slice of pizza in his hand.

Shirley said, "Bug off, square eyes."

But Ho was looking at the CDs scattered round the bin. "Piece of piss," he said.

It was clear, thought Marcus, that Ho hadn't absorbed many life lessons from the bruise Shirley had left on his cheek last night.

Shirley said, "You reckon? Seriously?"

"First time. No problem."

"You got a fiver says the same?"

"Shirley," Marcus began.

"What about you, old man?" she said. "You want a piece of that action?"

"I need to handicap him first."

"Hasn't life already done that?"

"Jesus, Shirley. He's standing right there."

Ho came into the room, squeezed another fold out of his pizza slice and ambitiously wedged it into his mouth. From Marcus's desk he picked up a CD, held it to the light, squinted, shook his head, and put it down again.

"Grandstanding," Marcus explained to Shirley. "You want to let him take a practice shot?"

"Nnng grrrrff," Ho said, or something like. He picked up another CD, made a noise like a traumatised python, and the pizza was history. "I don't need to practise."

"He doesn't need to practise," Shirley told Marcus. "Fiver?"

"Quid."

194

"Chicken. Okay, a quid." She looked at Ho, who was positioning a CD on the edge of Marcus's desk. "Hit it, pizza boy."

Ho hit it.

The disk shot vertically upwards into the light bulb, scattering dandruffy fragments of glass everywhere, before cartwheeling into the window frame, from which it excised a wedge Shirley later discovered in her coffee cup.

Almost as an afterthought, it dropped into the bin.

"*Yesssss!*" screamed Ho, dropping to his knees.

Marcus laughed so hard, it was a full minute before he realised Louisa had entered the office.

"Sorry," he said. "Are we making a noise?"

"A body's been dumped in the street. Broad daylight."

"Here?"

"Central London."

"What does narrow daylight look like anyway?" Shirley muttered, brushing a light glittering of bulb glass from her shoulder.

"More specifically," Louisa said, "outside a fuck-off restaurant near the Mall."

"That'll be exciting the Met," Marcus said. His eyes had narrowed: bodies in the street. There'd been a time he'd have been on standby.

"And guess who was dining in the fuck-off restaurant?"

"Well, probably not Her Madge," grumbled Shirley. But she slumped back into her chair, and clicked on the BBC website. "Peter Judd. So what?"

"Did you notice what he had to say?"

A moment's silence. Then Shirley said, "He's not quoted here."

"Precisely." Louisa came further into the room. "When's the last time Judd was in spitting distance of the media and slipped out the back door?"

"Is that what he did?" Ho asked.

"Figure of speech."

Marcus said, "He's Home Secretary. Law and order. It's got to be kind of embarrassing to be on the scene of a body dump."

"Embarrassing? This is Peter Judd we're talking about."

Roderick Ho said, "What's your point, Louisa?"

Everybody looked at him.

"What? What did I say?"

Under her breath, Shirley hummed, "Ho and Louisa, sitting in a tree . . ."

Louisa said, "Judd, our new lord and master, avoiding the press, the same day Catherine goes missing? And River's at the Park, he's under arrest. For stealing a file and God knows what else."

"Beating his chest in a built-up area?" Shirley asked.

"Whatever, all this happening, the same day? I can't be the only one thinks they must be connected."

Marcus said, "We're in the middle of a heatwave, did you notice? The temperature rises, crazy things happen. It's a well-known phenomenon. It doesn't mean there's a pattern."

"Yeah, right, sorry," Louisa said. "I mean, Christ, you're so busy. Didn't mean to interrupt."

"Easy, tiger."

"So let's all get back to making lists. What you working on, Longridge? People with the same make of car the 7/7 bastards drove?"

He raised his hands in surrender.

Shirley asked, "Where's Lamb?"

"Out."

"Well, duh. Any clue where?"

Louisa shook her head. "He got a phone call, and he vanished."

"He's answering his phone? We're through the looking glass, people."

"This isn't funny. Something's going on. Make all the jokes you like, but I'm going to find out what."

"I'm not busy," said Ho.

"What?"

"They were playing some stupid game. I just wanted to know who was making all the noise."

"Snitch," said Shirley.

"You owe me a fiver."

"Okay, then, do something for me," Louisa told Ho. "Make your computer dance. Find out who the corpse is."

"I can do that."

He left for his own room, wiping his hands on his trousers.

"K-i-s-s-i-n-g," murmured Shirley.

"Do you have a problem?" Louisa asked.

"God, no. Happy as Larry."

"Because you're uncannily twitchy and snarky as shit. Is it past time for your fix, or what?"

"*I'm* twitchy? Who turned your lights on? You've spent the past year —"

"Shirley," Marcus warned.

"— wafting round like a ghost on downers. All of a sudden you want to start giving orders?"

"Shirley," Marcus repeated.

"Because I'm not taking them from you. And don't you start, either." This last to Marcus. "*Partner.*"

She left the room and stomped up the stairs. A moment later, they heard the lavatory door slam shut.

After a while, Louisa said, "Another happy day in the office."

"You really think Judd's involved in whatever's going on?"

"No, I just wanted to wind Shirley up."

"Not exactly a challenge." Marcus fished a handful of CDs from the bin. Casually as he could, he said, "You all right?"

"I'm fine."

"You seem a bit —"

"I'm fine."

"Lighten up, girl. I saved your life, remember?"

"Didn't I thank you? At the time?"

". . . I guess."

"Well then."

"Okay." Marcus's focus shifted. "Fact is, I'd have shot him anyway."

"I know."

"He got on my tits."

"I can imagine how you felt."

"Shirley's a little uptight right now."

198

"Shirley's a loose fucking cannon."

"She's just split with her girlfriend. Boyfriend. Whichever."

"I want an update on her status, I'll check Facebook. But if she keeps annoying me, I'll clean her clock. And Marcus? Call me 'girl' again, it's your own life'll need saving."

"What was that about?" Shirley asked, coming back into the room as Louisa left.

"Office banter."

"You could repurpose that woman. Use her as a fire blanket. She can kill an atmosphere stone dead."

"Were you in the loo just now?"

"Yeah. I'd give it five minutes."

"You weren't . . ."

"Weren't what?"

"Nothing."

"Oh Christ, not you too." She stomped back to her chair. "I'm not a junkie, all right? I like the odd recreational high, that's all."

"That shit fucks with your reactions."

"Yeah, that's a real danger in this job." Shirley manhandled her keyboard, coaxing a satisfactory yelp out of it. "I get a rogue paper clip, I'm toast."

"You need to take things more seriously."

"And you need to lighten up."

"Yeah, well. You owe me a quid," he said, but she pretended not to hear him.

Outside, sunlight was a shock. Lamb found a patch of shadow overlooking a channel of water that was still

199

and green and pasted with a layer of thick round leaves the size of dinner plates. The occasional bloom was a defiant gesture, a doily the pink and white of a conjunctivitis-riddled eye. In a nearby flower-bed a scatter of feathers betrayed where a fox had caught a pigeon, unless the pigeon had simply exploded. He lit his cigarette at last. His phone had fallen silent before he'd left the church, but it would ring again soon. When it did, he raised it to his ear without looking at the screen and said, "Diana."

"What are you up to, Lamb?"

"Church visit," he said. "Have you let Jesus into your life? He does house calls, but it's nice to pop round his place."

"Tearney's just signed a release on your boy Cartwright."

"I doubt that."

"I've just had Nick Duffy on the line. He walked Cartwright out of the building himself. Not happily, I might add."

"I doubt Tearney signed anything."

Pause.

"Yeah, okay, she didn't do that."

Lamb watched as the smoke from his cigarette struggled upwards into the heavy, heat-struck air. "What's on your mind, Diana?"

"Judd's planning on overhauling the command structure," Diana Taverner said. "Apparently he thinks Second Desk level would be better served by ministerial appointees."

200

"You can see his point," Lamb said. "I mean, if the current system works, how come you're senior to me?"

"If it goes ahead, you'll be answering to some party hack whose sole aim in life is inching up the greasy pole. Well, I say answering. But the first thing any politico would do on taking the Slough House brief would be to shut it down."

"And you're telling me all this because . . .?"

"I have your best interests at heart. You know that."

"It's never occurred to you I might welcome retirement?"

He spent the silence that followed this question easing his underwear from the crack of his arse.

At length Taverner said, "If you're not going to take this seriously, there's no point my trying to warn you."

"Just lightening the moment."

"Because the image of you in retirement, leafing through the *Angling Times* or whatever —"

"I appreciate your input. But if I'm going to get a cake baked before young River gets home, I'd best be on my way."

"Jackson . . ."

"Diana."

"You know what I've spent the past few months overseeing? Reshelving paperwork. I'm serious. Off-site storage for the whack-job files, for black-ribboned folders, for anything deemed no longer necessary for, and I quote, quotidian objectives. That's daily business, in case you were wondering."

"I can't stress how much I wasn't."

201

"Carry on finding it funny. But I'm Second Desk Ops, Jackson, and I'm doing an intern's job. They won't just close down Slough House. They'll turn the Service into a work experience factory for Foreign Office wannabes." She paused for effect. "If you're asked to choose sides, I hope you pick the right one."

"For your sake or mine?" Lamb asked, and rang off.

Ho said, "His name's Sylvester Monteith. He ran a security outfit, Black Arrow?"

"Never heard of it," Louisa said.

Marcus said, "They're not top level, but they've picked up a couple of government contracts . . ."

He tailed off, trying to dredge up a detail.

"And now he's a stiff," said Shirley. "Who whacked him?"

Ho said, "You know what? His CV doesn't say."

It was ten minutes since the blow-up in Marcus and Shirley's office, and now, without arrangement, they'd gathered in Ho's room to find out what he'd discovered. Sometimes, it happened like this. It didn't always augur well.

"Whoever it was," Louisa said, "they weren't trying to keep it a secret. Dumping a body from the back of a van, the middle of London. That's gang behaviour."

"The van didn't get far," Ho said. "It was abandoned three streets away."

"Any CCTV?"

"Middle of London? Let me think."

"Thank you, smartarse. Have you got the feed?"

"Not yet," Ho admitted.

"Peter Judd," Marcus said.

"What about him?"

"Monteith's firm picked up government contracts because he had a handy mate somewhere. That's how the story went."

"And the mate was Peter Judd?"

"Be interesting if it was, wouldn't it? Given he was a bystander."

Ho's upper lip had curled. It was the face he usually wore when he was wading into the web, and accounted for a large proportion, though not the whole, of his unpopularity.

Not many keystrokes later he said, "They were at school together."

"I'm guessing it wasn't the local comp," Shirley said.

"God bless the Establishment," said Marcus. "But what's any of this got to do with Catherine's disappearance?"

"I don't know yet," said Louisa, tension in her voice. Marcus made a mental note to stand well back. The recoil from a woman's stress could have a finger off, if you weren't careful. "Let's find out more about Black Arrow."

"You mean, you want me to," said Ho.

"There's no *I* in 'team'," Louisa reminded him.

"But there's a *U* in 'cunt'," Shirley muttered.

Ho rubbed his bruised cheek with one finger.

Marcus opened a window, and for a brief moment enjoyed the fantasy that a cool breeze would rush in, dispersing the general funk of sweat and stale energy that hung around Ho's office. Then a blast of air and hot noise put him right. He closed it again, and made a mental note to badger Catherine about getting fans that worked. Except Catherine wasn't here ... A figure peeled out of the bookies a few doors down the road, paused by a bin, and dropped something into it, or nearly did. The bundle of paper slips bounced off the rim and fell into the gutter. Someone having a bad day, thought Marcus. He'd had a few himself, but one lucky afternoon was all he needed. And then he'd walk away from it all: the cards, the horses, the damn roulette machines.

"Did you say something?"

"We need some working fans," Marcus said.

Ho recited what he could find on Black Arrow. Founded twenty years previously, it wasn't what you'd call a blinding success, except that anything that hadn't actually gone tits up in the last five years was a hymn of praise to the free market. Currently employing just over two hundred "officers", it held a few smallish government contracts, and provided security to a second-tier supermarket chain. This probably involved ferrying takings and salaries around more than keeping an eye on stock, though it might mean that too.

"Employee records?" Louisa asked.

"Why?" said Shirley.

"Intelligence gathering. I haven't time to explain the concept, but —"

"Oh, any time you want start explaining *concepts* —"

Marcus said, "That was the door. Lamb's back."

204

So all four of them set about looking idle, because looking busy, they'd learned to their cost, meant that as far as Lamb was concerned, they were up to no good.

But it wasn't Lamb who appeared a minute later, it was River.

CHAPTER
NINE

The Thames looked low. Years gone by, there were stories of the river freezing; of ice fairs thrown in the shadows of the bridges, and skaters weaving past long-lived landmarks, but Sean Donovan didn't remember hearing it had ever dried up. When that day came, the stink would surely drive the capital out of its mind.

If that hadn't already happened. The fury of the pace, the anger of the traffic, had a sociopathic buzz.

And think of the secrets that would come to light, when the cracked, flaking ooze of the riverbed lay exposed to view. Everything the Establishment tried to flush away, to drown in the dark; it would all lie choking in the sunshine. There'd be nowhere to hide anything.

He was standing under a tree on the Embankment. The tree was sad and brown, and offered little in the way of shade; the Embankment was cloaked with CCTV coverage, and offered nothing in the way of privacy. But Donovan had faith in organisational chaos, and knew that while a match would eventually be made between the figure loitering here, early for an appointment, and the hooded man abandoning a van from which a body had been dumped a mile or so distant, this wouldn't happen for some time yet. He checked his watch as if to verify this, then looked up at the sky. The sun was working on plan B; the one where it cut the crap, and just frazzled everything in reach.

Momentarily dazzled, he didn't see Ben Traynor until the soldier was upon him.

"Sean."

Though they'd parted only hours ago, they shook hands.

"All okay?"

"I'm fine," Donovan said. "The woman?"

"Stop worrying. It's a rest cure." Traynor glanced round, a 360-degree sweep. He saw nothing to alarm him. "And Monteith? Not a happy bunny, I presume."

Not a happy bunny at all, Donovan thought.

He said, "Ben, it went wrong. My fault."

"How wrong?"

"The worst."

Traynor nodded. He glanced away again, towards the South Bank, and his eyes clouded over as he mentally adjusted to the new situation. Then he looked back at Donovan.

"Okay," he said. "So he's not trussed up in the van, cooking like a chicken. Tell you the truth, Sean, he's not the biggest loss to humanity."

"Walk away now," Donovan said. "Call the kid. Tell him it's over. He knows the drill."

"Aye, and what then? We've come this far."

"Kidnapping was bad enough. Murder's over the line."

"What did you do, snap his worthless neck?"

"He made a break for it, for Christ's sake. Have to hand it to the little bugger. I thought he'd fold and whimper."

"We'd all expect that."

"I caught him. Hit him. One punch, you know?"

"You don't know your own strength."

Donovan probably did, near as damn it. What he hadn't taken into account was his anger, the constant companion of the last few years, always glowering below the surface. Anger had been at his elbow in the car park, making sure he didn't pull his punch. He'd hit Monteith as hard as he'd ever hit anything. Even as he'd made contact, he'd known things had tipped over an edge.

A passing siren caught their attention, but it was an ambulance. Some poor sod collapsed in the heat. He waited until its clangour was wrapped inside the city's other noise, then said, "You're still here."

"We can still make it work."

"Maybe. Maybe. But we won't walk away from it."

"Sean," Traynor said. "We were never going to be able to walk away from it."

River Cartwright felt as if he'd had his insides scooped out, tossed like a salad, then reinserted any which way. Trying to move naturally, but keep himself from jostling, he looked like he was balancing an invisible egg on his head.

Nick Duffy had known what he was doing.

"Your grandfather won't be around forever," he'd told River as he'd escorted him out of the Park.

River was still dazed by the sudden turnaround in his fortunes. "What's that mean?" He was clutching his phone in one hand; his self-respect in the other. Any unexpected movement, and he'd lose his grip on one or both.

"Someone pulled your nuts out of the fire. And it's not like you've any friends round here."

"And everyone speaks so highly of you."

"Take some advice." Duffy dropped an arm round River's shoulders in a gesture that might have looked like friendship, from a distance. He squeezed, knowing where to apply pressure. "Don't bother going back to Slough House. All those forms and pointless reports, they must be doing your head in. So just fucking give up, why don't you? Try something else, like maybe McDonald's. Pretend you don't speak English, they'll take you like a shot. Because your spook career? It's deader than your mate Spider."

"He's not dead."

"No, but they hold a mirror to his lips every morning, to check."

They were out of the door by this time, over the road from the park in which mothers wheeled prams and some mad joggers ran, but mostly people slumped in groups in whatever shade they could find. Whether it was torpor or tranquillity, it felt strange to be looking out on it while hearing thinly veiled threats.

River said, "My grandfather's into his eighties. Some days he has difficulty on the stairs, you know? When his joints are troubling him."

"You're not gunna be taking them two at a time yourself any time soon."

"But on his worst day, he'd scrape you from his shoe without a second thought," said River, and he'd walked off down the road arms swinging freely by his sides, hardly at all like someone who'd recently had a professional going-over. He was round the corner before he'd dropped between parked cars and vomited into the gutter.

And now he was back in Slough House.

"We thought you were Lamb."

"Thanks."

Louisa said, "You've been at the Park. Why'd they let you go?"

"I don't know. Catherine still missing?"

Marcus said, "Do you know where she is?"

River showed them his phone.

Louisa took it and moved nearer the window, holding it at an angle to the light. The picture didn't change — Catherine, handcuffed, gagged, sitting on a bed.

"So that's why you went haring off to HQ?"

But River was looking at Ho's monitors. "Who's that bastard?"

"I don't like you walking behind me," Ho said.

"Name's Sylvester Monteith," said Louisa. "What makes him a bastard?"

"He's the one took Catherine. How come you've got him on-screen?"

"I don't like you —"

"Shut up."

210

Marcus said, "His body was just dumped in SW1."

"Someone killed him?"

"They were fly-tipping too. Don't leave that out."

River wasn't in the mood. "He was on the bridge. Earlier. He's the one sent me to the Park. He wanted a file."

Marcus remembered a figure on the bridge when he and Shirley went looking for River and found ice creams instead. Probably best not to mention that now, or ever.

Louisa said, "If he took Catherine and he's dead now, what's happened to her?"

Shirley took the phone, and studied the picture.

River said, "This bastard wanted the PM's vetting file."

"Did you get it?"

"Not hardly."

"She's sitting up," Shirley said.

"What?"

"Catherine. In this photo. She's sitting up."

"So?"

"Usually, victim photos, they're lying down."

River stared at her. "Is that a fact?"

"Yes. No. I don't know. This looks unusual, that's all. Staged."

"You think it's faked?"

She shrugged. "I don't know. It just doesn't look . . . desperate."

River shook his head.

Marcus said, "In what way?"

Shirley handed him the phone. "She doesn't look frightened."

"She's handcuffed, for Christ's sake," River said.

Marcus said, "Yeah, she's handcuffed. But Shirley's right. She doesn't look frightened."

"You don't seriously think she's part of whatever's happening?"

"I can't see her dumping a body from a van," Marcus admitted.

Roderick Ho said, "Would you just get away from behind my desk? I don't like being crowded."

"Keep your hair on," Louisa told him, and he scowled.

River retrieved his phone from Shirley and examined the screen again: Catherine, with her wrists in cuffs. Did she look frightened? It was hard to tell. Catherine, mostly, didn't give much away: she could be screaming on the inside, and you'd never guess. Maybe that's what she was doing, most of the time. But the fact was, he hadn't stopped to consider it. Seeing the photo had been enough to light his fuse.

Louisa said to Ho, "Have you found the CCTV yet?"

"No. Because I haven't started looking."

"Might now be a good time?" River said.

"You're not the boss of me," Ho announced loudly, making it clear he was addressing everyone present.

"Grow fucking up," Shirley suggested.

"Amen to that," Jackson Lamb announced, having scaled the stairs soundlessly.

Everybody froze.

* ★ ★

The two men were on Hungerford Bridge, crossing the sluggish river. The South Bank skyline, so enticing after dusk, looked brutal this time of day. On the railway bridge a train had come to an unscheduled halt, and sat in the sunshine, its passengers slowly poaching. Donovan and Traynor observed their plight with detachment. Both had been in hotter situations.

"So where's the body?" Traynor asked. "Monteith's. You left it in the van?"

"No, I dumped it outside Anna Livia Plurabelle's. You eaten there? It's supposed to be good."

Traynor left it a beat before he said, "You're not kidding. Are you?"

"If I'd left him in the van, they could have made it never happen. He'd have just disappeared. Or had a heart attack in bed. This way they can't cover it up, not so easily. So they'll have to play along."

"Have you made contact?"

"With Dame Ingrid Tearney, yes." Donovan stopped walking, looked up at the sky. "This bloody weather. The heat. It's not natural."

"In the circumstances, that's quite fitting, wouldn't you say?"

"Good point."

They moved on.

Traynor said, "So what'd she say?"

"That we use the Slough House crew, Standish's team. That's how I know she's keeping this off the books. This Slough House, it's where they put the fuck-ups."

"That fills me with confidence."

"It's not like we need them for anything. They take us where we want to be. We get what we're after and fade away."

"After dark, then."

Donovan nodded.

Traynor said, "So now we play the waiting game."

"You'd rather be under fire, wouldn't you?"

"Every time."

And the two men, who had sheltered under walls together while bullets chipped at the brickwork, shared a laugh that carried them the rest of the way across the Thames.

Lamb threw his jacket at the coat rack and missed. "Hang that somewhere," he instructed nobody in particular, and pulled the chair out from the room's second desk, the one on which Ho collected software packages and grease-stained pizza boxes. As he dropped into place he swept them to the floor. "That's better. Now. I could have sworn you all had jobs to do."

Ho said, "I told them to go back to their own rooms, but —"

"Yeah yeah, shut up." Lamb folded his hands across his stomach. He'd brought in odours of tobacco and sweat from the great outdoors, and seemed happy for them to circulate. "So. What are we all looking at?"

Louisa said, "We've found the man who snatched Catherine."

"Sylvester Monteith," said Lamb. "Former chum of Peter Judd, current mess on the pavement." He

214

observed their bewilderment with a practised sneer. "What, you wanted to surprise me?"

"Judd's involved, isn't he?"

"My, my," said Lamb, admiringly. "Here's me thinking you'd been banging your brains out every night, and it turns out they're still functioning."

Ho threw Louisa a puzzled glance.

Shirley stifled a giggle.

Lamb said, "What about you, Cartwright? Fun day so far?"

"It's been . . . different."

"I'll bet. Taking a run at the Park? You're in the Secret Service, not the Secret Seven. You should know that by now."

"Monteith sent me this."

He showed Lamb his phone. Something passed across Lamb's eyes, then flitted away. His lip curled. "She look frightened to you?"

"That's what I said," Shirley announced.

"Yeah, and when you tie a woman up, I'm sure you do it properly." Lamb threw River's phone back at him. "Monteith's crew was a tiger team. Hired by Judd. And you, you moron, played right into his hands."

Marcus said, "So who whacked him?"

"That's the thing about tigers, isn't it? Some of them turn out to be real."

"So who were they testing?" River asked. "Us or the Park?"

Lamb stared at him for what felt like a full minute and, Lamb being Lamb, might well have been, before starting to laugh. Still being Lamb, this was a full-body

215

exercise: his frame shook, and his guffaws filled the room. Head flung back, he looked like an evil clown. Where a shirt button had popped, a hairy patch of stomach winked at the room.

"Jesus wept," he said at last. "Sorry, but that is just so fucking funny. Us or the Park. You'll be wanting a licence to kill next." He wiped his eyes on his sleeve, and humour vanished. "Do you seriously think Judd wants to test how effective or secure Slough House is? He wants this place packed into a skip, and when I say 'this place', I'm including you comedians."

"But evidently his plan backfired," Marcus said.

"Silver linings," Lamb agreed. "His old chum Monteith is tomorrow's compost, but you, you lucky devils, live to play another day. Because guess what? Now the tigers have eaten their owner, they've got a whole new agenda, and it turns out you're on it. Slough House just went live. The four of you are up."

"There are five of us," Ho pointed out.

"Oh, are you here too? Put the kettle on, there's a good lad. I'm parched."

Ho chuckled.

No one joined in.

Ho dragged himself reluctantly out of his chair, and shuffled off to the kitchen.

"'Up'?" Marcus said.

Lamb said, "Ever heard of the whackjob files?"

"It's what they call the Grey Books," River said.

"Might have known you'd know. One of grandad's bedtime stories, was it? Go on, then. Floor's yours."

River said, "They're the records the Service keeps on conspiracy theories. 9/11, 7/7, the Lockerbie bombing, WMDs — they're a paranoid's treasure-chest."

"And don't forget the creepy shit," Lamb said.

"Right," said River. "Downing Street's run by lizards, the Royal Family are aliens, UFOs visit regularly, and the Soviet Union never really collapsed and has been running the world since '89."

"And these are official records?" Marcus said. "Seriously?"

River said, "They're an overview of what's out there. Back in the war it was noticed that improved communications don't just let information travel faster, they let bullshit off the leash too. There was a rumour about Churchill being assassinated and replaced by a double; it went what we'd call viral today. And damaged morale."

"Disinformation," Louisa said.

"Except this is the crap people make up for themselves," said River. "And with the internet, you can have a paranoid fantasy at breakfast and a cult following by teatime. Anyway, the Service learned long ago that when you know what people are prepared to believe, it makes it easier to bury uncomfortable truths. Hence the Grey Books."

"So some of it's *true*?" said Shirley.

Louisa, thinking aloud, said, "Throw enough darts, you're bound to hit the board."

"Uh-huh," River said. "A couple of years ago, if you'd suggested that western intelligence agencies were hoovering up people's emails, you'd have been laughed at."

"So some of it's true," said Shirley.

River shrugged. "Even the complete bullshit, it's useful to know who's buying into it. Because they're the type might decide to strap on a suicide belt and pop down the local shopping centre. So if it's out there, the Service keeps track. Monitors, records, stores."

"And I thought we had dipshit jobs."

"It's mostly outsourced. There are people happily spending their lives paddling about the internet, researching bonkers theories. The Service keeps a few on retainer. It's like having ready-trained dung beetles."

"Doesn't sound too secure," Marcus objected.

"Well. They're probably not told they're doing it for MI5."

"They probably think they are, though."

"But who's gunna listen to a twenty-four-carat nerd?"

"Speaking of which," said Lamb.

Ho paused in the doorway, mug in hand. "What?"

"Never mind." Lamb took the tea and used a surviving software package for a coaster. Ho swallowed an objection, and resumed his seat. "So, now you know. The tinfoil-hat tomes, bedtime reading for teenage boys and middle-aged virgins. Thank God we won the Cold War, eh?"

"What's any of this got to do with us?" Louisa asked.

"It's what they want. Monteith's so-called tiger team." Lamb scratched an armpit, then slid his hand

218

under his buttocks. "They want the whackjob files, and you're going to help them get them."

"Why us?" said River.

"Well, we've established they're fucking idiots," Lamb said. "Who else they gunna call?"

Marcus said, "And where are they kept? These files."

"I'm so glad you asked." Lamb levered himself out of the chair a few inches, and hovered. They braced themselves. Then he shook his head, and lowered back down. "Not gunna happen," he said. Then: "Yeah, where are the files? Go find out, will you?"

"Can't Ho do that?"

"You've changed your tune. Weren't you calling him a useless twit this morning?" He looked at Ho. "His words. Not mine."

Ho nodded gratefully.

" 'Twat', I told him. You're a useless *twat*." He looked back at Marcus. "You still here?" Now he pointed a finger at Shirley. "And you go keep him company, or whatever it is you do round here." He aimed the finger at River next. "And as for you —"

"Can't Ho do it?" River said.

"Ho, Ho, Ho," Lamb said. "It's like Santa's ghetto round here."

"Grotto."

"*Gesundheit*. As for you, and also you" — including Louisa — "go find out who's behind this tiger team. He's the one we're dealing with. All clear?"

A monstrous fart erupted without warning.

219

"Ah, good. I was worried that was trapped. Right, fuck off, the lot of you. Back here with answers, five sharp."

This addition to the atmosphere made them glad to troop out, but Lamb called Louisa back. "You ran online interference last year, right? Loitering in rest rooms?"

"Chat rooms."

"Whatever. When you've worked out who our Mr X is, see if you can find his footprints in any of the likely places. Bananas hang in bunches, so maybe he's been seeking company. He wants the whackjob files. Be good to know why."

Louisa said, "You do realise, whoever he is, he probably doesn't use his own name online?"

"Is that a problem?"

"Well, it's a bit like looking for a car without knowing the make, colour or registration."

"If you're not challenged, you won't grow."

Louisa stared.

Lamb shrugged. "I get emails from HR. Some shit's bound to rub off."

"How deep is the Park into this?"

"What difference does that make?"

"Whenever we get mixed up in one of Diana Taverner's schemes, somebody gets hurt."

"I hope you're not questioning my judgement."

"Just an opinion."

"Well, you know what they say," said Lamb. "Opinions are like arseholes." He showed yellow teeth. "And yours stinks."

220

When Louisa left, he turned to Ho, who was staring sullenly at his screens. "Ready to do some real work for a change?"

". . . Suppose."

"There's a good little monitor monkey."

He told Ho what he wanted.

It was the heat. It was the heat and the bottle, but mostly the heat.

But also mostly the bottle.

Catherine was hungry but couldn't eat, because eating would disturb the unity of the tray. If she ate the sandwich, the apple or the flapjack, or drank the water, she would bring the wine into focus, so it was best if she left things as they were, allowing the wine to blend into the background. If she continued not to notice it, its threat would be neutralised. It would offer no danger.

She had run a bath a while ago — what kind of kidnapping was this, where they served you drinks in an en-suite prison? — but the action had dredged up unwanted images, because the bath was where she'd found Charles Partner's body. A shot to the temple was not as neat as it could be made to sound. The contents of a head were untidy when displaced. She let the water drain away, and wearing only her slip returned to the bedroom, where the tiny bottle of Pinot waited like a hand grenade.

Partner had called her Moneypenny occasionally, an offhand note of affection. She had been sober for some time when he killed himself, and had remained sober ever since. So why did the wine bother her now?

No sober day is wasted.

A familiar thought — it was a bedtime mantra, a grace note on which to end her days. No sober day is wasted, meaning that whatever else she'd done or failed to do on any given day, there was always this achievement to reflect on in the violet hour. Every sober day was one more to her total, and though she did not keep a tally in the manner of many recovering alcoholics, she did not need to: each individual day was the only one worth counting, because the present was where she lived.

It occurred to her now, though, that her mantra had another aspect. If no sober day was wasted, then nobody could take one from her. Even if today brought a slip, the total would stay the same. All that would happen was that she would not be adding to it. It was like money in the bank. If you missed making a deposit, that didn't mean the sum grew smaller.

She returned to the bathroom to splash water on her face. Perhaps she should eat the apple, drink the water. The wine would remain camouflaged by the sandwich and whatever it was, the flapjack. What kind of kidnappers brought flapjacks? It was beyond absurd. She could mix the wine with the water; it would barely be noticeable. Like taking medicine. And then it would be gone, and she need think of it no more.

There was no mirror in which to talk herself down. Look herself in the eye, and ask what she thought she was doing.

And really, she was past this stage. No alcoholic, she knew, was ever past this stage, but in the comfort of her own head she allowed herself to believe she was, in the same way that her colleagues allowed themselves to believe that their careers might yet revive. Because belief was not about actually believing; belief was simply somewhere to shelve hope. But in her own defence, she had passed every test she had set herself, or been set. For some time, Jackson Lamb had been in the habit of pouring her a glass of whisky when they sat in his office at night. She had never yet succumbed, but often wondered what his reaction would be if she did. She thought he would snatch the glass away. Perhaps all that meant was, she hoped he would. But she suspected that he enjoyed testing the limits of other people's survival instincts, probably because his own had been subjected to rigorous examination over the years. The forms this had taken, she'd never heard him speak about — a thought she'd once had about Lamb was that when they'd pulled the Wall down he'd built himself another, and had been living behind it ever since. Hard to understand another human once they'd bricked themselves up like that. So she might be right, might be wrong: it was possible that when Lamb tempted her, it was because he wanted her to fall. The important thing to remember was that she'd not yet done so.

Besides, one night — the odds were in her favour — he'd run out of booze, and be forced to reclaim the glass he'd poured her. That was going to be sweet. And once he'd drunk that, she'd fetch the bottle she kept in her desk drawer, provided he hadn't found and drunk it before the opportunity presented itself. That, too, would be a kind of victory. Though, of course, to aim for victory would be to admit she was playing the game.

Back in the bedroom the bottle of wine sat waiting for her, obdurate on its untouched tray, and shimmering in the heat.

CHAPTER
TEN

Caviar had been on the menu at Anna Livia Plurabelle's, and while Judd had refrained from indulging, now, as he brushed a vacant bench with a rolled-up copy of the *Standard*, he recalled an article he'd read on how the roe was harvested. Sturgeon were big fish, four foot long, and kept in tanks significantly smaller than that. When their time came, they were dispatched by hand, this, apparently, ensuring minimal damage to the roe. Given the size of the fish, those tasked with its demise tended towards the muscular, as well as — by implication — the violent. The resulting image had been indelible: stocky bruisers, sleeves rolled up, punching fish to death. Thuggery run riot in the kitchens of the rich.

The article had been intended to inspire shock, but Judd had barely managed surprise. That a delicacy for the pampered was acquired through brutality was hardly news. By any civilised standard, it was how luxury ought to be measured — wealth meant nothing if it didn't create suffering. Because the standard liberal whine that the rich were cushioned from life's harsh realities was laughable ignorance: the rich created those realities, and made sure they kept on happening. That was what kitchens were for, along with prisons, factories and public transport.

So the rich, by which he meant the powerful, took messy violence in their stride — it was the cost of doing business — which was one of the reasons Peter Judd hadn't wasted time grieving the loss of his school friend. The traditional press, hanging on Twitter's coat-tails, was no doubt picking up the threads of the story now, and he'd be called on to comment: pointless to deny there was a delicious irony in an old chum of the Home Secretary falling victim to public savagery. But he'd never had difficulty in counterfeiting anger or remorse — *appalling barbarism, whose perpetrators, I am confident, will feel the full might of British justice* — so wasn't fazed by the prospect, and wouldn't lose sleep over Sly's death either. People died. It happened. How Monteith's dropping the ball affected his own game plan mattered more to Judd right now.

Satisfied the bench was as clean as it was going to get, he sat. It was shaded by trees set in a railinged square, which wasn't actually square at all but oblong: near Praed Street, not far from Paddington, and off the refined map. Hotels lined each side, but they were for downscale foreign tourists or out-of-town businessmen, neither of whom were likely to be haunting the area in the early afternoon. This made it a safe spot for a one-off meeting, and while waiting for this to happen, Judd paged through the *Standard*. As usual, he featured within, which was good news — the day the Mickey Mouse papers ignored him, he'd know his career was

226

over. What it actually said didn't matter. So long as it carried a photo, he was golden.

He heard the clacking of her heels on the path a full minute before she appeared.

Judd rolled the paper again, and used it to tap the space on the bench next to him. "It's reasonably dirt-free," he said. Then added, "The bench, I mean. Not this rag."

"I'd rather stand."

"Would you? Would you really? Well, how very nice for you." His tone slipped from penthouse to pavement. "But when I say sit, you sit."

Diana Taverner sat.

Sean Patrick Donovan.

That was the name River found, a recent recruit to Black Arrow; hired as Chief Officer i/c Strategy-Operations, a suitably pseudo-military title for one of these outfits — River had no trouble imagining a bunch of Territorial Army vets, Prison Service rejects and ex-community coppers making up the ground crew. Probably unjust but he hurt almost everywhere, Nick Duffy's blows having had the cartoon-like quality of spreading the pain of their impact outwards, until every available inch felt tender and ill-used. His grip on his mouse tightened, but he had to keep thoughts of vengeance at bay, focus on the task at hand — Sean Patrick Donovan.

The name hadn't been hard to come by: Sly Monteith had announced it in a release to the trade press back in February — *delighted to announce* and *formidable experience in the armed forces*, etc. etc. A brief online trawl revealed that Donovan's *formidable experience* included a stretch in a military prison prior to dishonourable discharge, a fact that received significantly less coverage. There was a photo, Donovan and another appointee, Benjamin Traynor, flanking their new boss, a champagne flute between two pint mugs. Neither of them cracking a smile, though Monteith's superior expression more than made up. *Look at my dancing bears*, thought River. Well, he'd had that smirk wiped off his face good and proper.

Ex-army; high rank; hard time. That ticked a lot of boxes as far as River was concerned: there might be other suspects, but this one would do to start with. He winced as another flash of pain lit up his body's circuitry, bit down until it passed away, then emailed what he'd found to the other slow horses, yards away.

Long past the hour Marcus Longridge mumbled something about getting lunch, and slipped out of the office pretending not to hear Shirley Dander's response, which involved a chicken baguette. The yard smelled worse than ever; the street was hot as hell. In the bookies by the station he filled out a betting slip for the 3:20 at Towcester, which he'd diligently researched under cover of work, and while he waited, stood and glared at the tin bastard of a roulette machine. It kind of looked alive, with a demon's eyes and grinning mouth . . . Wrapped up in this, Marcus forgot to follow the race, and glanced up just in time to catch the closing moments, which was like being sucker-punched by a supermodel: a beautiful moment nearly like pain. One hundred and sixty pounds straight to his trouser pocket. A sweet return on twenty quid.

He collected his winnings and patted the machine on his way out; insult to injury.

Marcus could, and should, have gone straight back to Slough House, but he was buoyed by success. This was the turning point he'd been waiting for. And there was a row of Boris bikes over the road . . . He thought: what the hell. Quicker than Tubing it. Excavating his debit card from his newly thickened wallet, he released one from its rack. Regent's Park, here he came.

Louisa Guy tucked a lock of hair behind her ear, briefly tugged at her blouse to fan her skin; suffered a brief, unasked-for memory of last night's stand — a bachelor pad in the worst sense, with month-old sheets and dishes in the sink, but still: enthusiastic and vigorous sex, leading to three hours' dreamless oblivion — and shook her upper body once, refusing to allow Lamb's gibe headspace.

Here's me thinking you'd been banging your brains out every night, and it turns out they're still functioning.

Which they were, but seriously, she didn't need brains for the task Lamb had set her. She needed blind faith and the devil's luck.

Roderick Ho abhorred Google, Yahoo, Bing and all the other popular engines: they searched, he claimed, less than 0.5 per cent of the internet's contents, and he'd sooner eat a vegan pizza than use them. But since

Louisa would sooner bake him one than ask him for a tutorial on the Dark Web, they were all she had to rely on. Still, what else was she going to do? Sean Patrick Donovan was her target, if Cartwright's guess was on the money. Closing down all other programs, in the hope this would free up enough space to allow her ancient machine some speed, she set to work.

Conspiracy theorists, she knew, were paranoid by definition, and usually with good reason — they were indeed being watched, largely because they were standing on an upturned bucket, haranguing the sheeple about their wingnut delusions. For months the previous year she had monitored message boards for suggestions of terrorist activity, and while she'd never entirely thrown off the suspicion that every other poster she encountered was an undercover cop, she'd grown used to eavesdropping on tin-hat conversations, from how the government was controlling the weather to the thought-experiments carried out on anyone who rang HMRC helplines. And all of these philosophers, without exception, were convinced they were under surveillance, their every online foray or mobile chat recorded and stored for future use. That this was probably true was an irrelevance, of course; they were simply caught in the same net as everyone else. Louisa had never trapped a terrorist; never stopped a bomb. She'd read a lot of discussions about 9/11, obviously, but contributions from structural engineers had been conspicuous by their absence. And while the helpline thing was probably true, that was just the law of averages at work.

230

And speaking of paranoia, how did Lamb know what she got up to outside work?

It didn't matter. Was just the law of averages again. Sod him, anyway.

The point was, anonymity was the paranoid's cloak — during her months treading those boards, Louisa hadn't come across anything remotely resembling a real name. Donovan could be venting three times daily on a host of sites, and if his username was SpaceRanger69, she'd never know about it. But Lamb had spoken. So here she was.

"Getting anywhere?"

Jesus! How did he do that?

Suppressing the start he'd given her, she said, "Give me a break. I've only been at it five minutes."

"Huh." Lamb came into the office, sniffing the air suspiciously. "Why does this room smell of cheese?"

"It doesn't. What have you got Ho on?"

"Why do you ask?"

"Because you'd be better off with him doing this."

"Shame he's busy, then." Lamb peered out the window at a passing bus, then rested his buttocks on the sill.

"You going to watch me all afternoon?"

"Is that how long it's going to take?"

"We don't even know for sure it's Donovan we're after."

"No. But we'll look stupid if we ignore him, and it turns out he took Catherine."

"What's Ho working on?"

"Above your pay grade."

"That reminds me." Louisa found a receipt on her desktop. "Taxi fares from this morning."

"Yeah, you might have to wait a while. I've been getting grief about the expenses you lot claim." He stood.

She said, "Is this all on the level? Or is something going on we don't know about?"

"I think it's safe to assume there's always something going on you don't know about," Lamb said.

He was nearly out the door when Louisa said, "Catherine."

"What about her?"

"Nothing. You called her Catherine, that's all."

"Huh."

Louisa settled back to her impossible task.

Five minutes later, she'd cracked it.

Do something, was what Longridge had said. *You want to make a mark, you want impress people, do something.*

So here he was: doing something.

Just so long as it's not sitting at a screen crunching . . . data.

Well, okay, crunching data was what he was doing, but still: it was what the moment demanded.

Roderick Ho paused to chug what was left of his Red Bull, then tossed the empty can at his wastepaper basket. It dropped neatly in, confirming what he already knew: that he was a superstar.

Crunching data, Longridge had said. As if this was something just anyone could do.

There were three properties registered to Black Arrow, one of which was a flat in Knightsbridge, clearly for Sylvester Monteith's own use, not that Monteith needed much room any more. His next lodging would be about the size of a fridge. The other two properties were larger, functional: Google Earth showed Ho they were both on industrial estates, one on the outskirts of Swindon, the other in Stratford, east London. The day the images were captured there were seven vans visible at the former; three at the latter. These were black, rugged-looking trucks, with windowless panels on which the firm's logo, a black arrow in a yellow circle, was displayed, and looked more substantial than the prefabbed buildings they were arrayed outside. Monteith chummed up to cabinet ministers, but his business didn't look blue chip. Ho printed off screenshots, left them in the tray, and focused on Monteith's personal life.

All the things kept behind firewalls — bank accounts and mortgage details; shopping baskets, mailboxes, porn domains, insurance payments — they were all low-hanging fruit. Passwords were made to be captured, and a basic crossword-solving algorithm could lay bare a life's secrets in the time it took to microwave what was left of a lunchtime pizza. So that's what Ho did while his privacy-shredding program ran the numbers on everything Sylvester Monteith wasn't using any more, beginning with where he'd kept his money, then running through what he'd spent it on. The pizza was a Four Seasons. Monteith's life was an open book. He had his wife and children; he had his business; he took holidays; he kept a mistress. Discovering how much each had cost him was just a matter of parsing his credit card statements. Crunching . . . *data* — yeah, right. This was something, and here he was, doing it.

And as he was doing it, Ho thought about what Lamb had said about Louisa banging her brains out. That had been cruel. Louisa was currently single. If she had a boyfriend, she'd talk about him: something Ho had learned not just from Mama Internet, but from listening to women talk — on the Tube, on buses, in bars, on the streets. Granted they weren't actually talking to Ho, but he had ears and facts were facts, and the ones with boyfriends never shut up about it . . . No, Lamb had been way off base, but Ho had to admit: the thought of Louisa banging her brains out was one he'd return to later, back home.

Meanwhile, he was accessing hard intel.

On one of Black Arrow's business accounts nestled a reference to *temp. prop.* — a substantial payment two months back, and another for half that amount on the same day of the following month. A deposit plus rental, Ho surmised. Temporary property. Lots of reasons why a security firm might want temporary possession of a property, especially — this was a few moves later, back on Google Earth — especially one out in the long grass, somewhere north of High Wycombe; a three-storey building with a few barn-like structures nearby, and there, slap in the middle of a courtyard, what looked like — and indeed was — a double-decker London bus.

234

Ho hit PRINT again, and this time collected the results.

Not far from the Park was a recently renovated swimming baths, its façade now boasting a row of hoarding-sized photographs: kids splashing about, an old fellow with goggles that made him look like a beat poet, a mother holding a child while its eyes blazed with delight. All very wholesome. Round the back was a metal-studded fire door marked NOT FOR PUBLIC USE. Marcus flashed his Service card at the topmost stud, and there was a short pause before the door emitted a low buzzing noise and a click, then opened.

He let himself in. Technically, like the other slow horses, he wasn't allowed here, but he had an advantage over the rest of the Slough House crew in that he'd once kicked doors down and pointed guns at bad guys, the kind of CV that impressed those who manned exits at Service facilities. This particular example greeted Marcus with a complicated handshake topped off with a toothy grin, and let him sign the log with his usual squiggle, a barely decipherable *Jackson Lamb*.

The shooting gallery was seven levels below the surface, beneath the baths, the gyms, the changing rooms. Marcus felt pumped heading down. Money in his pocket; his skin glowing from his bike ride — his shirt was soaked through, but he felt good, his muscles moving in smooth rhythms. He took the stairs three at a time, enjoying the sense of separation that increased with every flight. You could spend too much time in the world. Every so often you needed to check out, and if you could do that somewhere with live ammunition, so much the better.

So in the gallery he glad-handed another old comrade and shared an ancient war story; stole a bottle of water from the staff-only fridge, and drained it in one unbroken swallow; then mopped his still-sweating upper body dry with a handful of paper towels. After that he donned safety goggles, wrapped a pair of ear protectors round his head, signed for a Heckler & Koch, and planted ten straight bullets into the outline bad-guy-torso target thirty yards down the shooting corridor.

Yeah, he thought. Turned a corner.

Back in control.

Peter Judd said, "The way this was supposed to end, I'd have your boss's balls in my pocket. Instead, she's holding mine. Care to explain how that came about?"

"I know as much as you do," Taverner said. "Sean Donovan — what can I say? He went off-message."

That earned respect. Monteith had suffered, Judd's best information suggested, a single massive blow to the head; chances were, he was dead before he hit the ground. He was certainly dead before he was tipped from a van in SW1. Either way, "off-message" was as pithy a summation of that process as Judd had recently encountered.

"You're sure it was Donovan?"

"No. But if it wasn't, he'd have come forward by now. He must know his boss has been murdered."

236

Judd nodded, and pursed his lips. "Sly was a hero-fucker. He probably wet himself when Donovan applied for a job." He tapped the newspaper against the bench. "When you brought this tiger team idea to me, you knew I'd use Monteith."

Diana Taverner said, "It was *because* you had a contact in private security that I suggested it. You know that."

"I know you told me that. It's hardly the same thing. Did you know Donovan then?"

She shook her head.

"I have this weakness. Call it a foible. I like people to use words when they answer questions. That way I know whether they're lying or not."

Taverner looked him in the eye. "I'd never heard of Sean Donovan when I came up with the tiger team plan."

Judd regarded her without speaking. It was rare for him to spend long with a woman without making a pass — and "long", in those circumstances, could mean anything over a minute — but he knew how to prioritise. Besides, it was only postponing the inevitable, and the way things were going, when he did get round to bedding her it would be in the nature of a punishment, which suited him fine. Her too, if he read the signs aright. At last he said, "Tearney says whoever contacted her, who we assume's Donovan, is after the Grey Books. Is there anything damaging in them?"

"To national security?"

"To *me*."

"Not that I'm aware of. Do you have reason to think there might be?"

"If I don't feature in the paranoid fantasies of the internet's bedsit warriors, I'm not doing my job properly. And as long as mud's being flung around, some of it'll stick. What do you think he intends doing with this nonsense once he's acquired it?"

"I have no idea."

"You're supposed to be in Intelligence. Hazard a guess."

"I can only suppose he's looking for confirmation of whatever pet theory he's adopted."

"And we have no idea what that is?"

"Something military, I'd imagine. How important can it be? This is junk material. He might be researching a screenplay for all we know."

"I do enjoy levity in its right place. Which does not include when I've just been fucking compromised by the head of my own security service."

Diana Taverner knew enough not to respond to this.

Judd worked his way through a train of thought, carriage by carriage. At last he said, "Tearney will let Donovan get away because then I'm well and truly on her hook. As far as she's concerned, my scheme backfired and left one man dead and a mentalist with his hands full of Service secrets. The fact that they might as well be toilet paper's neither here nor there, because the press'd lap it up either way. So all I can do is kiss her arse and pretend I'm enjoying it." He slapped the bench with the rolled-up paper, frightening a pair of pigeons into flight. "If, on the other hand, she finds out the tiger team was your idea, she'll skin you slowly and feed you to spiders. So I might be in her pocket, but you're in mine, Diana. Which means my interests are yours. I trust you'll keep that in mind."

"Depend on it," she said.

Without warning, he reached out and clasped her right breast with his free hand. He squeezed hard. "If I thought this was all part of some game you're playing, I'd be very disappointed. I hope you appreciate that."

He'd expected fear, or at the least alarm. What he didn't expect was her hand on his crotch, and a reciprocal squeeze.

"Are you sure?" she said. "You don't feel disappointed to me."

The returning pigeons fluttered away again at Judd's raucous, earthy burst of laughter.

Chicken baguette. It wasn't much to ask.

But Marcus had been gone forty-five minutes, and it looked like lunch would have to be an office daydream: one of those brief reveries where you remember what it was like, last time you'd had something decent to eat. The past few weeks, supper had been whatever Shirley could scrape out of the fridge, eaten standing up. Drink: she was okay for drink — she couldn't remember the last time she hadn't had one of those. But food, she pretty much relied on getting something solid into her at lunchtime, which meant a local sandwich or a full-on takeaway. Unless Marcus came back with something pretty soon, she was going to faint with hunger.

Okay, so they'd been out earlier. But ice cream didn't count.

Bloody Marcus. He was supposed to be doing this: she was supposed to be watching.

Find out where the Grey Books are, Lamb had said, waving a pudgy hand, as if evaporating the difficulty involved.

Like she had the inside track on where the Service kept its crap.

Shirley scrabbled around her desk drawer for a while, unearthing the used envelope she scribbled her passwords on from a snowdrift of credit-card receipts and flyers for DJ nights. The Service intranet was a bland blue screen with a royal seal in the centre: she clicked on this, supplied her ID number and password ("inyourFACE") then navigated to a staff list with direct email and extension numbers.

So far so good.

The Queens of the Database were her first bet: they knew everything, and more besides. Shirley didn't know for a fact they spent their downtime trawling through personnel folders for dirt, but you had to figure. Unfortunately they took most other aspects of having signed the Official Secrets Act to heart, which meant even the one she thought she'd had a good relationship with, back when they worked in the same building — the one with the cheekbones, and eyebrows so fine they disappeared in a good light — wasn't prepared to let her know something as basic as information storage facilities.

"More than my —"

"Jobsworth. Yeah, I know."

"— Sweet thing. Are you having a torrid time over there? I hear Slough House positively *reeks* of disappointment."

Shirley's password drifted into mind as she broke the connection.

She went to the kitchen in the hope of finding something loose in the fridge, but River Cartwright was there, so theft wasn't on the agenda. He was holding himself in a painful fashion, but then he'd been given a seeing to by the Dogs — never a happy experience, Shirley gathered.

"How far did you get?" she asked him, genuinely interested.

"Archive level," he told her. He was drinking a glass of water, maybe checking for leaks.

"That's whatsername, right? The old bat with the wheels?"

"Molly Doran."

Shirley remembered the name, though had never encountered the lady. Another of those Service legends dimly whispered about; the subject of semi-thrilled speculation. She stalked back to her PC still hungry, an imp dripping mischief in her ear — she had a wrap of coke in her bag, so tightly tied it resembled a scrap of paper. Nothing like a snort to drive away hunger pangs. Plus, it would sharpen her up nicely; give her an edge . . .

But Jesus, no. No. She'd turned up at work slightly glassy once or twice: who hadn't? But she wasn't going to turn a teatime break into a launch pad, for God's sake. She sipped water from the unsmeared side of the glass on her desk, and felt it all the way down. That would do for now. It would have to. She found Molly Doran's number on the staff list, and called it.

Heading back from the kitchen, River paused at Louisa's open door to watch her gazing intently at her PC, head unmoving. In the rare moments he saw her — actually saw her, as opposed to being aware of her presence — he was struck by how much she'd changed her appearance since Min's death: different hair, different clothes, as if she were systematically erasing the person she'd been. If he knew her better, he'd have talked to her about that. But this was Slough House.

He was about to move on when she spoke, her eyes still fixed on her screen.

"Was it true what Lamb said?"

"Sounds unlikely. Which bit?"

"About you visiting Webb. In hospital."

River said, "Not sure you could call it visiting. Wouldn't he have to be aware of it to count as that?"

"But you go."

". . . Yeah."

"Why?"

He didn't answer.

She said, "He's the reason you wound up in Slough House. More to the point, he's the reason for that mess last year. What happened to Min. And you're taking him flowers?"

Her voice cracked on the closing word.

River said, "I know all that. You think I don't? He's a back-stabbing bastard, no question. I sometimes wonder if I'm only there to see if he's dead yet."

"That's a punchline, not a reason."

Now was the moment to leave, he thought; back to the safety of his room. He could ease into his chair, dose himself with aspirin, and hope they'd iron out his wrinkles before he was called upon to do anything energetic. But he couldn't, not while she was refusing to look at him. He'd always thought her borderline difficult, by which he meant she didn't take crap. Which in turn, he realised, meant he shouldn't offer her any.

"No . . . Yes, okay. It's not a reason."

"So why do you do it?"

"I talk to him. About this." *This* being Slough House. They both knew that. "About what it's like, day after day . . . About the gap between where we were and where we've ended up." He let that hover for a while. She didn't reply. He said, "I doubt he hears me. But if he does, he'll get it. I mean, Christ. You think this is bad? He can't even see out the window."

She redirected her gaze at last, and subjected him to a full quarter-minute's silence.

"So anyway," he said at last. "It's not like I cheer him up. Other way round, if anything."

He wasn't entirely sure that was the whole truth of it, but it felt as near as he could get.

After a while, Louisa said, "Got any painkillers?"

"I've got some aspirin. Want some?"

She shook her head, reached into her drawer, and tossed a packet at him. "Try those. They're stronger."

He caught it. "Thanks."

She looked back at her screen.

River returned to his office.

Marcus left the Boris bike at the baths and caught the underground back, and even the Tube stalling at Farringdon — signalling problems: these were often caused by heat, when they weren't caused by cold, or by things being wet, or dry — couldn't ruin his mood. He circled Smithfield, popped into an Italian deli for a chicken baguette, then headed up to Slough House, ringing home to tell Cassie he'd be late, he had a *work thing* on — an established code.

"You haven't had one of those for a while."

She didn't know about Slough House. She knew he'd been transferred, but not what that meant. He hadn't been able to bring himself to tell her.

"Yeah, well. It's not the kind of thing you schedule far in advance."

"Be careful."

"Always. Kiss the kids for me."

He felt coordinated — one up on the world. This morning's blues were someone else's soundtrack.

Sometimes, sitting at his desk, Shirley grumbling at her keyboard next to him, Marcus would zone out, reliving former glories with the crash squad. "Kicking doors down" was how Shirley referred to it. Which was accurate, up to a point, but left out how you never knew what was going to be on the other side, pointing a gun or strapped in a Semtex vest. In fairy tales, when you were offered a choice of doors, there was generally a tiger behind one of them. That was why it was best to kick them down. Even the thought of it made his muscles tense, and his grip on the baguette tightened — *Way to go*, he thought. Turn up with a peace offering that he'd mangled into paste. But with luck, Shirley would be too hungry to care.

Which was what he was thinking when he realised he'd been coasting on automatic; that instead of rounding the alley to the back of Slough House, he'd just entered the bookie's again, where the roulette machine still wore its demonic grin, daring him to take one step further — to come on in and kick its door down.

Marcus could still feel the weight of his wallet in his jeans pocket, its new thickness filling him with confidence that his world had turned a corner.

Okay, you bastard, he thought. *Bring it on.*

Molly Doran said, "My my. Two in one day."

"Yeah, Cartwright said he'd spoken to you."

"And how is the young man? He's back at . . . 'Slough House'?"

"Walking a bit crooked, but he's okay"

"How unexpected. I imagined he'd have had rather a business of it, explaining this morning's antics."

Shirley was bored already. "He has a knack for getting off lightly. Anyway, reason I called —"

"Not simply a social call, then."

Well, duh. Who did that?

But Molly Doran was a kidder, it seemed. "I'm sorry. The novelty of encountering *two* of Jackson's protégés has made me rather skittish. Do carry on."

"It's about some files."

"Oh dear. Are we going round this particular mulberry bush again? Perhaps Jackson could just call me himself and explain what he's up to."

"No, he doesn't do that. Anyway, this isn't about him, it's just a general query. About information storage?"

"You know, I always encourage junior officers to approach me if they have questions, but only in the certain knowledge that they're not actually going to do so. Couldn't you address your problems to the, ah, *Queens* of the *Database*?"

"Yeah, they're not that helpful? It's a simple question. I just need to know where the Grey Books are."

"The Grey Books?"

"The whackjob dossiers. The nutcase notes."

"I'm aware of what they get called. I'm just not sure why you feel the need to ask me."

"Well, you're a document shuffler yourself," Shirley couldn't keep from saying. "I thought you might know."

There was a lengthy pause.

"Prolonged exposure to Jackson evidently has its drawbacks," Molly said drily. "I suppose, like him, you eschew most official communications?"

If eschew meant what she thought it did, Shirley probably did, yes.

"You really ought to check your inbox, young lady."

246

And Molly Doran was gone, her voice replaced by the windless vacancy of a dead connection.

She had kind of a bite to her, that one. Maybe, Shirley thought, she'd chewed her own legs off.

Which had got her nowhere, except she might as well check her inbox, just in case that was a clue. But when she looked there was nothing there bar the latest all-Service newsletter circulated by HR: in-house transfer possibilities (slow horses need not apply); health and safety; promotions and retirements. Shirley had never encountered anyone who opened these, let alone read them. This was a personal first.

And there it was, under Miscellaneous Information: *recent info-storage issues have now been resolved . . .*

If Marcus had been there, she'd have raised a palm for him to slap, or at the very least to deposit a chicken baguette in; as it was, she had to settle for a quick victory lap round her desk — you *go*, girl, she told herself. *inyourFACE*. It felt like a natural high, making up for all the bullshit of her personal life these past few weeks, and as soon as that thought occurred to her, she knew she should have kept it at bay longer; should have enjoyed the moment for what it was, rather than taken it as consolation for the bad stuff . . . There wasn't anybody back home she could share this with later. There wasn't even Marcus, now, to high-five or fist-bump. Jesus, this switch in mood; it was sudden as gravity. She sat down, read the email again, tried to recapture the sense of achievement, or at least of blind stupid luck. But it was gone. You couldn't fake that sort of high.

Luckily, there were other kinds you could rely on.

Judd watched Diana Taverner leave the small park, enjoying the sway of her hips, and the way she paused briefly at the gate, giving him an extra second or two to study the goods. It was important to treat women with respect, but crikey, he was looking forward to rattling her bones — so much so it was politic to remain seated for a while. Last thing he needed was some citizen journalist bagging a shot of him in this state. Unrolling the paper he spread it on his lap as an extra precaution, and tried to concentrate on the matter in hand: Dame Ingrid Tearney. All outward appearances to the contrary notwithstanding, her Dameship currently had his dick in her handbag, a situation he couldn't allow to continue — one word from her to Number Ten, and he'd be out on his ear before you could say reshuffle. Disloyalty was the one political sin you couldn't survive being discovered committing; though of course, without it, your career would be one long tug at your forelock. That's what made public life such a balancing act. Which, let's face it, was why it was so exhilarating.

It's not so much that you have to go waltzing across the occasional minefield, my boy, some old fart had told him, his first week in the House. *It's that you've got to do it with a smile on your phiz.*

Yes, well, anyone who didn't have a game face for the plebs didn't deserve their vote in the first place, was Judd's view. Not that he'd say it out loud, of course — always important to stress that. Never say "plebs" out loud.

248

These ruminations having calmed him somewhat, he felt able to get to his feet.

Heading for the gate, he called Sebastian, his chief scout and bottle-washer — the ghost in his machine, you might say. Some of the bottles Seb had washed over the years weren't the kind you put out for recycling — more the sort you buried at night, in landfill — but his admittedly rather limited range of solutions had seen his master safely over a number of minefields in the past. You never could tell when the need to impose such a solution might arise. And Judd didn't plan to be caught with his trousers down a second time.

Maybe it was that phrase that triggered it, but while waiting for Seb to answer, Judd experienced an almost physical memory of Diana Taverner gripping his crotch, her tone as calm as if she were choosing an avocado. *You don't feel disappointed to me.* Ha! He hadn't felt that much innocent pleasure since choosing Clash tracks for all eight of his Desert Island Discs. He'd afterwards learned that an old Trot in the Isle of Dogs had literally had an apoplectic fit while listening. Which just went to show you couldn't please everyone.

It's said of Churchill that he'd catnap in an armchair with a teacup in his hand, and when he dropped off the noise of the cup hitting the floor would wake him. He claimed this was all the rest he needed. Jackson Lamb was much the same, the difference being he used a shot glass rather than a teacup, and didn't wake when it fell. Catherine would sometimes find him in the morning, sprawled on his chair like a misplaced squid, the air smelling like water from a vase of week-old flowers.

That was his condition when the slow horses, minus Marcus, gathered on his landing at the appointed hour.

River put a finger to his door, which hung ajar, and pushed it just enough to give them a view of Lamb's corpulent slumbers. A stray piece of paper, marooned on his desk, fluttered with each meaty exhalation.

Shirley said, "Shall we wake him?"

She seemed unnaturally bright; her volume a touch awry. On the other hand, Lamb had told them they'd gone live: maybe, Louisa thought, this was just what Shirley was like, with the prospect of action looming.

"Where's Marcus?" she asked.

Shirley shrugged. "Went for a bagwich. A sandwich. Baguette sandwich."

Louisa and River exchanged a glance.

Ho said, "He said five. He'll be mad if we don't go in."

"After you," River suggested.

Way down below the back door scraped open and slammed shut, and they all thought *Catherine*. But it was Marcus, stomping up the stairs as if they'd done him personal injury. He arrived at the top to find the others huddled there like a praetorian guard.

"What?"

"You're late for the meeting," Ho said.

"So are you," said Marcus. "Unless this is it."

"Where've you been?" asked Shirley.

"Out."

"I had to do all the research on my own. You know what that's like?"

"If it's like working, yeah. Here." He handed her a paper bag of indeterminate shape.

She squinted at it suspiciously. "Did this used to be a baguette?"

"Do you want it or not?"

"Whatever."

Louisa watched fascinated as Shirley tugged a squashed object from the paper bag and peeled away its Cellophane membrane. It was so much no longer baguette-shaped, she was able to eat it sideways.

River asked Marcus, "You okay?"

"Why?"

"You look . . . peeved."

" 'Peeved'? What is this, Hogwarts?"

"Pissed off, then."

"I'm fine."

"This is actually pretty tasty," said Shirley, or so the others assumed. Her mouth was too full to be sure.

"Good," said River to Marcus. "Because you might want to be on your game tonight."

"Trust me, Cartwright. I get the opportunity to shoot anyone, I'll be on my game."

"Nice to know."

"Not fussy who, either."

"I think they put paprika in it or something."

"Christ," Louisa said. "Nobody said anything about shooting. We're a glorified escort service, that's all."

"For a crew who took Catherine," said River.

"Precisely. Until we know she's safe, no one's shooting anybody."

"I nearly asked you to get me a tuna, but I'm glad I didn't now. Chicken's definitely my favourite."

"I think we should go in," said Ho.

"I think you're right," said River, pushing him through the half-open door.

Ho went sprawling onto the carpet.

Without opening his eyes Lamb said, "You're ten minutes late."

"Five," said Ho.

Lamb pointed at the clock on his shelf.

"That's fast," Ho objected.

"It's always fast. Do I have to specify local time?" Lamb opened his eyes, and his tone changed to a roar. "Get in here."

They trooped in while Ho scrambled to his feet, shooting daggers at River.

"Jesus," said Lamb, wiping a paw across his face, blurring his features to a screaming pope's. "One of these days I'm gunna wake up and it will all have been a bad dream."

"That happened to me once," Shirley said, her mouth full.

"What are you eating?"

". . . Chicken baguette."

"Give."

Shirley looked at what was left of her lunch, then at Lamb's implacably outstretched hand. She glanced at Marcus for support, but he was having none of it.

"Don't look so glum," said Lamb. "You could do with skipping a few."

"Are you even allowed to say stuff like that?" she complained, surrendering the sandwich.

"Not sure. Haven't read the manual." He examined her offering suspiciously. "Did this get hit by a bus or what? You can buy them new, you know." He took a bite out of it anyway, reducing it by about half. "All done your homework?"

There was a muttered chorus of assent.

"Right. Cartwright first. Sean Donovan. What have you got?"

"Sean Donovan," River said. "He's a career soldier, a combat veteran. Sandhurst, tour of duty in Northern Ireland, then an attachment to the Ministry of Defence. After that, he served with the UN Protection Force in the Balkans, then with NATO during the Kosovo War. He was a lieutenant colonel once that was over, and reckoned to be in the running for higher things."

"How high?" Shirley asked, then giggled abruptly.

Lamb stopped chewing to train a basilisk stare in her direction.

River said, "He was well thought of at the MoD. Sat on some high-level commissions, including one on domestic terrorism which had Regent's Park connections, and was on an advisory body to the UN in '08. A newspaper profile of him that year called him the perfect modern soldier, part warrior, part diplomat."

"I do like a man without faults," Lamb said, scrumpling greaseproof paper into a ball and tossing it over his shoulder. "Reminds me of me."

"Only he had a reputation for being a drinker."

"There you go," said Lamb. "A real prince."

"What," said Marcus, "he's in the closet? In the arms trade? Or likes dressing up as a Nazi?"

Lamb glared. "What's your problem? You look like you've lost a fiver and found a button."

". . . A button?"

"Forgive my folksiness. Woodstock generation."

River trundled on. "Donovan's career went to hell overnight. Not long after his UN stint he visited an army base in Somerset to give a lecture to an audience of cadets. Apparently there was a party afterwards, a knees-up in the mess, following which Donovan left the base in a car. He lost control, wrote the vehicle off, and his passenger, a Captain Alison Dunn, was killed. He was tried before a military court, and served five years, dishonourably discharged upon release. That was a year or so ago."

"Okay," Lamb conceded. "Maybe not entirely without faults." He held up one fat finger: "So. He has a Regent's Park connection." And a second: "And he's a drinker. Well?"

Nobody offered a comment.

"Jesus, do I have to do everything? He didn't pick Standish at random. He already knew her." He pointed at River. "How'd Sergeant Rock end up with Black Arrow?"

"Remember the Spider-Man incident?"

254

"Some idiot dressed as a cartoon fell off a building," Lamb said.

This had happened back in the winter, not far from Slough House. It had made headlines for a few days, and had figured in a few comedy routines too, because the guy hadn't actually died and, well, had been dressed as Spider-Man.

"Was thrown off a building," River said. "It was a demo, Fathers 4 Justice sort of thing. He was divorced, and had been denied his visiting rights."

"Was he complaining or celebrating?"

River ignored that. "Name of Paul Lowell, one-time DI with the Middlesex Constabulary, and more recently Sylvester Monteith's second-in-command at Black Arrow. He never knew who threw him onto London Wall. They'd made contact through the Fair Deal for Fathers website, and whoever it was came dressed as Batman. He was never caught."

"Well well well," said Lamb. "Wonder who that could have been?"

"Donovan," said Shirley.

"Yeah, that was rhetorical. Jesus, if I didn't know the answer to something, you think I'd ask you lot?"

When he was sure Lamb had finished, River said, "Monteith hired Sean Donovan the same week."

"Nothing like creating a job vacancy. Hope none of you think that's the way to the top."

"We'd never fit you through the window," Louisa muttered.

Lamb rubbed the palm of his hand on his whiskery chin. Which he was scratching was open to question.

"Okay, that's who he is. What's he want with the Grey Books? You." He pointed at Louisa. "Go."

Louisa said, "There's a number of message boards where conspiracy theorists gather to swap stories. We're not talking Dark Web here, this is all out in the open — well, they're passworded, obviously."

"But we have the passwords."

"We have the passwords."

She listed some of the sites, to blank indifference from her audience, except Shirley, who nodded vigorously throughout.

"About a year ago, around when Donovan would have been released from prison, a poster calling himself BigSeanD crops up."

"Is that what gave you the clue?" Lamb asked.

"Thanks, yes. That and hints at a military background. It's not unusual for online warriors to big themselves up, but he makes comments that chime with Donovan's experience. About the Balkans, and the UN."

She talked them through it. To all appearances, "BigSeanD" fitted snugly into the online community, where the prevailing attitude resembled what you'd get if you spliced the DNA of an only child, a *Daily Mail* reader and a viciously toxic bacillus: an organism that was self-obsessed, full of pent-up rage, and sprayed poisonous shit everywhere. Symptoms included a tendency to lapse into CAPITALS, the dismissal of all dissent as Establishment toadying, and a blinding ignorance of Occam's razor.

"So what's his bag?"

"It's the weather."

"The what?"

Louisa said, "He's got a thing about the weather. He thinks it's being controlled by . . . someone. The government. *Them*."

This was met with a moment's silence.

Then Lamb said, "Christ, and they let him carry weapons."

"He posts a lot about Project Cumulus, a government operation in the fifties, which had military backing. It was all about cloud-seeding, artificial rainmaking."

Lamb squinted towards the window, where the blind was doing a half-arsed job of keeping the sunlight out. "Yeah, that's working nicely."

"In 1952 there was a serious flood in Lynmouth, in Devon. Thirty-five people died. There are those, BigSeanD among them, who think this was the work of Project Cumulus. What was meant to be a demonstration of rainmaking potential got out of hand."

"Fifty-two's a long time ago," Marcus observed.

"But the theories continue. There's an American outfit, military-funded, called HAARP — something about high frequency transmissions — which is reckoned to be developing a weather-control system. Floods, hurricanes, tsunamis — a lot of big stuff has been laid at their door. Man-made climate change, according to the webheads, isn't a by-product of over-consumption. It's a deliberate attempt to interfere with weather patterns. Specifically, to weaponise them."

Shirley said, "That's like . . ."

What it was like escaped her.

Lamb said, "And there'll be stuff in the Grey Books relating to this?"

"Well, evidently they're a Looney Tunes jukebox. A one-stop shop for the conspiracy brigade. The Lynmouth flooding — there are still classified government documents on that one, the findings of a Select Committee investigation. If they're included, that'd be exactly the sort of thing Donovan's after. Apparently."

"You don't sound convinced. You're not sure it's him?"

Louisa shrugged. "It fits the dates. Like I said, BigSeanD didn't start posting until Donovan came out of prison. I'm guessing they don't let you have the internet in a military chokey."

"No, the brass band accompaniment is punishment enough." Lamb leaned back in his chair, always a potential Buckaroo moment. But its springs held. Staring at the ceiling, he said, "Okay. Golden Boy finds his career derailed, gets banged up for five years, and develops an obsession with *X-Files* mumbo jumbo. And now we have to help him get his hands on it. Have you finished fizzing yet?"

"Has who finished whatting?" Shirley asked.

"Give me strength."

Marcus said, "He's asking where they're kept. The Grey Books?"

"Oh, right, yeah, you know how I found out? It's actually on an email, one of those corporate-type Service catch-ups HR send round? With job vacancies

258

and promotions and links to where you can find out about your pension —"

"Any time you feel like it, jump right in and shoot her," Lamb said.

Marcus rested a hand on Shirley's shoulder. "Where? Are? The Grey Books?"

"I don't know, but a new off-site confidential info-storage facility has just gone operational where all Ops's quote non-key data unquote is now being housed, so they're pretty likely to be there, wouldn't you think?"

"You want to be any more specific about where 'there' is?"

Shirley said, "Out west of Hayes. That's still London, isn't it?"

"Depends whether you're an estate agent or a sentient being," Lamb said. "But yeah. That's where they'll be, all right." *You know what I've spent the past few months overseeing?* Diana Taverner had said. *Off-site storage for the whackjob files . . .* He surveyed his crew. "Jesus. An ex-soldier with a screw loose versus you lot. A bunch of losers with fewer moves than an arthritic tortoise. Wonder how this is going to pan out?"

"We can take him," Marcus said.

" 'We' aren't taking anyone," Lamb said. "Reason being, the whole point is to let him get away with it. Or did you forget that part when you were out pretending to be the Sundance Kid?"

"Oh."

"Yeah, oh."

"So I got a little practice in. Keeps me sharp."

"No, what you got was out of order. Next time you take my name in vain, do it while you're sitting my medical. Meanwhile, when I give you a job to do, you do it. Even if it involves sitting in front of a monitor."

"Hey, the job got done. Shirley just told you where the books are kept."

"And I'm amazed she stopped talking long enough for us to make sense of what she was saying." Lamb's gaze swung her way. "I've tasted what passes for coffee round here. And that's not what's got you buzzing."

"We're technically outside of work hours," Shirley muttered.

"Yeah, that was then," said Lamb. "But as of now, you're just technically outside of work."

Marcus and Shirley exchanged a puzzled look.

"Christ," said Lamb. "It's getting so you can't sack anyone round here without a phrase book."

River, Louisa and Roderick Ho unconsciously shuffled a little closer together.

Marcus glared at them, then at Lamb. "You can't do that."

"I just did."

"It's unfair dis —"

"You disobeyed a direct order, not to mention forging my name on a Park register. And her eyeballs are still spinning from whatever she's put up her nostrils. You seriously think you've a case for unfair dismissal?"

"You need us. Need me. How you gunna get Catherine back without —"

Lamb's coffee cup spun past Marcus's shoulder and shattered on the office wall, the spatter from its dregs Pollocking Marcus and Shirley en route. Marcus's words were swallowed by breaking crockery and the sympathetic ringing of the windowpane.

When the noises faded away, Lamb's voice held more menace than the slow horses were used to.

"You went AWOL. She got stoned. Do you want to explain how that helps? Because you might have been hot shit once, but here and now you're just another fuck-up and I am *not* risking you being involved while I've got a joe behind the wall. So take your glove puppet here, clear your desks and fuck off out of my building. I'll deal with the paperwork tomorrow."

For a long while Marcus stared at Lamb, whose eyes were cold as stone. On the wall, coffee dribbled a pattern between the cracks in the plaster; a new coastline being etched onto a map. Shirley snuffled once, a doglike noise, as if a thought had occurred to her, but she had yet to work out what it was. And then Marcus opened his mouth once, closed it again, and turned to leave.

"Watch yourselves," he said to River and Louisa as he left.

He might have been talking to Ho too, of course.

Shirley said, "Yeah, fuck," and disappeared in his wake.

River felt something uncomfortable wriggle down his spine: that sneaky feeling he'd just dodged a bullet.

An office door slammed downstairs, and a piece of furniture crashed to the floor.

Lamb produced a cigarette out of thin air, and waved it in their direction. "Leaving you two. And believe me, that says more about the alternative than it does about you."

"There are three of us," mumbled Ho.

"You still here?"

Louisa said, "Was that necessary? Donovan's a pro, and we already know he's not averse to violence. We —"

Lamb gave her the same basilisk stare he'd granted Shirley, and she faltered.

"We could have used Marcus," River said. "That's all we're saying."

A match flared, and Lamb's features shimmered in its heat.

They heard footsteps leaving Slough House, and the scratch and thump of the back door being prised open. They didn't hear it close. After a while, a warm draught climbed as high as the top floor, and curled around their ankles like a cat. Lamb smoked, and his office took on the blue-grey hue of late-night jazz piano. The light coming slantwards through the blind picked up motes and dust spirals gyrating in the air. When you could see what it was you were breathing, River thought, it really was time to be somewhere else.

At length, he said, "Okay, it's just us. So what do we do now? Wait for Donovan to make contact?"

"I doubt we'll be waiting long," said Lamb.

And because, as River later speculated, Lamb had long ago sold his soul in exchange for the occasional display of omniscience, River's phone chose that precise moment to chirrup.

Catherine, his caller display read.

But it was Donovan.

CHAPTER
ELEVEN

It was the Violet hour once more, and still the heat had not lifted. As River eased out of the car he felt his stomach muscles complaining, and before he was fully upright had reached into his jeans for the painkillers Louisa had given him. Four left. He popped them from their plastic sheath and dry swallowed. The last one stuck in his throat, which would keep him entertained for the next minute or so.

Louisa shut the door on the driver's side. "I think we were followed."

"Yeah?"

"It was keeping back, three cars behind. And disappeared for a stretch. But it was there."

River nodded, though he wasn't convinced. That kind of tail sounded professional, and if it was professional, he didn't think Louisa would have spotted it. But voicing that opinion might be dangerous, and his testicles hadn't fully recovered yet. "You should have said."

"Yeah, well, I wasn't entirely sure." She threw him a look which was a barely disguised challenge. "But I am now."

"Okay," said River. But if they'd been followed, whoever it was had now dropped off the radar.

They were within what Lamb would have called pissing distance of London's westbound railway lines, which ran alongside a corridor of airport parking, gas holders, cement works and heavy plant depots, and had parked on a patch of wasteland surrounded on three sides by long low office blocks: low by the capital's standards, six storeys tall, and originally white. These were set at a higgledy-piggley angle, with gaps between wide enough to drive a car. Two, joined at third-storey level by a walkway, were derelict, glassless, tagged high and low with faded swirls of paint; the stuttering, repetitive squawks of urban discontent — *Tox, Mutant, Flume*. At ground level each block was unwalled, with thick round pillars every few yards; these were scorched black where homeless wayfarers or partying teenagers had made camp, and the floors were strewn with bottle glass and random litter. Toilet smells drifted out to where they stood, on a pitted and rubbly patch of concrete, with thuggish plant life sprouting from its cracks. River could feel its heat seeping up through the soles of his shoes, and the ground trembled as a high-speed train thundered past.

The third block looked to be in the process of being reclaimed, though how far advanced this was was open to question. Its paintwork, if not fresh, hadn't yet succumbed to distemper, and glass shimmered in its windows, but a distressed air hung over it, as if it had fallen into bad company, and knew things wouldn't end well. The fourth side of the more-or-less square was a disused factory — paint or vinyl, River thought — which had a squat, rectangular tower at one end, next to which a tall whitewashed chimney reached up to about the height of the nearby blocks. An extension had been added, long ago; a slant-roofed corrugated-iron and sheet-plastic construction, from whose guttering barbed wire dangled like an ill-fitting crown of thorns. Pictures of Alsatians were studded at intervals, indicating that trespassers would be eaten, or worse. A jagged hole in its wall at ground level suggested that this threat hadn't been taken entirely seriously.

Three fridges and a mattress formed a nearby cairn, next to which ten-foot lengths of metal fencing were stacked in a pile, chained to each other by their end-poles, and secured to the earth by an iron hoop. An orange skip lay on its side, like a Tonka toy cast off by a giant.

Louisa's car ticked, as if counting down to something ominous.

"I think I saw this place in a film once," River said. "It involved zombies."

"West of Ealing," Louisa said. "It might have been a documentary."

River's phone rang. It was Lamb.

"Why's your phone on?"

"It's on vibrate," River lied. "We've just arrived. Place seems quiet."

"Well, it was until your phone rang."

River waited, Lamb's breathing rusty in his ear.

266

At length Lamb said, "These soldiers, Donovan and . . ."

"Traynor."

"Traynor. Once they've got what they want, back off. Don't try to follow them. Let them leave."

"What about Catherine?"

"Just focus on your end," said Lamb. "Remember, Ingrid Tearney's pulling the strings here. And when it suits her, she'll cut them."

"We'll beware of falling puppets," said River.

"Don't get cocky. You're desk drones, not the Dynamic Duo."

"And we should know that by now," River finished for him.

Lamb hung up.

Louisa said, "What's he want?"

"For us to be careful, believe it or not." River tucked his phone away. "But he's run out of Enid Blyton analogies."

Another train rumbled past, picking up speed out of Paddington, and sounded its whistle; an old-fashioned, reliably forlorn noise. A crow, picking at something near one of the abandoned fridges, looked up, emitted a sullen cough, and went back to its meal.

"There was definitely a car," she said. "But I didn't get the make or colour."

"Okay," River said.

He was saved saying anything more by the sight of two shadows emerging from behind a pillar in the nearest of the wrecked buildings.

* ★ *

Roderick Ho was finding it quiet in Slough House, now the others had gone. This didn't usually bother him. Most days, he saw as little of anyone as he could manage, except for the moments he engineered in the kitchen with Louisa, who had given him a look before she left — an amused glance, telling him she'd rather stay behind than set off on a ludicrous exercise: babysitting a pair of ex-soldiers while they stole the X-Files. He'd mirrored this with a look of his own, a slight raising of an eyebrow meaning *You and me both, babes*, but she was out of the door before he'd delivered it. He needed to practise that look. If he'd been quicker off the mark she'd have caught it, no problem.

He powered his computers down, and cast a goodbye look around his kingdom. Now that Longridge and Dander were history, he ought to check out their office, see if they'd forgotten anything worth having. Longridge had a nice silk scarf; he wasn't likely to be wearing it in this heat, so might have left it on a hook. Ho got as far as the door before this plan underwent sudden revision.

"And where do we think we're going?"

"Uh . . . home?"

Lamb placed a paw in the centre of Ho's chest and kept walking. Ho shuffled backwards until the backs of his thighs met the edge of his desk. Then Lamb let his hand drop and went and stood by the window, his back to Ho.

The street outside was starting to droop. Traffic was heavy still, but tinged with exhaustion: poor sodding

268

workers heading home from battle, rather than the go-getting warriors of the morning. Across the road, a woman stepped out of the dental laboratory, which had an industrial aspect, as if large-scale experiments took place within, rather than individual acts of dentistry. She shook her head, dispelling an unpleasant memory, and walked off towards the Tube.

"High Wycombe," Lamb said.

The farmhouse Ho had found. The one Sylvester Monteith had rented.

"Uh, yeah. A little way past it on the motorway. Satnav'll find it no problem."

"I prefer natsav," Lamb said.

"Huh?"

"Natural savvy. It allows me to avoid demeaning tasks when there are others to perform them for me."

"Uh . . . Cup of tea?"

"Where's your car?" said Lamb.

Marcus was driving a black SUV with tinted windows: a vehicle designed for urban military ops, but usually driven by harassed mums caught between the school run and Waitrose. Shirley had pointed this out to him in the past, but didn't think it was a good subject to bring up at the moment. When Marcus had stopped swearing about Lamb, it had only been so he could pick on her instead.

"You straight yet?"

"Are we back on that?"

"This is not a fucking joke, Dander. You were high earlier. Are you straight yet?"

Shirley thought about lying, but only for a second. "Jesus, it was one tiny toot. Didn't even kill the hunger pangs."

"Fuck it, Dander. *Fuck* it."

"Keep your hair on. Christ, half an hour, max. It was a half-hour lift, no more."

"Did you forget what we said earlier?"

"No, *partner*. It was what kept me going all afternoon, after you'd disappeared on your jolly."

They were in bad traffic, progress stalled by a breakdown up ahead, reducing the road to a single lane. This had not improved Marcus's temper.

"So now it's my fault?"

"Hey. I take responsibility for my own fuck-ups. I'm not carrying yours too."

Marcus swore under his breath, and then swore out loud, and slapped his hands against the wheel. "*Hell!* Have you any idea what kind of shit I'm in?"

"Same kind I am," Shirley said. "The kind where you haven't got a job and life sucks."

"I have a family. You're aware of that, right? I've got mouths to feed and a mortgage to pay. I *cannot* lose my job."

"Good strategy, Marcus. Shame you didn't put it into action earlier."

"Don't get gobby with me, girl. Or you can get out here and walk."

"Call me girl again, you won't be *able* to walk."

The pair seethed in silence while the SUV crawled past the broken-down vehicle, from whose windows a forlorn young woman stared.

270

"Just anywhere up here," Shirley said at last. "Christ. I'd have been quicker on foot anyway."

"Yeah, because you're in a real hurry, aren't you? No job, and nobody waiting at home."

"Thanks for the update. But I hadn't actually forgotten my life was crap."

"Look on the bright side. Maybe you'll find some crystal meth down the back of the sofa. You know, the way people find loose change —"

"Don't fucking judge me, Longridge. You don't catch me losing a week's salary to a one-armed bandit."

"I don't do one-armed bandits!"

"And I don't do crystal meth!"

Marcus swerved abruptly into a parking space, and Shirley's head banged against the back rest.

"Shit!"

"Shit!"

They sat in silence, their anger trying out different shapes. Traffic rumbled past through almost visible heat, and the clock on the dashboard experimented with making time stand still, every second dragging itself over innumerable obstacles. Marcus was the first to surrender.

"So okay," he said. "We both screwed up."

Shirley seemed about to offer footnotes but changed her mind at the last moment. "Maybe."

"You think that fucker Lamb'll change his mind?"

"He was mad."

"I know."

"Really mad."

"I know," said Marcus. "So now what?"

"I hear Black Arrow has vacancies."

"Great."

Their renewed silence was only slightly less uncomfortable; Shirley tugging at the strap of her seatbelt and letting it slap back into her chest; Marcus drumming his fingers on the steering wheel in a series of broken rhythms. At last he said, "Cassie knows I'm on a job tonight."

"So?"

"So she's not expecting me back."

Shirley let the seatbelt slap against her again, then said, "If you're about to make a pass, I'll peel your face with a spoon."

"Jesus, Dander. No offence, but I've been sacked, not lobotomised."

"Yeah, none taken. Only you're too old and baldy for me."

He shifted in his seat. "This op of Lamb's."

"The Grey Books."

"It's Looney Tunes."

"Well, duh."

She pulled her seatbelt out again, but Marcus caught it before it slapped against her chest.

"Stop doing that. It's Looney Tunes, yeah, but what if it's not?"

"Meaning?"

Marcus said, "This Donovan. Before he was kicked out of the army, he was a high-flier, right?"

"You heard Cartwright," Shirley said. "MoD attachments, UN committees, meetings at the Park. He wasn't a squaddie, that's for sure."

272

"And he's got a thing about the weather."

"Everyone's got a thing about the weather, Marcus. The weather's Looney Tunes too. Floods and heatwaves, Jesus. I'm just waiting for hurricane season."

He ignored her. "So everyone thinks what he's after is worthless, and he only wants it because he's a headcase. But what if he's not? What if he knows something we don't? All that high-level Ministry of Defence stuff, he must have had access to a lot of black bag ops. What was Louisa saying about that HAARP project?"

"I don't remember."

"Well it was something about weather manipulation. So what if Donovan's not as fucked-up as he's pretending? What if there's something in the Grey Books that actually matters? Proof these weather projects are really going on?"

Shirley shook her head, and looked across the street. In a bar opposite, a young man wearing denim cut-offs and a leather waistcoat was polishing tabletops. She wondered whether they needed cleaning, or if this was part of the floor show.

Marcus said, "There's Select Committee reports in there too. Documentation, maybe other kinds of official paperwork."

"So?"

"So Donovan was kicked out of the army, remember? Maybe this is payback. He's planning on going Assange on someone's arse."

"Yeah, you might want to choose your words more carefully." Shirley withdrew her attention from the barman. "Besides, what's it got to do with us? Unemployed, remember?"

"Maybe."

"Right. That Lamb. What a kidder."

"Seriously, Shirl. If Donovan's not the tin-hat he's made us think he is, then this isn't just a hand-holding operation. Because once he's got what he's after, he won't want to leave witnesses."

"Lamb's not about to reinstate us just for looking keen."

"Maybe not. But what else are we gunna do? You expected home? Because like I said, I'm not."

Shirley gazed at her thumb for a while, as if contemplating biting it off. Without looking up, she mumbled something.

"Say what?"

"Say fuck it," said Shirley, more audibly. "Fuck it, then. Let's go."

Walking out of the sunlight into the shadow of the crumbling office block was like stepping from a live oven into a dead one: the heat was dirtier, wrapped in all the stink of a derelict building — rot and mildew, beer and piss, overlaid by something sweet and sickly, which River suspected might be a dead animal. Random bits of brick and lead piping suggested local turf wars. The two men were waiting by a pillar, and something in the way they held themselves reminded him of Marcus. The bigger of the two, a broad-shouldered man with a grey crew cut and a boxer's nose, late fifties, stepped forward at their approach.

274

"Cartwright?"

An Irish note to his voice contained less warmth than the accent usually carries.

River nodded.

"So you're Guy."

Louisa simply looked at him.

River said, "And you're Sean Donovan. Making you Ben Traynor."

The second man was cut from the same wood as Donovan, but younger, and where Donovan was greying Traynor was mostly bald, his chevron of hair razored to a light stubble. He didn't respond to River's identification, seeming more interested in Louisa, who had come to a halt shoulder to shoulder with River.

"You know what we're after," Donovan said.

Before River could reply, Louisa said, "We know what you say you're after."

"Let's not get complicated. It's a straightforward collection job."

Neither he nor Louisa had weapons, it occurred to River. Earlier, this had seemed a detail: the job wouldn't, shouldn't, require them to be armed. But in the face of the two Black Arrow operatives, the wouldn't/shouldn't aspect of the job lost ground to the might-just-possibly element. Because if these two weren't armed, he thought, they were breaking an ingrained habit.

Though calling them Black Arrow operatives was pushing it, he conceded. Killing the boss was definitely grounds for dismissal. Lamb reminded the slow horses of that on a weekly basis.

"How did you know about this place?"

Donovan regarded him without emotion. "Same way I know about Slough House. I do my homework, Cartwright. How about you? Or do you make a habit of setting off half-cocked?"

Since an honest response to that would be "Yes", River left it unanswered.

Louisa said, "Where's Catherine?"

"She'll be released unharmed once the Grey Books are ours."

"And we have your word for that," she said flatly.

"Our word's good." This was Traynor, speaking up at last.

"That what you told Sylvester Monteith?"

Donovan said, "Monteith signed up for it. He should have known the risks. Catherine's a non-combatant. She'll be released unharmed when we get what we want."

"She'd better be."

River said, "So how's this going to work?"

"You go in, make sure it's all as advertised. Once it's secure, you open the doors and we follow."

"Sounds simple," Louisa said.

"I gather you're the special needs crew. Anything more complicated than opening a door, I'd probably have looked elsewhere."

River was getting tired of having the horses' lowly status underlined. "But maybe kidnapping an unarmed woman seemed the easiest option. Was it just the two of you, or did you have help?"

276

Donovan's smile didn't reach his eyes. "Feeling sparky now? There's a good lad. Time to chat up the doorman, right?"

It was on the tip of River's tongue to say he hoped they'd have a chance to continue this later, but it struck him he'd had this conversation once today already. So he just glanced at Louisa, nodded, and the pair of them walked back out into the sunlight, towards the old factory building.

Nick Duffy watched their progress from the third floor of the other derelict block. Tailing them from the Barbican, he'd thought they'd spotted him, despite his car being an anonymous silver hatchback like every second set of wheels on the road; there'd been a definite phase when Louisa Guy had exhibited paranoid tendencies: slowing excessively for one amber light, pedal to the metal for another. When that happened, Duffy knew, you kept your cool; assumed that the usual traffic inhibitors would do their job, and a regular, even speed would bring the target back into focus at the next crowded junction. Failing that, you always had back-up.

Except, like now, when you didn't.

What he did have was the next best thing in the circumstances, which was knowing where they were headed, because Dame Ingrid Tearney had told him.

"They're aiding and abetting an ex-convict in the commission of a crime involving a breach of national security."

This with her usual, unflappable delivery. Duffy suspected that if Tearney were ever to break news of imminent nuclear catastrophe, it would be in the same style, though in those circumstances she would no doubt resort to calling him "dear boy", her invariable way of sweetening a pill.

"And you want me to stop them?"

"That won't be necessary."

They were in Dame Ingrid's office, with its view that had once been green, but was now mostly brown: since the hosepipe ban, the plantlife in the park opposite had been dying. This had happened before, but this time it was hard to believe that things would revert to normal. It was as if a tipping point had been reached, and the city, maybe the planet, was sliding into irreversible decline.

But since there was nothing he or anyone else could do about this, Duffy shrugged it off, and listened to Dame Ingrid's story of Sylvester Monteith's tiger team, and how it had turned on him and bitten his head off.

Since speaking to Lamb, Dame Ingrid had conducted a little research of her own, following the exact same path River had taken. One Sean Patrick Donovan, she explained to Duffy, was the chief suspect.

"Dumping the body in central London," he said. "Sounds like he was trying to make a point."

And it explained what River Cartwright thought he'd been doing this morning. But the fact that Cartwright had walked away unaided indicated that whatever was happening now, it wasn't going to be written up on official notepaper.

That was fine by him. Duffy had been head Dog long enough to know which end did the wagging. If Dame Ingrid needed something done under the bridge, then under the bridge he'd go.

"The files are of no consequence," Tearney said. "Archived material of a rather lurid nature. I suspect that Mr Donovan's wide range of experience, either in the military or in its house of correction, has left him somewhat paranoid. It's always a shame when a career goes so spectacularly awry."

"But you're happy to let him get away with it?"

"When you get to my age, dear boy, you'll understand that nobody really gets away with anything. But in this very specific instance, yes, I'm happy for him to appear to have got away with this."

The word *appear* swam between them for a moment or two, then vanished in its own slippery coils.

"I want you to track him to his lair, Mr Duffy. To run him to earth. And ensure that his paranoia doesn't lead him into more serious misadventures."

"I see."

"I very much hoped you would. You're happy to undertake this without support?"

"Without back-up? Yes, Dame Ingrid. I'm happy to do that."

Because acting without back-up broke every rule in the Service's code of practice, which meant she'd be putting a very big tick on his side of the ledger. And given his earlier run-in with Lady Di, Nick Duffy was feeling the need for a friend in high places.

Besides, this was what he was born for. Leaning on agents who stepped out of line was one thing. Squashing potential enemies of the state was entirely another.

When Cartwright and Guy disappeared through a side door into the abandoned factory, Duffy lowered his binoculars and wiped the sweat from his eyebrows. It wasn't dark yet, though shadows were lengthening on the wasteground below. Whatever played out here in the next short while, there was no danger he'd miss anything.

Nick Duffy, in fact, prided himself on missing very little.

"Where's your car?" said Lamb.

"Why?"

"Because I thought it might need a wax and polish. Jesus, answer the question."

Ho pointed through the window, in the direction of the nearby estate. He had a local resident's parking permit in the name of an actual local resident, though as the resident in question was ninety-three and homebound, she was never likely to discover this. Come to think of it, she might be dead by now. Either way, there was probably a law said your boss couldn't make you lend him your car.

On the other hand, if such a law existed, it almost certainly didn't apply to Lamb.

"Good. I'll have a dump while I'm waiting."

"Waiting?"

"For you to fetch the car. Are you awake? Because sleeping on company time's a sackable offence."

A glint in his eye suggested Lamb had acquired a taste for firing his staff.

Ho's reluctance to reach the obvious conclusion was being worn away by the inevitable. "You want to go to High Wycombe."

"And to think your annual appraisal says you're slow on the uptake." Lamb's melancholy headshake might have been more convincing if he wasn't responsible for the said appraisal.

"And you want me to drive you?"

"Christ, no. But there's nobody else around."

"Well, if you hadn't sacked . . ."

Ho's voice tailed off in the face of Lamb's benign expression. "You go right ahead, son. I've always prided myself on being able to take criticism."

"I just don't think I'll be much help."

"Neither do I. So you'll have to prove us both wrong, won't you?" Lamb plucked a can of Red Bull from Ho's desk, and shook it to gauge its contents. There were none. He sighed, and dropped it. "Look. If you were kidnapped, would Standish help?"

Ho broke with his usual habit, and gave this question some thought. Standish called him Roddy, which nobody else did; she would occasionally praise him for his computer skills without immediately following this up with a request that he perform some digital task; and one lunchtime had presented him with a homemade salad in a Tupperware box because he "ate too much pizza", whatever that meant. When his

281

resentment had worn off, Ho found he was quite touched; so much so that he had disposed of it where she might not find it. And he thought, too, how of all the slow horses, she was the one most likely to be pleased when she found out about him and Louisa. Of course, there were fewer slow horses than there used to be, but that altered the percentages, not the facts.

Having thought all this, he muttered, "I guess."

"You'd better hope so. Because no other bugger round here will, I promise you that. Now go get your car. Chop chop."

Ho was halfway down the stairs when Lamb called out, "Oh, and when I say 'chop chop', I hope you don't think I'm being racially insensitive?"

"No."

"Only you Chinkies can be pretty thin-skinned."

It was going to be a long drive to High Wycombe.

The details of the off-Park storage site were on the Service intranet, if you knew where to look; passwords were available to agents in good standing, which didn't include the slow horses, but applied to Jackson Lamb. Neither Louisa nor River had seen fit to pass comment on this back at Slough House while Ho had retrieved the relevant code. From the summary this accessed, they had learned that the facility was below the semi-derelict industrial estate; an underground complex that had started life as a bomb shelter in the thirties, and been refitted two decades later. At this time, it was hugely expanded to allow living room for a hundred and twenty local government officials, these being

282

deemed, for reasons perhaps not unconnected with their having been involved in the planning, necessary to the survival of civilisation in the aftermath of a nuclear exchange. The subterranean network now stretched for more than a mile westwards from its originating point, its connecting corridors carved into abrupt dips and bends to avoid the underground line — the work had been passed off as maintenance. Here in this system of caves and caverns, the important work of means-testing and rates assessment would carry on even as the world outside shivered through nuclear winter.

That had been the plan, anyway, but in the late seventies the site was repurposed and moved into Service hands. Given that Armageddon was still on the cards then, council officials had evidently been downgraded to expendable, but little fuss was made. Natural wastage, generous early retirement packages and the notoriously abbreviated attention span of local government officers had combined to allow the facility's existence to pass into the status of myth; and it was deep enough, and its walls thick enough, to pass undetected while the work of the industrial estate lumbered on overhead. And when that fell victim to the economic miracle that had transformed Britain into a service industry, the facility continued on its quiet course, upgraded by now to cope with more contemporary threats than a nuclear exchange: viral outbreaks, extreme weather events, and the righteous indignation of a pissed-off electorate.

It was hard not to think in terms of James Bond-type hit.

"You think there'll be crews wearing silver tracksuits?" River said as they made their way into the abandoned factory.

"You mean blondes," Louisa said.

"Well, obviously blondes. But, you know. Redheads too."

"And a secret railway?"

"And a control panel with a countdown window and a big red button."

Louisa's mouth twitched and she seemed about to say more, and then, exactly as if some big red button or other had actually been pressed, the moment was erased and her lips flatlined. "You realise the place is now basically a warehouse."

"I hadn't forgotten."

"Minimally staffed."

"Yeah, I read that bit too." It was on the tip of River's tongue to tell her to lighten up, and then he wondered if James Bond-type shit was the kind of thing she used to laugh about with Min, so didn't. "The south-west corner. Which one's that?"

Louisa was already pointing, phone in hand, compass-app working.

"I'm hoping for a nicely oiled trapdoor."

What they got was a drain cover, its handle packed tight with dirt.

"Oh great," said River, looking round for a stick or something to scrape it clean.

"Maybe we should try the main entrance."

This was at the southernmost point of the complex, and doubled as an access tunnel to the city's Victorian

284

sewage system. As such, it was something of a tourist attraction. It had closed for the day by this hour, but remained more likely to be populated than the old factory; besides, it was a long hike from there to the complex's nerve centre, directly below them. Unless there really was a secret railway.

"We're here now," River said. He'd found a foot-long length of metal siding, and used it to prise up the drain cover, releasing various stinks into the already fetid air. "Jesus."

Louisa said, "You thought it would be all shiny metal? It's a secret entrance."

He pushed the cover aside, feeling at the base of his spine the noise it made scraping the floor. "Want to go first?"

"I think I'll let you do that."

She produced a torch and aimed it down the hole. With this to guide him, River dropped into darkness.

Dame Ingrid was signing off the minutes of that afternoon's Limitations Committee meeting, each set of initials at the foot of each column a work of art; her pen never leaving the paper as she bestowed approval upon a series of opinions that the act of transcription had somehow rendered gnomic . . . Each member invariably left a session convinced that his or her criticisms had been taken on board, and a window opened on a grubby corner of the covert world that would henceforth gleam untarnished. Only with the passage of time would it become apparent that the window remained closed, its curtain securely drawn.

And were this state of affairs ever drawn to Dame Ingrid's attention, she would express surprise that anyone might think otherwise, and produce the minutes to prove that it had never been intended so.

An ability to think round corners was often cited as a prerequisite for Service work. Perhaps more critical was the ability to bend other people's thoughts through 180-degree angles. Come to think of it, that was why Peter Judd represented such a threat: he knew how to play a meeting as well as she did. Luckily for Ingrid Tearney, his attempt to short-circuit the process had left him vulnerable.

Though even as she framed the thought, it struck her that luck was not an element she usually relied on.

Capping her pen, she reached for her glass of water and sipped from it, considering. As things stood, the upper hand was hers. Judd's tiger team, intended to demonstrate the shaky grasp Dame Ingrid had on the Service, was now an object lesson in how ministerial arrogance could leave blood on the streets: a career-ending fiasco, even for the so-far impermeable PJ. Mopping up was under way, with Nick Duffy primed to trace Donovan to his lair once the Grey Books were in his possession. It was one thing to allow the ex-soldier to waltz off with his fool's treasure — that was another nail in Judd's coffin: *look what your hare-brained scheme let happen* — but to allow things to go further was to license anarchy. So Duffy was the stopgap: Donovan would die a soldier's death; the files would be returned to their subterranean cabinet; the slow horses, ridiculous name, could go back to their humdrum existence; and Dame Ingrid herself would resume the even tenor of her way, comfortable in the knowledge that the ministerial hand apparently on her tiller was in fact responding to her instructions. And as for the future, Judd's ambitions need not necessarily be thwarted; if having a whipped Home Secretary rendered her position bulletproof, having a PM in her pocket guaranteed beatification. So all in all, a good day.

But still, there was that idiot whisper loose in the room now, the one that kept reminding her that luck was the grease in the wheel. If Donovan hadn't proved a wild card, everything would have gone Judd's way.

Ingrid Tearney realised that she was uncapping, recapping, uncapping her pen in a way that in a lesser mortal might reveal uncertainty. She placed it firmly on her desk. Time for a walkabout.

By dint of a brief, illegal shortcut up a one-way alley, Marcus had changed direction and was heading west, manoeuvring his black tank through the city streets like he was piloting an image on a PC, and the worst that could happen was game over. Twice, as he strayed into oncoming traffic, Shirley stopped breathing, and her grip on the door handle was tight enough it would take a monkey wrench to loosen.

Her voice squeakier than she'd have liked, she said, "We going fast enough yet?"

"Sooner we get there, sooner I'll slow down."

Shirley was hoping this would come to pass without any pedestrians smeared across the tarmac; or, worse, her own sweet self propelled through the windscreen.

She looked across at her partner. Was that still the word, now they'd been sacked? Or was he just another semi-stranger; one of the increasing number in her life who buggered off when things got tricky? Except he hadn't, had he? Things officially turned tricky about an hour ago, and here he still was, skyrocketing her through the city streets; heading full-tilt for what might turn out to be just another windmill.

Maybe he could read her mind.

"Back in the crash squad, we had a joke," he said. "When is a door not a door?"

". . . When it's ajar?"

"When it's a pile of fucking matchsticks," Marcus said. "We weren't especially subtle."

"No, I get that."

"If there's a chance something bad is happening, we want to be there before it starts. Otherwise we're already on the defensive, and that's not anywhere you want to be when the bad shit's going down."

He was slipping into the macho rhythms of his Service career, Shirley realised, and in a rare moment of tact decided not to call him on it.

An amber light turned red maybe two seconds before they cruised past, leaving an angry squall of honking in their tracks.

"Hence the need for speed."

"So we can arrive before the bad thing starts," Shirley said.

"Yep."

"And maybe get our jobs back."

"Maybe."

"And keep Cartwright and Guy from getting toasted."

". . . Yeah. That too."

"I still think you should slow down," Shirley said.

"Why?"

"Because that's a cop car you just passed," she told him; information immediately rendered old news as the car in question flashed its bar-lights and the familiar two-tone lament began its upward spiral, demanding everyone's attention, but specifically theirs.

Roderick Ho was proud of his car. Some other horses he could mention (he was thinking of Cartwright) didn't even own a set of wheels, let alone a Ford Kia, electric blue with cream flashing, and seriously punishing sound system — Ho favoured music that came with health warnings, in Gothic lettering. The seats were cream too, with reciprocal electric-blue seaming, and the windscreen ever so slightly tinted, to keep onlookers guessing. Online, where Ho mutated into Roddy Hunt, DJ superstar, he referred to it as the chick magnet, and in real life kept it immaculate, regularly treating it to squishes from a spray can of new-car smell. In return for which it had obstinately refused to live up to its nickname, but then that was the problem with pre-owned wheels: the previous owner had used up its luck.

Still a great ride, though. Probably every bit as good as the other kind, he thought, coming to a halt at the kerb where Jackson Lamb stood waiting.

Waiting, holding a polystyrene coffee cup, and shaking his head: "Jesus wept."

Ho wound down his window. "What?"

"If you have to ask," Lamb told him, "you wouldn't understand the answer. Would it make you feel like a lackey if I sat in the back?"

"Yes."

"Excellent." Lamb squeezed into the rear, spilling not very much coffee as he did so. "Why does it smell of cheese?"

The evening was darkening at last; one or two streetlights had popped on; others remained dormant, either on a different schedule or broken. The home-goers on the pavements had given way to pleasure seekers, heading into the Barbican for an event, or drifting towards bars on Old Street. Roderick Ho checked his rearview and caught Lamb on one of his fishing expeditions, hands emerging from both pockets; one clutching a cigarette, the other applying his lighter.

Lamb said, "Keep your hair on. It's one of those e-cigarettes."

"No it's not," Ho pointed out.

"It's not?" Lamb examined the burning end suspiciously. "Crap. I've been ripped off."

Ho cut his grumbled protest short when he realised Lamb had spotted the parking permit on his windscreen. "It's cover," he said.

"Cover," Lamb repeated.

"And a safeguard against identity theft."

Lamb's laughter was two parts cough. He exhaled so much smoke he resembled a damp bonfire. "Identity theft? Trust me, kid. You couldn't give yours away."

Ho scowled.

Behind him, Lamb settled back and closed his eyes. Something erupted from his lips — the beginning of a snore or the end of a chuckle, hard to say — but after that he fell more or less silent while Roderick Ho, guided by satnav, drove them through and then out of the city, towards where Catherine was being held, or where they hoped she was being held.

"Diana," Tearney said.

"I was just leaving."

"Of course, my dear. Absolutely no need for you to stay late."

"It's already after —"

"But I was wondering whether you'd signed off on the invoices for the Data Removal people."

Data Removal, rather than simply removal: these people were, after all, specialists, even if the end result was that boxes had been taken from one place to another.

Dame Ingrid followed Diana into her office, whose lighting automatically came on; a cool blue which approximated to spring sunshine, though caused the hairs on the back of one's neck to prickle; a sensation Ingrid ascribed to an excess of electricity in the air, as if it leaked out through ill-fitting sockets. Strange how those hairs kept up their work, stoking creepy feelings, when the hair on the rest of her head had parted company with her when she was in her teens. No completely satisfying reason had ever been put forward for this, though Dame Ingrid would reluctantly admit that that was less a failing of medical science than an indication of her own disinclination to be, in the circumstances, completely satisfied.

Diana Taverner ran a word search without sitting down, frowning slightly as she bent over her screen, watching a jumble of folder names weave in and out of themselves, none of them yielding the information she sought. "It's somewhere here."

"No hurry, my dear."

She had learned long ago that the best way to fluster a subordinate was to assure them there was no need to hurry.

While waiting, Dame Ingrid gazed through the office's glass wall at the kids on the hub; "kids" being the term regardless of age and experience. Loyalty had brought them to work here, though loyalty was an infinitely variable term; it began with a commendable desire to serve queen and country; could ascend to the even more virtuous heights of swearing fealty to the head of their service, but at its worst could degenerate into a no-questions-asked desire to please their immediate superior, in this case Diana Taverner. If more than luck was involved in today's sudden reversal of fortune, then whatever it was was likely to have its roots in this department: Ops. Of course, Diana was more than capable of implementing skull-duggery on her own, but if it turned out she'd suborned her crew into helping with the dirty work, there'd have to be a purge. Which was fine: a good purge never hurt anyone. Well, except for those it hurt, but that was rather the point.

All of which was jumping the gun. If there'd been more than luck involved, she needed to know why, and what the endgame was.

"Here you go."

The abruptness with which she spoke suggested that Diana Taverner was keen to be on her way. So Dame Ingrid waited a moment longer, lost in contemplation, before saying, "Ah, good. Yes. Would you print it out for me? I do find screens a nuisance, don't you? At our age?"

Diana ate that one, but didn't enjoy it. Two seconds later, the printer on the shelf behind her burped into life, and she handed the product to Dame Ingrid.

Who, after a moment or two's study, said, "Expensive."

"It was a problem," Diana said. "It's been solved. Anyway, I thought Finance were pleased? Didn't you say so this morning?"

"I may have sweetened their response for the benefit of the gentlemen present," Tearney said. "We girls have to look out for one another."

"We certainly do."

Dame Ingrid folded the invoice, glanced through the glass wall at the kids again, then said, "Does the name Sean Donovan mean anything?"

"Should it?"

"It's a simple question, Diana."

"I can have him checked out —"

"Personally. Do you have any personal knowledge of Sean Donovan?"

"The name rings a vague bell," Taverner said. She adopted a thinking-about-it expression, swiftly replaced by one of dawning comprehension. "Didn't he sit on a joint intelligence committee years back? Carrying bags for the MoD?"

"And you've had no contact since?"

"We didn't exactly have contact then. He was just another uniform, one with hands-on experience of tackling insurgency."

"I see."

"Why do you ask? Is there anything I should know?" She indicated her team. "Anything we should be doing?"

Dame Ingrid subjected her to a long abstracted stare, as if she were trying very hard to remember something, and Diana happened to be in the way. It was a technique that could drag information from the most unwilling subordinate, but in this instance Diana maintained an expression of very slight concern mingled with willingness to help which at no point lapsed into speech. At length, Dame Ingrid shook her head. "No, my dear. His name came up, that's all." She waved the sheet of paper. "I'm sure this is fine. As you say, it's a problem solved. Short-term cost, long-term benefit."

"As per the brief."

"Material up to Virgil level, correct?"

294

"Up to and including. Again, as per the brief," said Diana. "Is there a problem, Ingrid? You look alarmed."

"Alarmed? Of course not. I'm sorry to have kept you, Diana. Enjoy your evening."

The corridors were quiet now. Even the clacking of her own heels sounded disjointed to her ears, as if slightly out of synch with her legs.

Back in her office she sat, not at her desk, but in the armchair in one corner, next to which was a low coffee table. It was where she sat when she took a gin and tonic of an evening: a quiet reward for a day well spent. Where she sat when preparing for her occasional public appearances, gingering up a phrase or two to be tweeted and tittered about in equal measure. And it was where she sat when she needed cover; when her desk felt too exposed.

There was a general belief among her staff, Dame Ingrid knew, that she was unaware that the current security codes were based on Thunderbirds, but it suited her to be underestimated in matters of no consequence. She was certain that the majority of her staff regarded her as pen-pusher-in-chief. She was also certain that the brief handed to Diana Taverner did not include relocating files classed Virgil, since Dame Ingrid had long determined that second-level secrets formed the perfect hiding place. Scott was where the sexy stuff hid: the cloak-and-dagger material that was any service's crown jewels. Virgil, for the most part, concealed data only of interest to a devoted number-cruncher with a fetish for budgetary matters: how much was spent on upgrading software, or subsidising the canteen, or replacing carpets. So, if Dame Ingrid had any black secrets hidden among the Service archives, Virgil was where they would be nesting.

And any keen Ingrid Tearney watcher knew that, far from being a mere pen-pusher-in-chief, she had black secrets.

After a while, she produced her mobile from her bag.

Nick Duffy answered on the first ring.

"There's been a change of plan," she said.

CHAPTER
TWELVE

River didn't drop more than a foot or so, landing on the cement floor with enough of a bump to remind every last bone of the debt he owed Nick Duffy. A thought filed away for later.

He called up to Louisa. "Okay."

She followed, landed with more grace, and immediately played her torch beam around the chamber. Up and down the walls blue and red cables ran in banded clumps, disappearing at floor and ceiling. In the middle, a wheel-shaped handle set horizontally on a concrete block looked like it would open a sewer.

"What's that?" River asked.

"Some kind of drain?"

"No, what you're holding."

"A torch."

"I can see that. Why's it shaped like a pig?"

"It just is."

"Okay."

"It's the torch I keep in my glove compartment, all right? If I'd known we'd be exploring, I'd have packed more appropriately."

"Fair enough," said River. "Point it over here a moment."

He'd found what looked like a fuse box on the wall, held shut by a metal clasp.

Louisa held the beam steady while River tugged at the clasp, which looked at first like it was going to defeat him. But when it gave, the box's door swung open to reveal a remarkably pristine-looking rotary dial phone.

"You or me?" he asked.

"You do it."

He reached for the receiver, but before his hand got there, the phone rang.

She'd heard once of a long-distance hiker, way before the days of e-readers, who'd carried a novel over the Alps, tearing out and discarding each page as he read it, to lighten his load. There was a lot to be said for that. For a baggage-free existence, each moment of your story jettisoned as soon as done; your future pristine, undiluted by all that's gone before. You'd always be on the first page. Never have to turn back, relive your mistakes.

Here in the hot room, Catherine had grown mildly delirious, but not so much that she couldn't appreciate this for what it was. It was ever so slightly like being what people called "drunk". Amateurs, that is; those who'd never really been drunk a day in their lives — and anyone who'd only been drunk a day hadn't come close to being drunk.

The bottle still sat on its tray, barely camouflaged by the sandwich, the apple, the flapjack, the water. These, she had mentally discarded. The colour of the sky

298

through the window told her it had been a full day since she'd stepped onto the street to hear a ghost's whisper: *Catherine?* Like most things, this whole episode could have been avoided by minute adjustment. If she'd turned, like any good spook should have done, and headed back into Slough House the moment Sean Donovan appeared, this wouldn't be happening. One word from her to Charles Partner, and the wheels of the Service would have ground into action. That was the advantage of being close to the man at the top. When there was trust between you, a simple word got things done.

Except Charles Partner was dead, having emptied his head in a bathtub. Her boss now was Jackson Lamb, and stirring him into action required more than trust.

She had mentally discarded the water, the flapjack, the apple, the sandwich, because this was not their fight. In the struggle for control of the room, there was only herself and the bottle of wine. And for some reason this was no longer on the tray, but had managed to spirit itself across the space between them, like a spooky puppet in a horror film, and now nestled in her hand.

Well, that was fine. If there was to be a struggle, it made sense that she kept a tight grip on herself; and keeping a tight grip on the bottle too underlined the symbiotic nature of their relationship. The bottle held the key to her past; all those pages she'd tried to throw away, she could reread every last one simply by unscrewing its cap and draining its contents. Of course, in allowing her to do that the bottle would be giving up its own future — becoming nothing more than an empty vessel — but that was the nature of co-dependency: one of you had to die. Look at Charles Partner.

She was upright on the bed, her back against the wall. The bottle felt comfortable in her hand, its contours moulded to fit, and the seal on its cap was such a flimsy thing, so very ripe for twisting . . .

All those evenings in Jackson Lamb's office, watching him punish much larger bottles: that should have been the sterner test. Instead, here she was, on her own, and in danger of falling. Which was starting to feel not so much like falling, but simply relaxing; subsiding into who she'd always been, despite her efforts to convince herself otherwise.

It wasn't such a very grave betrayal, was it?

She cocked her head and listened, as if expecting the voices to return and whisper the answer in her ear. But nothing happened. A far-off car changed gear somewhere, and that was all. The room seemed to grow a shade darker. But this always happened to rooms, this time of evening. There was nothing to be read in that. It was simply another moment to tear off and throw away.

Almost involuntarily, Catherine twisted the cap and broke the seal.

The voice was electronically treated, and sounded the way a dustbin might.

"Hold your Service card up in front of you."

"I can't see a camera," River said.

300

"You don't need to see a camera. The camera sees you."

Behind him, Louisa rolled her eyes.

Fishing his card out, River held it up at eye level. Despite the receiver tucked to his ear, this felt like having a conversation with a ghost.

In the same electric monotone, the voice recited his Service number.

"Okay," River said. "I believe you. There's a camera."

"Your card's not biometric."

"Yeah, they didn't get around to renewing ours yet." Or ever.

"River Cartwright," the voice said. "Now the woman."

River moved aside, still holding the receiver, and Louisa showed her card to the empty space above the phone.

In River's ear, the voice recited numbers again, then said, "Louisa Guy. But her hair has changed colour."

"Your hair's changed colour," River told her.

"Yeah, that happens."

The voice said, "Where is Slough House?"

"Is this a quiz?"

"Where is Slough House?"

"Aldersgate Street."

"You're not from the Park."

"No," he said patiently. "We're from Aldersgate Street. We need to consult the records that were moved here last month."

Silence.

"You know which records I'm talking about?"

"I wasn't told this was happening."

"Yeah, but you were probably told it might," River said. "At an unspecified time in the future."

Silence.

"This is that unspecified time," River said.

"You have authorisation?"

"Verbal."

"I can't let you in without seeing written authorisation."

Louisa, leaning in close so she could hear, said, "You've seen our cards. They check out with what's on your screen, right?"

"Except I've never heard of Slough House."

"No, well, you wouldn't. You're hired help."

River gave her a warning nudge, and said, "Slough House is need-to-know. I can't say any more over an open line."

"This isn't an open line."

"Yeah, okay. But you're familiar with the protocol."

"I did a course," the voice said.

"He did a course," Louisa murmured.

"If our cards were fakes, you'd already have sounded the alarm. We all know you haven't done that. So let us in, okay?"

Louisa leaned in again. "This is an important mission we're on. It's Scott level. Okay?"

"Scott level?"

River said, "Not on the phone. Let us in, we'll explain everything."

There was a pause, a not-quite silence during which the speaker's breathing was translated into the same electronic dustbin whisper. And then the click of a connection being broken.

And then another, louder, grating noise, as the wheel-shaped handle on the concrete block behind them, released from its hidden locking mechanism, shifted upwards an inch or two.

Lamb gazed with dismay at fields on both sides of the motorway; thankfully disappearing into gloom now, they still covered more of the near-distance than was acceptable. Dotted among them were houses; sometimes in small bunches of four or five; more often set by themselves, surrounded by open spaces.

"You'd better be right about this," he told Ho. "If you've dragged me into this godforsaken wilderness on a fancy goose chase, you can say goodbye to your annual bonus."

This particular stretch of godforsaken wilderness was six lanes wide and medium-busy.

Ho said, "I get an annual bonus?"

"No. Weren't you listening?" Lamb was visibly toying with lighting another cigarette, though possibly even he had started to notice that the air in the car was barely this side of toxic. "God, look at it. There are folk living out here have probably never seen a taxi."

This depressed him enough that he went ahead and lit his cigarette anyway.

"It's the kids I feel sorry for," he went on, words he'd almost certainly never used before in a single sentence. "Growing up miles from civilisation. Learn to hot-wire a car, or you're stuck here till they plant you."

"I can hot-wire a car."

"Huh. I always assumed it was Longridge had the criminal youth," said Lamb. "Not to resort to stereotypes or anything. But he is, well . . ." He paused. "You know."

". . . Black?"

"From the East End. Jesus, you immigrants are quick with the racist jibes, aren't you?"

"I —"

"Where'd you learn to hot-wire, anyway? I thought all you did was exercise your wrists." Lamb supplied a demonstrative gesture, halfway between working a keyboard and milking a cow, then leered. "One way or the other."

"The internet's full of information," Ho said. "That makes me an expert at lots of things."

"It's full of pornography too," Lamb observed. "Doesn't make you Casanova. What's your thingamajig say?"

Ho checked his satnav. "Exit after next."

"Good. And I hope you've been working on a plan." Lamb collapsed back into a Toad of Toad Hall slump. "Because I haven't."

Ho grinned nervously, caught sight of Lamb's face in the mirror, and stopped.

It was somehow inevitable, Louisa thought, that the dustbin voice, decoded, would belong to a man who looked like a broomstick: one of those straight-up straight-down bodies on whom elbows, wrists and knees look painful, as if grafted on in the aftermath of tragedy. He wore a short-sleeved white shirt buttoned to the neck over brown corduroy trousers, and was compensating for the thinness of his pale red hair by growing a moustache. It was impossible to tell how long he'd been working on this, and nearly as difficult to refrain from suggesting he stop. Even to Louisa's mind, and men weren't currently anywhere near the top of the list of things she cared about, the sparse carroty wisps on this one's upper lip seemed like an act of self-harm.

His name, he'd told them, once they'd opened the airlock-type hatchway and climbed down the metal ladder to the air-conditioned facility beneath, was Douglas.

"First name or last?" she asked, as the hatchway door swung shut above them, and locked itself in response to a switch Douglas threw.

"First."

"Okay."

"I'm not going to tell you my last name."

". . . Okay."

"Can't be too careful," he explained.

Which was true enough, but it would be unkind to point out that that particular ship had sailed, where Douglas was concerned.

The room was large and bright, most of its visible surfaces one type of shiny metal or another. Against one wall was a work console, its swivel chair bobbing jauntily now Douglas had vacated it, and the panel of monitors he'd been looking at were evidently CCTV, because Louisa recognised on one screen the chamber they'd just left. Others showed various angles of the wasteground outside, already looking gloomier than ten minutes ago; others still must have been internal, and displayed doors, corridors, and several warehouse-like spaces filled with industrial-sized shelving, on which were ranged rows of packing crates, boxes, and what looked like miles of paperwork in box files and cardboard folders. Among them, no doubt, the Grey Books. She wondered how the cataloguing worked — without a system, they could pick through that lot from now until Christmas, and never find what they were looking for.

Still, at least she'd be cool . . . Louisa couldn't help what she did next: she raised her arms, aeroplane mode, and allowed refrigerated air to creep under her blouse and stroke her skin.

Douglas was watching her. "Your hair really has changed colour, you know," he told her.

"It was deliberate."

"Disguise, sort of thing?"

"Yes," she said. "That sort of thing."

River said, "How big's your team down here?"

Douglas gave him a superior look which fitted him about as well as his moustache. "That's classified."

"Classified," said River. "Gotcha." He paused. "Can I see your Service card?"

"My what?"

"Your Service card. To verify your security rating."

". . . I don't have a Service card."

"Right."

"I'm not Service. You already know that."

"Right," River said. "But see, that's where the whole classified thing gets complicated. Because my security rating's higher than yours. You know, because you haven't got one."

"I've been vetted," Douglas said.

"That's obvious," Louisa began, but ran so smoothly into her next sentence that River's warning glance was unnecessary. "You're in charge of this facility, you've got a lot of . . . equipment, there's no way you got here without undergoing pretty vigorous assessment." She tugged at her blouse again, allowing more air to circulate. "But we get ridden pretty hard too, Douglas, which is how come we're cleared for the serious stuff. You know, the full-on hardcore action . . . Do you know what I mean, Douglas?"

Douglas cleared his throat. "Ungh. I mean, I think so."

River seemed to be having an allergic reaction to the chilled air: he'd put finger and thumb to his nose, and was squeezing hard.

"That's good, Douglas." Louisa released her blouse, and ran a hand through her hair. "So that puts us on the same side, doesn't it?"

". . . Um, yes. I guess so."

"That's lovely. How many others are down here with you, Douglas?"

"Er . . . right now? Or usually?"

"Right now."

"None."

"How about usually?" River asked.

"Well, usually . . . none."

"None," said River.

"Except there's a walk-through once a week. My boss does a sweep, makes sure everything's how it should be." He raised a finger to his upper lip, checking on his moustache's progress. "The rest of the time, we're on our own."

"We?" said Louisa.

"Me and Max." Douglas coloured slightly. "It's what I call my computer."

"You've given your computer a name," Louisa said, without inflection.

"It's voice-responsive."

So was Louisa's keyring, but she hadn't formed a club with it.

Douglas tugged at his collar, in unconscious imitation of Louisa's cooling-down procedure. "So, er, what exactly is it you guys are after? Is it about that pair who were here earlier?"

"Which pair's that?" River asked.

"Wandering around up there. Between the buildings."

"One in his fifties, grey hair, well built? The other one shaven-headed?"

"Yeah, that sounds like them. Only we get a lot of hobos up there, well, obviously. But these guys were different."

"Don't worry," Louisa told him. "They're not a problem."

"We get film crews too sometimes. It's a good place to blow up a car."

"I'll bear that in mind."

308

"It's funny, they'll be out there making a movie, and here I am watching, and they don't even know I'm here. It's like . . ." He meshed fingers, demonstrating the interconnected complication of real life and fantasy playing out in parallel, some of it above ground, some of it underneath. "I get a kick out of that."

"Uh-huh," said Louisa.

"Kids screwing in cars, too. That happens a lot."

"How long have you been here?"

"Three years."

It was on the tip of Louisa's tongue to ask how long the shifts were, but she decided she didn't want to know. The possibility that Douglas had spent three years on his own here, without a break, was seeming likelier by the minute.

River was looking at the bank of monitors, and the lifeless scenes they displayed. He indicated the one showing the warehoused crates and box files. "Is that the stuff that was delivered last month?"

Douglas reluctantly shifted his gaze from Louisa. "Yeah. It took them two days."

"That must have been exciting," Louisa said. "I mean, compared to . . ."

Absolutely bugger-all happening is what she meant, but Douglas begged to differ.

"Oh, it's always exciting. *Nobody knows I'm here.*"

This last in a whisper, as if the surreptitious nature of his role extended to all discussion of it.

"But it was pretty cool when the phone rang," he admitted. "I thought it had actually, you know. Happened."

"... 'Happened'?"

"Yeah, you know. I mean, this place was designed as a survival facility. I thought maybe there'd been an . . . event."

A dirty bomb or a toxic splash, he meant; something to drive city dwellers underground. Or at least, those whose security clearances allowed them access to survival facilities.

"But it turned out a false alarm."

"That must have been very disappointing."

"Yeah, well. Shit happens."

River said, "So how far away is it?"

"The stuff they delivered? Other end of that corridor." He pointed to a pair of doors on the far side of the room. "You need some of it back?"

"Something like that."

"Yeah, well. I guess you got the clearance."

"Oh, and another thing," Louisa said. "That pair you noticed earlier? Up in the world? They're going to join us."

"They're with you?"

"They are," said River.

"No problem. All they have to do is show their passes, I'll let 'em in."

"Yes, see, that's where we go off-book," Louisa explained.

Douglas looked from one to the other, waiting for the punchline.

"It's okay, Douglas," River assured him. "We're from Slough House."

310

Evenings were long now, but hardly endless; shadows had crept across the scabbed and tacky concrete apron between the derelict buildings, and the trains that trundled past increasingly resembled boxes of light, more strongly outlined the darker it got. The two soldiers had followed the Slough House pair into the factory five minutes ago, and the phone in Nick Duffy's hand was now a grenade. Dame Ingrid's call — *There's been a change of plan* — had primed it, and the calls he'd made since had set the timer running.

To a few of the Dogs he could trust: those who knew how the real world worked, and how sometimes you had to tie a black ribbon round events without asking awkward questions.

To a suit the website listed as a company director of Black Arrow, and who it didn't take long to persuade to unleash his cut-price commandos.

And to his girlfriend, cancelling their evening. That was the one he'd end up paying for, but nobody had ever pretended his job was an easy one.

From his window on the third floor, Duffy tried to picture forthcoming events. There was no such thing as a watertight plan, and any operation had the potential to go tits up, but he'd had a clear go-ahead from Dame Ingrid: that the worst-case scenario involved Sean Donovan walking away. Whatever else, that wasn't to happen.

So: flood the area.

Because if Black Arrow weren't anyone's idea of crack troops, there were at least plenty of them. Plus, they'd be fired up by notions of honour and revenge: Duffy had told the suit that tonight's target was the man responsible for murdering Sly Monteith. *We'll be taking him off the board.* They loved that talk, the deskbound warriors: they were all for pouring men onto the field of battle. *Let's do this thing,* he'd replied, like a man buckling on a holster and heading for the O.K. Corral. It hadn't worried him that his Black Arrow team were amateurs, barely kitted out for crowd control: truncheons, tear gas, maybe Tasers, a flash bomb or two. Still, they'd soak up whatever ammo the soldiers were packing. Then Duffy would step in with his hand-picked pros and finish the job.

He surveyed the ground through his binoculars again, getting a mental fix on lines of approach and areas of cover: the skip, that pile of fencing. The complex that lay beneath stretched way into the distance, but he'd factored that in: there was a main entrance a mile or so south, and a Black Arrow crew should be arriving there — he checked his watch — any minute now.

Right on cue, his phone trembled in his breast pocket.

"Can I speak to Alice?"

"Sorry, wrong number," said Duffy.

If it had been Betty who was sought it would have meant things were Buggered, but Alice signified A-okay, meaning the other team was at the front entrance. There were fifteen of them, Black Arrow irregulars, plus two of his own. His pair were coordinating events, but the Black Arrows themselves

312

would take out the security guards, which was only fair: security here, as at other low-priority Service posts, was outsourced, so it was one set of dobbins against another.

That done, they were essentially drain cleaner: they'd flush through the system, pushing the blockage towards the only other outlet: the hatchway in the dead factory down below. When Donovan and the others emerged back onto the wasteground, Duffy was here to make sure they got no further. Chances were, things wouldn't go the distance: a bit of luck, there wouldn't be bodies left in the open.

Bodies there would be, though, and no one was getting a free pass. He mused briefly on River Cartwright and Louisa Guy. Cartwright was a pain in the neck, overdue an accident, but Duffy couldn't help feel a niggle when he thought about Guy. It wasn't so long ago her boyfriend was smeared across a road round Blackfriars way: something of a professional embarrassment for Duffy. So maybe that niggle was guilt, or maybe just irritation at a bad memory, but either way, wiping the slate clean tonight would put it behind him. So no hard feelings to Louisa Guy, but really, she should have made the effort to be luckier.

"The Slough House crew too?" he'd asked Tearney.

He hadn't wanted any ambiguity hanging over this one.

"All of them," Tearney had said. And then, just to be clear, "The Slough House crew too."

So be it.

Phone stowed in his pocket, Duffy continued his appraisal of the ground below, while light crept away and shadows spilled out from their corners.

Fourteen minutes by the clock on the dash, and Marcus was still on the pavement, arguing with the policeman. It would have been quicker to take the points, pay the fine, do a short jail sentence, but any of that would have involved admitting culpability: not something that came easily to a man who used to kick down doors, and would probably do so again, if aggravated enough. Which could happen, if the fourteen minutes stretched out much longer.

Standard procedure, Shirley thought — watching from the passenger seat of the SUV — should have had her out there with him, because arguments with uniforms were one of the things she did best, even — especially — when her side didn't have a leg to stand on. But cops have a sixth sense for naughtiness, and she didn't want to face a drugs test: not for a couple of hours, or maybe a fortnight. Besides, Marcus could handle himself. Worse came to worst, he probably knew fifteen ways of killing an unarmed opponent. More, if he was allowed to use both hands.

Such talents had been wasted in Slough House, of course. And even that was history now. Awareness of this was starting to penetrate: tomorrow, Shirley would wake up, groan at the thought of what the day held, then realise it didn't any more. That what she'd become was worse than a slow horse: she was an ex-slow horse, with neither plans nor prospects.

314

And if Marcus decked the policeman, he'd find out the hard way what being cut loose from the Service meant.

The road was still busy, because other people still had occupations. Pedestrians slowed as they passed, lit by schaden-freude, and Marcus had folded his arms, which made Shirley want to adopt the crash position. If he blew his top, if he got arrested, they weren't going anywhere, and if they weren't going anywhere . . . It was a sentence that didn't require completion.

No, what they needed was for something bad to be going down, for River and Louisa to be in dire peril. What Shirley and Marcus needed was to turn up just in time to rescue them, or failing that, only very slightly too late — casualties would be acceptable, but only if Shirley and Marcus bagged the villains at the scene. Because any blood would be on Lamb's hands: his operation, his disaster. And nothing would give Shirley greater pleasure than to rise like a phoenix from one of that bastard's mattress fires; to stage the greatest comeback since Lazarus, and be welcomed home to Regent's Park for averting a national security disaster. First thing she'd do would be send Lamb a postcard. *Wish you were here?* Ha-de-fucking-ha.

But before any of that could happen, Marcus had to not blow his top.

While she was waiting for him not to do that, Shirley bent to her smartphone and accessed the Service intranet. It was a damp-squib moment of relief to find her password hadn't been cancelled, but that was Lamb all over: without Catherine Standish to keep him organised, it wouldn't occur to him to follow through on his drive-by management decisions. Thanks for nothing, Shirley thought, navigating her way onto Citizens Records, the database the Service maintained on those it existed to protect, and who at the same time represented the greatest threat to national security: the people. This was one of those ironies you were encouraged to get over early in your spook career. One Snowden per generation was reckoned one too many.

Trying to focus, trying not to feel the fizzy moments still coursing through her bloodstream — Jesus, one little taste: it's not like Lamb didn't hobble round on a nicotine crutch — she pulled up the file on Sean Donovan, and found everything just as River Cartwright had summarised: the military career, the MoD secondment, the UN posting. And then the night it went to hell, when he crashed a jeep on his way home from delivering a lecture to a bunch of cadets. His passenger, one Captain Alison Dunn, had died when the car rolled into a ditch; Donovan was reckoned lucky not to have written himself off too, though there'd doubtless been times since when he'd wished he had been. From international postings to a brick cage. That ever happened to Shirley, she'd find a way of offing herself. Or at any rate of hurting herself badly enough to be put on a morphine drip while her sentence played out.

The files were cross-referenced, hyperlinked, so it was a moment's work to run down Donovan's connections.

And this, Shirley discovered, was a moment Cartwright obviously hadn't taken, because if he had, the information he'd have found would have been up front and centre when he laid out Donovan's CV.

Marcus was still arguing with the cop. The cop was still visibly wondering whether, if he Tasered Marcus, the paperwork would take all week. Shirley watched them for a moment, glanced down at the smartphone again, and decided enough was enough.

She leaned on the horn.

Obedient to his satnav's demands, Roderick Ho left the motorway at the next exit, and immediately the world became darker, quieter, the ambient hum of the mindless traffic fading to a mosquito buzz. The exit inclined towards a roundabout from which Ho peeled off onto a minor road, its edges potholed and broken, and over which trees dangled foliage like fishermen hoping for a bite. Theoretically trees were a good thing, lungs of the planet, and Ho didn't mind them in parks, but out here they loomed too large, the way unleashed dogs acquired extra menace. They cast their shadows as if it were only by their permission that traffic was allowed to pass beneath, and Roddy Ho felt what he'd have called a threat to his sense of self, were such terms available to him. Instead, he simply noted that they were fucking creepy, and constituted a hazard. He made a mental note to do something about them, saved it in the folder *When I'm King*, and checked satnav again. Their target location was half a mile ahead.

"Slow down," Lamb said.

"I am slowing down."

"Well slow down faster."

Ho came to a stop in what passed for a lay-by.

"Kill the engine."

Silence followed, though it was only silence if you were used to city noise. The car ticked, and nature rustled. Through Ho's open window, warm sticky air trickled in.

He couldn't see the farmhouse they were heading for. Half a mile: Ho didn't really have a sense of what half a mile meant. The trees lining one side of the road were just that, a line of trees. On the other, they were a wood; trees hiding behind other trees, so all he could see was darkness getting darker. He glanced in the mirror. Lamb's face was immobile; his eyes somehow absent. Ho wanted to ask what they did next, but didn't dare, so just sat gazing at the empty road, which turned a bend a short distance ahead, leaving him looking at even more trees.

Do something, Marcus Longridge had said.

Well, here he was, doing something. It was just that he didn't precisely know what. But if Catherine Standish was being held prisoner in the house up ahead, however far away it was, then the something was going to involve getting out of the car, and Ho wasn't sure he liked the sound of that.

Lamb was foraging about in the footwell, and when he straightened was holding the polystyrene cup. He'd been using it as an ashtray, which at least meant some of his filth had been contained, but even as Ho

318

watched he dumped its contents onto the seat next to him.

"Got any change?" he asked.

". . . Change?"

"Loose coins. Any kind'll do."

Ho found some silver in his wallet.

Lamb put it in the cup and jiggled it, so the coins splashed against each other. Then he opened the door. "If I'm not back in twenty minutes, do something."

". . . Like what?"

"Well I don't fucking know, do I? Google 'cunning plan', see what the internet suggests."

"What are you going to do?"

"I haven't decided yet. But it'll involve fetching Standish back. I'd forgotten what it was like not having a buffer between me and you lot, and I'm not enjoying it one bit."

"Have you got a gun?"

"No."

"What if they have?"

"Your concern is touching. I'll be all right."

"But what if . . ."

Lamb leaned through Ho's open window. "What if they come after you? With guns?"

"Yes."

"You'll be fine. Getting shot's like falling off a log. It doesn't take practice."

He walked off down the road and melted into the twilight as if it owned him; as if country shadows were no more foreign to him than any other kind. And Lamb, Ho reflected, belonged in the shadows — not a thought he'd formed himself, but one he remembered Catherine Standish articulating. Lamb was a creature of the half-light. The notion made Ho shudder. He checked the clock so he'd know when his twenty minutes were up, and when he looked back at the road, Lamb was gone.

Do something.

Roderick Ho hadn't the faintest clue what.

He hoped Lamb returned before it became an issue.

Douglas said, "You're bastards, you know that?"

River partly agreed, but sometimes being a bastard was the best way of getting things done. Even slow horses know that. Douglas hadn't wanted to cooperate, and neither of them had wanted to hurt him, but in the end it didn't take more than a minute to work out how to open the hatchway, because the switches on Douglas's console were neatly labelled, one reading HATCH. Douglas had watched the monitors with a bitter expression as Donovan and Traynor dropped into the chamber beneath the factory floor; had snorted with disgust when they descended the ladder into the facility itself.

"This'll all be reported," he told them.

"Even the part where you groped my tits?" Louisa asked.

"I never — I wasn't —"

River said, "Douglas. Keep your cool, don't be an idiot, and you might come out of this with your job intact."

Reaching the floor, Donovan and Traynor scanned the facility like they were used to such places.

"Is he all there is?" Traynor asked.

"Yes," Louisa said.

"And is he going to be a good boy?"

"Yes."

"Well make sure he sits somewhere quietly and touches nothing."

"They want you to sit somewhere quietly," Louisa began, but Douglas snorted again.

"I heard."

River said, "The files are that way." He indicated the doors Douglas had pointed to earlier: swing doors with glass portholes, through which only darkness could be made out.

Traynor said, "Thanks. Now go sit with Igor."

Douglas said, "Igor?"

"I'm not sitting anywhere," River said.

"Nobody puts Baby in a corner," Louisa muttered.

River ignored her. "The deal is, we let you have the Grey Books, then everybody leaves. Nobody said anything about letting you wander round —"

"If he doesn't shut up, can I pop him?" Traynor asked Donovan.

River, being River, took a step forward at this, a move Traynor seemed to be expecting. They were an inch off bumping chests when Louisa laughed. "Why don't you just get them both out? I expect Douglas has a tape measure."

Donovan said, "Okay, pack it in. That includes you." This to Louisa. Then to Traynor: "Wait here. Don't shoot anyone unless you have to."

Traynor nodded, and dropped his hand to his belt, brushing his shirt tail aside. The movement revealed, as it was intended to, the handle of a gun.

River rolled his eyes, making sure Traynor noticed.

Donovan said, "I'm not going to say it again. Behave yourself or he'll put a bullet in your knee."

Then he strode to the swing doors, pushed through, and disappeared into the corridor beyond.

"Marcus."

"Fucking moron copper. That light was amber. I had *ample* time."

"Marcus."

"He's lucky I didn't —"

"Marcus."

"What?"

Asking the question but not in a way that suggested he wanted an answer: it was one of those *whats* that mean *I'm still talking*. But as he asked it he registered the expression on her face, so he said it again, "What?" and this time meant it.

"There were two soldiers, right?" she said. "Donovan and Traynor."

"Yeah, they joined Black Arrow at the same time." He started the car, and glanced bitterly into the mirror, where he could see the policeman at the kerb, studying Marcus's departure as if willing some further infraction to be made: a failed indicator, mirror neglect, high treason.

"Benjamin Traynor served with Donovan," Shirley said. "He was honourably discharged about the time Donovan came out of the clink."

"So? They were mates. Soldier buddies, they're not gunna let a thing like a little jail time come between them."

"Yeah, right. Except. Alison Dunn? The woman who was killed in Donovan's car that night?"

"What about her?"

"She was Traynor's fiancée," Shirley said.

Lights through windows leaked a pallid yellow into the evening sky; an hour from now they'd be beacons, but for the moment seemed an admission of weakness. The farmhouse was stone, with a brick addition on one wing, and the front door had a small porch arrangement, a wooden afterthought which one big storm or one bad wolf might easily render kindling. And there was a bus on the forecourt, a London familiar made strange by dislocation; an open-topped tour bus, its upper deck swaddled in canvas to keep the rain off, a gesture that embraced both caution and optimism, given the heatwave.

If it had been a working farm, Lamb noted, there'd have been dogs barking. The only sound he could make out was an insect-like chirping.

He studied the house again. It would have an attic and cellar, and any hostage would be in one or the other. Himself, he'd have opted for the cellar. But there was something off about this whole affair — it had been tainted with unreality since the Grey Books were thrown into the mix — so chances were Standish was in the kitchen, brewing up a cuppa for whomever

Donovan had left in charge. Probably happier than she was in Slough House.

But she was one of his, and you messed with Lamb's stuff at your peril. Besides, the joes you didn't bring home were the ones who never let you go.

He rattled the polystyrene cup, and was rewarded with a silvery tinkle. If you were going to storm an enemy citadel, you might as well do it with flair — he kept a gun at Slough House, illegal, unofficial, and it might have been a useful piece of kit right now, but Lamb hadn't survived this far by getting into firefights with soldiers. Well, maybe just the once — and memory tugged at him again: the burning church, and gunfire in the snow. He shrugged it away.

In the porch he found a doorbell but used the rapper instead, pounding it as loudly as he could — a steady, unforgiving thunder that rattled the door on its hinges and travelled every inch of the building, swarming along its boards and beams as fluidly as a family of mice. *Bam bam bam bam bam*, and if it wouldn't raise the dead it might at least disturb the worms enjoying their corpses.

Without warning the door flew open, and the knocker was wrenched from his grip. "What do you want?" the answerer snarled. He was younger than Lamb might have expected: stocky, in an off-white short-sleeved shirt; his arms writhing with black-and-blue designs; his head hairless; his expression halfway between anger and alarm. Which was fine, thought Lamb, this was an audience he could work with, and without further warning he began to sing:

324

"We wish you a merry Christmas, we wish you a merry Christmas, we wish you a merry Christmas and a happy new year."

Not the most musical rendering ever, but, all things considered, not a bad stab at the melody.

Then he rattled the cup in his hand.

"It's for the kiddies and orphans," he explained. "Early, I know, but I like to beat the rush."

The man said, "What the *fuck*?"

CHAPTER
THIRTEEN

Catherine Standish admired the empty bottle. They were undervalued objects, empty bottles. In her time, she'd wasted fond glances on full ones, regarding the empties as little more than markers on a journey to oblivion: either the dark, dreamless cellar of sleep, or the labyrinth of alcoholic blackout, where hours were peeled invisibly away. Afterwards, you could examine yourself for clues to where you'd been and what you'd done there, but there was no retracing your steps through that maze. And empty bottles held no messages. Spin them any way you liked, they always pointed in the same direction: back into the darkness, to the discarded hours.

But this one she held now had a peculiar beauty of form. She knew it had rolled off a production line somewhere, that no glassworker had ever cradled its new-crafted shape in his hands; but still, looking at it, feeling it, enjoying its lightness in her grasp, she thought that of all the bottles she'd emptied in her life, she'd never encountered one with quite this much *amiability* — that was the word she'd been hunting. Amiability. Through all the afternoon's struggles, ever since Bailey had appeared with the tray, she had been thinking of this bottle as her enemy; something to be overcome, the way you would a snake in your garden. She hadn't appreciated that they were on the same side; that it had desired emptiness the same way she had wanted to empty it. Desire lies at the heart of all that's made of glass, she decided; glass is simply need given substance. You blow into it, and it assumes new shapes. Strike it in the wrong place, it shatters.

Well, she had fulfilled this one's secret desire, she thought. Its contents were now history.

A moment ago, she had thought she'd heard singing — you could almost call it singing; it had sounded like a Yuletide brawl — and wondered if this heralded the return of the voices. But all in all, Catherine decided, it didn't seem likely: a single day spent locked in an attic wasn't enough to send her spiralling back into the depths she'd spent years emerging from. And she had, after all, just poured the fucking Pinot down the sink. After a triumph like that, she was due a victory parade, not a relapse.

So she refilled the bottle with water and screwed its cap on tight. It balanced nicely in her hand, felt reasonably weighty. Bailey was young and fit, but Catherine Standish had wielded bottles before, and knew that an unexpected tap with even a small one could stop a fight before it started.

And next time he came through that door, gracious host or not, she'd show him what a journey into oblivion felt like.

Heading west, free of city traffic but snarled up among the heading-out-of-town kind, Marcus had slowed to a crawl. Another hold-up ahead. When they reached it, it would turn out to be nothing — a grease-spot on the tarmac; a balloon tied to a railing — but until then they'd shunt and curse like everybody else, which at least gave them time to argue about the significance of Shirley's discovery.

Marcus said, "It doesn't necessarily mean anything."

"You reckon?"

"They'd known each other a long time. They're soldier buddies. That's not the kind you break with easily, not after you've been in combat."

"Donovan killed Traynor's wife-to-be, Marcus. That's hardly the same league as, I dunno, crashing his car."

"Some men get very attached to their cars. But either way, she died in an accident. Maybe Traynor's got a forgiving nature."

"He fought in Afghanistan," Shirley said. "I don't think turning the other cheek was a big part of their training." She was still looking at her smartphone, tracking Alison Dunn through Service records. "She sat on that UN committee with Donovan," she went on.

"Do they even let soldiers marry each other?" Marcus wondered.

"There's a redacted bit here."

"Saying what?"

"It's redacted, stupid."

"I heard you the first time, dummy. But which bit precisely is redacted?"

Shirley said, "Right after she got back to the UK, after the UN thing I mean, she filed some kind of report. Whatever it said got stamped on from on high."

"Huh," said Marcus.

"Huh," Shirley repeated. "Very illuminating. What does 'huh' mean exactly?"

"In this context," Marcus said, " 'huh' means, sounds like political bullshit. And a good kind of bullshit not to get mixed up in is the political kind."

For no obvious reason, the traffic started to move more freely.

Shirley said, "So what's the new plan, you gonna turn around and drive us home?"

"No, I figure we'd better catch up with Louisa and Cartwright fast as we can."

"Why so?" Shirley asked, looking up from her screen.

"Because you see that black van up ahead?"

Shirley did.

"It says Black Arrow on the side," said Marcus. "And it looks like it's heading for the same place we are."

"Fuck off," said the man.

That was all, but he seemed to think it enough. He moved back, the better to slam the door in Lamb's face, but Lamb could move fast when he wanted, and a scuffed leather brogue, battle-hardened by years of contact with Lamb's foot, wedged itself into the gap before the wood hit the jamb.

"Not even a thruppenny bit?" he said. "It's in a good cause."

"Move your feet, old man."

"Sorry. Dancing's extra." Lamb pushed, his opponent stumbled backwards, and Lamb was inside, kicking the door shut behind him. In the same movement, he tossed the polystyrene cup at the man's face, relying on an instinctive reaction, and was rewarded by the man catching it neatly, leaving his stomach wide open . . . Lamb had no desire to embroil himself in hand-to-hand combat. Make it quick, then. Swinging his fist sideways, like he was ringing a bell, Lamb buried it in the man's midriff, and when he folded in half Lamb slapped both palms against his ears, almost hearing the explosion that must have caused inside his head. And there was always the possibility, he reminded himself as he brought his knee up into the waiting face, that he had the wrong house, so he went easier than he ought to have done; kept his hands on the man's ears and lowered him to the floor reasonably gently, then stepped back sharpish as blood poured from a broken face.

"That takes me back," Lamb said, though it was doubtful the man could hear him.

Rolling his victim over, Lamb found a gun in the waistband of his trousers. Well, that solved the problem of whether this was the right house, or at least excused the violence he'd just done the householder if it turned out not to be. Anyone who answered the door to a carol singer armed deserved all he got, thought Lamb piously. Ejecting the magazine, he slipped it into a

330

pocket, and tossed the gun through the nearest doorway. There was nobody else here, Standish aside. He'd have been shot by now otherwise.

He cleared his throat noisily, and glanced around as if for a spittoon. Then swallowed instead: good manners, as he was fond of explaining to his slow horses, cost nothing. There were stairs to the left, and several doorways other than the one he'd just tossed the gun through, but he'd almost certainly end up climbing the bloody stairs, so might as well get to it. He paused on the first landing to light a cigarette, but before doing so sniffed sharply. Why did this place smell of cheese, he wondered.

Not important. Cigarette in mouth, Lamb stomped his way upstairs.

River said, "So what's your bag, exactly?"

Traynor threw him a sardonic look, but didn't reply.

River was on the floor, back against the wall, a position which offered his sore stomach muscles some relief, though not so much that he was likely to think of Nick Duffy with fondness in the foreseeable future. Douglas, a yard or two away, looked like he was trying to will himself into a different universe; one in which he hadn't allowed River and Louisa through the hatch. That, or he was trying not to burst into angry tears. As for Louisa, she had disappeared into what River had come to recognise as her silent space: the one into which she wandered whenever her presence was unavoidable, but her full attention wasn't required. It was somewhere she'd spent a lot of time when she'd first been exiled to Slough House; now, since Min's death, it looked like she was planning on moving back there. Like revisiting a flat you'd once lived in, River thought: certain it was pokier than you remembered, but give it a day or two, it would be like you'd never left.

Above their heads, the CCTV monitors continued their automatic surveillance; blinking from coverage of the derelict estate through a montage of the empty corridors and rooms that stretched a mile beneath the western fringe of the capital. Traynor kept glancing at these, presumably checking on Donovan's progress.

He tried again. "UFOs? Most of the people who've had alien encounters, it's amazing they can spell 'UFO'. That your thing, Traynor? Or no, let me guess, it's Lady Di. You're one of those idiots thinks the Secret Service had her taken care of, on the orders of the Lizard Duke."

This time Traynor didn't even use the look. He just stared at River, unblinking, as if River were a buzzing insect: not worth the effort of getting up to squash.

"Because I've got to tell you," River said, "of all the sad-arsed nutjob theories out there, that one's got to be the saddest. You think word wouldn't have got out around the Service if that had been a hit?"

Traynor said, "From what I hear, you wouldn't get to know about it if the Service decided to put vinegar on its chips."

And then, just as River was congratulating himself on having provoked a rise out of him, Traynor's expression changed, and he gave his full attention to the monitors.

332

At the same moment Louisa came back from her silent space; she was standing, staring at the screens.

"Who the hell are they?" she asked.

Only Douglas remained sitting. The other three were on their feet, watching the monitors; specifically the one showing a corridor that had previously been empty but was now swarming with black-clad figures, masked and utility-belted, moving at a clip in what River could only assume was their direction.

After they left the main road the streets became narrower; tree-lined at first, giving way to rows of terraced housing, and then, as they approached the railway lines, increasingly run-down storage depots, warehouses, vacant yards. Traffic dwindled, and Marcus kept well back. When the Black Arrow van disappeared between a pair of darkened buildings, he carried straight on while Shirley twisted in her seat to observe its departure. "Some kind of industrial estate. That must be where the off-site facility is."

Marcus grunted, turned at the next corner, and parked in front of garage doors marked CONSTANTLY IN USE. "Wait here."

"Where —"

"I need something from the boot."

He got out and went round the back of the car. Shirley, about to follow, thought better of it, and sat pillaging her pockets instead, suddenly certain there was hidden treasure on her person — an overlooked wrap of coke was aiming high, but she'd been wearing the same jeans for a few days, and it wasn't unusual to come across the odd crumb of hash in its crevices, picked up on her night-time travels, and forgotten about in the heat of the . . . heat. But there was nothing. She reached for her jacket, ran her fingers down its seams — sometimes a pill could slip through to the lining. Nothing. Fuck. But it didn't matter. She was fine. Maybe Marcus kept something in the glove compartment — Jesus, aspirin, anything — but a quick rummage produced nothing more useful than an ancient roll of Polo mints and a few CDs that had lost their cases.

But she was fine, and didn't need a pick-me-up. Adrenalin would see her through. She didn't need Marcus telling her that; didn't even need the lecture from herself. So she flipped through the CDs as a way of clamping down on jittery feelings, and found an Arcade Fire bootleg from last year's Hyde Park show: way too cool for Marcus, so presumably one of his kids', which meant asking permission to borrow would result in tedious negotiation. On the other hand, it was a bootleg: the kid obviously had no copyright issues, rendering the "property" thing moot. She wasn't feeling jittery at all now, she noted, slipping the CD into her jacket pocket, and nearly jumped out of her skin when Marcus reappeared at the window.

"Don't *do* that."

"You okay?"

"I'm fine. Jesus." She squinted up at him. "You seriously planning on wearing that?"

That was a black baseball cap of the kind Marcus had worn in the crash squad, though without the skinny comms mic. He had it low over his brow, but with the peak upturned.

"It's what I'm used to."

"It stops the light reflecting off your bald patch, you mean." Shirley dumped her jacket on the seat behind, and clambered out of the car.

"You should put that on," Marcus told her.

"It's hot."

"A white T-shirt? You seriously want to do this wearing —"

"O-*kay*, okay." She grabbed the jacket and pulled it on. "Just because you're old enough to be my dad, you don't have to act like him."

"I am not old enough — forget it. You sure you're ready for this?"

"They're just a bunch of Saturday soldiers."

"Never underestimate your opponent. Especially when you don't know how many of them there are."

"It was a big van," Shirley admitted. "What do you reckon they're here for?"

"They're Donovan's crew. Or they were until he killed Monteith this afternoon. So maybe they're cool with that, and are here to help him with whatever it is he's doing. Or else —"

"Or else they're narked he whacked their boss and they're here to piss in his whisky."

"Yeah, something like that. Are you armed?"

"No. Are you?"

"No," said Marcus. "Well, a gun."

"That's kind of armed."

"It's not a big gun."

"You bring a spare?"

"What am I, your nanny? No I didn't bring a spare. This is a family car, not a roving arsenal. Now do your buttons up. Your T-shirt's showing."

Shirley did her buttons up, and the pair of them set off round the corner.

Nick Duffy checked his watch, wondered again where the hell the Black Arrow crew were, then exhaled when he saw the van appear below, coming to a halt with an unnecessary squeal of brakes near the pile of mesh fencing. Amateurs: they spilled out the back the way they'd seen it done in Vietnam movies, as if they'd set down in a chopper, and Charlie was lurking in the reeds.

But they didn't need to be good at what they did. They only had to be there, in large numbers.

Duffy counted a dozen before letting the binoculars fall to his chest. They were in full-on Cowboys and Indians mode, peeping out from behind whatever shelter they could find: the van itself, the skip, that pile of fencing. The Slough House crew's vehicle was available too: Cartwright and Guy were that keyed into undercover work, they'd parked it in full view of the slowly appearing stars. In a sense, he'd be doing everyone a favour, taking them off the board. And even as he had the thought, he was aware that this was the mood required for this kind of job: you had to be clear that what you were doing was for the common good, even of those you were doing it to.

All of them, Dame Ingrid had said. *The Slough House crew too.*

He watched the black-clad wannabes at work, some unpacking equipment from the back of their van — a pair of quick-assembly scaffolding towers on which Klieg lights perched — while others hopped and jumped from shadow to shadow, preparing their ground, and looking like they were having fun, but only because they'd never done this for real before. If he were of a sentimental persuasion, Duffy might have mused that once upon a time he'd been like that himself, but he wasn't, and he hadn't, so he simply stooped to the holdall at his feet and pulled out a black silk balaclava. Black for night, silk for coolness — even now, the heat persisted; like a bakery where the ovens had only just been turned off — but most of all, a balaclava so his face wasn't on show. When this was over, the Black Arrows were going to be left holding the body bags, and it would be nicer all round if they had no descriptions to chuck about.

Then he checked his guns, checked his ammunition, and went down to take charge.

On the top landing, Lamb found a padlocked door and thought: okay, that resembles a clue. The key was no doubt in Sunny Jim's pocket, and it wouldn't take two minutes to pop back downstairs and collect it, but it didn't look like anyone was about to volunteer, so he simply bellowed, "Standish? You might want to step back," and without further warning applied his foot. The first kick threw splinters and pulled the metal clasp holding the padlock halfway out of the frame. The second completed the job, and the door slammed inwards, hit the wall, and bounced back closed. In the split second between, he saw Catherine Standish, framed in another doorway, holding something in her hand. When he pushed the broken door open once more and stepped through it, she was still there, but her hands were empty.

Lamb looked at her, looked around the room, looked at her again, and said, "Thought this was a kidnapping, not an away-day."

"The lock was on the outside," she pointed out.

"I've seen more secure rabbit hutches." Walking past her, he poked his head through the doorway into the bathroom. "It's en suite, for God's sake."

"Maybe. But I requested non-smoking," she told him.

"That's a really bad habit, that passive-aggressive shit." But he lobbed his cigarette at the toilet anyway. It bounced off the seat, and disappeared behind the sink pedestal, where it probably wouldn't start a fire and burn the building down.

Catherine said, "What did you do with Bailey?"

"If he's the work-experience type they left in charge, he's having a lie-down. Another old flame, is he?"

"How much of a lie-down?"

"I didn't kill him, if that's what you're asking." Lamb had spotted the tray now, and made a beeline for it. "Don't get me wrong, I disapprove of Service

338

personnel being abducted. But it's not like you're important."

Deliberating for a moment, he scowled at the apple, pocketed the flapjack and tore open the sandwich.

"Who's with you?"

"Nobody."

"You came by yourself?" She couldn't keep the incredulity out of her voice.

"Yes. Well, Ho drove." Lamb bit into the sandwich and made a face. "Christ. How long's this been sitting there?"

"What did Donovan want?"

"In return for you?" Lamb chewed for a moment, swallowed, then took another bite. Once his mouth was full, he went on, "Well, he says he wants the Dipshit Chronicles."

Catherine looked confused, then more so. "The *Grey Books*?"

"Yeah, that was my reaction. On the other hand, if, as seems likely, he shagged you back in the way-back-when, it's more plausible." Another pause for chewing. "On the grounds that he's obviously a nutcase, I mean."

"Can we leave now?"

"I haven't had my flapjack yet." He paused, and sniffed the sandwich. "Has this got cheese in it?"

"Oh God, not again. Turn round."

Lamb did so, and a moment later felt her peel something from the seat of his trousers. When he turned back, Catherine was holding a flattened disc of what looked like mozzarella. "Always check before you sit down in Roddy's room. What are your laundry bills like?"

"What's a laundry bill?"

She left the room ahead of him, and paused on the landing for a moment to look back. Lamb didn't bother. It was an ordinary room, and nothing much had happened in there. There were worse things to endure than boredom.

From the next landing, they could see Bailey's comatose body in the hallway. He looked like he might have been asleep, Catherine reflected, if people generally smashed their faces against an anvil before settling down for the night. "He's only a kid, Jackson," she said.

"He had a gun. Why d'you call him 'Bailey'?"

"He had a camera too."

Lamb thought about that for a moment, then dismissed it. "Well, you're gunna have to wake him up now. I want to know what Donovan's really after."

"Because you don't think he's really a nutcase."

"Well, he's probably that too. But that doesn't mean he hasn't got a hidden agenda."

She said, "Thanks for coming to get me, Jackson."

"Did you think I wouldn't?"

"Oh, I knew you would. I just thought there'd be more mayhem involved, that's all."

And that was when Roderick Ho drove a bus through the front door.

"They're Black Arrow," Traynor said.

Black Arrow, and they were moving down the corridor the way it was done in the movies; one forging ahead a few yards then dropping to a crouch, allowing another to overtake him, and secure the next few yards. Most held nightsticks; some carried what might be guns, but looked too clunky. Tasers, River thought, triggering a sense-memory at the base of his spine. He'd encountered Tasers before.

Louisa said, "Your crew?"

"They wish." Traynor looked at Douglas. "Where are they? Where is that?"

Douglas, who was still on the floor, shrugged sulkily.

"Christ on a bike," Traynor muttered. He grabbed Douglas by the collar, hauled him to his feet, and pointed him at the screen. "That. Where are they?"

It took Douglas's voice a moment or two to catch up with his lips. "That's C Corridor."

"A big help. Where's C Corridor?"

"This side of B," Douglas explained.

"How far are they from the warehouse room?"

"That's just after E Corridor."

Traynor said, "Okay." Taking his gun from his belt he checked its load, then held it loosely by his side. "Right, change of plan. I'm going that way." He pointed towards the corridor down which Donovan had disappeared. "Make sure you're not in our way when we head back."

"You still have our colleague," Louisa said.

"She'll be released at nine come whatever. Unharmed. You think we're animals?"

"Jury's still out."

River's eyes were on the monitor on which the Black Arrow crew were securing the complex. "You plan to shoot them?"

"I plan to back up my CO."

"They're Noddy squad," River said. "They've got sticks and stones."

"Some of them are ex-forces," Traynor said. "And they're not all unarmed. Ever worked private security?"

"Not yet," Louisa muttered.

"Trust me. The types who do are the kind to squirrel away illegal handguns."

"What are you really after?"

But Traynor was gone; through the swing doors, and off down the corridor at a trot.

River looked at Douglas. "Do you keep weapons down here?"

"Are you kidding?"

Only sort of, thought River. He looked up at the monitors again. Armed or not, there were plenty of men out there. Probably more than enough to deal with two ex-soldiers.

Probably.

Douglas had thrown the lever that opened the overhead hatch.

"When you get up top," River said, "call your boss. Tell him there's been an incursion. Tell him he needs to sound the alarm."

"Her," said Douglas.

"What?"

"My boss is a her."

"Yeah, right. Whatever." He looked at Louisa. "What about you?"

"I'm a her too."

"Funny." But it was as near as Louisa had come to the attempt in a long time, so River gave her a brief smile before saying, "You going up?"

"Are you?"

"I'm going to hang on here a while. I want to know what's happening."

"Yeah, well. So do I."

Douglas was already halfway up the ladder. They watched as he disappeared through the hatch, then River threw the lever that locked it once more.

A moment later he was on the monitor that displayed the chamber overhead.

On one of the other screens the Black Arrow crew were approaching a set of doors, and making much use of hand signals and pointy fingers.

Watching them, Louisa said, "Remind me whose side we're on?"

"That'll be easier to work out once the shooting starts," River said. "Anyone who's not aiming at you."

Together, they headed off through the swing doors, down the corridor.

The room was a long one, high too, and from the end Traynor entered seemed stacked nearly to the ceiling with crates, some of them in evidence cages, each neatly padlocked. But about halfway along, the crates gave way to rows of shelving, no more than two feet apart, with an aisle running down the centre as far as the next set of doors, in front of which a wide area had been left empty, though large metal filing units lined the walls either side. Sean Donovan was halfway along a shelf full of cardboard folders: he was plucking them one by one, checking the top sheet, then — like a dissatisfied library user — dropping them to his feet. The spillage ran right back to the aisle, so when Ben Traynor reached him, it looked like Donovan was wilfully sowing disorder; turning a neat expanse of ordered history into a snowstorm of confused event.

Without breaking off from this task, he said, "Problem?"

"We have company."

"Who?"

Traynor was already past him, heading for the doors to E Corridor, slipping his belt off as he ran. Looping it through the door's handles he pulled it tight, buckled it, then turned his attention to the filing cabinets.

Donovan emerged. "Who?" he said again.

"Monteith's crew."

Donovan thought for a moment, then shook his head. "They're lightweights, Ben."

"They don't have to be good, they just have to be numerous," Traynor said. "Give me a hand with this."

Donovan helped him tip a cabinet onto its side, then slide it in front of the doors.

"That's not going to hold them long," Traynor said.

Donovan said, "I don't know. Just opening a door is a stretch for some of them." He was already heading back to the shelf he'd been working on.

Traynor peered through the fraction of porthole window unobscured by the cabinet and said, "They're here already. We'd better go."

"I'm not running from those clowns. Not till I get what we came for."

"Sean, look around. This place is the size of a fucking church. You could spend all week and not find it."

The older man shook his head: he was out of sight, between the shelves, but Traynor could tell that's what he was doing. "The catalogue numbers tell you where to look. V for Virgil, plus Tearney's initials. Then the date, then a four-figure reference. It's between six and eight years back, so we only need to go through this section here. And I'm halfway done already."

"What if all this is a set-up?"

"What would be the point, Ben? I was just out of prison, I was drinking myself half to death. And Taverner approached me, remember? It's not like I was on a crusade."

"I don't trust her."

"She's a spook. You'd be mad to trust her. But she's a spook with an agenda, and she wants to destroy Tearney as much as we do. For Alison, Ben. Remember?"

". . . I'm not likely to forget."

"So how long are you prepared to give this?"

Traynor said, "Okay, okay. As long as it takes."

Gun in hand, he went back to the doors, observing fractured slices of motion from the crew outside through his paring of window. They looked like they were getting ready to mount an assault . . . He had been here before, it occurred to him, by which he meant not here but in just this scenario: hostiles two breaths away, and defences no thicker than a brick and plaster wall.

The difference was, the quality of the enemy.

He checked his gun again, though didn't need to, and settled to wait. When they made a serious attempt on the door, he'd give them something to think about. But it was important to remember that they weren't all clowns — one or two of the Black Arrow squad had been boots on the ground: Iraq, Afghanistan. If they were out there, he didn't want to be loosing bullets in their direction, but that was a soldier's life: you couldn't always choose your enemies. Besides, Ben Traynor was no longer marching under a flag. The nearest he had was a photograph, of Captain Alison Dunn, and with the thought he kissed a finger and tapped his breast pocket. He could hear Donovan leafing through folders — plucking, glancing, discarding — but he let that sound fade into the background and focused on the world behind the blocked doors: alert, on duty, and tense as a trigger.

When Douglas emerged from the disused factory he stood blinking for a moment, like a rat freed from a maze, then froze as a train whistled past, as if becoming motionless would see the danger off. It appeared to work: the train was gone already, a bar of noise and light heading for the suburbs. Douglas looked up at the sky, in which stars had now appeared, shook his head in disapproval, then reached into his pocket for his mobile. He checked the screen, scrolled down for a number, but before he found it was flattened by one of the Black Arrows: an illegal tackle any way you looked at it, and the only way Douglas was looking at it was from underneath. With his mouth against the concrete he couldn't shout, couldn't scream: all the breath within him had been scattered into the dark. A voice barked harsh instructions into his ear, but Douglas couldn't understand them: it wasn't a foreign language, just a mode of experience he wasn't accustomed to. A memory exploded in his head of watching while a middle-aged couple did the business, right out here in the open, folded over the back of their car. Knowing these things happened, invisibly observing them, had rendered Douglas untouchable, he thought. The things that people did were jokes to which he alone supplied the punchline. But now the joke was on him: he was being hauled upright, an arm around his throat. He hadn't been in such close contact with another human since lifesaving lessons at his local pool, in 2007.

"Okay. I'll take him."

Him was Douglas; the speaker was a newcomer, not the man who'd flattened him.

Breath was trying to find its way back into his lungs now: the air out here was hot, and felt even hotter as it forced its way inside him.

It seemed that he had thrown up, too.

"Can you walk?"

He nodded, though he was fairly sure he couldn't.

The newcomer wore dark clothing, but not the paramilitary gear that the vicious bastard who'd just

347

taken him down wore. He did, though, have a silky-looking black balaclava. "Come on then."

Douglas could walk, kind of, or at least couldn't prevent himself being half-dragged, which had the same effect. He was being taken towards a black van, which appeared suddenly out of the gloom: everything was dark now, and shapes were only slowly making themselves understood. Deep breath. And exhale. The trick of it, he was discovering, was not to try too hard: breathing was one of those things you could only manage if you thought about something else while doing it. The problem was, the only other topics he could think of involved being dragged towards this van, shoved into the back of it, its door being closed with a heavy *ker-thunk*. Then it was just him and the man with the balaclava, together in solid darkness, until the man did something which made a small electric lantern light up. The van was large: a windowless people-carrier with bench-seating around the sides, in proper military fashion. Douglas could still taste vomit on his tongue, and was worried he'd done something to his teeth on that concrete.

A small worry, though, compared to being here with this man.

Who said, "You okay now?"

Douglas nodded. Coughed. Nodded again.

"Sorry about that."

Worry thinned, like fog becoming mist.

"The guys are overexcited, and you can't blame them. Those are some serious bad actors you let into the facility. You want to tell me why you did that?"

348

"I'm — it's — can't. Classified."

"Yeah, sure. Listen, son, you really don't need to worry about that right now." The man pulled the balaclava off, and became ordinary looking. "I'm from Regent's Park, name's Duffy. You can call me Nick. There's been an incursion, we both know that. An unauthorised incursion into a Service facility. And you know what? It's not the first time that's happened today. So don't worry about what you did or didn't do, and whether protocols were observed, because we're all feeling a little foolish at the moment, and all that matters is that this gets cleared up. So tell me, how many of them are there?"

"Four," said Douglas.

"Good, that's what we thought. And your crew, how many of your crew are down there?"

"Just me," Douglas told him, and then said, "Shouldn't you know that? If you're from the Park?"

"Yeah, we're not exactly on the same page today. You know how it gets. Tell me how that back entrance works. Some kind of hatchway?"

Douglas did so.

"And there's no way of working it from the outside?"

"None. It's totally secure."

"Yeah, right, good. That's also what I thought. Thank you, Douglas."

Douglas nodded, and noticed that he was breathing normally again, which was a relief, though in the same instant became irrelevant. His body hitting the floor of the van made more noise than the gun. Duffy was pleased: he was using a Swiss-made suppressor, and hadn't been entirely sure it was one hundred per cent effective, but there was no arguing with results. He knelt and pushed Douglas's body under the bench. Given five minutes and a bucket of soapy water, he might have done something about the head-splash on the panels too, but time was what he didn't have.

One down, he thought. Four to go.

Busy night.

He pulled his balaclava on, turned the lantern off, and stepped out into the gathering dark.

CHAPTER
FOURTEEN

The pub was off Great Portland Street, and she remembered being here once before, a wake for a dead agent, Dieter Hess. The usual pious utterances, when the truth was, like most doubles, you could trust the man as far as you could chuck a ten-pound note: where it fell, he'd be waiting. But that was the nature of the beast. A spook threw shadows like a monkey puzzle tree's; you could catch whiplash hearing one describe yesterday's weather.

Diana Taverner was drinking Johnny Walker Black Label — a special occasion tipple — and trying to work out how special the occasion was.

That Dame Ingrid had heard the sound of one big penny dropping was beyond dispute. Whether she'd heard it in time to catch the penny on the bounce was another matter. If she had, Taverner's career would probably not see out the week. It was one thing to plot and seethe in corners: that was what office life was about. But to actually set wheels in motion was a declaration of war, and the only war you could win against an enemy like Dame Ingrid was one that was over before the starting gun was fired.

But it had been too good to miss, this opportunity . . .

She sipped slowly, trying to ignore the sudden craving for a cigarette that alcohol inevitably spiked. Somewhere right this moment, under London's crust, Sean Donovan was hunting down evidence that would not only ease Ingrid Tearney from her seat of power, it could result in her trial and imprisonment. That the evidence was in the archives was an odds-on certainty: she knew how Dame Ingrid's mind worked. Ingrid was committee-clever, had boardroom smarts; ultimately, she thought like a civil servant. Which, she should have realised, was something of a liability when surrounded by civil servants. Burying documents within a tsunami of documents must have seemed like a no-brainer, because there were always documents — there were always documents. This was the saving grace, and ultimate downfall, of every civil servant. Because there were always budgets to balance and third parties to pacify; there were flight plans and requisition forms; there were waivers, contracts, guarantees — anything that took place outside the jurisdiction, you needed paperwork to cover your arse; anything that happened within it, you needed to sign the overtime chitty. And all the paperwork had to be initialled in triplicate and copied to file; stored against the day you were called to account for actions you didn't remember performing ... Paperwork was how the Service, like every corporation, ran. Paperwork, not clockwork, kept the wheels turning. And this happened because nobody had yet thought of a convincing way of stopping it happening; or not convincing enough to convince a civil servant. Who were notoriously set in their ways, and displayed all the flexibility of a rhinoceros in a corridor.

So the evidence was there, among the information recently relocated to a secure site off-grid, and while it was true that Diana might herself have gone rooting for it any time these past few years, that would have been to lay herself open to the risk that Donovan now faced on her behalf . . . Besides, leaked evidence would have resulted in a whitewash, or a Select Committee Inquiry as they were also known; the inevitable investigation would have focused on the leaker, not the leaked. Several whistle blowers of the recent past served as object lessons to this effect: icons of the internet generation they may well be, but Diana Taverner saw no future for herself holed up in an embassy box room, or eking out an existence in a foreign capital. No, if the evidence surfaced through another's machinations, that would allow her to watch in horror as her Head of Service's corruption was revealed; to offer her support to a dumbstruck minister; to humbly accept a caretaker role until the dust settled . . . If she wanted to take on Ingrid Tearney, the way to do it was sideways. Which meant using someone like Sean Donovan, whom she could trust because he was no spook but a soldier, and held to a different notion of loyalty: one that involved revenging himself on a Service that had done him harm.

Of course, if he discovered that it was Taverner herself who was responsible for that, things might grow awkward . . .

She finished her drink, considered her immediate options, and decided she didn't have any. The only course of action open to her was to have another drink.

It didn't take her long to get served, because the bartender was male. When that stopped happening — Diana didn't know what she would do when that stopped happening. It was like contemplating death. While he poured she glanced round the bar, then noticed her own reflection in the nearby mirror, and saw with horror what looked like a grey streak in her chestnut hair . . . It turned out to be a trick of the light, thank God, but underscored her current situation: time was stomping on regardless, and opportunities had to be seized. Better to go down in flames than timidly fade.

Thinking all this, she didn't pay as much attention as she should have done to a figure in the corner; a smooth man — sleek even — with dark hair brushed back from a high forehead, and brown eyes. He had a newspaper spread in front of him, and appeared to be studying it, but what he was mostly doing was watching Diana Taverner.

"I told you I could hot-wire a car."

"Buses weren't mentioned," Lamb said.

Ho had made tinder of the porch, and punched a sizable hole where the front door used to be, which, given the speed he'd been going at, said much for the durability of the good old London bus, and not much for whoever had put the house up. The hallway was littered with chunks of masonry, shattered glass, and splinters of wood. Part of the door frame was lying across Bailey's back. If the bus had intruded much further, it would have flattened him like a bug.

"I thought you might be in trouble."

"Yeah. Because crashing a bus would have been a big fucking help if I had been."

"He was doing his best," Catherine said. "Thanks, Roddy. That was a good plan. Now go and fetch some water, would you?"

"I'm not thirsty."

"No, well, it's not for you. The kitchen's back there somewhere."

"Try not to level it to the ground," Lamb said.

Ho moved sulkily off, just in time for a dinnerplate-sized chunk of plaster to drop from the ceiling and hit him on the head.

Lamb tilted his chin heavenwards. "Owe you one."

Catherine bent over Bailey and brushed debris away. "Leave him alone. If you'd driven a bus through a wall, we'd never hear the end of it. What are the others doing?"

"Cartwright and Guy are helping your pal Donovan out."

"Helping?"

"Seems the Grey Books are in some off-site storage place near Hayes. Donovan needed Service help to get in." Lamb was fiddling in his pocket while he spoke, and when his hand emerged, it was clutching the unwrapped flapjack. He bit it in half then said, "Well, that or he didn't fancy Hayes on his tod."

"What about Marcus and Shirley?"

"I incentivised them."

"What's that supposed to mean?"

Lamb gave a long-suffering sigh. "Am I the only one who understands man-management round here?" He crammed the rest of the flapjack into his mouth, and a moment or so later said, "And when I say 'man', I'm most definitely including Dander."

"She's big-boned, that's all. How, precisely, did you —"

"I fired them."

Catherine pondered this for a moment. Marcus and Shirley, more prone than River even to banging their heads against walls while waiting for something — anything — to happen.

"That might work," she allowed.

"Yeah, and the beauty of it is, if it doesn't? They're already fired."

"But on the other hand, you could have just given them instructions."

"They haven't fucking learned to follow instructions."

Ho returned from the kitchen with a glass of water. He looked at Lamb, then at Catherine, then at Lamb again.

"It's a glass of water," Lamb said. "Take a wild guess."

Ho handed the water to Catherine.

"Thank you," she said.

She was on her knees now, cradling the still-unconscious Bailey's head in her lap. Opening his mouth with one hand, she poured water from the glass into it.

"You're going to drown him?" said Lamb. "Seems a bit harsh."

"I'm not the one who broke his face."

"I think I've got one of his teeth in my knee."

"He's just a kid."

"Shouldn't be playing with grown-ups then." Bending low, Lamb went through Bailey's pockets. Finding a wallet, he sat back on his haunches and flipped through it: some small change, a pair of ten-pound notes, a credit card and a driving licence.

The notes disappeared in Lamb's meaty fist.

"What on earth are you doing?"

"Petrol money," said Lamb. He glanced at the licence. "Well well well. Craig Dunn."

"He's waking up," Ho said.

The young man's eyes were moving under their lids. Catherine tapped his cheek gently with the flat of her hand.

"Is that actual first aid?" Lamb asked suspiciously. "It looks like what you'd do with a puppy."

"Why don't you do something useful and call an ambulance?"

"I've already been useful," Lamb said. He looked at Ho. "What's the matter now?"

"I paid for the petrol."

"You'll need to file an expenses claim," Lamb said. "Louisa'll show you how."

Craig Dunn groaned and opened his eyes.

At first sight, the wasteground was empty of people. The Black Arrow van was parked near a car which looked like Louisa's, and there was a skip, various heaps of masonry, and a pile of tumbled-over fencing, but the crew they'd seen drive in had melted away.

"Where did they go?"

"Don't look for people. Look for movement."

It was like one of those children's puzzles: you stare at a picture of a tree until you can make out the squirrels.

They were in shadow themselves, more tree than squirrel, and speaking in whispers. Shirley had buttoned her jacket up, to prevent her white T-shirt showing; Marcus had pulled his cap low. They were huddled by the entrance to the misshaped quadrilateral formed by the buildings; a pole designed to block ingress had been fixed in an upright position, and a wooden sentry box where a car park attendant once lurked was empty, save for a heavy stink of piss. There were lights beyond the furthest building, signals for passing trains, but the sky overhead had given way to a thoughtful deep blue, and nothing shone in the foreground.

Then something shifted across the far side, between the pillars on ground level of the furthest building, and Shirley realised she was looking at a pair of Black Arrows.

"I see two."

"I've got seven," Marcus said.

"Show-off."

"They're not much good," he said. "This kind of terrain, this much cover, I'd be invisible."

"I can see you," Shirley muttered. Then: "What are they? Are they Klieg lights?"

There were two sets of them, scaffolding towers that loomed a few metres tall with searchlights affixed to the top: one by the Black Arrow van, and the other a few metres away, neither lit, but both aimed at a hole in the factory wall. They looked like outsized anglepoise lamps. They also looked like you could tip them over with a broomstick.

"Yeah, that's exactly what — oh, Christ."

"It's a killing ground," said Shirley.

"Looks like."

"They're gunna flush River and the others out of the facility. They come up, the lights go on — blam blam blam."

"Hush."

A figure emerged from the back of the van. A balaclava obscured his face, though he was too far away for that to make much difference. After a brief survey of the area, he trotted towards the block to their right.

"Eight," said Marcus.

"Are you just gunna count, or do you have a plan?"

"Well, in situations like this I ask myself, 'What would Nelson Mandela do?'"

". . . Seriously?"

"Dude survived twenty-seven years in a maximum security prison," Marcus said. "I'm pretty sure he could take care of himself."

"Yeah, that's not what most people think of when — oh, forget it. What would Nelson do?"

"He'd take those towers out before the lights came on. You up to that?"

Shirley was, and would have said so, but a figure appeared behind Marcus wielding a truncheon. The alarm in her eyes gave Marcus half a moment's grace, and he moved just enough that the stick, instead of swinging into the side of his head, caught him on the neck. He bounced full body off the wall and hit the ground with a thud. Shirley had time to note that his baseball cap remained fixed in place; almost time to step forward and launch a chin-bound kick at his assailant; no time at all to do anything but fall flat on her face when her legs were taken out from under her by a second man. *Roll*, she thought, and took a mouthful of gravel as his kick came in to take her head off.

Running along the corridor, Louisa noticed her heart rate . . . It had been a while since she'd been conscious of the beating of her heart.

Two paces ahead, River barely slowed before launching himself through a set of swing doors; they banged off the walls and swung back at her, and she fended them off with her forearms. Any of the instructors they'd had, back before their fall, would have had seven kinds of fit watching this: they were more like schoolkids having a race than agents on an op . . . If that's what they were. If that's what this was.

What it mostly felt like was an unholy mess, but there was nothing unusual about that. Last year, she and Min had had the sniff of an op: little more than a handholding exercise, but it had made them feel more alive than at any time since being kicked out of the Park. As things turned out, they were playing someone else's game: Min died, and all she'd had since was the daily grind of make-work and nightly stands with strange men; so many strange men, she was near to forgetting there was any other kind.

And now this.

More doors. She'd lost track of which corridor they were in, F or E, but that didn't matter because here they were, in the room they'd seen on the monitor, with its rows of newly assembled shelving, and crates packed in what looked like cages, as if the information they contained was savage, and needed to be kept behind bars. A lot of it probably was. At the far end of the room, visible along the aisle between the rows, Ben Traynor was by the far set of doors: he'd erected a barricade, and was standing on an overturned cabinet, sighting through a fraction of a porthole window. His gun hung loosely by his side, but on their arrival he spun round, aiming it in their direction.

River and Louisa leaped in opposite directions, taking cover behind caged crates.

Traynor lowered the gun. "What the hell are you doing?"

River emerged, hands raised to shoulder level. "Was about to ask you the same thing. Where's Donovan?"

The sound of a box file hitting the floor betrayed his position.

Traynor said, "I thought I told you to go."

"And I thought you said you were after the Grey Books."

Louisa joined River as he lowered his hands. "Are they showing signs of coming in?" she asked.

He hesitated. Then said, "There's a room a few yards down the corridor. They're in there at the moment. I imagine they're planning their next move."

Which presumably involved all-out assault, thought Louisa. That or surrender, which didn't seem likely. "Have they got guns?"

"Maybe one or two of them. They haven't fired any yet."

Another box file hit the floor.

River said, "If he's going through them one by one, we might be here a while."

"We know what we're doing."

"They won't need guns. They can just wait for the hinges to rust off the doors."

Louisa moved down the aisle towards Traynor, and stopped when she reached the row where Donovan was. There was something incongruous about the scene: like watching Rocky play librarian. In his hands was a box file. Before she opened her mouth he'd dropped it and was reaching for the next one.

She said, "I found your online musings."

"BigSeanD," he said, without stopping what he was doing.

"BigSeanD has a thing about the weather," she said. "He seems to think They've weaponised it."

"Uh-huh."

"Wasn't too clear on who *They* were."

"I expect They're the same crowd putting chips in people's heads to track them when they're abducted by aliens." He looked at her briefly. "They get up to creepy shit, They surely do."

He'd reached the end of the row of box files; next up were manila folders, of varying thickness; some bound with ribbon, others paper-clipped closed. They had catalogue numbers stamped in red ink on the cover; Donovan checked each before unbowing the ribbon, discarding the paper clip. A quick glance at the top sheet seemed to be all he needed, and the folders joined the mess on the floor.

"You have to admit," he said in a conversational tone, "it doesn't sound that far-fetched. If the weather's not being controlled yet, you can bet your life someone's trying to make it happen."

"But you don't care about that, do you? You were just building a legend to get you access to this place."

"What's the matter, don't I fit your image of a conspiracy nut? What have you been told we look like?"

"I gather they come in different sizes," River said. He stood in the aisle, with a sight line on both Donovan and Traynor. "But whatever you really want, we can't let you take it."

"Is that so?"

"Making a move now," said Traynor.

"How many?" River asked.

"Six. More. I have limited vision here."

Donovan looked unmoved. He said, "You might want to leave. One or two of them have real guns. They even know which way to point them."

River said, "You took Catherine Standish. Sent me her photo."

"I took her," Donovan said. He plucked another folder from the shelf.

A glance, the barest shrug. The folder hit the floor.

"You knew her from the old days," Louisa said. "Back when she was at the Park."

Donovan opened another folder. He looked at the front page, seemed about to drop it, then looked again, more closely.

"But what I want to know," Louisa said, "is how come you knew about Slough House?"

Glass splintered, and she turned. Through the gap on the shelves left by Donovan's predations, she saw Traynor raise the gun to the window he'd just broken: two shots ricocheted down the corridor. In immediate response came a louder bang, and a flood of light which filled the room before receding, leaving a dark blur in its place. Traynor was thrown from the cabinet, which juddered across the floor with a heavy scraping sound. The doors bulged inwards, the left-hand one torn free of the wall by the blast, and the rows of shelving toppled like dominoes, as those nearest the blast collapsed onto their neighbours. Donovan dropped to the ground; Louisa followed when he pulled her arm, and the falling shelves spewed files and folders onto their heads. What had been an aisle was now a tunnel, and the overhead crashing continued until the last of the shelves came to rest on the first of the rows of crates. River had gone. For two seconds Louisa was blank confusion, her ears full of noise, her eyes full of light, and then a survival instinct kicked in: on her hands and knees, she scuttled through debris to what had been the central aisle, where she could make out figures pouring through what was now a hole in the wall where the doors had been. Scrambling upright, she found herself grabbed by a stranger, his features obscured by black wool. When she rapped his throat with the side of her hand he backed off two steps, comically choking for breath, and another man, identically clad, took his place. This time Louisa was flung to the floor, with something like a cosh swinging down towards her. It would have connected if a box file hadn't hit the man in the face first. He staggered sideways, then fell when River punched him in the head.

Louisa got to her feet. A light haze had filled the room, smoke, but mostly dust. Some of the Black Arrow crew didn't appear to know what to do now they'd broken through; a couple of others, more proactive, were sitting on Ben Traynor; had rolled him over and were cuffing his wrists. Sean Donovan emerged from behind her, and she saw him reach for the folder he'd been looking at when the doors had blown open. He tucked it inside his shirt before standing up.

River shouted. "You okay?"

She thought that's what he shouted. Her ears were still ringing.

He shouted, "Time to go," and then his body went rigid and the light in his eyes went out.

The way he hit the floor, she was sure he was dead.

Shirley rolled sideways, and the kick that should have taken her head off did no more than graze her ear. In the same movement she hooked her foot around her assailant's leg and brought him to the ground. From the corner of her eye, she saw the first man bring his truncheon down on Marcus's stomach, but that was yards away — another time zone — and she had her own enemy to worry about. She threw herself upon him, pinning his elbows with her hands. He was several stone heavier, and clad in combat-ready gear; she wore jeans, a tee and a jacket, but if she lacked a well-packed utility belt and a nightstick she at least had a hard head, and when she brought it down on his nose she heard the satisfying crunch of bone on bone. The coward screamed, and his stick went rattling across the concrete. Pushing herself semi-upright, Shirley punched him twice, very hard, in the exact same spot she'd just butted him. She'd have done so a third time, but had to throw herself sideways to avoid the first man's truncheon, which whistled so closely past her face she could taste it. She rolled over twice then sprang into launch position, like a racer waiting for the starting pistol. Facing her, he slapped the truncheon into his open palm, once, twice, like an invitation. The second man was wheezing heavily, bubbling with blood;

Marcus was prone and didn't look like he'd be moving soon. And there were more people heading this way: she could hear the rustling of gear, the heavy tread of hot men. Another slap of the truncheon — *Come and get it*.

She could take him. Five seconds' untrammelled movement from her, and he'd spend the rest of the night removing that stick from his arse.

But there was more than just him to contend with. Before the noises got closer, she feinted left, moved right, spun on her heel and ran.

Sorry, Marcus.

Shadows swallowed her, and she vanished inside darkness.

She didn't see Marcus being gathered up and carried to the black van.

Dame Ingrid sat in the aura of her standard lamp, and to an observer might have looked serene, saintly even, given the halo effect of her blonde wig. Though if the same observer had moved closer, ignoring the soft focus, she'd have noticed that any calm in Dame Ingrid's eyes was the kind that rocks contain, comprising a sublime indifference to the forces that produced her and a stubborn intention to endure, come what may.

There was no observer, but Ingrid Tearney rubbed her cheek anyway, as if disturbed by a stranger's breath, then patted her wig, assuring herself it remained in place. After today's events, she would not have been surprised to find strands of it falling about her shoulders, the way her real hair might, had it not been lost to her long ago. Today had been a day of surprises; of sandbaggings and sudden reversals. Peter Judd's plotting had not been unexpected: PJ was a known quantity — public buffoon and private velociraptor — and Dame Ingrid had been girding her loins for an attack since his elevation to the Home Office. Diana Taverner's machinations were hardly out of character either, but what startled Dame Ingrid was that Taverner's plan had evidently been germinating for years.

Half an hour's research had proved this much.

Sean Donovan was a name that would have rung bells, had Dame Ingrid ever concerned herself with the sharp end of operations. Donovan had been a career soldier, destined for laurels; his non-combat duties had included a session at the UN, where he'd advised on crushing resistance, or counter-insurgency as it was also known, depending on whose foot the boot was on. He'd been accompanied by a Captain Alison Dunn, who was engaged to Donovan's subordinate, Lieutenant Benjamin Traynor. All very cosy, and it didn't require much imagination to conjure up myriad ways in which things could have gone pear-shaped, but what actually happened wasn't romantic entanglement but political indiscretion. In a Midtown bar, Alison Dunn had been approached by a junior delegate from one of the former Soviet republics. Dunn had known enough to stay sober in this company; the junior delegate had either been unencumbered by such wisdom or was pretending to be drunker than he was to excuse his flapping tongue. Or possibly — you couldn't rule it out — his motives had been honourable. Either way, the information he passed on to Dunn had been alarming enough for her to submit a report to the Home Office, stamped MINISTER'S EYES ONLY, on her return home.

That had proved to be something of an error.

Dame Ingrid pursed her lips, giving her the appearance, had she but known it, of a disappointed fish. Doubtless, in recruiting Donovan and Traynor, Diana had claimed that it was Ingrid herself who had been responsible for the death of Alison Dunn, and Donovan's consequent imprisonment; doubtless, too, she had provided them with precise instructions for laying hands on Virgil-quality documentation which would corroborate the story Alison Dunn had heard in New York. Information that would be more than enough to end Ingrid Tearney's career.

The Grey Books indeed . . . She should have seen straight through that decoy. Would have done, except that it came gift-wrapped: if Peter Judd's tiger team were a pair of reality-impaired conspiracy buffs, then they presented no real threat; an outcome so welcome Ingrid had accepted it without question. She sighed . . . She had been too willing to believe in others. It was an abiding weakness, her one great character flaw, and might prove her downfall if her eleventh-hour attempt to eliminate the whole pack of them proved unsuccessful.

Darkness was edging further into the room now, painting her lamplit corner brighter. Nothing to do but wait. And as she did so, she couldn't quite suppress a sneaking admiration for the tenacity with which Diana Taverner had pursued her aims.

Not the least audacious aspect of which, as far as Dame Ingrid was concerned, was that she had managed all this without paperwork.

CHAPTER
FIFTEEN

A tidy battlefield is a good battlefield, thought Nick Duffy. He wasn't positive that particular gem appeared in those art of war texts City dickheads read on the Tube, but it fitted his mood. From his current perspective, the fencing, the skip, the mounds of urban debris had transformed into landmarks: areas of cover for what was yet to come, which, ideally, wouldn't last more than a minute. The Klieg lights were poised to turn the area outside the derelict factory into a stage, and once that happened, anyone treading the boards would find their dramatic career cut short. They called it dying when it happened on stage. They called it that when it happened elsewhere, too.

He was deep in the shadows of the building nearest the railway tracks, leaning against a pillar, and while he didn't know precisely what was happening in the complex below his feet, he had a calm feeling nevertheless; the sense of everything going to plan. Pulling the trigger on the red-headed kid had done that. You'd think it would push him in the opposite direction, that he'd have a hollowed-out feeling now, be all butterflies and shit, but that wasn't how it worked. How it worked was, everything was going to be okay, because the alternative, now he'd killed that kid, was unthinkable. And Nick Duffy didn't do unthinkable.

One of the Black Arrows approached, not even attempting to look stealthy. In a shaky voice, he said, "We've got a prisoner."

For a second, Duffy thought he'd missed something. "They've come up?"

"No. He was spotted on the perimeter, checking us out."

Perimeter, thought Duffy. These toy soldiers loved their vocabulary.

"He's a big guy, black. Thing is, there was someone with him."

Duffy mentally ran through Slough House personnel. A big black guy would be Marcus Longridge; someone else was either Shirley Dander or Roderick Ho. His money was on Dander. Ho was a desk-jockey.

"And they got away."

"Fuck. Anyone go after her?"

"She's in block one, far as we know."

The Black Arrow gestured behind him, in case Duffy had forgotten which block was which.

"Thing is . . ."

Another thing? Duffy said, "What?"

"They've put him in the van. Where we put the first prisoner?"

"Good."

"Only . . . the first prisoner?"

"What about him?"

"He's dead."

"And?"

372

"Jesus, I mean . . ." From toy soldier to boy soldier: Duffy could tell that any moment now, his lower lip would wobble. "Nobody said there was going to be killing."

Duffy nodded. The Black Arrow couldn't see his face, which was probably as well, because his expression wouldn't soothe worries away. He leaned in closer, and just to erase any ambiguity from the situation wrapped one gloved hand round the man's throat as he did so. "Well what the fuck did you think we were going to do? Tag them and release them into the community?" His voice had dropped an octave, a grace note he'd always found effective when explaining grim realities.

"But it's just —"

"It's just nothing. For the past six months your crappy little operation has been headed up by someone who today turns out to be an enemy of the state. Now there's two ways we can deal with this. We can have a nice tidy discussion followed by a full-scale investigation, after which none of you will have a job ever again. Not to mention having MI5 so far up your arses you'll spend the rest of your lives whistling when the wind blows. Or we can do it my way, which is quick, quiet and leaves no mess. If you're not man enough for that, say so. But get your head round this first. If you're not part of the solution you're part of the problem. Understand?"

The Arrow nodded.

"Didn't catch that, son."

". . . Yes."

"Welcome aboard. This new prisoner, is he cuffed?"

"Yes."

"Good. I'll deal with him. You get to your position. Anyone comes out that factory, the lights go on, and you bring them down. Understand?"

This time he didn't wait for an answer. Leaving the Arrow in the stench of the dying building, he headed for the van.

In Roddy Ho's opinion, he wasn't being given enough credit for taking charge. *Think of something,* Lamb had told him. *Do something,* Marcus had said. Any way you looked at it, driving a bus through a front door was "something". The fact that it turned out unnecessary was one of those wise-after-the-event outcomes it was hardly fair to pin on him.

In his mind's eye, it had played out differently. He'd rolled straight out of the driver's cabin, disarming the thug holding Lamb at gunpoint; bit of the old natural grace coming into play as he'd brought said thug to his knees with a quick *one-two* . . .

Later, with Louisa: "Really, Lamb said that? All I was doing was reacting, babes."

"Jesus, Roddy, when someone calls you a hero, just accept it, yeah? Is that his gun in your pocket, by the way?"

"Hell's teeth. Did the impact fuck your hearing up or what?"

And this was Lamb, bringing Roddy Ho back to reality.

"Dunn. Alison Dunn. That was the name of the woman Donovan killed."

Ho said, "Yes. No. I can't remember . . ."

"Give me strength. If it was your brains I needed, we'd all be in trouble. All I want is your typing skills. Look her up. Is this guy related?"

For a moment, Ho couldn't lay hands on his smartphone, and his life flashed before his eyes. Most of it involved *Grand Theft Auto*. Then he located it — new holster attachment, duh — and keyed in his password for the Service intranet. Typing skills, typing skills. What Lamb didn't realise was how much more was involved than simple typing skills.

Alison Dunn, deceased. Military. Scroll down to find her surviving family.

"You know," Lamb said, looking round at the mess the bus had made of the hallway, "when I first met you, I had you pegged as a waste of space."

Busy as he was, Ho couldn't prevent a smirk. He recognised a third-act moment when he heard one. "And when did you change your mind?"

"When did I what?"

Catherine emerged from the room where they'd put Dunn. "As long as you've got your phone out, call an ambulance."

"Like hell," Lamb said. "We'll cuff him to a radiator and let the Dogs pick him up. Things are messy enough without a trip to A & E."

"He's a civilian," Catherine said. "Not our jurisdiction."

Ho looked up from his phone. Standish was glaring at Lamb in a way that made him glad it wasn't happening to him. *Babes,* he told Louisa, *that lady can be mighty fierce, you hear what I'm saying?* Surviving family was her mother and a brother, Craig. There was a fiancé too, one Benjamin Traynor.

Traynor . . .

"Something else you should know," he told Lamb.

Shirley found a staircase, its fire door hanging by one hinge, and bounded up to the next level. Smells of piss and weed: you didn't have to abandon a building long before nature stepped in to reclaim it. Even here: not quite the heart of the city, but its appendix or something. Its bladder. She almost tripped at the top, but didn't; stepped out onto the first level, and ran lightly down a corridor with a view of the wasteground through its glassless windows. Bitching dark now, one big shadow, but Shirley could make out shapes. There was the Black Arrow van, where they'd have taken Marcus. She hoped it was where they'd taken Marcus. The alternative — that they weren't taking prisoners — didn't bear thinking about.

Because apart from anything else, there was at least one of them on her tail right now.

At the end of the corridor she swung a hard right: more windows, now with a view of the railway lines, behind a breeze-block wall topped with lengths of wire, the topmost one barbed. A digger was parked against the wall, its tool semi-upright, angled like a stepladder.

376

Those things were always yellow or red. This one was yellow.

An open doorway. She spun into it, dropped to a crouch. Waited. Private security operations aimed to hire the brightest and the best: they wanted fitness, smarts and enough nous not to go belting into the dark after an unknown subject without checking out the terrain. What they mostly got, though, were lumbering wannabes who thought duffing up a Goth in a pub car park made them Jason Statham. The one on Shirley's tail trundled past her wheezing like Thomas the Tank Engine, the gear on his utility belt slapping his thighs in cumbersome counterpoint, before erupting into a brief solo when she thudded into him waist height, sending him flying through the unglassed window. He didn't fall far — it was only the first floor — but he hit the ground like a sack of spanners. Shirley tried to remember how many Arrows Marcus claimed to have seen, but couldn't. One down, anyway.

Hearing more feet on the stairwell, she slipped back out of sight, noticing as she did so a strange sensation in her face; an unaccustomed tautening of muscles. She used her hand to check — yep. She appeared to be grinning.

Nothing like a drug-free high, she thought, and waited in the shadows for the next Black Arrow to make his move.

River wasn't dead.
River might be dead, but act like River's not.
So: River wasn't dead.

That, or something like it, was the burden of Louisa's thoughts as she stood face-to-balaclava with the Arrow who'd just brought him down. Sometimes you can tell when a man in a mask wears a smirk. She wiped it off him by feinting a blow to his stomach, hindsight letting her know that a feint wasn't necessary — the blow might as well have landed for all his ability to parry it — then punching him in the throat instead, because that had worked well for her so far this evening. While he windmilled backwards, she stepped over River's prone body and took two lengthy strides down the aisle, towards the ruptured doorway.

Dive and ro-o-o-ollll . . .

She could almost hear the instruction bellowed at her as it had been time and again one long day in hell, issuing from an instructor who looked like a sex doll: five foot nothing, curly blonde hair, ruby red lips never seen closed . . . But boy, could she bellow. *Dive and roll!* Anyone not diving, not rolling, to her satisfaction spent the next fifteen minutes doing squat thrusts. And like any good sex doll, she was never really satisfied; always wanted more.

But you learned to dive and roll all right, and it wasn't a skill you forgot in a hurry.

So Louisa dived and rolled, and when she came upright again she was holding the gun Traynor had spilled when he fell. First she shot the man who'd put River down, then the two who were securing Traynor. The rest had scattered by then, back through the ruptured doorway or behind collapsed shelving.

Two shots came back at her, but she was somewhere else already, pulling River's body behind cover.

"Fuck was that?" he drooled.

Not dead, then.

"That," she told him, "was a Taser."

"Not again . . ."

"Good shooting," someone said, and she almost proved his point by shooting him too.

It was Donovan.

"Where's Ben?"

Louisa pointed with the gun. Traynor was still where he'd been dropped and cuffed: in a heap ten yards away. Of the two bodies next to him, one was twitching and the other not.

"Alive?"

"Think so," she said.

"How many?"

"We saw plenty on the monitor. Twelve? Fifteen? Three are down."

River mumbled something, *fuckin Taser*, she thought it was.

Donovan had a gun too. "I've worked with these guys," he said. "Some of them won't stop running until they reach the sea. And some will think Christmas just came early."

Another shot was fired, the bullet hammering into a wooden crate, porcupining splinters from its side. Louisa briefly stood and fired twice in the direction the shot had come from, then dropped back under cover.

As if she hadn't moved, Donovan indicated River. "Is he okay?"

"He's been Tasered before," Louisa said. "I think he kind of likes it."

"You shot the man who did it."

Louisa didn't reply.

"That's good soldiering in my book," Donovan said.

"We're not on the same side."

"Maybe not," he said. "But I'd sooner have you as an enemy than these clowns as friends."

One of the clowns took offence at that, and loosed another shot in their direction. Louisa flinched, but the bullet went wide.

River pushed himself up to a sitting position, and dry-retched. "*Jesus.*"

"Keep your head down," Louisa hissed. Then she nodded at Donovan's shirt front, where he'd tucked the folder he'd taken. "Whatever you've got there, someone definitely doesn't want you to have it."

"That's right," he said. "And whoever that is didn't send the cavalry, did you notice? They sent a bunch of mercenaries instead. You might want to think about that."

"When we get out of here, I'm going to have to take it from you."

"That's a discussion I'll look forward to. Meanwhile, cover me. I'm going for Ben."

And without waiting for her reply, he was off.

The temptation was to stay in the pub all evening. By the time she emerged, it would be over: Donovan and Traynor would have the evidence to bury Ingrid Tearney, or would be buried themselves in the caverns below Hayes. If the latter, Diana would have to prepare for Tearney's wrath. It was as well, she thought, that the Dame had no sense of humour. If she did, Diana might find herself facing exile to Slough House . . .

A knife in the back would be preferable. No metaphor intended.

The strange thing was, the event which had set all this in motion had been engineered for the good of the Service. It had been shortly after Dame Ingrid had taken up the reins, a post Diana Taverner hankered after, but had been clear-eyed enough to admit she wasn't ready for. Back then time had appeared to be on her side, and an unrocked boat was a sane and sensible course. So when a report had landed on the Home Secretary's desk which threatened to hole that boat beneath the waterline, Diana had acted.

The minister at the time had been every senior spook's wet dream: spineless, indecisive, terrified of bad press, and anxious never to be caught in the vicinity of a decelerating buck. Back then, before Ingrid Tearney had begun her programme of stripping power from the Second Desks, Diana had had weekly meetings with him: he liked to keep abreast of developments, he asserted, his choice of wording corroborated by his focus. But on that particular day, he'd been too rattled by the report he'd received to spare her bosom more than a wistful glance. *This*, he'd told her. *Make this go away, can't you?* Which Diana had taken as carte blanche.

It was the kind of op that was under the bridge in all the right ways: no paper trail, no oversight; just a slush-fund payment to a pair of crash-squad near-retirees eager to build a nest egg before leaving Spook Street for civilian life. The target being military, it was best to have her die in an accident; the combination of a spiked drink and tampered steering had done the trick. It wasn't even Dunn's drink they'd spiked — a bit of lateral thinking there. So in the eyes of the world, Sean Donovan had wound up responsible for Alison Dunn's death, but then, as a soldier, he'd understand the nature of collateral damage. His protestations had been muted — impossible to deny he had a drink problem — and he'd disappeared into the military justice system, his once successful career a pair of skid marks in the dark.

Diana left the pub. She did not notice the sleek-looking man in her wake. Outside, it had barely cooled with the going down of the sun; the pavements were sticky with heat, and the air hung in hot pockets. It required little imagination to think something was going on with the weather. A detail that had leaped to hand when concocting this new op's legend . . .

Because in the years since dealing with Alison Dunn, Diana's own career had stalled; not as spectacularly as Donovan's, but just as decisively. Her role had become that of another middle-management drone, while Tearney's crusade to transform the Service into a bland, national security delivery system, with herself as CEO, had marched on relentlessly. Budget meetings. Corporate branding. The whittling away of power from individual departments until *a more vertical structure was achieved*; one in which the traditional routes to power — long service, qualifications, a willingness to crawl over the bleeding bodies piled up in front — had been rendered null. Little wonder Diana's thoughts had turned to alternative methods of advancement. And she had always prided herself on the elegance of her schemes. When looking for an off-the-book joe, who better than one with a grudge and a skill set?

It had taken little effort to persuade Donovan he'd been the victim of a conspiracy; little more to convince him it was of Ingrid Tearney's making. Diana had handed him the opportunity for revenge, and he'd brought his service chum, Alison Dunn's fiancé, along with him.

At the corner, next to a row of bikes, she lit a cigarette and checked her phone. Nothing. And then, before she could change her mind, she called Peter Judd's number. When she'd fed Judd the tiger team idea, she'd told him nothing of the underlying scheme. This afternoon, he'd made it clear he suspected her of holding out on him . . . He'd be a dangerous friend to have, PJ, but sometimes you were left with little choice. Lovers were the only true enemies. All the others were constantly shifting.

He answered on the second ring. "Diana."

"PJ. I have a small confession to make."

"You mean you weren't being entirely honest with me earlier?" His tone was flat as a road. "I'm shocked, Diana. Shocked to the core."

"I do know your tigers. Operationally, I mean." No names on an open line. "But what they did this morning, that was no part of their mission."

Sentiment didn't play a large part in Peter Judd's world, or not when the cameras weren't running. "Can't enjoy a scone without spreading a little jam," he said. "But really, Diana, we'd be much more comfortable discussing this somewhere private. Why not have Seb call you a taxi?"

"Who's Seb?" she asked a dead connection, then started as a sleek-looking man with dark hair brushed back from a high forehead materialised at her side.

"Cab, Ms Taverner? Your lucky night. There's one coming now," and he raised an arm to flag it down, his other hand ever so lightly on her elbow.

You don't get lucky twice, Shirley learned.

Her second opponent was a harder proposition.

She hit him with the same tackle that had produced such splendid results two minutes back, already picturing a heap of broken Arrows piling up below, as she dispatched the whole platoon one by one. But instead of toppling through the window he threw himself onto the floor, regaining the advantage by pulling her with him. She landed hard, felt a sharp metallic crack. For a moment they were spooning almost, and she could smell his body odour, rank in the evening's heat. The cosh he held looked like something you might buy under the counter; short, fat, ugly. But he couldn't swing it while they were wrestling, and when he tried to wrap an arm around her throat she bit his wrist. He howled like a dog, and she pushed free from his grasp only to fall flat on her palms when he grabbed her foot. Shirley let her leg go limp then kicked viciously, catching him somewhere, she hoped his face, but the impact wasn't squishy enough. Her foot came free. She scrabbled forward a yard or two, regained her feet and turned to him, her palms stucco-rough with grit and glass. She brushed them on her trousers, her gaze not leaving the man in front of her.

Bigger than her, but most men were. What mattered more was that he'd tossed the cosh through the window; had produced in its place a wickedly grooved knife.

He grinned, his teeth showing whiter than reality against the black of his balaclava. "I am gunna skin you alive, sweetheart."

Save your breath, she warned herself.

"Gunna make *holes* in you."

She backed along the corridor, feet scrunching on the floor.

"Make you squeal like a piglet."

He lunged and she parried, her forearm knocking the knife aside, and she slapped the flat of her hand into his face. It should have been enough, but she'd lost some balance and didn't connect with the force she might have done. He reared backwards, and she reversed too.

"Doing the old quickstep, eh?"

He'd watched a lot of movies, she thought. That was fine. The more they talked, the less breath they had.

"Let's see what you got, darlin'."

What I've *got* is anger management issues. Apparently.

"Because we can go easy or we can go hard."

Fuck it then. Let's go hard.

385

She aimed a punch at his sternum, high and fast, but not fast enough. He leaned back, grabbed her arm and reeled her in backwards, crushing her against his chest, the tip of his knife suddenly pushing into her chin.

"Got you right where I want you now, honey."

"Yeah," said Shirley, "me too," and flexed her free left arm up over her shoulder to drive the splintered edge of half a compact disc into his eye. When he screamed and released her, she turned and landed a kick where her punch had been aimed. He staggered backwards, his thighs hit the window ledge, and over he went, still screaming.

Shirley made a crosshatch sign with her fingers. Hashtag epicfail, dickhead.

He'd taken the knife with him, but when she patted her jacket pocket the other half of the Arcade Fire CD, broken in her recent fall, was still there. Might come in handy.

On the ground below, a shadow was heading towards the Black Arrow van.

Shirley ran back to the stairwell.

Donovan fired three times on his way to where Traynor lay, his shots directed at the space where the door had been. When he reached his friend he dropped to his knees and cut the plastic ties binding his feet. Louisa stood and fired twice, both bullets carving chunks from the already battered door frame.

I killed a man three minutes ago, she thought. *Maybe two. Possibly three.*

The thought felt like an intrusion from an onlooker; someone not immediately involved in the action, and thus able to adopt judgemental attitudes.

A figure popped briefly into sight through the doorway and squeezed off a shot at Donovan that went wide.

He was cutting Traynor's wrists loose now.

River said, "He won't make it."

"Thanks for the input." Louisa stood again and fired twice, thinking *two, three, two, two, two*. The magazine held fifteen. If Traynor had fired more than the two she'd witnessed, she was going to be out of ammo very soon.

"Welcome."

And then River was gone again — he was doing that a lot — had leaped from their cover and was running towards where Donovan was struggling with Traynor. The figure in the doorway popped into sight again: he fired once, then jerked back to safety when Louisa shot back. River shouted Donovan's name, and the soldier stooped and slid his gun across the floor, then hauled Traynor to his feet. River scooped the gun up and slid to a halt behind the overturned filing cabinet just as the figure behind the broken wall appeared again and rattled off three shots at the two soldiers. Donovan and Traynor collapsed. River stood, aimed, and fired at the precise moment Louisa, somewhere behind him, did the same. The Black Arrow with the gun jerked backwards as if his strings had been cut.

There were smells now: cordite, blood. The dust that hangs around archives was swimming in the air.

A baton slammed into the cabinet next to River's head, but it had been hurled, not swung. A shape disappeared behind a stack of crates. River thought about shooting, but didn't; if it was armed, it would have fired at him.

Louisa joined him. "There's at least one loose in here," she said. "No idea how many through there."

The corridor behind the blasted door, she meant.

River said, "They're sitting ducks if that's the only way they can get in."

"We don't have much ammo."

"They don't know that."

He plucked a ledger from the floor and lobbed it at the doorway. Neat throw: it sailed right through unmolested.

"Good shot," Louisa said. "Proving what exactly?"

"Maybe they don't have much ammo either. Cover me."

She stood and took aim at the doorway, arms steady on the top of the cabinet, but nobody appeared there. River ran in a crablike crouch for Donovan and Traynor, who were in a heap on the floor; when he pulled Donovan up his face was covered in blood.

But the blood was Benjamin Traynor's, the back of whose head was missing.

Donovan had been hit too, but a good-guy wound — good guys get shot in the shoulder. His eyes were out of focus, though, and River struggled to get him off the ground. He half-dragged half-carried him back to the cover of the overturned cabinet, then dropped him, panting.

388

"They're either mustering their forces or have no fucking clue what to do."

"Or they've gone," Louisa said. She was unbuttoning Donovan's shirt; to check his wound, River assumed.

Donovan came awake, and he seized her by the wrist with his good hand. "Don't."

Louisa laid her gun aside, and unclamped his hand. "Your friend's dead," she said. "And an unknown number of hostiles are shooting at us. I think we can safely say your operation's fucked."

"Ben's dead?"

"I'm sorry."

He closed his eyes again, and she undid another button, then pulled free the folder he'd been carrying. An ordinary manila one, its top corner stained with his blood, or his friend's.

She handed it to River. "Let's keep this safe."

"By which you don't mean re-shelve it," River said, tucking it inside his own shirt, jamming the unbloodied edge into the top of his jeans.

"No, well. It might repay study. Seeing as how people are trying to kill us." She pulled Donovan's shirt aside and looked at his wound. "This doesn't look too bad," she told him.

"Nice to know," he said through gritted teeth. "How's the other one looking?"

Uh-oh.

He'd been hit in the thigh, too; not so much a good-guy wound, with bone showing through his trousers.

River was peering round the edge of the cabinet. "There's movement."

"Oh good."

"We might need a plan soon."

"No offence," Louisa said, "but I wish Marcus was here."

"None taken," River said. "I was thinking the same about Shirley."

Something hard and round came flying through the shattered doorway, and bounced off the cabinet.

Then everything turned to white light.

Marcus Longridge's hands were secured behind him, with a pair of those plastic cuffs that were so popular these days, and he'd been similarly bound at the ankles. He lay on his side in the back of the Black Arrow van, and had clearly clocked that he wasn't alone, and had registered the very *former* nature of his companion. A bullet to the head was a decisive punctuation mark. He couldn't be in much doubt that he faced the same full stop.

What was odd, though, was that his damn baseball cap was still on his head.

Nick Duffy didn't remove his balaclava because there were rules, and they kept you alive, but he knew Longridge had recognised him. Duffy had approached him once, in fact, before his fall, to see if he fancied a role with the Dogs: they could always use men with Marcus's skills. The people they were sometimes called upon to apprehend often didn't want to be apprehended, and were highly trained in methods of resisting said apprehension. So having people on your side even more highly trained in smacking heads off walls was a plus. Hence the offer.

To which Longridge had replied, "Does my arse smell like bacon to you?" which Duffy had paraphrased in his subsequent write-up, but hadn't needed Google Translate to catch the drift of.

"Is that thing Velcroed to your head?" Duffy asked now.

Longridge had taken some heavy blows, and been dragged a few hundred metres across rough ground; the sleeve had been ripped off his sweatshirt, and his right cheek was a mess. He should have lost his cap by now. Duffy leaned down and ripped it from his head. Not Velcro but parcel tape, the thick brown kind. Partly fastening the cap to Longridge's head, and partly securing his gun inside it: small revolver, sissy-looking piece, which frankly Longridge should have been ashamed to be carrying.

"You keep your gun in your *hat*?"

"Didn't look there, did they?" Marcus said.

"No, well. I swear, you just can't get the help."

"Fuck you, man. If you're gunna do it, do it."

"Okay."

"Prick."

"Thanks," said Nick Duffy. "That makes it easier."

CHAPTER
SIXTEEN

The motorway was quiet in the way motorways sometimes are, its traffic buzz little more than static, with only the occasional comet of oncoming headlights. Catherine sat in the front next to Ho; Lamb in the back. They'd left Craig Dunn at the farmhouse, having called — at Catherine's insistence — an ambulance. Lamb was toying with a cigarette, rubbing the filtered end absent-mindedly against his cheek, occasionally losing it in his thinning mat of hair. Catherine had made it clear that if he lit it, he'd be dumped on the hard shoulder.

"This car already stinks like an eighties pub."

"You could smoke in pubs then?" asked Ho.

Lamb sighed heavily, like an elephant deflating.

"It's a revenge thing," Catherine went on. "Must be. Dunn's death wasn't an accident."

"That's quite a leap," said Lamb.

"Fine. Let's think of another reason they'd be working together. Her brother, her fiancé, and the man supposedly responsible for her death."

"Tribute band?"

"They must think it was some kind of conspiracy," Ho said. "Whatever happened to Dunn. And that's why they're after the Grey Books."

"Roddy," said Catherine, before Lamb could speak. "They're not really after the Grey Books. That was a ruse. To get them into the place where the Grey Books are kept."

"You sure?"

"Sean Donovan is a lot of things," Catherine said, "but he was never a conspiracy nut. Whatever they're looking for, it's not in the Grey Books. They're after proof she was murdered. Murdered by the Service, I mean."

Lamb said, "They'll be lucky. If it was a Service hit, there won't be an order on file. Tearney's a paper-pusher, but even she wouldn't ask for a receipt for wet work."

"Then what?"

Lamb stared out of the side window for two minutes, his face squashed into a scowl. When he spoke again, his voice was flat and final. "Tearney didn't come up through the ranks. She's a committee animal; she runs meetings, not joes. Dunn died six years ago. Back then, Tearney wouldn't have known her way under the bridge, certainly not well enough to have someone bump off army personnel. Even just a captain."

"You mean, it's not Tearney they're after?"

"I mean, if it's Tearney they're after, there's someone else pulling their strings. How'd they know about Slough House, for a start?"

"Oh," said Catherine.

"Yeah, right. Oh."

"What?" said Ho.

"Above your pay grade," Lamb said. "Stop at the next services."

"We're okay for petrol."

"It's not the car's fuel I'm worried about," said Lamb, putting his unlit cigarette in his mouth. "It's mine."

In their ears, nothing but ringing. In their eyes a shadow-show; everything silhouetted against everything else.

But it would have been a lot worse if the flash bomb had cleared the cabinet and landed on their side, instead of bouncing back the way it had come.

River, eyes screwed shut, reached out and felt for Louisa.

"*Oy.* Hands."

"You okay?"

"Uh-huh. You?"

He nodded, then said, "Uh-huh." The thing about a flash bomb was, it preceded an attack. But maybe that only happened when you threw it in the right direction.

"And they call us special needs," he muttered.

"What?"

"We need to get out of here." He looked at Donovan. "Can you walk?"

Donovan shook his head. His features were glazed with sweat.

"You got another magazine for this thing?"

"Left-hand pocket."

River fished it out and reloaded. Donovan reached out his hand.

394

"You're kidding, right?"

"Uh-uh. You two go. Back the way we came in."

Louisa said, "You're losing blood. I mean really, a lot."

"So I'll just lie here and bleed quietly. But leave me my gun. I'll deal with the rest of this crew."

River and Louisa exchanged glances.

Donovan grabbed River by the shirt. "You think we did all this for nothing? Ben knew we might be killed. Well, he's dead. And if that folder stays down here, he died for nothing."

Louisa said, "I already told you. We're not on your side."

"You're on theirs?"

"It's not as simple as that."

"We're only in this because you took Catherine," River said.

"Then give it to Catherine." He closed his eyes briefly.

River unpeeled Donovan's fingers from his shirt front.

Louisa peered round the cabinet. A pair of figures were cautiously making their way through the wrecked wall, one holding a gun. She fired once, over their heads, and they scuttled back to safety.

Donovan opened his eyes again. "Give it to Catherine," he repeated. "And when you do, tell her I'm sorry."

Louisa said, "Another minute, two at most, they'll try again."

River said, "We'll have to carry him."

"Like hell you will." Donovan reached for River again, but River batted his hand away. "You try taking me anywhere, I'll resist. How far do you think you'll get?"

"You seriously want to die?"

"I seriously want that information out there in the light."

"Louisa?"

She said, "If he won't come willingly, none of us'll make it."

"If we take the gun, he's dead for sure. And if there's anyone between us and the exit, they can't be armed. Or they'd have made a play by now."

Louisa said, "There'll be more of them up top."

"You think?"

"Don't you?"

River said, "Yeah, probably. But they're not all armed."

"They don't all have to be," she said. "One'll do."

"Your call," he said.

She looked at Donovan, then back at River. "Oh, for Christ's sake. Leave him the gun," she said.

"Prick."

"Thanks," Nick Duffy said. "That makes it easier."

The windscreen of the van collapsed inwards in a storm of metal.

Marcus arched his back and kicked out with both bound feet, catching Duffy mid-chest: he flew backwards into the van's rear doors, which opened to spill him onto the ground. His gun disappeared in the dark just as the tumbling Klieg light completed its bounce off the roof of the van. With a loud crash the floodlight shattered in a shower of glass. Marcus lay on his back, legs in the air, and tried to ease himself through the loop of his cuffed hands. It was like performing yoga on a bus. He focused on the mess on the side panels, the smear of brain matter oozing floorwards. *Do this now, in the next three seconds, or that's what your future looks like.* It was all about taking control again, being in charge of the situation. But he couldn't even take charge of his own damn legs, and he was still caught in that position, bound hands locked behind his arse, legs in the air like a chicken, when a figure leaped through the open back doors of the van, wielding a gun.

He blinked, ready to die.

"Found this," Shirley said, her voice bright.

Then she said, "*Ha!* What do you look like?"

The domino collapse of the shelves had been halted halfway, where the crates had blocked their fall. Getting that far was a scramble over tumbled boxes, files, a snowdrift of paper; not an easy journey to undertake without a lot of noise. When Louisa tripped on a length of wood River risked looking back. Their view of the doorway was obscured by the fallen cabinet, but Donovan had hauled himself upright, gun at the ready. Horatius at the bridge, River thought, pulling Louisa to her feet. He couldn't remember what had happened to Horatius. He got to be a hero, but that was true of a lot of dead folk.

"You okay?"

"Yes." Short sharp answer. "Run."

They'd reached the back half of the room, where the crates were still in ordered rows; crates containing God only knew what. More documents, more relics of a covert history. Conscious of being in a narrow aisle, a straightforward target for anyone at either end, they took it at a gallop, and had almost reached the far doors when they heard the first shots. River leaped for cover; Louisa kept moving, throwing herself into a dive at the last moment, hitting the doors, sliding through them, head and shoulder first. The doors swung shut behind her. She rolled onto her back. A Black Arrow stood over her, a truncheon in his hand. He raised it to bring it down upon her. She, in turn, raised the gun in her hands, the gun she was only half-sure was empty, and pointed it at his face.

"Don't," she said.

". . . You don't either."

"I won't. So long as you drop that and go."

He hesitated a moment longer, probably weighing the truth of her words more than he was his own chances. Then he sagged at the knees slightly, let the truncheon drop to the floor, and made for the doors. He opened them just as River pushed through from the other side, and for a moment the two stared at each other in crazed horror. Then the Black Arrow was gone, back inside the chaos of the storage room.

"I knew there was one behind us," said River.

"Yeah, well. You were right."

"Nice bluff."

"If I was bluffing," she muttered, holding the possibly empty, possibly not empty gun two-handed as they headed down the corridor, towards Douglas's room, and its hatchway to the world.

"It was Duffy."

"*Nick* Duffy?"

"*Nick* Duffy."

"Nick Duffy, head Dog?"

"Jesus, Shirley, how many ways you want to say it? It was Nick Duffy, head Dog. Either he's gone way off reservation, or we've walked into a mop-up."

She had severed his bonds with the jagged half of a CD ("Lucky you found that." "Yeah. Lucky."), and the first thing Marcus had done was grab his cap and peel his revolver free. He felt happier with a gun in his hand. Less happy thinking about the possibility this was a mop-up.

Shirley said, "Those Black Arrows aren't Service issue. They're not trained and they don't bounce."

"Let's get out of here."

They ran for the cover of the skip in a half-crouch, expecting to be fired upon. But no shots came.

"You tipped the light onto the van," he said, stating the obvious.

"It's what Nelson would have done."

"That was smart."

"For a cokehead, you mean?"

"Wanna bet?"

She grinned.

"That's Duffy's gun?" Marcus asked.

"Uh-huh."

"Which way did he go?"

"Not sure. I was avoiding tumbling debris."

He peered round the edge of the skip, towards the block bordering the railway line.

Shirley said, "If it's a mop-up, it's a half-arsed one. Like I said, these Arrows are strictly part-time. And they don't have guns."

"Some do," Marcus said. "Duffy did. And that kid in the van was shot."

"Well, okay, some do. But most of them have scattered. Should we take the other light down?"

Marcus looked at it, twenty yards away. "It's aimed at that building." The factory. "At that hole in its wall."

"Must be where the entrance is. Wanna take a look?"

"What I want," Marcus said, "is to find Duffy."

"Separate ways?"

"Be careful."

They bumped fists, and split.

Lamb walked away from the pumps, round the side of the 24/7 — DVDs, overpriced groceries, and pornographic magazines wrapped in coloured plastic — and lit his cigarette leaning against the free air dispenser. He checked his phone for messages: nothing. Which meant that whatever Cartwright and Guy were up to, either they hadn't finished yet, or it had all gone fine, or it had all gone badly wrong.

Gunna be a lot of empty desks at Slough House in that case.

He was unsurprised when Catherine Standish appeared behind him.

"They'll be okay," she said.

He put his phone away. "Who will?"

"Sean Donovan's an angry man," she said. "But it's not us he's angry with."

"Yeah, he's already killed one man today. Remind me not to piss him off." He dropped his cigarette and immediately produced another. "He gave you booze, didn't he?"

Catherine turned her gaze on him, her face expressionless.

Lamb said, "I could smell it, soon as I came through the door."

"I'm surprised you can smell anything, the fags you get through."

"What can I tell you? I'm highly sensitive." He leaned towards her, nostrils twitching, then pulled back. "Only I'm not getting anything now."

"Lucky you. When's the last time you changed your shirt?"

"No need to get personal. That's typical of you spinsters. Once you're past the menopause, you think you can get away with saying anything."

She sighed. "Is there a point you're trying to make, Jackson? Because what I really want to do is get home and have a bath."

"Did you drink it?"

"Did I drink it? You've just finished telling me you're 'not getting anything'. I took that to mean your highly developed sense of smell can detect no whiff of alcohol."

These last words delivered in a precise, schoolmistressy tone; a warning sign, if Lamb had cared to heed it.

"Yes, well, maybe you stuck your head under a tap or something. You alcoholics can be cunning, I've learned that much."

"Anything you've learned about alcoholics is self-taught. Would you mind giving it a rest now? I'm tired."

"Only he was one of your drinking buddies back in the day, wasn't he? Sean Donovan. That why he left you a bottle? Old times' sake?"

She said, "What are you after, Jackson?"

"Just concerned you're not about to have a relapse. Don't want to arrive at the office to find you naked and covered in vomit. Which is what we were expecting when you didn't show this morning, point of fact."

"Was it?" she said, in a voice that would cut glass.

"Pretty much. First place we looked was the local park bench."

"Thank you."

"Second place was under it."

"Shut up now, Jackson."

"So why'd Donovan give you booze, if he's such an honourable guy?"

"Did I say anything about him being honourable?"

"You seem pretty keen on painting him as a white knight. And this is all guesswork, remember? Could be, he's exactly what he seems to be. A killer drink-driver who thinks the country's run by lizard people."

402

"And this is because you think he left me a drink? Jesus." Catherine Standish rarely swore. "That's rich, coming from you."

Lamb curled his lip. "There's a difference between offering you a glass and locking you in a room with the stuff."

"Well pardon me for not getting that. Besides which, it wasn't Sean left me the drink. It was Bailey. I mean Dunn. Craig Dunn. And he thought he was being kind."

"Proper little gentleman. Good job I'd toughened you up, isn't it?"

"You did?" She laughed. Lamb had rarely heard Catherine Standish laugh. "Trust me, it was no thanks to you I kept sober. If I've anyone to thank for that it's my old boss. Because unlike you, Charles trusted me. He showed me friendship, he believed in me, and he kept me on when anyone else would have thrown me to the wolves. So it was Charles Partner let me pour that wine down the sink instead of down my throat, and the only thing you did was turn up and batter that poor boy senseless, when he was going to let me go anyway. Now finish that filthy thing and get back in the car. I want to go home."

Lamb removed the cigarette from his mouth and studied it for a moment, as if concerned it was as dirty as Catherine had suggested. Then he replaced it, and gave her the same brutal stare. Out on the forecourt a car door slammed, and music briefly blared into life. Then the car departed, and Lamb was still staring, still smoking. At last he dropped it and, unusually for him, ground it out heavily; kept grinding until it was a smear underfoot. All this with his eyes still on Catherine.

Only when she made a *tchah* sound and turned to go did he speak. His words stopped her in her tracks.

"You really do pick 'em, don't you? Your hero? Charles Partner? You want to know why he really kept you on?"

"Don't even dare, Lamb . . ."

"Charles Partner, your old boss and mine, spent the last ten years of his life passing secrets to the Russians. For the money. That was your hero, Standish. Your oh-so faithful friend. And he kept you on precisely because you're an alcoholic. You think he wanted someone at his side alert enough, together enough, to pick up on what he was doing? Uh-uh. No, he trusted you all right. He knew he could rely on you to take life one day at a time, and never see beyond the given moment. Once a drunk, always a drunk."

"You're lying."

"Does it sound like a lie? Seriously? Or more like something you've known all along and never dared admit to yourself?"

Catherine was frozen into place, looking beyond Lamb as if something monstrous lurked behind his shoulder. And then her gaze shifted, and she was staring straight at him, that sense of monstrosity still steady in her eyes. Her lips moved, but no sound came out.

"I didn't hear that."

"I said fuck you," she said, in a voice scarcely louder than silence. "Fuck you, Jackson Lamb. I quit."

"Of course you do."

But she turned and walked away without replying.

When he got back to the car, Roderick Ho pointed at the pedestrian bridge, on which Catherine had just crossed the motorway before vanishing from sight on the other side. "Where's she going?"

"She decided to walk."

Ho said, "It's like, thirty miles . . .?"

"Thank you, Mr TravelApp. Just drive the fucking car, will you?"

Ho started the engine. "Where to?"

"Where do you think?" Lamb snarled. "Slough House."

Halfway to the factory wall, Shirley took fire, two bullets ringing off the brickwork ahead, and veered away, coming to a crouch underneath the surviving Klieg light, whose frame afforded imperfect cover. For a minute she waited for another burst, and when it didn't come she removed the silencer from Nick Duffy's gun, rolled out into the dark, and fired at the sky.

The shots that returned came from the pile of metal fencing to her left.

Huddled on the ground she aimed, fired, three, four times. The bullets bounced off the fences with a firework display of noise, each ricochet a carillon . . . She paused then loosed another volley. When the noise at last faded, its echoes ringing off the walls around, she heard someone running for the safety of the nearest building.

"Chicken," she muttered.

On her feet again, she ran for the factory, and the jagged tear in its corrugated-iron wall. Before going through, she turned for a moment, and surveyed the wasteground. Nothing moved, that she could see. However many Black Arrows there'd been, most were probably back out on the streets, hastily constructing alibis. There were only so many gunfights you could have in London before someone called the police. Sooner or later, there'd be sirens wracking the evening.

She took a deep breath, smiled another secret smile, then froze as she felt a gun barrel pressing into her neck.

Then: "Shirley?"

". . . Fuck."

The gun withdrew and Louisa came through the hole in the factory wall, followed by River.

"Fuck," Shirley said again. "You guys okay?"

"What are you doing here?"

"This and that."

"Marcus with you?"

"Well, duh. Yeah, he's over there somewhere." Shirley waved her gun at the building on the far side. "Chasing after Nick Duffy."

"After who?" Louisa said.

But River was already away.

A train hurtled past, headed for London, its passengers tired, hungry, irritable, alert, eager, excited or happy, depending, but none paying much attention to the derelict building briefly to their left, with dead windows, spray-tagged walls, and an armed man hunting another on its shadowy ground level.

Marcus, arms rigid, sissy gun in a two-handed grip, and Nick Duffy nowhere to be seen.

Grit underfoot betrayed every movement, but still he moved between the pillars with as light a tread as possible. From here he could see the breeze-block and wire wall keeping the railway line at bay, the yellow digger parked against it, but he couldn't see Duffy. Duffy was either lighter of tread than he was, or stood stone still in the shadows. Or had doubled back, and was out on the streets; stuffing his fancy silk balaclava into a pocket and hailing a cab.

The time for silence had probably passed.

"Duffy?"

No response.

"I'm gunna make it easy for you, Duffy."

No response.

Marcus could feel sweat on his neck, and tension in his thighs. It had been a long time since he'd been here: in the dark, expecting trouble. A long time since he'd been as near death as he had been three minutes ago. And he couldn't remember death ever wearing the face of a former colleague.

"Step out now, hands up, and I won't shoot you dead."

No response.

The sweat was welcome, and so was the tension, because they reminded him he was alive. All those days spent chasing money down various machines, across countless counters: cards and horses and numbers on a wheel. All he'd been doing was looking for a door to kick down. All he'd wanted was someone to be on the other side.

"I'll kick the living shit out of you, but I won't shoot you dead."

Half a brick came out of nowhere, bounced off a pillar and spun into the dark.

Marcus turned and nearly fired, but didn't.

Control.

"That was fucking pitiful," he said. Revolving slowly, covering all angles. "Makes a difference, doesn't it? Me not being shackled on the floor, I mean."

No response.

"Mind you, you couldn't even manage that, could you?"

This time, the brick hit his head.

He staggered back, but kept his grip on the gun, and when Duffy hit him waist height, a classic rugby tackle, he fired three times, each shot punishing the ceiling. Then he was on the ground, Duffy on top of him, Duffy's fist about to pound his face.

Marcus caught the blow with the open palm of his left hand, and with his right levelled the gun, but even as he squeezed the trigger again, Duffy's elbow nudged his aim aside. And then there was a tight grip on his forearm, and Duffy was smashing his hand on the ground twice, three times, four, and the gun went skittering into the shadows. He was free suddenly, Duffy's weight lifting from his chest, and he rolled and scrambled to his knees, lunged for Duffy's feet before Duffy could reach the gun. He missed one, caught the other, and Duffy hit the ground flat, but a moment later his foot smashed into Marcus's chin. Marcus bit the tip of his tongue off and his mouth swam with blood, but he didn't let go of Duffy's foot until the second kick arrived, this one catching him square on the nose. His eyes filled and the world went watery, and Duffy broke free. Everything slowed. Marcus was on his hands and knees, dripping blood onto the ground, and Nick Duffy, breathing heavily, was getting to his feet, the sissy gun in his hand. He looked down at Marcus, shaking his head. "You are too fucking old," he said. "And too fucking dead." But before he could shoot, a length of metal piping hit the side of his head, and he went down.

River dropped the pipe and bent over, panting. "I'm gunna pin a note to his jacket," he said, "so when he wakes up he'll know it was me did that."

"If he wakes up," Marcus said thickly. He spat a huge red gobbet, but his mouth immediately filled again. "You hit him kind of hard."

"You're welcome."

"Any more around?"

"I think they mostly ran away," River said.

"Huh."

"Louisa shot a few."

"Good." He spat again. His tongue was numb. He had a sudden memory of eating ice cream that morning — strawberry and pistachio — and wondered if he'd ever know flavour again.

River prodded Nick Duffy with his foot, to see if he was conscious or alive, and then kicked him very hard for no special reason. It had been a long day.

"Is he breathing?" Marcus asked.

"Fuck knows. Don't care."

"A hand here?"

River helped him up, and they stood for a moment, breathing hard, as yet another train went past, casting brief slices of light through the gaps in the breeze-block wall, and rustling through the litter with its draught. And then it was dark once more, and the air hung heavy with heat, and the distant wail of the city throbbed and stammered. Marcus collected his gun, spat again, and shook his head.

"I'm kind of disappointed nobody went under a train."

"Yeah, you'd expect that, wouldn't you?" River said. "Place like this."

Then they walked back across the wasteground to where the others were waiting.

CHAPTER
SEVENTEEN

It was the hour after lunchtime, and the heat had changed its tune; a subtle variation that brought the promise of release, if only because it seemed unlikely it could keep up this tempo forever. In the misshaped square near Paddington the trees hung listlessly over desiccated garden beds, and pigeons hunkered in their shade, more like stones than birds. They barely fluttered when a dog barked in the road, and didn't stir at all when Jackson Lamb stomped down the path, his shirt untucked, one shoelace undone. He wore a pair of plastic sunglasses and carried a manila folder, tied shut with a length of pink ribbon. Anyone else would have been taken for a lawyer. Lamb looked like he'd just lifted it from a bin.

He slumped heavily onto the bench next to Diana Taverner, who herself looked like she'd wandered in from the right side of town; her blouse hanger fresh, her grey linen trousers immaculate. Only her eyes, when she looked at him over the top of her Gucci shades, betrayed any hint of misplaced cool.

"Jackson."

"You couldn't have picked a bar? Somewhere air-conned?"

"It seemed best to be somewhere we won't be overheard."

"So thanks to your guilty conscience, I'm damp as a bimbo's cleavage." He slumped back, and fanned himself with the folder. "Gets any hotter, I'm going topless."

Taverner suppressed a shudder and said, "So. It seems your crew had themselves quite the little party yesterday."

"You know what it's like. Sun's shining, school's out. Seemed a shame to keep them cooped up inside."

"Quite a lot of bodies littering our facility near Hayes."

"Sounds like my local," Lamb said. "Saturday nights get a bit hectic."

"Can we be serious for a minute?"

Lamb made an expansive gesture with his free hand.

"Traynor dead, Donovan dead. He took quite a few Black Arrows with him, it seems, along with two of Nick Duffy's men. And as for Duffy himself . . ."

"Yeah, Cartwright was asking after him. Sore head?"

"Limited brain function."

"Anyone noticed?"

"You licensed a small war, Jackson. There are going to be questions."

"I licensed nothing." He produced a pair of cigarettes from his pocket, stuck one behind his ear and lit the other. Taverner waved smoke away. Lamb said, "Ingrid Tearney approved yesterday's outing, and I'm guessing it was her who then changed her mind and

412

sent the troops in." He waggled the folder. "When she realised exactly what it was Donovan was after."

"Not the Grey Books."

"Not the Grey Books. And before you start spinning fairy tales, Diana, this's got your fingerprints all over it. Those soldier boys didn't find out about Slough House from the phone book. Everything they had, from the names of my crew to Ingrid Tearney's private number, that all came from someone on the inside."

Diana let her gaze wander the square, perhaps wondering if Lamb had brought backup. But nobody caught her attention for long. She turned to look at him instead. "Shame. I was rather hoping to convince you it was Ms Standish did all that. Did she enjoy being . . . 'kidnapped'? Rather more attention than she usually gets, I'd have thought."

Lamb said, "You even told me where they were, the whackjob files, when we talked on the phone. Talk about signposting."

"No discussing Ms Standish, then? All right, Jackson, yes, hands up to this one. The tiger team was my idea, and I sold it to Judd. I brought Donovan on board, though his method of creating a job vacancy at Black Arrow was his idea, not mine. As was killing Monteith. That's the trouble with going freelance. You can't always keep the talent on the straight and narrow."

"But you had to go out of house, because you needed a third party to bring this to light." Lamb waved the folder again. "Everything you always wanted to know about the Service's use of black prisons, but were afraid to ask."

413

"Don't act like you're surprised."

"Trust me. I'm not."

He might as well not have spoken.

"We've used them for years, Lamb. Project Waterproof. A way of deporting undesirables without going through all that tiresome legal bullshit. And it hardly makes us outcast among nations. They've long been doing it in the good old US of A."

"Maybe so," said Lamb. "But I thought we'd denied using them in the UK of E, S, W and NI."

"That's the whole point. We've denied using them. Most categorically, and in front of Parliamentary Committees. More to the point, we both know precisely *who* has denied using them."

"Ingrid Tearney," said Lamb.

"Whose name's so plastered over the paperwork, you'd think it was the logo. Flight plans. Transport requisition. Fuel . . . You can't conjure an international flight out of nothing. And it's not like these places come round and collect. Have you got a spare one of those?"

Lamb checked his second cigarette was still tucked behind his ear, and said, "No."

"Too hot to smoke anyway . . . And we're not talking registered charities here, either. They're actual prisons. Or used to be. They're . . . special purpose now. And require payment."

"In return for the permanent removal from circulation of various miscreants," Lamb said flatly. It was impossible to tell from his tone whether he approved or not.

414

"Well, you can't have a parole hearing if you've never been sentenced." She gave a short, bitter laugh. "I don't mean to sound judgemental. These are people who, on the whole, we don't really want loose on our streets."

"On the whole?"

She shrugged. "There's rumours Tearney's used Waterproof to vanish people for personal reasons."

"Perks of the job."

"I'm sure the PM will see it that way."

"He'll probably ask her to use it on Judd. And this is what the Dunn woman learned that night in New York."

"The guy who approached her, he was a delegate from . . . Well, let's just say one of the 'Stans. Some while back, he'd brokered a deal for the use of a couple of his nation's particularly remote high-security facilities." She paused. "Their version of high security's not as high-tech as you might imagine. It mostly involves thick walls and no plumbing."

"I know," said Lamb. He lit his second cigarette with the stub of his first, which he then flicked, still burning, at the nearest pigeon. It failed to respond.

"And evidently, some years later, saw the light and felt the need to come clean. Or maybe he just wanted to impress Captain Dunn."

"Effectively signing her death warrant."

"We've all touched pitch, Lamb. Don't pretend your hands are clean."

He didn't reply immediately. The pair sat watching the discarded stub of his cigarette blackening the already frazzled blades of grass it had landed among.

Given time, given time, such a start could burn a city down.

Eventually he said, "So what now?"

"Documentary evidence of the project's existence is more than a career embarrassment for Tearney. It's an international incident waiting to happen. So it'll be blanketed from a great height. Judd will encourage her to retire. That'll leave a vacancy at the head of the service."

"To be filled by . . .?"

"I couldn't possibly comment."

"And in return," Lamb said, "you'll ease Judd's passage into Number Ten. Which should be a doddle, what with your having access to all sorts of confidential material. Such as the PM's vetting file."

"He'll be a safe pair of hands, I'm sure," Taverner said. "We had a meeting yesterday, point of fact." She brushed her palms the length of her thighs, stretching the linen as she did so. "He assured me that he holds the Service in high regard. That any ideas he had regarding reorganisation, he's now shelved."

"He's a fucking psychopath," Lamb said.

"All the more reason to have him inside the tent pissing out."

"This is Peter Judd," said Lamb. "I'd be more worried about him taking a dump. Besides which, you're overlooking something. You don't have the evidence. I do."

Again, he tapped the folder that River Cartwright had given him.

416

"Because of course," he said, "if this all went public — if it found its way to, say, the *Guardian* — well, that would be different, wouldn't it? A public explosion instead of a controlled detonation. Tearney would still go, but Judd would be caught in the blast. And without a friendly minister to grease your wheels . . . What do you reckon, Diana? Think you'd still find yourself First Desk?"

Taverner said, "This is not the sort of juggernaut you want to walk in front of, Jackson."

"Oh, I don't know. Don't forget, I have my team to consider."

"Really? That'll be a first."

"They have a natural respect for me."

"That's not respect. It's Stockholm syndrome."

"How do you think they'd feel if I said we'd just let it go, all those folk trying to kill them? They have a right to know what was at stake." He scrunched his nose up and sniffed noisily. "Maybe take a vote on it."

". . . You have got to be kidding."

Lamb turned heavy eyes on her, his expression momentarily obscured by the cloud of smoke he'd exhaled. Then he said, "Of course I'm fucking kidding. Getting shot at's a day at the races as far as they're concerned."

"Jesus, Lamb . . ."

"And I wouldn't let them vote on their favourite breakfast cereal." He extended the folder to her, but didn't relinquish it when she took hold of it. "But I'm serious about Judd. You've got a real tiger by the tail there."

"I can handle him."

"Sure?"

"I said I can handle him."

He sneered at that, but let go of the folder anyway. Diana all but snatched it from his grip.

Lamb stood, and this time the pigeons took fright: with one thought between them they clambered clumsily into the air, where they wheeled about in confusion for a while, and were forgotten about.

Taverner said, "Seriously, Catherine Standish. She's okay?"

"Apparently she quit."

"Sorry to hear it."

"It evens out," Lamb said. "I thought I sacked a pair yesterday. But it looks like they've changed their minds."

He walked away down the path, a bulky silhouette against the silvery white heat of the day.

Diana Taverner watched until he'd disappeared from view, a trick he achieved surprisingly quickly for a man his size. Then she undid the folder's ribbon, pulling it loose so that it ran through her fingers for a long silky moment, and opened its cover. The topsheet was blank, save for a V-for-Virgil scrawled in marker pen, and a catalogue number stamped in red ink. She removed it.

Underneath lay a copy of the *Angling Times*, and nothing more.

"Oh, Jackson," she said. "You stupid, stupid man."

She looked for the pigeons, which were gone, looked up at the sky, which was still there, then looked in her bag for her phone.

Peter Judd answered on the first ring.

"That worst-case outcome we discussed?" Diana said. "It just happened."

The weather is breaking on Aldersgate Street. It is breaking in other places too, keen to wash the smells of hot tar from London's roads, but it is over Aldersgate Street that it appears angriest, and here the violet hour has given way to early darkness. Thunder rumbles, so near it might be just over the page. As yet there is no rain, but residents in the Barbican towers hover by their windows, hoping for dramatic skyscapes, while on the pavements pedestrians — still dressed for that morning's dry heat — hurry towards shelter, wherever it might be found. In the alley that leads to Slough House's back door a freak wind stirs hot dust, and beneath the sound of clouds crashing together (which, as every child knows, is the true cause of thunder) might be heard that of a door scraping open; a door which jams in all weathers, even weather so close to breaking as this . . . But if someone has entered Slough House, there would be noises on the staircase, which there are not. And only a ghost, surely, could climb Slough House's notoriously squeaky stairs without the slightest whisper.

If a ghost it is, it's a peculiarly inquisitive one, and pauses at the first landing to test the air. Here, as always, the doors hang open, and while the rooms are empty, even a spectre would have no trouble spotting which was Roderick Ho's room; which Marcus Longridge and Shirley Dander's. The latter is tainted with conflicting emotions tonight, as if the recent male occupant has been reflecting that for all his combat experience, he basically had his nuts pulled from the fire twice yesterday, both times by people he regards as light-weight. So much for taking control . . . And as for the female, there's a suggestion that her recent physical exertions, satisfying as they were, are perhaps no long-term substitute for intimacy — and as a short-term measure, postpone, rather than obliterate, the need for any other kind of high. But there is a tangible sense of relief here too, that yesterday's sackings appear to have been reversed; or, at any rate, were not referred to during the lengthy post-mortem of last night's events. A strange quirk, perhaps, to be relieved by the prospect of remaining among the slow horses, but as every ghost knows, there are few more complicated creatures than the living.

In the former office, meanwhile, a particularly perceptive shade might catch a trace of a fragment of conversation; the words *A bus? Okay, that's old school* — words spoken by Marcus and lapped up by Roderick Ho; words Ho repeated silently to himself over and over, until they gave way to another mantra, equally silent: *So, babes, fancy a drink?*, this too practised over and over, mimed to a window in lieu of a mirror, and mimed long after their intended recipient had appeared on the street below, leaving Slough House, and Roddy Ho, equally unthought-of behind her.

More stairs now. Onward and upward. On the next landing two more vacant rooms, again heavy with the late presence of their incumbents, one of these being the just-now alluded to Louisa Guy, who is currently sitting on a barstool, and, as usual, is being approached by the usual man with the usual line, though tonight finds herself saying, *Sorry, not interested*, recalling as she does so a snapshot memory from yesterday evening: not the men she shot, not poor dead Douglas, nor even brave, doomed Donovan, but River Cartwright pulling her to her feet when she fell, a brief moment of contact that somehow overrules the possibility of going home with anyone tonight, a feeling which might outlast her third vodka, but then again might not. As for River himself, that lunchtime, for reasons he couldn't articulate, he made the hop across town to Spider Webb's bedside once more, only to find the room vacant, its bed remade, its eternally beeping machines removed; a discovery that prompted the queasy suspicion that yesterday's trip to Regent's Park, and his alibi-forming lie to Diana Taverner, *if he ever wound up plugged into a wall-socket, if that was all that was keeping him alive, he'd want to be switched off*, has produced an unintended consequence, a thought so bowel-shrinking he prefers not to entertain it, so has instead opted to visit his grandfather, the O.B., and hear familiar tales of Service myth and Spook Street legend, and lock all self-examination away.

Again, the thunder sounds, so near it might be crashing off the roof, and this time it is accompanied by, yes, a flash of lightning; a sudden electric burst that fills the uncurtained rooms, and if there were anyone here they would surely be seen now, captured in that flash as by a photograph . . . But there is nothing.

Nothing, unless that shadow in the corner is darker, thicker, more substantial, than it should be . . . Unless it moves like a ghost, soundlessly flitting up one last staircase to the uppermost floor, where the rooms are smaller, and closer to heaven . . .

The first of these, though just as empty as the others, seems somehow emptier tonight, as if its condition has acquired permanence; as if Catherine Standish's absence is the latest in a long series of absences that Slough House thrives upon; as if the building will only be satisfied once it has driven each of its inhabitants away. As if it fattens on loss. A ghost, surely, would speak this language. A ghost would choose this threshold to hover on, savouring the desolate air, the abandoned umbrella on the hatstand, the dust already gathering on desk and window frame. But the ghost — if there is a ghost, and if it's there — doesn't seem interested in the last of Catherine Standish. The ghost, instead, hovers on the landing, outside the only door in the building that's currently closed, and from behind which rumbles something reminiscent of a barnyard presence; the snoring, perhaps, of a discontented pig. Thunder rumbles once more overhead, and has its echo in this upper room, but the thunder is alert and purposeful, while the pig sounds deep in slumber.

Rain at last begins to fall, perhaps summoned by mention of an umbrella. A thick pattering on the windows at first, and then faster, and then everywhere; drumming off the roof, battering the walls. Aldersgate Street, like the rest of London, has long been waiting for this moment. If city streets could sigh, that's what this one would be doing. And of course they can, and they do, and it is. This is the noise rain always masks; the grateful sighing of the pavements.

But still, inside Slough House, the snoring persists. And perhaps the line between worlds blurs for a moment, for a ghost would pass through this door unproblematically — a door presents no obstacle to any spook worthy the name — but instead there's a gloved hand on a door handle, a quiet twist and push, and in these last moments of somebody's life a sleek-haired presence becomes visible at last. It is Peter Judd's man Seb — the ghost in PJ's machine — come to claim what Jackson Lamb withheld; come to silence that barnyard rumble too. Lamb can torment his underlings to his heart's content, but when you bother the mighty, there's always a bill to pay.

The door swings open, surprisingly quietly. There is Jackson Lamb, slumped behind his desk, and the air is suddenly full of his odours: old and new farts, ancient and recent cigarettes, and clothes which have seen better days, or even weeks. His mighty, regular snores have not been disturbed in the slightest by Seb's entrance, and the task that lies ahead would be painfully simple, no more than the washing of another bottle, were it not for the fact that Lamb's eyes are open, and that in Lamb's hand sits Lamb's gun.

The last Seb learns of this world before his ghost departs it is that, if you open enough doors, you'll eventually find a tiger.

Lamb ceases his snoring, puts his gun in his drawer, and fishes a cigarette from his pocket. Before lighting it, though, he reaches for his phone.

A bloody nuisance, getting rid of bodies.

Good job he's got slow horses to do that for him.

Other titles published by Ulverscroft:

DEAD LIONS

Mick Herron

London's Slough House is where disgraced MI5 spies go to while away what's left of their washed-up careers. Now they have a chance at redemption. An old Cold War-era spy is found dead on a bus outside Oxford, far from his usual haunts. Slough House's head honcho, the despicable, irascible Jackson Lamb is convinced Dickie Bow was murdered. As the agents dig into the circumstances, they uncover a shadowy tangle of ancient Cold War secrets that seem to lead back to a man named Alexander Popov, who is either a Soviet bogeyman or the most dangerous man in the world. How many more people will have to die to keep those secrets buried?

SLOW HORSES

Mick Herron

Slough House is Jackson Lamb's kingdom; a dumping ground for members of the intelligence service who've screwed up: left a secret file on a train, blown a surveillance, or become drunkenly unreliable. They're the service's poor relations — the slow horses — and bitterest among them is River Cartwright, whose days are spent transcribing mobile phone conversations. But when a young man is abducted, and it's threatened that he'll be beheaded live on the Internet, River sees an opportunity to redeem himself. Is the victim who he first appears to be? And what's the kidnappers' connection with a disgraced journalist? As the clock ticks on the execution, River finds that everyone involved has their own agenda . . .